A DANGEROUS SILENCE

A DANGEROUS SILENCE

Catherine Palmer

TYNDALE HOUSE PUBLISHERS, INC.
WHEATON, ILLINOIS

Library of Congress Cataloging-in-Publication Data

Printed in the United States of America

07   06   05   04   03   02   01
9   8   7   6   5   4   3   2

May the words of my mouth

and the thoughts of my heart

be pleasing to you, O Lord,

my rock and my redeemer.

PSALM 19:14

Do not be afraid of the terrors of the night,

nor fear the dangers of the day,

nor dread the plague that stalks in darkness,

nor the disaster that strikes at midday.

Though a thousand fall at your side,

though ten thousand are dying around you,

these evils will not touch you.

PSALM 91:5-7

The Sixteenth Day of the Yellow Flower Moon, The Year of 1869

I must write words that speak of death. The ge-ta-zhe has come to Yellow Dog's village on the river called Ni-Shu-Dse, and it eats our people one by one. Even while the ge-ta-zhe devours my mother, she instructs me to write in the manner I learned at the mission school in Pawhuska. She believes that if I mark down on paper the tale of this terror, it will never be forgotten.

She is wrong. The writing of words was brought to us by the Heavy Eyebrows, and so was the ge-ta-zhe.

The ge-ta-zhe first attacked my mother with fire. Like white flame that burns close to the wood, the ge-ta-zhe began to curl deep inside her body. She had been weaving a blanket for my father, Walks-in-the-Night, but soon the fire consumed her strength. She lay down inside the lodge she had built of hickory saplings and buffalo skins. Since that moment, she has not moved from her pallet.

Because I am ten years old and have no sisters, Walks-in-the-Night instructed me to care for his wife. I am honored to do this. When my mother coughs, I wipe the spittle from her lips. When her arms and legs begin to ache, I rub her muscles. Today, she begins to vomit. She tells me she is trying to rid her stomach of the fiery spirit of the ge-ta-zhe. I clean her mouth and rub her back to ease the pain. Her skin burns my fingertips.

As the sun sets, my father comes into the lodge and kneels beside my mother. He is a handsome man, tall and well formed, with dark eyes that can flash in anger like lightning on the dry prairie. In the days before my birth, he hunted the buffalo. Now the buffalo have disappeared from the grasslands. The Heavy Eyebrows killed them, just as they are killing my mother.

This night my father's eyes do not flash. Instead, they pour with a soft rain of sorrow, for he loves my mother, his beautiful White Hawk Woman. As he holds her, she begins to writhe. Her voice cries out in fear at the terrifying visions the ge-ta-zhe attacks her with.

My father's voice is gentle as he whispers to my mother. "Wah'Kon-Tah thi-ga-xe don-da-don a-ni-ge thi-k'i thin-kshe i-thi-gthon thin ha," he says softly. "Think of Wah'Kon-Tah, who made you and gave you all you know." By these words he intends for my mother to take courage because of her children and her husband who love her so much.

But I know that his words are useless. I have seen too many die. Soon the fire will cool, and the ge-ta-zhe will begin to eat my mother's flesh.

Yesterday, the Heavy Eyebrows agent came to our village to give us the cure he had promised. But he brought nothing. He told us that the medicine to fight the ge-ta-zhe had been killed in the heat of the summer sun. This is a lie. As we all know, Grandfather the Sun, to whom we pray each morning, is the source of life, not its destroyer.

The agent ordered my father to bury White Hawk Woman and all the others beneath the ground after their deaths. This, the Heavy Eyebrows agent told us, will prevent the ge-ta-zhe from spreading through the rest of the tribe and killing everyone.

This order we will never obey. Instead, Walks-in-the-Night will gather the body of his wife against his broad brown chest and curl her as tightly as a baby. He will place her on a hill and cover her with stones. This cairn will point the way for Wah'Kon-Tah to find my mother.

Even though Wah'Kon-Tah will find my mother after death, I know he cannot save her life. As I sit beside her now and stroke my fingers through her long, blue-black hair, I see the red stain of the ge-ta-zhe begin to spread across her flesh.

Within my own heart I feel the first flicker of a white-hot fire, and I know that soon I, too, will die.

From The Journal of Little Gray Bird, unpublished
Central Kansas Museum of the Native American archival
collection

1

Cowley County, Kansas; Present Day

Big Ed Morgan stepped backward off the edge of his
barn loft into thin air. He fell twelve feet to the dirt-
packed floor and landed with the crunch of a shattering
pelvis, the snap of breaking ribs, the pop of a shoulder
being wrenched from its socket. Sunlit hay from the
bale he'd been tugging scattered across him like leaves
on an autumn morning. A piece of frayed twine drifted
downward, settling finally on his barrel chest.

He took a ragged breath and lifted his head to peer
across the barn. Taking the movement as a signal to
play, Gypsy bounded from a corner of the barn where
she'd hidden, tail waving in delight. Plopping her front
feet onto her master's chest, the black-and-white dog
licked his face, pushed her cold nose under his chin,
and danced on his injured rib cage.

"Down, Gyp!"

The dog sank to her belly, still panting happily. Her tail brushed wide arcs across the dirt floor. She was smiling.

In rapid succession, three certainties entered Ed's mind, imprinted as if they'd been inked with the forty-year-old rubber stamp he used to address payments of the farm's bills. First, Edward Donald Morgan *wasn't* going to die. Not a chance. Second, he wouldn't be able to milk his small herd of dairy cows this evening. And third, no one would find him.

The telephone was in the rock house, fifty yards away. His pickup sat over by the pond. Pete Harris, the nearest neighbor, was in Wichita attending a conference on wheat diseases.

As Ed lay on the dirt floor trying to focus his thoughts, trying to come up with a plan of action, the smell of the barn draped over his face like a wet washrag, gagging him. Though he'd lived on Morgan Farm all his life, he realized he had never given the odors much notice: moldy hay mixed with cow droppings, the sweet scent of oats, the dry pinewood bins that held leftover winter-wheat seed from the past fall's planting. A tang of metal flared his nostrils, pulleys that dangled from the barn's old beams, shovels and rakes, old tractor parts.

And suddenly Ed remembered Korea, Company C and the ambush at the railroad tunnels south of Chipyong-ni, the metallic smell of his gun, and the musky scent of damp, half-frozen rice paddies. A grenade had exploded a dozen feet away, leaving him shredded like so much hamburger meat. The first thing that had come to him was the scent of an army boot lying near his face, smelling of leather and sour socks and mildew, a boot empty of the foot that had belonged to his buddy Jim.

Somehow, Ed had managed to drag what was left of Jim to safety that morning, hauled him down into a ditch, and held his hand as their blood pooled together in the chilly dirt. Later, after the helicopters and the hospital and the months of recovery, Ed had been given a medal. He was a hero, the army said, though he hadn't felt heroic that day in Korea. Not unless heroism had something to do with making up your mind to stay alive. To live one more minute, and then the next. To refuse to give in to death's clutching fingers.

Big Ed Morgan, his fellow soldiers called him, because he was tall and brave and as tough as that leather boot. And he would live through this, too. Now as he lay in the barn remembering, he felt the numbness begin to fade. Pain shot into his hips and traveled down his legs, making them tremble. A knife twisted through his shoulders. His left eye began to twitch, as though a flea had burrowed down under the skin and was trying to get out.

In the old days, someone would have found Ed right away. Pop and Grandpa, one or the other of them, had sauntered in and out of the barn all day as they worked the cattle or tended the crops. Maybe a brother would have wandered by, Tom or Ben. But they were all gone now, buried in the cemetery in town. Tom was killed in a car wreck, drunk, his fault. And young Ben hadn't been tough enough to survive Vietnam.

There'd be no wife calling Ed to lunch, either. Ruby had died years before, left him alone to manage everything. And he had. Each of their four daughters had up and abandoned the farm almost the day she was grown. At the memory of his children, the crushed bones in his chest began to throb. Gypsy was all he had.

The Border collie scooted closer on her belly and nudged his hand. Ed ran his fingers across her warm silky head. Some people would be praying like crazy right about now. Not Big Ed Morgan. Oh, he believed in God, all right. He just figured the Almighty had more or less lost interest in his creation a long time ago. If folks were going to survive in this world, they'd do it on their own.

"Well, Gyp, looks like it's just you and me." Her tail thumped the floor. "Let's get a move on."

Edging up onto one elbow, Ed began to drag himself toward the barn door. His fingers raked the hard dirt, burying grit under his thick, flat nails. One leg was strong enough to push off with. The other scuffled along, the heavy leather work boot slowing his efforts. Once he made it out into the sunlight, he paused to catch his breath. His fingertips were bleeding.

He braced himself and began to pull again. Gyp raced around him in circles, barking encouragement. The sun rose in the sky, grew hotter, beat down on Ed's back, baked him inside his overalls. He stopped and retched. Then he wiped his mouth on his shirtsleeve and continued on.

❦ ❦ ❦

Northern Wyoming

The medical compound had once been a small elementary
school built to serve the farming community. Far from any
town, poorly heated and electrified, the wood-frame structure
butted up against the foothills of the Bighorn Mountains. Each
of the six classrooms had held a single grade.

When Dr. Milton Gregory purchased the property, he found
scattered textbooks, palettes of cracked watercolor paints, and
bottles of dried ink scattered across the floor like remnants of a
parade that had passed through long ago. The wooden floors
and walls exuded the scent of sweaty bodies, mingled with the
smell of pencil shavings, chalk dust, and a bygone lunchtime's
cooked cabbage. But the windows were boarded up; the play-
ground equipment had rusted.

Dr. Gregory deemed it perfect.

In a single year's time, the physician and his colleagues
had moved into the building and remodeled it to serve their
purposes. Nineteen men and women devoted to a single cause
built bunks in the classrooms, rewired the entire building,
rehabbed the plumbing, and transformed the cafeteria into a
laboratory. Long wooden tables embedded with the grime of
countless lunches had been scrubbed, bleached, and painted.
Computers, microscopes, incubators, test tubes, culture plates,
and flasks now lined the room—a laboratory as sophisticated as
many hospitals could boast.

Gregory was aware that few of his colleagues could fully comprehend the vast scope of the work they had undertaken, its import for the future, its ramifications to humanity. None of them was as well trained or as experienced as he, yet in the passing months, they had become essential to him, more of a family than he had ever known. Young and idealistic or old and embittered, each individual in his organization had been following a dream. Now, with Milton Gregory as their guide, they had dedicated themselves to this quest. They were, in a sense, knights seeking a holy grail. And he was their lord.

Dr. Gregory enjoyed his colleagues' dedication, and he had worked hard to earn their respect. Yet, despite hours logged on the Internet, intensive experimentation, and two field tests, the first phase of the project had failed. A mixture of anger and disappointment flooded through the physician as he studied the group gathered on metal folding chairs in the lab.

"Good afternoon, everyone." He paused to regard them, their faces strained with concern. "I want to thank you all for stepping away from your work schedules for a few minutes to gather here with me for this time of debriefing and reassessment."

His colleagues shifted in their seats. Restless. Disheartened. "As you all know, Phase One has been completed," the physician continued. "Team A, our research experts, pinpointed the excavation site in Utah. Team B, those of you involved in our actual scientific experimentation, accomplished the harvest, albeit on a small scale. I know we all appreciate the dedication and long hours both teams put in."

He began to applaud, and the others joined him. There was no point, he felt, in discouraging everyone to the point of resignation. They had, in fact, worked very hard.

"And Team C administered the viability test," he resumed as the applause died. "Then they attempted to carry out the destruction of the test sample. I'm afraid *attempted* is the operative word here."

Gregory spotted Mike Dooley, hunched over as if studying the pattern on the linoleum between his feet. The physician knew the young man was troubled. He had been active on both the excavation and the experimentation teams.

"Obviously, the sample we used in our experiment was not strong enough," the doctor said, as Dooley began to pick at a hangnail on his thumb. "Either it was the weaker strain of the agent, or we did not harvest enough particles to attack our test sample fully. Without a scanning electron microscope, I find it difficult to make a conclusive determination."

Gregory let out a breath of frustration. Had he not already exhausted most of his financial resources on this endeavor, he would have been able to afford the microscope. As it was, he had been forced to rely only on the polymerase chain reaction analysis of the volume of particles in the sample.

"Furthermore," he went on as he began to walk around the room, "the viability of transporting the agent to our target population on a wide scale is unproven. I'm sure you all recall Desert Storm and the toxins used by Saddam Hussein. They were subtle, indefensible, and deadly, and they moved through our troops in ways the United States government has yet to determine. In many cases, the government continues to deny these weapons were even used. Our mission is clear, ladies and gentlemen. We cannot allow such treachery against our people. We must protect ourselves from the threat of destruction. Now, as you are all aware, September 15 is our final deadline for this project. I cannot stress that date strongly enough. If we fail to accomplish our mission by September 15, my friends, we fail altogether. Summer knocks on our door. Time is running short."

"Dr. Gregory, may I ask a question?"

"Of course, Bob."

Bob Harper was a new member of the organization, and Gregory noted that he and Mike Dooley had struck up a friendship. Worrying the hangnail back and forth, Dooley turned in his chair so he could see more clearly.

"Sir, where can we get our hands on more of the agent?" Harper asked. "Sounds like we're going to need a lot of this stuff if we're going to be able to protect people the way you said."

"I'm glad you asked that question. It leads me directly to the topic of this meeting." Gregory turned and pulled down a rolled school map with the continents in bright, primary colors. "Once again our dedicated research team has done some great work, narrowing the focus of our next excavation first to the United States, and then to a single state, to a single county, and finally to a single farm. This is quite an accomplishment in itself. But in addition to that, the team has calculated the specific site for our new probe. Along a hilly ridge beside a river that runs through this farm, we believe we'll find what we need."

Mike Dooley spoke up. "Are there any towns close by, Dr. Gregory? In Utah, it felt like people were breathing down our necks the whole time we were trying to work."

"There's a small community nearby, but the farm itself is owned by a single man who has no family to speak of. I understand your concerns about interruptions, Mike, but I would ask you to keep in mind the importance of maintaining a clear focus on the goal of this project. Our work is of global importance. What we're doing together as a team will benefit mankind throughout the future."

Gregory noted that Dooley had yanked too hard on his hangnail and was blotting the blood on his jeans. He crossed to Dooley's chair. Removing his wallet from his pocket, the physician spoke softly. "Give me your hand, young man."

Dooley did as he was told. Gregory took a sterile Band-Aid from his wallet, peeled back the protective paper, and stretched the adhesive wings over the young man's thumb.

"Is that better?"

Dooley swallowed. Clutching his bandaged thumb into a fist, he mumbled, "Yes, sir."

"Infection can creep into open wounds like that, Mike. The results are often painful, even dangerous. We'll find you some antibiotic lotion after the meeting."

"Thank you, Dr. Gregory."

"Focus, Mike," Gregory said gently. "You'll do fine on

this new effort, I know you will. As long as you keep your focus."

"Yes, sir."

"Then pack your bag, Mike. You, too, Bob. We'll leave in the morning."

"Where are we going, sir?" Harper asked, dropping his cigarette and grinding it out with his heel.

Gregory turned and pointed to a small yellow rectangle in the center of the old school map. "Kansas."

🐾 🐾 🐾

Odd that Ruby's face swam before his eyes, Ed Morgan mused as he crawled toward the barbed-wire fence that lined the gravel road. He hadn't thought much about her in years. His late wife had been pretty enough. Dark brown hair, fair skin, strong hands. Ed recalled that Ruby's fingers had been rough from her constant dishwashing, laundry, mopping. In and out of water all the time, you'd have imagined them as soft as soap. But through the years her skin had grown dry and hard and cracked, like sandpaper when she touched his cheek. There always seemed to be a little dirt in the crevices, too, from her gardening.

Ed had never understood what Ruby loved so much about her rock-lined flower beds, but when she came in from weeding, her eyes always sparkled like morning sunlight on the pond and her cheeks glowed bright pink. "The purple cone-flowers are up," she'd say. "I can see the leaves poking through the dirt, dark green and all ruffly. Oh, Ed, we're going to have masses of flowers this year!"

He hadn't paid much attention to Ruby's flowers, though she arranged them in vases and glass jars all over the house. But he did remember one time, an evening when the girls were all away at a ball game, when she had pinned a cluster of pale pink asters in her hair and dabbed on some perfume. He'd been watching *Bonanza*, but Ruby had come into the living room, sat down on his lap, and kissed him right on the lips.

Spikes of sharpened steel tore across Ed's forearm, opening slender rivers of bright blood as he worked his massive body under the fence. The barbs caught his blue chambray shirt, trying to hold him back. He ripped the fabric loose and dug his path slowly under the wire. Gyp followed, tufts of black hair clinging to the barbs as she wriggled through the narrow opening.

Ruby had been soft that night, all gentle curves and the taste of lemonade as Hoss and Little Joe and Ben Cartwright chatted quietly in the background. Times like that, Ed had felt sure he loved Ruby. Loved her with a passion that drove out the memories of his losses, filled in the emptiness, healed the hurt.

After Korea and his long recovery, Ed had chosen a young wife in much the same way he had selected the 1959 Chevrolet pickup he still drove. And through the years of their marriage, he had grown to care about Ruby. He had given her all he had, and he had expected the same in return. By all that was right, his wife's wide, comfortable hips should have borne him a son. Was that asking too much?

But four squalling daughters was all he got. Ed rested his cheek on the dusty gravel driveway that led to the old rock house his great-grandfather had built. Marah had come first. Then Deborah. And finally the twins, Sarah and Leah. Sara Lee Cupcakes, he'd called them. Ruby had laughed, but she knew he'd been counting on sons.

"I'm sorry," she had whispered in the hospital, her eyes bloodshot from straining to give birth to the twins. And he hadn't been able to comfort her.

"I'm sorry, too," was all he'd been able to muster.

Pausing on the road, Ed allowed Gyp to lick the sweat from his face. After the twins, Ruby had gotten sick. Female troubles. She was a religious woman, always carting her daughters off to church, and she prayed for God to heal her. The doctor took out her parts anyhow.

"How's a man supposed to run a farm without a son?" Ed had growled at Doc Benson. "Our land has been in the Morgan family more than a hundred years. I need a son."

But the doctor had just shrugged.

Marah, the oldest daughter, could have taken over the farm. She was strong enough, smart enough, stubborn enough. She had the Morgan backbone and the Morgan looks—thick black hair and eyes as bright blue as chicory blossoms. He could almost see her now, shinnying catlike up a tree, long legs and skinny arms everywhere. Ed had taught his oldest daughter to drive a tractor, drill wheat, work the cattle, even pull a calf.

Now look at her. A doctor. What a waste!

The gravel on the road cut through denim and scraped skin from his knees. Ed glanced over his shoulder once and saw the trail of slick blood that marked his progress.

A doctor. There were more than enough doctors in this world.

"What we need is more good farmers," he said. His voice sounded far away, the words muffled. Something bitter and metallic filled his mouth, but he couldn't bring himself to spit.

Black spots swirled before his eyes. Vultures, probably. He'd show them. He reached the first step of the front porch. His chin dropped suddenly, cracking hard against the splintered wood. Gyp bounded onto the porch, barking, yapping, whining.

Ed hefted his good leg up onto the step. White-hot pain exploded through his hip. The vultures descended.

🐾 🐾 🐾

Jal, New Mexico

"Ugly sign, ain't it?"

"Nah. It's a work of art."

The neon cactus on the Saguaro Motel flashed alternating pink and green light across the fake adobe walls. One-room cottages rented by the night, the week, or the month. Television, pay phone, private bathrooms. Not mentioned in the advertising: no maid service, no restaurant, infrequent hot water, three billion cockroaches, and the occasional scorpion.

"You nervous about tonight?"

Judd Hunter shook his head.

He stuck his hands in the pockets of his jeans, leaned one shoulder against the door frame of his bungalow, and regarded the cactus that gave the place its name. A decent saguaro wouldn't set foot in this part of the state. The roadside inn, with its row of crumbling cottages, was lucky to have a few mesquite bushes and an occasional prickly pear to break up the endless sea of dry grass that filled the landscape.

Odd how in three months a man could go from thinking he'd stepped off the end of the earth to believing he'd discovered a rare treasure. A sunrise in these parts boiled across the sky in shades of orange, blue, and pink. Noontime heat sent waves that rippled the horizon in bands of gold. Night brought a symphony of crickets, barn owls, toads, and the chilling howl of the coyote. Hunter was going to miss this place.

"I didn't figure you'd be nervous." The older man set a hand on Hunter's shoulder. "You've proven yourself one of my best boys, you know? It's not everybody'd be willing to hunker down here in the middle of nowhere, not with the Feds sniffing our tails every time we turn around. But you've done good, son. I'm real proud of you."

"Thanks, Jim."

"Reckon you'd like to come visit me and the wife after this deal goes down? We've got ourselves a nice little house, and the wife's a bang-up cook. It'd be real homey for you."

"Sounds all right." Hunter couldn't picture "homey" if he tried.

"We got a spare bedroom. Now that the kids are all grown

and gone, the house gets awful lonely. You just make plans to stay awhile, why don't you?"

Hunter nodded, aware of the headlights on the straight stretch of road that ran past the motel. "Here's the bus."

Jim stiffened. "OK, all right. Let's stay calm."

"Yes, sir."

"You look in on the teenagers who checked into that other cottage down the way. We don't want nobody stepping into our business unexpected. I'll check the main desk, make sure they're watching TV, like always." Jim leaned back into Hunter's small room and called to the eight men who waited inside. "Boys, the bus is here!"

Hunter felt for the pistol under his denim jacket. Then he scanned the endless blanket of black that surrounded the motel. Heart hammering, he crept to the window of the cottage occupied by the motel's only other customers. The curtains were drawn; the black-and-white television set cast a square glow through the thin cotton fabric.

A long yellow school bus left the highway, crossed the grass, and pulled to a stop behind Hunter's cottage. In silence, the men who had arrived at the motel with Jim the day before began to file out through the back door.

Hunter drank down a deep breath. It looked like the operation would go off without a hitch. For three months he had lived at the motel, receiving small shipments of ammonium nitrate brought by individual members of the group until his room was stacked to the ceiling with the explosive fertilizer.

He had written down names of couriers, noted sources, kept track of everything. Finally, Jim had arrived. The shipment was due to go out at last.

Missouri had been chosen as the target state for this operation. Because of its recent failure to pass a law allowing citizens to carry concealed weapons, Jim and his men felt that Missouri needed to be taught a lesson. Such a violation of constitutional rights could not be tolerated.

Jim's plan seemed faultless. The school bus, pencil yellow with tinted glass windows, would provide an ideal cover. Groups of fifth-graders always visited Missouri's capitol in the springtime. Their buses were seen throughout the city during that season. After Jim and his men hid the explosive under the seats, the driver would pass the adjoining security building and park beside the capitol. At 3 P.M. sharp, with the legislature in session, a radio signal would activate the detonator.

"Get over here, son." Jim motioned Hunter to the back door of his cottage. "We need your muscle on these bags."

Hunter nodded. "Grab that end, and we'll get this one together."

Jim had been standing to one side, keeping watch on the empty roadway. He shrugged and bent over the bag of fertilizer.

"I reckon I'm good for a bag or two," Jim said. "The ol' back ain't what she used to be, but—"

A semicircle of headlights suddenly flicked on. The nearly loaded school bus glowed brilliant yellow. Men stood out like wax statues. No one moved.

"This is the FBI." The amplified voice drifted across the dry grass and echoed against the motel walls. "You're under arrest for—"

"It's the Feds!" The line broke as men dropped their bags, fell to their knees, scrambled toward open ground.

Hunter watched shock drain the color from Jim's face. Nostrils flaring, the older man let his half of the bag fall to the ground and began to run. Hunter took off after him. The door to a cottage they'd thought was empty burst open, and uniformed men poured into the motel's open courtyard. Gunshots popped like a string of firecrackers. A bullet whanged into the school bus. Another sent up a puff of dust at Hunter's feet.

"Jim!" Hunter shouted as he crashed into the man's shoulder. "Get down!"

Both fell, their legs tangling, their arms clutching, pushing. "Let me go!" Jim cried. "What are you—"

"Just stay down. Don't move." Hunter reached into his back pocket. At that moment, a bullet grazed his thigh and buried itself in Jim's abdomen.

"I'm hit!" The older man coughed. "I'm bleeding."

Hunter rose to his knees. "Stay calm, Jim. You'll be all right."

"Get me out of here! You got to help me, son, or I'm—"

"Hold on, you two." A flashlight beam lit up the pain etched across Jim's face.

The man moaned as he clutched his stomach. "Officer, I'm hit. You got to get me some help."

The federal agent flicked the beam to Hunter's bleeding leg. "Looks like you took a bullet, too."

For a moment, their eyes met, and Hunter saw the other man's eyebrows rise slightly. His own face remained implacable. "Get over here with some stretchers!" the agent called. "We winged a couple of 'em."

Hunter pressed the wound on his leg as Jim was lifted onto a stretcher and rolled toward the ambulance now pulling up at the scene. Sirens blared as the agent knelt to slip a pair of handcuffs on Hunter's wrists.

🐾 🐾 🐾

Forcing himself out of his blackness, Ed tried to muster the strength to move. The sun was sinking. Time to get the cows in. Time to milk.

Never missed a milking. Those pretty guernseys of his wouldn't appreciate this delay. He could see their faces now, their big brown eyes.

Taking a ragged breath, he pulled himself up the steps . . . up the rocky slopes of Hill 453, Lieutenant Mitchell in command, shouting orders. Company C rifle platoon, Second Infantry Division, United States Eighth Army, and Lieutenant Mitchell in charge of the drive toward the railway tunnels south of Chipyong-ni. Grenades and mortars and screams all around. The Chinese scrambling up Hill 453, and all forty-four members of Company C climbing the frozen ridges, too. Big

Ed Morgan, a hole in his stomach and his fingers all broken, climbing and climbing . . . climbing up to the front door and sliding inside the cool rock house.

The black telephone sat on a low table beside the sofa. Ed stared at it. Unplugged, as usual. That ringing could drive a man buggy.

Gyp watched her master, his big fingers trying to insert the plug into the phone jack. It slipped into place with a tiny click.

"See there?" Ed picked up the receiver. For a moment he lay beside the sofa, breathing hard, fighting nausea, trying to stay conscious.

Who could he call?

Lieutenant Mitchell was dead. Ruby was dead, too. His neighbor Pete was out of town. The four daughters had all gone away. Left the farm as though it were diseased. Marah despised her father. Deborah, married and living in Oregon, was due to have a baby this month. Sara Lee Cupcakes had both joined the army.

Ed swallowed the bile that rose in his throat.

Then he punched out a sequence of numbers he'd memorized long ago, the way he had memorized the numbers on his dog tag, the serial numbers on his brand-new tractor, the scores of the Royals and the Chiefs through the years.

A nasal voice came on the line. "Gateway Pediatrics, may I help you?"

"Get Morgan."

"I'm sorry, sir, I can't hear you clearly. Could you repeat—"

"Morgan!" he barked.

"Dr. Morgan is not on call this afternoon. May I take a message, or could one of our other pediatricians—"

"You tell Marah to call me." A dark veil began to slip over his eyes. "Tell her . . . her daddy needs her."

🐾 🐾 🐾

St. Louis, Missouri

The high-pitched beep of monitors, the whoosh of ventilators, the gurgle of fluid-filled lungs barely registered as Dr. Marah Morgan studied the chart in her hands. This was odd. Two young patients had been brought in nearly a week ago from the same incident— a state-subsidized day-care center had burned to the ground in an arson blaze attributed to a worker's angry boyfriend. The patients had both suffered third-degree burns, smoke inhalation, broken bones. Despite the severity of their injuries, the little girls had begun to rally. As always, Marah fought for professional detachment as she watched the children struggling to survive. But she knew a part of her would die, too, if they lost the battle.

Then an unexpectedly high fever began to rage through each tiny charred body. There was no sign of pneumonia, the burns were healing at a normal rate, and yet the children hovered on the brink of death.

"What do you think?" Dr. Sam Girard, head of the hospital's burn unit and Marah's most persistent admirer, took the chart of one of the youngsters. "It doesn't make sense to me."

"It must be a secondary infection of some sort," she said.

"I don't think it's bacterial."

"Viral?" Marah shook her head. "Look, Sam—"

"Dr. Morgan, please dial 103." The intercom cut off her words. "Dr. Morgan, dial 103."

"Gotta go." She started for the door. A child's life might be hanging in the balance.

Sam caught her hand. "Marah, we're set for Friday night? The Fox Theatre?"

"Sam, 103 is my emergency code."

"It's probably just your father again."

Marah gave a sigh of agreement. "What's playing at the Fox?" she asked Sam.

"*Phantom*, remember? I've had the tickets for a couple of months. You told me you'd go."

"And I will." She swung through the door and hurried down the white-tiled hallway, her open white coat flapping from side to side. She didn't mind spending time with Sam Girard when she had nothing better to do. But frankly, she had to admit, it was only the Phantom of the Opera himself who could lure her out on a Friday evening when she could be soaking in a warm bubble bath, reading the latest Grisham.

"Dr. Morgan here," she said, balancing the receiver.

"They're killing me."

She groaned. It was him. Ever since her father's accident a week and a half earlier, she had yet to get through a day without several long-distance tirades, either in person or on her voice mail.

"They're trying to kill me," Ed repeated. "They won't let me get out of bed. They want me to lie here and die."

"You're in the best hospital in Wichita," she told him, trying to stay firm, trying to keep distant. "Nobody's killing you. Now, will you please stop calling me when I'm on duty?"

Marah was setting the receiver down when her father spoke again. "It's almost June. Wheat'll be turning."

"I guess it will."

Wheat. Like a dousing of warm water, the memory swept over her. How long since she had thought of the vast fields of windblown winter wheat, rippling like a yellow gold blanket across an unmade bed? For more than fifteen years, Marah had avoided returning to the family farm. She skipped her sisters' birthdays, high school graduations, even Deborah's wedding. Though Marah once had taken the role of mother to the three younger girls, they understood her absence. They had left the farm, too, as soon as they could.

In the years since Marah had left home, with God's help, her broken, lifeless spirit had been reborn. Her father's consuming presence went into remission, pushed so far away she considered herself healed. Like the parents of her pale little leukemia victims, she prayed for healing, wanted healing, convinced herself she was brand-new and cancer-free.

But these past few days, each time she heard her father's voice, Marah felt the sickness inside her stirring to life, curling and stretching like a little larva that has lain dormant in the ground all winter, like a small, anemic white worm that wriggles and nudges at the dirt and thinks about looking for something to eat.

Her father was still speaking. "Pete Harris tells me the calves are all out to pasture."

"I'm sure they are." Marah set one hand on her hip, willing away the image of the guernseys' brown eyes and long, silky lashes. Though eighteen years had passed, she might have left the farm yesterday. "Look, I'm really very busy here. I'm trying to save the lives of two victims of a day-care fire, and I need to—"

"Pete can't do his work and mine, too. I gotta get out of this place."

"You're not going to be pulling calves any time soon."

"Beans."

"Your doctor told me you'll be using a walker." Marah made her voice hard, tough, and soldierlike against him. "You might as well get used to the idea. You're out of the farming business."

She almost put the receiver down, but the silence on the other end of the line made her pause. Her father was a mean old buzzard, often thoughtless and sometimes cruel, and Marah had long ago stopped allowing thoughts of him to dominate her life. In this situation, she felt she'd done her part. After his emergency call, she had made sure he was airlifted to Wichita and placed in the hands of a reputable orthopedic surgeon. Why hadn't his doctor told him his farming days were over?

"Marah," he said.

"Yes, sir?" She twisted the cord around her finger. She'd

heard this tone before, knew well the power in his voice that could leave her helpless. Somehow she always did what her father asked, and she hated herself for it. *Please, not this time.*

"Marah, I need you to run the farm until I'm on my feet again," he said.

"That's impossible."

"It's the least you can do."

"I have responsibilities here."

She rubbed the perspiration from the back of her neck. Did he even know she was a pediatrician in St. Louis? Was he at all aware that she had built a full life without him? She owned a calico cat, taught a kindergarten Sunday school class, sang in the choir at her church, grew fifteen varieties of daylilies in her garden, and dined out with friends every Tuesday evening. She drove a new silver BMW, shopped at the Galleria, subscribed to five magazines, walked thirty minutes on her treadmill four times a week, and read every novel that hit the best-seller list.

"Listen to me, Marah, you better come help out." His voice grew more persistent. "You've got to see the farm through the summer."

"I have important work to do here."

"Important work." He was silent for a moment. "Then I guess I'll do it myself. On my walker."

Beans, she thought.

"Come to Kansas, girl," he said. "I'll be waiting for you."

The receiver in her hand went dead.

2

"You're not going to Kansas."

"Excuse me?" Marah's fingers tightened on the Styrofoam coffee cup.

"You're not going." Sam Girard stared at her face, his eyes as intense as if he were examining one of his patients. "If you head back to that farm, you'll be buckling under the old man's will just like you always did when you were a kid. You told me how your father ordered you around, made you work like a farmhand, forced you to take care of your sisters, practically ran you into the ground. You said that when your mother died—"

"I know the story of my own life, Sam." Marah tossed the half-full cup into the hospital cafeteria's trash bin. She had no desire to discuss this with him. Her focus was on the young patient fighting for life in the burn unit upstairs.

One of the two children under Marah's care had gone into cardiac arrest just as Marah was finishing her rounds the day before. The child's death hadn't been unexpected, though the cause was not yet known. The physicians tending the two victims of the day-care fire couldn't agree on what was taking place in their badly burned bodies.

Marah felt certain the illnesses were unrelated to the injuries and smoke inhalation the children had suffered in the blaze. She wondered if perhaps the patients were already coming down with something at the time of the fire—the flu, chicken pox, a case of mild food poisoning? Marah's mentor, Dr. Luis Jordan, a veteran pediatrician whom she had called in for consultation, insisted that the secondary infection had been burn induced. Influenza was a possibility, he acknowledged. But the course of the illness bothered him. It just didn't act like any flu he'd ever seen.

"Look, I'm not saying I *want* to go to Kansas," Marah told Sam as she headed for the cafeteria door. "I *don't* want to go. I'd do just about anything to *keep* from going. But I feel I have a certain moral responsibility to help my father."

"Why?"

"Because it's the right thing to do." She pictured a dusty glass case that had hung on the living-room wall in the old white house. How often had she studied the display, the solid bronze and silver medals hanging from faded ribbons? They had fascinated her and somehow given her hope.

"My father once saved someone's life," she said. "He has a

little plaque that tells about it. During the Korean War, his company was hit by mortar fire. In spite of his own injuries, my father dragged another wounded soldier straight up a frozen mountainside. They hid in a ditch until rescue helicopters came. That's the kind of thing my father would do. He might not like you, but he'd save your life."

"And so you're supposed to abandon your own life for him?"

Marah stared at this man she thought she knew. "My father taught me about sacrifice."

"And he sacrificed *your* childhood in the process. I don't know why you even think of the guy as a father figure. Anyone can be a father, Marah. It takes someone special to be a dad."

"Shall I needlepoint that for you?" She shook her head, instantly regretting the sarcasm in her voice. "Do me a favor, Sam. The next time you want to give your opinion about my life, try using words that don't sound exactly like something Big Ed Morgan would say."

As she strode down the hall toward the elevator, she could hear him hurrying behind her. Why couldn't the man buy a pair of shoes that didn't squeak? No, Sam Girard had to wear his polished black wing tips every day as surely as Ed Morgan had to wear his Big Mac overalls.

Marah knew the hospital in Wichita had released her father two days earlier. He had been given instructions to go to a clinic in town for physical therapy three times a week. An outpatient social worker had arranged for a senior citizens' van to pick him up at the farm. Marah had arranged for the state to send someone from Family Services to check on him, and she set up an account with the local grocery store owner to take him food if the need arose. But she felt like she was trying to organize the habitat for a willful, geriatric hamster who refused all instruction, all order, all assistance and instead scurried around taking care of his own matters just as he always had—burying seeds in little piles, shuffling cedar shavings here and there, and occasionally rearing up on his hind legs to chitter loudly at anyone in the vicinity.

At least three times a day—sometimes four or five—her father left messages insisting the farm was going to rack and ruin. Hobbling around with his walker, Ed informed his daughter that he had refused to set foot in the senior citizens' van. He couldn't afford to be gone that long, he said, not with things falling apart all around him. He had inspected fences and studied his wheat crop and tried to milk his cattle. His graveled voice always stated the same command: "Girl, you better come home."

Home. Marah pictured the empty clapboard house with its peeling white paint, the weedy yard and barren flower beds, the scruffy dog pausing occasionally to scratch at fleas, and the father who considered himself lord and ruler of his little universe. Kansas was the last place on earth she wanted to go. But she was going to have to make a decision—and soon.

"Now what's that comment about your dad supposed to mean?" Sam asked, catching Marah's arm as she stepped into the elevator. "Are you equating me with your father?"

"You *ordered* me not to go to Kansas."

"I *advised* you not to go."

"It was an order. Believe me, I know the difference."

The elevator slid silently upward. Sam brushed back Marah's dark hair and ran his hand behind her neck. "You're tense."

"Demetria's going downhill."

"This is not about your patient, Marah."

"I've asked Dr. Jordan to take another look at her."

"I love you, Marah. I'd like to think we could have a future together. Maybe that's why I'm expressing myself a little strongly on this situation with your father."

Marah looked across the elevator at the man she thought she'd been dating only casually. *Love? A future together?* Sam Girard was intelligent, nice looking, a gifted physician. But Marah had no intention of marrying—him or anyone. Ever. Why would she?

Her mother had rarely been happy, ever subservient to her husband's demands and irrefutable opinions. Ed hadn't been happy either. The wife who could produce nothing but baby girls had failed him in the most crucial way, as he was quick to remind her. It was clear he had never really loved his wife for who she was. Marah had watched her parents' marriage crumble before her eyes. The tension, the arguments, and finally the silence.

"If you go to Kansas," Sam went on, "I'm afraid he'll trap you. Tie you down there. You said he's a powerful man."

"And I'm a powerful woman." She gave him an empty smile

as she got off the elevator. "He taught me well. I'll let you know what I decide, Sam."

Detaching herself, she hurried down the corridor toward the hunched figure of Dr. Jordan. Small in stature, as bald as a tomato, and surely smarter than King Solomon himself, the elderly physician had earned a prominent spot on Marah's shelf of heroes. As he moved toward her, his long white coat billowing slightly behind him, she had the impression she was in the presence of an angel. Dr. Jordan headed the pediatrics group she had joined fresh out of residency, and he had quickly become her mentor. Somehow the man always knew what those around him needed most. And he gave it without hesitation.

"Dr. Morgan," he said, lifting a gnarled hand. The heavy accent of his native Colombia hadn't faded during all the years he had lived in the United States. "I'm thinking maybe I have written down the wrong time of our meeting."

"I'm sorry I'm late. I was speaking with Dr. Girard." She flipped through her files to Demetria's chart. "How's she doing tonight?"

He shook his head. "Do we have parents in this case?"

"She's been in foster care. Mom's in prison. Drugs, I think. There was no father listed on the inpatient information."

"And the foster parents? Do they visit?"

"No." She looked into Dr. Jordan's brown eyes and read the pain. How was it that despite years of practice on thousands of patients, this man still cared so deeply for each child?

Sometimes during her internship and residency, Marah had

lain awake at night, alone in her apartment, fearing she might one day shrivel up under the constant demands of her career in exactly the same way she had shriveled under her father's domination. She pictured herself exhausted and skeletal again, viewing her cases as puzzles to solve instead of as human beings who needed her healing touch. What if she became analytical and logical rather than compassionate? What if she grew hard and self-absorbed and detached?

Marah studied her mentor's stooped figure as he hobbled into the patient's room. She had literally prayed that God would transform her into a female version of Dr. Jordan. She had worked to become like this man, warm and gentle and caring. But now, with her father's voice nudging at her again, the old worry came back. The anemic white grub worm began to burrow through the roots of her spirit, and she felt something sour and hard growing inside her. Something that she had tried to kill and bury and forget. But it was still there. Alive. What was wrong with her?

Dr. Jordan bent over the stainless steel bed rail and took the child's bandaged hand.

"Demetria," he said softly. "Hello to you, my sweet girl. How do you feel this evening? Can you look at Dr. Morgan and me?"

To Marah's shock, the child who had been unresponsive for three days suddenly opened her eyes and stared at him.

"Oh, we're happy to see you now." Dr. Jordan moved his hand away and took Marah's wrist. Drawing her to the bedside, he laid her palm on the child's bare fingers and motioned her to stroke them. "Can you feel that? This is the way Dr. Morgan gives you a big hug."

Two glistening tears filled the child's eyes.

"Now, Demetria, I want to ask you not to be afraid," Dr. Jordan continued as Marah caressed the tiny fingers. She could feel the painful, raised blisters, the peeling skin. In the room, the smell of singed flesh lingered beneath the antiseptic tang of new gauze bandages, sterile tubes, and ointment.

"You're here in the hospital, and we're taking care of you," Dr. Jordan said. "That thing on your face is a ventilator to help you breathe. And all the sounds you hear are just little machines checking on you and making you feel better."

Marah smiled as she thought of the way Dr. Jordan always talked about "ma-cheens." He knew the medical equipment frightened his little patients, and he would do all he could to allay their fears. He had been known to hang clip-on monkeys from his stethoscope and wear a pastel plaid doctor's smock. From Dr. Jordan, Marah had learned the trick of disguising her otoscope as a brightly colored parrot with a fascination for peeking into children's ears.

"Now I need you to do something for me, Demetria," Dr. Jordan said, gently touching the single spot on her forehead that had been spared the flames. "I need you to be very strong and fight this sickness. You're going to have to be brave, like a princess on a horse, fighting the dragon with a big spear. Can you do that?"

The child's eyes slid shut again. Marah's spirits sank.

"Well, I think we better bring your mama here to see you, Demetria," Dr. Jordan continued as he leaned over the rail. "I will promise to work on that if you promise to fight the dragon. OK? You hear me?"

A flicker of movement crossed the tiny forehead.

"That's good. That's very good, Demetria." Dr. Jordan took Marah's arm and stepped away from the bedside. "She doesn't have anything to fight for," he whispered. "Why should she fight? Would you fight?"

Marah tried to put herself in Demetria's place. No family, no home, no one who truly loved her. A chill washed down her spine as she recognized herself in the description.

"You find out which prison the mama's in," the elderly doctor said, "and I shall do the legwork to bring her here for a visit. Maybe the little girl can find a reason to fight."

With a nod that seemed to settle this outrageous and probably impossible plan, he started for the door. Marah touched his shoulder.

"Dr. Jordan," she said, "I've been wanting to talk to you. I need to . . . well, to take some time off. It's my father. He was injured not long ago, and he's asked me to go to Kansas."

"He needs you."

"He says he does, but he doesn't. Not in the way you think." The idea of Big Ed Morgan needing anyone was ludicrous. "I have to settle his situation—put the farm on the market and set him up in a retirement center."

"It's a difficult time to be away, Dr. Morgan. We need your

opinion on the HMO situation. And don't forget the plans to move our group into the new medical building next month. Can you return by the end of the month?"

"The end of June? I . . . uh . . . I need more time than that. I was thinking of a short sabbatical. Three months at the most. That would get my father through the harvest and give me a chance to sell the farm."

"But three months?"

"I haven't taken time off since I started working here. I could be back by mid-September at the latest. Believe me, I'm hoping to make this trip as short as possible."

"You don't want to go?"

"Well, I . . ." Marah felt about two inches tall. Why wouldn't a daughter want to help her ailing father? How could a doctor—in the business of caring for the ill and tending to the needy—be so callous?

"Dr. Jordan," she said finally, "you know my life is here in St. Louis."

"I see." He nodded, and she wondered if this man really did see beyond her words. "Dr. Morgan, you are one of our busiest physicians. Do you think the other pediatricians in the group will agree to take your cases while you're away for three months?"

"They will if you speak on my behalf."

Dr. Jordan stepped out into the hallway, bent his head, and fell silent. Beside him, Marah shifted from one foot to the other. The thought of seeing her father again, of looking into his hard blue eyes and touching his thick fingers and smelling the sweat on his worn-out overalls, made her feel sick inside. Sick and afraid and angry. But who else did he have? Who else did she have?

"I will speak on your behalf," Dr. Jordan said. "But I ask you to do something for me, too. I ask you to go into this patient's room right now and sit down on the chair beside her bed."

"Of course. And then what?" Marah tried to anticipate what her mentor would recommend next. A new form of treatment? A method of therapy? An observation chart?

"Then I ask you to take out that little Bible from the drawer beside the bed. You know the one I mean?"

"The Gideons' Bible?"

"That's it." He smiled, his face forming a familiar wreath of wrinkles. "You read that Bible to Demetria, Dr. Morgan."

"But—" She started after him as he walked away. "But what do you mean?"

"Read it." He waved a hand over his shoulder and vanished around a corner.

Marah let out a groan and checked her watch. She didn't have time to read the Bible to a semicomatose patient. She had admitted three children to the pediatrics wing that morning, and she needed to check on each of them. A two-year-old had developed serious croup, the parents were distraught and unhappy about the oxygen tent, and Marah was hoping to be able to release the child the following day. Another patient had been hit by a car while he was bicycling—no helmet, of course. The prognosis was grim. And the third had been brought in after his mother had discovered a hard lump in the groin area. Marah needed to evaluate the test results and probably refer him to a surgeon.

She glanced into Demetria's room, weighing her promise to Dr. Jordan. Though she regularly attended church and sometimes even made it to an evening Bible study, Marah couldn't deny that her private time with God had diminished with each passing year. Oh, she tried to skim through a few Scriptures and offer up a quick prayer each morning before work, but she was always in too great a hurry to actually ponder the verses' meaning or delve into deep prayer—just as she was in a hurry now.

With a sigh, she walked back into the room, opened the bedside drawer, took out the maroon Gideons' Bible, and sat down beside her little burn patient. The Twenty-third Psalm would be quick. It was short, and she had memorized it in Vacation Bible School long ago.

"'The Lord is my shepherd,'" she began. Her voice sounded too loud in the room, too hard and metallic, like the uncaring robot she feared she might become. Swallowing, she reached out, took Demetria's small hand in hers, and began to whisper. "'I shall not want. He maketh me to lie down in green pastures: he leadeth me beside the still waters.'"

Marah could recall her mother reading from the book of Psalms every morning at breakfast. No matter how loudly Ed griped, on this one matter Ruby Morgan stood firm. There

would be no breakfast until a psalm had been read and the meal
had been prayed over.

"'He restoreth my soul,'" Marah read, "'he leadeth me in the
paths of righteousness for his name's sake.'"

The paths of righteousness hadn't brought Marah's mother a
lot of outward happiness. But her faith had been her source of
strength. Every Sunday morning and evening, she had combed
and braided her four daughters' long dark hair, buttoned them
into starched dresses, and marched them off to church. On
Wednesday nights, they were allowed to wear pants to the
prayer service. Ed grunted in disapproval, though he never
went along.

"'Yea, though I walk through the valley of the shadow of
death,'" Marah said softly, her eyes on tiny Demetria but her
thoughts on her mother, "'I will fear no evil.'"

Evil. An image drifted through her thoughts almost too
quickly to capture. The big old white house. Her mother ill,
a burning fever like this child's . . .

Was that how her mother had died? Had a fever killed her
. . . or had something else happened? Why had Marah never
been told the story of her mother's death? Why hadn't she
asked?

She focused on the Bible. "'Surely goodness and mercy,'" she
whispered. "'Goodness and mercy—'"

A loud buzzing drowned her words. Marah glanced at the
monitors and leaped to her feet, dropping the Bible to the floor
as a young nurse raced into the room.

"Dr. Morgan, we've got a Code Blue in here!" the woman said. "Her blood pressure's way down."

"I can see that. Get me some gloves."

Alarms sounded, and the room filled with nurses, physicians, machinery, shouting, commands. Marah leaned over the bed and took the child's small hand.

Demetria was dying.

👣 👣 👣

"Beans." Ed eased his stockinged feet off the mattress as the telephone jangled from the living room. Gypsy began to bark, the white hair on her nape rising in defense of her master. The folded aluminum walker was in reach, and Ed snagged it with his good arm. Didn't take but a second to flip the thing into position, but standing up was another matter.

"Gyp, hush yourself, dog." Ed heaved himself off the bed, grimacing as the bones in his pelvis protested the weight they were forced to bear. All his life he'd considered his muscular, brawny body an asset. Now he'd give just about anything to be a skinny string bean like the fellow who came out from the Department of Family Services to check on him once a week.

Marah had set that up. Ed had tried his best to drive the fellow off, but he kept coming back. Even brought groceries once in a while. A good thing, but still an intrusion.

Pain shot through his back and down his legs as Ed rolled the walker into the living room. The phone would probably quit squalling just before he got to it. Whoever was on the other end would get tired of waiting and hang up. The government fellow had tried to bring him an answering machine, whatever that was. Ed said he had about all the machines he could take.

"What?" he barked into the receiver. "What do you want?"

"It's Marah."

"Well?"

"I wanted to let you know that I've made a decision. I feel like I ought to help you out, and I had a young patient who . . . anyway, she didn't . . . well, I've decided to come to the farm for a few—"

"When you getting here, girl?"

She didn't answer for a moment. He realized he'd made her mad, the way he'd cut her off. Well, Marah was mad at him all the time anyhow. Been mad at him her whole life. He didn't know why. Never had understood the girl. He'd been a good father to her, kept her fed and clothed. But she always wanted something more from him, the way she looked at him from a distance with her big, hungry blue eyes. She reminded him a little of Gypsy, always staring at him, unspeaking but begging and pleading all the same. A dog was easy. Just give her a pat and a scrap of bacon from the table. But Ed never could figure out what it was Marah wanted, and it frustrated him to try.

"I'll be driving down there," she was saying, "so it'll take a couple of days. I'm leaving tomorrow."

"Tomorrow? What's wrong with today? Still plenty of daylight left."

"I have a cat, my garden, mail—a lot of things to take care of."

"A cat?" Ed didn't like the thought of some scrawny feline invading his farm. He'd had a cat once as a boy—one of the wild little barn kittens had turned out to be friendly, and they'd taken up together. That tiny orange cat had slept on his bed for months, curled up at his feet for warmth. But then one day Pop caught it stalking chickens, and that was the end of that. Ed had been inconsolable as his father's rifle dispatched all the barn cats one by one. Sometimes at night when he was trying to get to sleep, he could still hear the crack of the bullets. As he had sat on the front porch crying over the loss of his orange kitten, Pop reminded him that cats were always getting run over by tractors or crawling up into the engine of a pickup and turning themselves into mincemeat. Cats and farms just didn't make a good mix.

"Don't you bring a cat out here," Ed warned his daughter. Then he thought he'd better add an explanation. "Gyp wouldn't like it."

"A friend is taking him." She was silent for a moment, as though he'd offended her at the mention of his dog. "Listen, I want you to start thinking about where you might want to live. You know, in town."

"Town?" He scowled. Now wasn't this just like his oldest daughter, coming up with something out of the blue? Ed

Morgan had been brought up to believe that children ought to be quiet and respectful, doing their chores and never making much of a ruckus. But Marah had her own ideas about things. He'd always felt she spent too much time reading and thinking, and that gave her an independent streak a mile long.

"What's all this about town, girl?" he asked. "I've got a good place right here on the farm. This rock house isn't going anywhere, and neither am I."

"You're living in the rock house?"

"That's what I said."

"But the rock house was Grandpa's. When did you move out of the white house?"

"When the roof started to leak." Ed thought about describing the situation to Marah, telling her all the details of the move and the condition of the old white clapboard house. Sometimes he felt that when he talked to her, giving her his opinions on one matter or another, he was able to reach out and touch her a little bit. But right now he was sore and tired, and he just wanted her to come home.

"So, hurry up and get yourself out here," he said. "Pete's about had it with milking my cows twice a day and keeping an eye on my wheat. And don't bring any cats, you hear me?"

"I wasn't planning to."

"Good."

He dropped the receiver onto the cradle and gritted his teeth as the knives in his ribs twisted through his chest. It was about time Marah got her head on straight. He pushed the walker back toward the bedroom. He hadn't fed and clothed four daughters all those years for nothing. A man did his duty by his family, and they owed him their loyalty in return. He never would forget the day Marah had driven off to college, shouting at him through the open window of her car. She'd said she hated him. Well, hate was one thing. Loyalty was another.

A rap on the door sent Gypsy into another frenzy. What now? Ed tried to look back over his shoulder, but the pain ripped through him. Laboriously, he pushed his walker in a wide arc until he was facing the front of the room. Good thing that skinny government worker had rolled up the rug.

"Hold on," he yelled. "I'm coming."

Every jolt of the rough wooden planks his great-grandfather had hewn to build the floor sent a stab of agony through Ed's body. Dumb thing, pulling on that hay bale. When the twine broke and he stepped backward off that loft, his life had changed forever. Still, he didn't believe in regretting the past. Never look back.

"What?" he growled, pulling open the door. A tall fellow in a suit and tie stood just outside on the porch with two younger men behind him. "You boys need something?"

"Good afternoon," the man said. He was wearing a pair of sunglasses with mirrored lenses that went clear around his face to his ears. "We're looking for a Mr. Edward Morgan."

Right off the bat, Ed took a dislike to those sunglasses. And the man himself was pasty, with the white, bread-dough hands of a city fellow. Probably didn't have a decent callus on his body. Ed decided the men must be from one of those religious groups that rode around on bicycles, though he didn't see their little name tags. Well, he hadn't been to any church in years, and he wasn't planning to start now.

"I'm Ed Morgan," he said. "Who's asking?"

"My name is Dr. Milton Gregory. I'm an archaeologist with the Bureau of Indian Affairs."

"No Indians around here. Not for a hundred years, give or take a few." He started to shut the door.

The man put out his bread-dough hand. "We're aware of that. All the same, our research shows that this area was a part of the Osage Indian reservation from 1825 until 1870. We have reason to believe that a large village once stood on land that is now part of your farm, Mr. Morgan."

"Do tell." He wondered what they were getting at. Never had felt kindly toward government types. Sneaky, was what they were. Even that skinny fellow who came to see him once a week. After the man left, Ed always checked things around the house just to be sure nothing was missing. You never could be too careful.

"Mr. Morgan," the archaeologist went on, "the Bureau of Indian Affairs recently received a formal request from officials of the Osage tribe that we try to locate the site of their former village. They intend to transport any human remains discovered there to the current reservation in Oklahoma for a proper burial. Although the tribe asked to do the work themselves, the bureau felt that the site might be of archaeological importance.

I have some medical training as well as a great deal of experience in anthropological analysis. Because of that, my team and I were assigned the task of locating the village, excavating the site, and preserving the remains."

Ed was getting tired of leaning on his walker. His right arm was still strong enough, but he'd dislocated his left shoulder. He had a feeling he knew what these men were wanting, and he didn't like it much. If he had his druthers, he'd send them packing.

Now Dr. Gregory was taking out a file folder and displaying a sheaf of papers imprinted with the seal of the BIA. Ed couldn't take the thing and hold himself up at the same time, so he just stared at the tiny rows of printing.

"This letter authorizes us to begin work immediately," Dr. Gregory said. "If you're comfortable with that, I'd ask you to sign on this line." The bureau man marked a small X at the bottom of the page and handed the pen to Ed.

He didn't take it. "I don't want government boys roaming all over my land," Ed said. "Forget it." He tried to shut the door.

The man held out his hand to prevent it. "I don't believe you understand, sir." The archaeologist smiled. "We are authorized to begin this excavation."

"Not on my private land, you're not."

"Yes, sir, we are. But we'd prefer to have your cooperation. Without it, we'll still continue. But with it, we can proceed more quickly and with less impact on your farming operation."

What farming operation? Ed wanted to ask. Ever since his

accident, the whole place had gone downhill. The last thing he needed was government folks out digging holes in his fields and scaring the cattle. On the other hand, those fellows standing behind the doctor looked mighty strong.

"Any of you boys know how to run a milker?" he called over the leader's shoulder.

"I do, sir. My daddy was an insurance man, but we owned a small farm, too. Dairy cattle, mostly." The man was of average build with a blond crew cut. "My name's Mike Dooley, sir."

"Mike, how about milking my cows for me tonight? You reckon you could do that?"

"Yes, sir. And I'll milk them tomorrow morning, too."

"That is, if we can have your pledge of cooperation as we move onto your farm," the archaeologist added.

"Hand over that pen." Ed balanced himself long enough to scribble his signature on the line. "There's a bunkhouse south of here a mile or so down that road. Got places for you to put your sleeping bags. Mike, get your backside over here to the rock house before long. My neighbor comes to milk of an evening, and he'll tell you what's what. Pete'll be glad to hand it off to you."

The archaeologist smiled again.

Ed shut the door in his face.

Odell, Nebraska

Judd Hunter edged onto a red vinyl seat and stretched his legs out under the table. "Been waiting long?"

"About an hour." Chuck shook his head as he glanced at a clock on the wall of the truck stop's diner. "Midnight. You ever been on time for anything, Hunter?"

"If I had a decent vehicle, I'd give it my best shot."

From the booth, Judd could keep an eye on his pickup through the plate-glass window that fronted the almost-deserted eatery. The rusty green rattletrap had no locks, and all his gear was stashed in a duffel bag on its grimy floor.

"You're a farmhand," Chuck said, handing over a manila packet fastened with a brass brad. "You need a pickup."

"Yeah, and I need a vacation, too. It's been two years since I've taken time off."

"I don't know what you're griping about, Hunter. You had all that time in the hospital."

"Four days. And I was recovering from surgery."

"OK, OK, but this'll be a lot like a vacation. Low-key, nothing sophisticated. Just keep your eye on things."

"I've heard that before."

"Seriously. They watch us. We watch them. That's about it."

"What can I get for you, cowboy?" The waitress wore a pale blue polyester uniform, white apron, snagged stockings, black utility shoes. Blond hair out of a bottle. Fortyish; five-three; one-thirty. Scar on the upper left biceps.

"Coffee," he said. "Black."

"This stuff is high octane," she said as she turned his cup over on the saucer and filled it. "You might be up all night."

"Planning on it." He noted she was left-handed.

"Something to eat?"

"Cheeseburger."

As she headed for the kitchen, Chuck gave a rueful grin. "You'll regret it. Enough grease to float the U.S. Navy. I've had two."

Judd gave his coffee a stir. He was glad to see Chuck again. The two men had worked together for the past seven years. Gregarious, loyal, dedicated to the organization and his colleagues, Chuck had earned something Judd extended to very few people—his trust.

"How's that leg anyhow?" Chuck asked.

Judd ran his hand over the still-tender flesh under his jeans. "Better."

"How many bullet holes you sporting these days, Hunter? Two or three?"

"Four, counting the bullet that's lodged near my spine. So, who's our boy?"

"Dr. Milton Gregory." Chuck handed over a second packet. "This is a different can of worms."

"How?"

"The guy is smart," Chuck explained. "Brilliant, some say. A week ago, he packed a lot of high-tech lab equipment into his van and drove to Kansas. Took two of his colleagues along."

"What's he doing on a Kansas wheat farm?" Judd wondered.

"No idea." Chuck passed a third envelope across the table. "Edward Donald Morgan. Wheat, a few cows, four grown daughters, wife died years ago. Wounded in the Korean War, Purple Heart, Medal of Honor. Seems his patrol was ambushed and he saved the life of one of his buddies. Other than that, the man has no background. Doesn't turn up anywhere but voting records, motor vehicle registration, and the IRS. Simple farm, simple man."

Judd let out a low whistle as a batch of photographs slid from the envelope into his hand. The first was a high school graduation portrait of a striking young woman with dark hair and big blue eyes. He flipped it over and read the notation: Marah Morgan. The other photos were obviously of her sisters.

Two were identical twins. The data sheet put Marah in
Missouri, Deborah in Oregon, and the twins in the army, both
of them hovering somewhere around the Persian Gulf. The
image of the farmer had been taken from a driver's license. He
was six-four, two hundred and fifty pounds, and he looked
about as friendly as a grizzly bear.

"Can't wait to meet him," Judd said.

"I'll bet. The two of you'll be like family in no time."

Judd shrugged as the waitress slid his plate onto the table.
He poured some ketchup on the fries. "Speaking of families,
how are Sheri and the kids?" He had spent a little time with
them at Chuck's home in Virginia, with his pretty wife and
three children.

Chuck dug in his back pocket for his wallet. "Take a look at
that. Jamie's senior picture. Is he a chip off the old block, or
what?"

The young man's grin mirrored his father's, their freckled
faces and carrot orange hair identical. Judd had to laugh. He'd
never known a father as proud of his children.

"Eighteen years old." Chuck gazed at the photograph of his
son. "Can you believe that? And here are my gals, Sheri and
the two little ones. Would you look at those sundresses? Sheri
made them herself. Sewed up three of them so they'd all look
alike. She's amazing, I'll tell you what. We're coming up on our
twentieth this year."

"Going to celebrate?"

"You bet. I'm taking her to Indiana. Now don't bust a gut

laughing and spit your coffee all over me. Sheri was born in Terre Haute, and she's always wanted to go back. So I'm making a big deal out of it." He fell silent for a moment, running his finger over the picture. "I love this little lady, you know."

"You're lucky to have her," Judd said. "Sheri's a great woman."

"It's not about luck. It's about a promise. A commitment."

Judd nodded. He had believed in such things once. Had trusted his wife, counted on their vows. He could still recall the way Marianne had tossed back her long blond hair when she told him about her new love, her dreams for her future, the baby she was expecting, the plans she had made. He had just returned from the Gulf War. A Desert Storm hero, he had thought. When he had argued with her, fighting in his soldier way, she had called him hollow. An empty man.

"I wish I could spend more time with Sheri and the kids," Chuck was saying. "I've been thinking of getting out. I'd like to work in the yard. Putter around the house."

"Putter? You?"

"Don't knock it. If we can nail this gig, I'd like to hang it up for good. Maybe find a cushy job someplace."

"The family means that much to you?"

"You bet it does," Chuck said as he put his wallet away. "Do you ever think about marrying again?"

"Nope, not on the agenda."

Though he had rejected the idea of another marriage, Judd sometimes wondered what it would feel like to hold a woman in his arms, certain she would never leave him. To tell her everything he held bottled inside. To argue and never fear that a disagreement would bring an end. To be weak, even hollow at times, and still be valued. What would it be like to know the truth of love?

"A wife would get you out of that shell more," Chuck said. "You keep to yourself too much, Hunter."

"I'm low profile."

"Sure, nobody sees you. But nobody wants you either. Nobody needs you." Chuck leaned forward. "You think your own intelligence, your instinct, are going to save you."

"Anything wrong with that?"

"They may get you through. But you'll be lonely."

Judd shrugged. "It's a life."

🐾 🐾 🐾

Marah pulled her silver BMW to the side of the road beside the black metal mailbox. Its owner's name had been crudely lettered in white paint: Ed Morgan. Leaning her forehead on the steering wheel, she drank in a deep breath. No wonder her mother had spent so much time on her knees in prayer. Just the thought of driving down the gravel road onto the Morgan Farm sent a wave of nausea crashing through Marah's stomach. When she left eighteen years ago, she had vowed never to return.

God, help me, she lifted up. When nothing more came to mind, she gripped the wheel until the blood stopped in her fingers. Conversations with God had always been a part of her life. As a child, she had regularly climbed a huge tree on the farm, one of the few that thrived on the windswept prairie. Escaping her earthbound father, she would scramble up the branches, curl her skinny legs around her favorite limb, and address her heavenly Father. Amazing how carefully he had always listened as her pain and longing and loneliness poured out.

Through the intense years of medical school and residency, Marah had relied on her faith in Christ to undergird her. Though she spent less time in prayer and Bible study now, she gave God the credit for all she had accomplished. With his help she had built a pediatrics practice, paid back her school loans, and had even begun to invest her money. She saw her medical work as her mission—a way to bring God's love and healing to the world. Most of the time she felt whole and fulfilled and purposeful . . . unless her father stepped into her thoughts.

Marah lifted her head and let her gaze slide across land that had belonged to the Morgan family for more than a hundred years. Like a flat, smooth blanket, its fields of ripe winter wheat seamed together with barbed-wire fences and quilted with bumpy dirt roads, the farm beckoned her. She didn't want it, she told herself. It was worn and frayed, like Grandma's old coverlet that Marah's mother had laid across the bed on cold nights. With its holes and bumps and tattered edges, the quilt held no appeal for her. But somehow she needed its warmth.

Nestled in the middle of the property sat the cluster of old buildings that formed the centerpiece of this hodgepodge farm. The rock house had been built of stone that Marah's great-

great-grandfather had plowed up from the prairie. Years later, Ed's father had constructed a white frame building with clapboard siding. Behind the two houses, the red, tin-roofed barn leaned to the left as it always had, sagging with the weight of years. The bunkhouse sat off in the distance, and the machinery sheds, pens, grain bins, and rusty pickups stood just where they had for as long as Marah could remember. Nothing added. Nothing removed.

She straightened and ran her manicured fingernails through her hair. She no longer needed that old quilt, she reminded herself. She had grown beyond Morgan Farm, transformed herself into someone new and completely different. Pearls at her neck. A casual spring suit, Jones New York. Taut silk stockings and beige heels. She was a successful physician now. A pediatrician with a thriving practice. Published in several medical journals. Popular conference speaker.

OK, OK. She could do this. She didn't even know what she was afraid of. Her father could no longer dominate her, could he? He couldn't order her around as though she were some low-ranking private in his patrol, making her work until she could barely drag herself to bed, giving her nothing of himself but his long-winded opinions or barked commands. She didn't need the man's affirmation to know who she was and what she could accomplish.

Maybe she was afraid that her anger would emerge, swollen like a red, infected boil she had seen once on a little patient. Maybe the fury inside her would rise like that pustule and then burst in a gush of foul-smelling, diseased rage. She had tried so hard to heal the anger in her heart, praying and praying for release. But maybe it still lurked beneath the surface, waiting until her father said something cruel or thoughtless or mean, just the way he always did. And then it would fill her with pus and contamination and make her sick again—so very sick.

Or maybe she was afraid she would begin to want him again, hoping against hope that he would become the daddy she had always dreamed of. Maybe her hard-won strength would drain away, and she would melt into a puddle of longing—longing for strong arms to hold her tight against sorrow and fear, longing for a gentle kiss on the cheek, a pat on the back, shared conversation and laughter and hugs. Marah didn't want to need Ed Morgan. She wanted to be sufficient and complete.

Lord, please help me.

She put the BMW in gear and turned in at the gate. As she passed the mailbox, she saw her mother's bright blue morning glories twining up the rough post. Beside them, the four-o'clocks were just emerging for the afternoon, hot pink flowers unfurling in the heat.

"Always try to keep something in bloom, Marah." Like the barest breath of wind on a summer day, a soft voice from somewhere in the past whispered to her. *"Just after the morning glories fold up for the day, the four-o'clocks will come out. A garden is such a lovely thing."*

Marah forced down the unexpected lump in her throat and pressed on the gas. *Keep something in bloom,* she repeated to herself. *Don't let him squash the beauty. Don't let him step on you.*

Ruby Morgan had been an avid gardener. Like fluffy yellow chicks, her four little daughters had followed their mama hen everywhere, helping her sow seeds and transplant tiny native flowers into her thriving plots. Fresh blossoms had graced the Morgan table at every meal, arranged in canning jars or dime-store glass vases. The bouquets stopped, of course, when Ruby became so ill. Once when Marah was eight, not long after their mother's death, six-year-old Deborah had pulled up a handful of goldenrod stems and put them in a vase on the table.

"Goldenrod?" Ed had snapped. "We'll be sneezing for the rest of the week," and he'd given Deborah a sound thrashing for her foolishness. Deb had never forgotten that. Years later she called to tell Marah that at the last minute she'd picked some stems of goldenrod and added them to her wedding bouquet. They had laughed together, savoring the small victory over him.

As Marah pulled to a stop in the barren front yard of the rock house, a cloud of fine dust settled on her car. *Beans*, she thought. She always kept her car spotless. But, she reminded herself, time would pass quickly and it wouldn't be long before she could drive to her favorite St. Louis car wash and rinse away every reminder of her three-month sabbatical. Not long.

"That you, girl?" The gruff voice was accompanied by a dog's excited barking.

As Marah stepped out onto the gravel, she saw her father rise from an old rocking chair and push himself upright, leaning on his walker. His whiskered flesh sagged around the jowls, and a pale knee showed through a hole in his overalls. *Oh no.* Something crumbled inside her. The dam she'd built up against him.

Big Ed Morgan had always been strong. Untouchable. Rigid. A fortress. Now look at him. He reminded her of the scarecrow she and her sisters once helped their mother erect in the vegetable garden, skinny and hunched with a wrinkled burlap face and a worn-out flannel shirt that had been chewed on by mice. Marah hadn't believed their scarecrow could frighten anything away. He was too old and mournful and broken.

"Hey there," she managed. She slipped her purse over one shoulder and walked toward the sloping front porch. "Wheat looks good."

"If you'd driven the way I taught you, you'd have been here two hours ago." He pushed the walker forward on its two little rollers, the scruffy Border collie at his feet. "Pete's coming over to set you up on the milkers. I figured you probably forgot how to do it."

She stood clutching her purse strap, staring at him, feeling the dam rise again inside her. Her father was no scarecrow. He was an old bull, his horns battle worn, his flesh scarred but still solid. He would never falter, never grow weak. She could sense her own willpower building against him—she, the young heifer, stronger and even more stubborn. Their blue eyes locked, and she knew they were a match. Two minutes together, and the Morgan blood inside them had heated to a low boil.

"Your doctor told me your ribs and shoulder are healing,"

Marah said as she stepped onto the porch. "But he says you need to stay off that hip."

"Doctor," Big Ed spat.

The word slapped her in the face. "You'd better sit down," she said.

"I'll sit when I'm good and ready." He looked her over, a mixture of surprise and regret suffusing his face. "Well, well. I guess you're all grown up now. Didn't expect you to be so tall and skinny."

"Skinny?" The word conjured images of her fragile childhood. No, she wasn't skinny anymore. She thought of her treadmill, her sit-ups, her power milk shakes.

"I'm in peak physical condition," she told him. "In fact, I ran in a 5K last month."

"You must not be eating right. 'Course, I reckon nobody does in the city."

"Actually, the social worker from Family Services is concerned about *your* eating habits. He suggested I arrange for meals to be sent out here. He says you eat ice cream all the time."

"Chocolate. With Hershey's syrup on top."

They stared at each other.

"And I hear you haven't been going to your physical therapy sessions," she said. "You know, the exercise program your doctor set up for you. To work your muscles. Help you get stronger."

"I check on my wheat and clean the milking parlor and oil the tractor engine and about a hundred other things. Why should I go all the way to town just so I can stretch some little pulleys and walk no place on a treadmill?"

"But there are specific muscle groups—," Marah began. And then she knew nothing she could say would make any difference. He had made up his mind.

She took another step toward her father, her heels echoing on the hollow porch floor. Age had softened him a little, or maybe it was just the walker. In spite of his blunt words, she felt sure his blue eyes had misted as he studied her. But she reminded herself not to fall under any false spell. This was Ed Morgan.

"I've come to help you put things in order," she said. "I'll stay until the first of September. While I'm here, you're going to need to decide what to do about the farm and your own future."

"This farm is my future."

"But you can't manage the place any longer. And you can't keep living out here by yourself. It's not safe."

"Safe? I've lived here all my life. Know the land like the back of my hand. There's no place safer."

"Not when you're alone. Not when you're disabled."

"Disabled?"

"Whether you like it or not, things have changed. You're going to have to make some decisions about your future."

He eyed her. "Is that why you came out here? To move me off my land?"

"I came to help you because you're my father. I'm your daughter."

He gave a snort. "A daughter stands by her family. She doesn't go running off to who-knows-where at the first chance."

"I went to college," she said. "Medical school."

The blue in his eyes glittered, hard again. "I know what you're after. You want to sell the farm and dump me in one of those old folks' homes, don't you? You want my money."

Her first reaction was fury. Blazing white-hot rage. With effort, she transformed it into contemptuous laughter. "I don't need your money. That's the last thing I would ever need from you."

"Well, what do you want from me then? What brought you all the way out here in your high-heel shoes and your uppity doctor suit? What are you looking to get from me, girl?"

Marah stared at him. What she had needed from her father years ago he hadn't had the power to give, she thought as hurt poured over the wall she had built to hold it back. She no longer needed anything from this man. It was too late.

"I came out here to tend to you the way you once tended to me," she told her father. "I came to make sure you have a roof over your head and food in your stomach."

"What's that supposed to mean?"

"It means I'm here to see that the land and the buildings are in good shape before they're sold. You'll need the money to pay for your care."

"You're not selling the farm, girl!" he bellowed. "This land has been in our family more than a hundred years. This dirt you're in such a hurry to sell off is soaked with Morgan blood and sweat. This farm *is* our family, and I'll be jiggered if I'll part with one acre of it!"

Marah gritted her teeth. Yes, the farm was her father's family. It had been that way from the beginning. And it was a family in which she could not survive.

"I won't stay in the rock house," she told him. "I'll put my things in the white house, our old house."

"Suit yourself." He hesitated a moment. "Roof leaks."

"Roofs can be fixed," she said. *A lot of things can be fixed,* she wanted to tell him. *Maybe you and I could be fixed. More than a patch—maybe we could build a whole new roof.*

"You've been gone a long time, girl," he said. "You and your sisters. If you'd stayed around, I might have repaired that roof. But you all ran off and left me here, and somehow I just made do on my own. I got used to doing without you."

Was there tenderness in his tone? Marah studied his face. Maybe she was just imagining he had spoken in a wistful way. Had he missed her and the other girls? Had he actually thought of her more than once in the last eighteen years?

"Well, what are you standing there for?" he said, his face firming up again, the old soldier back in formation. "The only way either of us is going to have a roof over our heads or food on the table is if you get busy running this farm. Now march!"

"March?" she said, incredulous. She gave a derisive laugh.

"Get moving, girl. How much more do I have to say?"

Marah stood before him, trembling with pent-up rage. There

was nothing gentle or kind about this man. He was hard and cold—straight to the heart. Everything inside Marah screamed in frustration. *Get back in the car. Drive away. Leave Ed Morgan to die in the miserable, selfish place he's created for himself.* She owed him nothing. Absolutely nothing.

"Hey, Marah!" The youthful voice cut the tension. "Your dad told me you were coming."

"Pete." She swung around, swallowing the lump of anger in her throat. "How are you?"

Husky, deeply tanned, and wearing a smile that outshone the sun, her childhood friend bounded up the stairs and gave her a firm hug. Pete Harris had inherited the neighboring farm from his parents. She'd heard sometime back that he was married and doing well.

"It's been a long time, Mar," he said. "I'm glad you're back."

She nodded. "You're looking great."

"Couldn't be better. Wheat's ripe, lots of calves, and a new tractor, to boot. Did you hear Hilda's expecting? She's due this fall. We're about to bust with excitement. The doc says she's carrying twins."

"Twins?" Ed said. "You might get more than you bargained for there, Pete. Let me tell you that from experience. Sara Lee Cupcakes—what a pair."

Once again surprised by the softer tone in her father's voice, Marah turned to find him seated in the rocking chair, a small golden-haired child nestled on his lap. Where had she come from? Like a pink-cheeked, barefoot pixie in ragged cutoffs and a baggy T-shirt, the little girl seemed to have materialized out of nowhere. All lanky arms and legs, she snuggled close against the old man's chest as she rubbed the dog behind its ears.

"You had a baby named Sara Lee Cupcakes?" she asked, focusing liquid blue eyes on Ed's face.

"Twin girls," he said, cupping her cheek in his calloused hand. "Sarah and Leah Morgan. Cute as bugs' ears, but ornery little critters. They're both in the military now, off to who-knows-where."

"Perky, did you say hey to Marah?" Pete spoke up. "I don't know if she's ever met you."

The large eyes turned on the visitor. "Hey," she said shyly. "I'm Pearl Kathleen Harris, and I'm seven years old."

"Seven going on twenty-one," Ed interjected. "Thinks she's too big for her britches."

"You can call me Perky," the child continued. "Everybody does."

"I'm Marah Morgan."

"Marah's a doctor," Pete explained. "A pediatrician. Marah used to tag around after me when we were growing up. She's Poppy's daughter."

"Poppy, you never told me you had any children." Perky tapped the old man's nose with a forefinger, as though to admonish a naughty boy. "How many do you have?"

"Four. All girls."

"Sisters." Perky beamed at Marah. Her front teeth were growing in, two large flat shingles that looked too big for her face. Wispy bangs framed her eyes, and two braids hung like thick ropes down her back. "Guess what! I might have twin sisters in the fall, if my mom can make it this time. Did you play together, like having tea parties and planting gardens and sledding down hills in the winter?"

"They played too much," Ed said.

"We worked very hard," Marah countered. "I did all the cooking and laundry after our mother passed away, and my sisters and I did chores every morning and evening. We spent our days in the fields and the milking parlor and the kitchen. We didn't have time for tea parties."

She realized she'd been talking to her father. He glared at her. Perky looked from one to the other.

Pete clapped his hands together. "Well," he said, "better get out to the pasture and bring those ladies in. Perky, want to help?"

"Daddy, would it be OK if I stayed here with Poppy? I haven't gotten to see him for three days."

"That's fine, Perk. Marah, I'll meet you in the barn in a few minutes. Need any help with your suitcases?"

She shook her head, still staring at the little blond girl snuggled up on her father's lap as though he were a kindly grandpa. The old man had closed his eyes and was stroking the child's hair as she hummed a tune. He was almost smiling.

Who was this stranger? All her life Marah had longed for just one gentle touch, a soft word, a smile from her father. She would have given everything to have been allowed to crawl into his lap. And here sat this elfin child, teasing him and calling him "Poppy," as though he were a blowsy petaled flower nodding in the breeze and smelling as sweet as a rare perfume. How had Perky transformed him? Why did he cuddle this little girl yet bark at his own daughter? Who was this child?

Jealousy, confusion, pain, and an overwhelming desire to trade places with Perky Harris swept through Marah. She leaned against the porch post as Pete started for the pasture.

"Glad you're back, Mar," he called over his shoulder. "Welcome home."

The Nineteenth Day of the Yellow Flower Moon, The Year of 1869

Today my mother left us. The ge-ta-zhe entered her head and grasped her mind, digging deeply inside her with talons that severed her sense and reason. This morning my mother began to leap and turn on her pallet, as though she were a frog that had been trapped in the hollow of a stone. I crawled toward her from my own pallet, where I now lie burning with the heat of the ge-ta-zhe as it eats my body. I tried to calm my mother, but she cried out and bit me and scratched my skin. My father says it is not his wife who does these things.

It is only the ge-ta-zhe.

My father tells me not to fear, but I am afraid. He says the Heavy Eyebrows agent will come with medicine to fight the ge-ta-zhe. Why does my father trust the agent? Why does he believe anything or anyone can have power over the ge-ta-zhe? My father hopes like a man clinging to a branch when the river rushes around him. He hopes, but in this he is foolish.

Though my mother's mind has gone, her body lives on. The ge-ta-zhe sweeps across her skin and paints it red. This is not the orange red of the columbine flower or the pink red of the setting rays of Grandfather the Sun. This is the red of new blood that pours fresh from an open wound. This is the red that sweeps over my mother as she screams and weeps and pleads for mercy.

I cough as I write these words. The cough comes from deep within my chest. The breath that leaves my body smells of death.

From The Journal of Little Gray Bird, unpublished
Central Kansas Museum of the Native American archival
collection

4

Milton Gregory was growing frustrated. The research team in Wyoming had narrowed the former site of the Indian village to this strip of rocky land along the river that ran through Morgan Farm. Gregory had historical documents and old maps to prove it. But thus far, their surveys, metal detectors, and shovels had turned up few signs of anything more significant than roaming cattle and prairie dog burrows. If there had been a village in the area, evidence of it seemed long gone. And there was little time to waste. September was approaching.

Spotting Mike Dooley, one of his two field colleagues, in the distance, Gregory decided it was time for an update on the young man's trips to the milking barn each morning and evening. The physician had visited Ed Morgan's rock house only once since they had moved onto the farm, yet he knew it was important to maintain a good working relationship with the farmer.

The team's mobile laboratory now occupied the entire loft area of the log bunkhouse. Bob Harper, the third research associate, was also a skilled electrician. He and Mike had enhanced the old building's wiring and installed a couple of new telephone lines. Computers, microscopes, and incubators had been set up behind a padlocked door. Though the sleeping quarters were camplike and therefore somewhat unsanitary, the arrangement was working well. Gregory wanted it to continue that way.

"How's the milking these days, Mike?" he called as he crossed the rocky pasture toward his colleague. As much as he resented the amount of time this aspect of the project was taking, Gregory enjoyed the vast, open vista of the prairie with its rolling wheat fields and rustic farmsteads. Having grown up in California and having spent the preceding winter in Wyoming, he welcomed the change. He removed his sunglasses and set them on top of his head. "I hope you're not going to be wooed away from us by the lures of pastoral life. You know how much we need you for this project."

Dooley grinned and took off his baseball cap. "I'm not helping out in the milking parlor anymore, sir," he said as he ran a hand over his blond crew cut. "Mr. Morgan's daughter showed up at the farm the other day. She took over the milking."

Gregory stiffened. "His daughter? Why didn't you tell me about this, Mike?"

"I didn't think it was a big deal."

"Have you met the woman?"

"No, sir, but I got the impression she's nothing to worry about. Mr. Morgan told me she'd wasted her life and was a big disappointment to him. She's not married. He said she just came to help him out until he's well enough to take over again."

"All the same, we need to keep a close watch on every resident or visitor to the farm."

"Yes, sir."

Gregory watched Dooley squirm, toeing the loose dirt with his work boot. The doctor was reminded of one of the insects in his boyhood collection. At first, concerned about their pain, he had put them in the freezer to kill them. But later, after his mother objected to the countless spiders, crickets, and cockroaches that had taken up residence with the frozen peas and ice cubes, he'd had no choice but to pin each specimen down while it was still living. Repulsed but fascinated at the same time, he had observed these small, inconsequential creatures struggling for life even as the sticky essence of their vitality seeped onto the cork display board.

Gregory took a step closer to his colleague. "Is there something else you need to tell me, Mike?"

He swallowed. "Well, there's a little girl who comes and goes. Perky's her name. She's about seven. Her dad owns the farm next to the Morgan place. Pete Harris. But he's busy all the time, and she's just a kid. I don't think they'd bother us."

"All the same, you'd better keep an eye out." Gregory crossed his arms over his chest. "We can't let our work be undermined by anything or anyone. You understand what I'm saying?"

"Yes, Dr. G, I do."

"Good, Mike. Let's never forget that we're working toward a goal that has vital significance for our nation. The future of humanity may be at stake here."

"I know, Dr. G. I realize that."

"And as for this newly arrived Morgan daughter, I think we might want to head over to the farmhouse and take a look at what's up. Why don't you give Bob a holler? We'll drive over to the rock house and join Mr. Morgan for a meal."

Mike beckoned Bob Harper, who had turned up a couple of rifle casings with his metal detector that morning, but nothing more. Piling into the large gray van, the three set out across the fields with their coolers and lunch sacks. As Gregory drove, the younger men continued their discussion from breakfast—sports scores and television shows. They had decided to root for the Royals while they were staying in Kansas. Make things more interesting that way.

As he pulled the van to a stop near the rock house, Gregory spotted Ed Morgan seated on his back porch, whittling a slab of wood. The man looked like an old fallen limb himself, all gray and hunched over and unmoving. His walker was propped against a sagging wicker table, its bright aluminum legs a stark contrast to the rustic rock walls and weathered porch.

"Hey there, Mr. Morgan," Gregory called. "How are you this fine summer day?"

Ed Morgan looked up, his bright blue eyes narrowing as the team climbed out of the van. Gregory suspected that the man was canny with an animal's wariness and instinct for survival, his nose held high as if he were sniffing the air for the scent of enemies.

"What do you want?" the farmer asked.

"Would you mind if we joined you for lunch? We thought you might like an update on our progress."

"I'm busy."

Undeterred, Gregory stepped up onto the porch. "We've brought sandwiches, apples, chips. We could sit out here at the table, or we could all go into the kitchen."

Morgan said nothing. Like slips of curled butter, wood shavings dropped to the sloping porch floor. Gregory could see that the block of pine in the farmer's hands was taking the shape of a human head, a child's face with large eyes and a smiling mouth.

"Clear yourself off a spot in the kitchen," Morgan said finally. "I don't hold with eating outdoors."

"I couldn't agree more." Gregory motioned the others into the rock house. "Nothing more uncomfortable than a picnic, in my opinion."

"Too many flies."

"I trust you'll join us at the table, Mr. Morgan."

"Name's Ed. Big Ed's what they call me."

"I can see why. It takes a strong man to manage a farm as large and complex as this one."

"What kind of sandwiches you bring? I don't like peanut butter. Sticks to your gullet."

"I brought ham."

"I'll be there."

Dooley and Harper were transferring open pickle jars and empty egg cartons from the red Formica dinette table to a trash bag as Ed manhandled his walker into the kitchen. The room reeked of unwashed dishes and unemptied garbage cans. Flies danced around the sink. A cloud of gnats hovered over a wooden bowl filled with blackened bananas. Gregory wondered why the daughter had done nothing to help her father clean up his house. She really must be a good-for-nothing, as Dooley had told him.

"Well, we've had quite a time finding that village," Gregory began. He had been hoping the farmer might provide a hint that would help the team locate the missing excavation site. Surely he knew this land intimately, and maybe he had seen or heard something that would give them the answer they were seeking. "I understand you own more than a thousand acres, Mr. Morgan." He felt as though he were playing a sort of game with the farmer, a little like solving a session of Clue. The body is in the conservatory, murdered by Professor Plum with the candlestick. Gregory already knew some of the key factors in the mystery. But the location, the location. That was the missing clue.

"The Morgan family has owned this land for more than a hundred years," Ed said. "Got it as part of the Homestead Act back in the sixties."

"That's the 1860s, I'm assuming."

"Yep." Ed spread mustard on his bread and began to layer slices of ham. "I reckon I've got the papers over at the white house someplace. My wife used to be interested in that kind of stuff. Ruby had plates and books and even some Indian junk from the old days. Thought it was important to preserve the past, she used to tell me. You take a look in the living room, and you'll see my medals from the Korean War hanging right there on the wall. Ruby had them framed in a glass box."

"I believe your wife was right about preserving the past."

"Well, that wouldn't surprise me too much. Ruby was right about a lot of things."

"Your farm takes up a huge area, Mr. Morgan. Our research team pinpointed the site of the former Indian village as some-where along the river that runs through your property."

Ed chuckled around a mouthful of sandwich. "That narrows it down, huh?"

"Our study of the Osage tribe indicates a preference for hilly ground, somewhat forested, with access to prairie hunting grounds. We've been searching along the knolls that run paral-lel to the river, and we've uncovered arrowheads, Civil War–era bullets, and a belt buckle. But so far we haven't been able to find any grave sites or concentrated artifact deposits. It's begin-ning to look like we could be searching for quite some time."

"I reckon." Ed Morgan wiped his whittling knife on his over-alls. He picked up an apple and began to peel it. The bright red skin came away in a long strip.

Gregory shifted on the cracked vinyl chair. The farmer's reticence and self-absorption annoyed him. Maybe he should move on to the topic of the newly arrived daughter.

"There was a spot we used to call Indian Hill," Ed said suddenly in a matter-of-fact voice. He dropped the apple peeling to the floor among the ants and dust. "I played on it when I was a boy. I always thought it had been given that name because the rocks were kind of craggy, you know, like the face of an old Indian chief. But maybe that's where your tribe used to camp."

"Where's Indian Hill?" Dooley blurted the question.

"Over west." Ed scowled at the young man, as though he were an impudent puppy tugging on a shoelace. Then he turned to Gregory. "With all those maps you probably own, you shouldn't have too much trouble finding it. Government planes been flying over my property for years, checking to see if I was growing what I ought and leaving fallow what I promised I would. You probably have aerial photographs of every inch of my place, don't you?"

The doctor nodded. "I suspect it was the colloquial name 'Indian Hill' that threw Mike. Can you give me a better description? Maybe you could specify some physical markers. A tree or a particular rock formation?"

"Physical markers." Ed muttered something under his breath. "Anybody who ever saw Indian Hill could figure out why it was called that. It's different from everything else around it. The whole pasture is different, covered with rocky mounds all over the place. No Morgan has ever plowed that land. Too many boulders. Indian Hill is west. Thataway."

He pointed across the room, and Dr. Gregory turned to find a woman standing in the doorway. A beautiful woman. This creature would have been the envy of his former patients. They flashed momentarily through his mind, women who tried so hard to be beautiful, tucking and peeling and plumping their skin. Lifting a little here, siphoning off a little there, certainly never anticipating nature's mistakes—small, annoying mistakes—that he had helped remove from their lives.

But Gregory knew that none of this woman's beauty came from a surgeon's knife. She wore her dark hair parted in the middle and hanging straight to her shoulders. Her eyes stood out in her face like a pair of blue sapphires. She had pale skin, a touch of sunburn on her cheeks. Tall, thin, wearing jeans and a shirt that matched her eyes, she walked into the kitchen and tossed a pair of leather gloves onto the table.

"Well, this is a surprise," the woman said as she glanced around the room. Gregory observed that she bore the same genetic traits as Ed Morgan, except that she was young and pretty and delicate. This must be the good-for-nothing daughter. "I hadn't heard we were expecting company. Who are your friends?" she asked her father.

Big Ed took a pull from a Dr. Pepper can. "Government."

"Oh?"

"I'm Dr. Milton Gregory," the doctor said, rising from his chair and extending his hand.

"Marah Morgan." She dusted her palm on her thigh before giving him a firm handshake. "Pleased to meet you."

"I'm a medical archaeologist," he said. "I work for the Bureau of Indian Affairs."

"Medical archaeology? What's that?"

"It's a branch of anthropology, actually. I was trained in anatomy, pathology, and other medical fields. But my focus was on historical human remains. You might say I'm sort of a medical examiner for the long departed." He smiled at her. "And this is my team—Mike Dooley, Bob Harper. We're searching for the site of an Osage tribal village that once stood on your father's property."

"You're staying here? On the farm?"

"In the bunkhouse. Would you care to join us for lunch, Miss Morgan?"

"Oh, no thanks. I'm busy."

"That's what your dad said, but we managed to entice him with the offer of a ham sandwich."

"It's OK. I'll grab something over at the white house." She studied him for a moment, and Gregory felt a familiar pull of attraction. He knew women liked him, enjoyed spending time with him and being seen in his company. Some of that had to do with his classic looks—the thick curling hair, square jaw, and affable smile. He kept himself physically fit and mentally alert, and at one time he had had a lot of money and the accouterments that went with it. But it had been several years since he'd allowed time for a relationship, and the flicker of desire he sensed in Marah Morgan's eyes felt strange yet somehow very welcome.

"You're not staying here?" he asked her. "With your father?"

"No, I'm . . ." She gestured vaguely behind her. "I'm over there. In the white house. It's where we used to live."

"I see."

Her cell phone rang and she left the room to answer it.

"That gizmo beeps all the time," Ed explained. "I keep mine unplugged. Jangles so loud a whittler could cut his finger clean off."

"Your daughter carries a cell phone?" Gregory asked.

"Yeah, she thinks St. Louis can't get along without her."

Just then Marah came back into the kitchen and gave the barest grunt of exasperation. "I'm monitoring the health of several patients. These are critical cases, and I need to stay in constant contact with the hospital."

A chill raced down Gregory's spine. "You work for a hospital?"

"I'm a pediatrician," Marah told him. "I have a practice in St. Louis, but I came down here to—"

"What have you been working on this morning anyhow, girl?" Ed interrupted. "I haven't seen hide nor hair of you. I hope you're not wasting time trying to fix up the old white house. I need you out in the field."

"I've *been* in the field." Her blue eyes sparked. "But we *will* need to address the future of the white house at some point. Nothing's been done to keep the place in order. There's furniture and debris everywhere. I can't even get up the stairs—"

At the sound of someone knocking, Ed shooed her off. "Get the door, will you, girl? It's probably that boy from Family Services. Tell him I don't need him anymore."

Gregory watched as Dr. Marah Morgan turned on the heel of her muddy work boot and left the kitchen. It was a shotgun house, with a view straight through, and he could see her opening the front door.

"Yes?" she said. "May I help you?"

A tall man with broad, straight shoulders and a black felt Stetson came into view. He took off his hat, but he didn't smile. "I'm looking for work," he said. "Name's Judd."

5

Judd reached down to pat the Border collie that nudged his hand for attention. Average-sized dog, long hair, typical markings, no collar. He hadn't owned a dog for years, but he liked animals. Always had.

"What kind of work are you looking for?"

The woman set one hand on her hip as she spoke. He sensed anger. Frustration, maybe. He recognized her at once from the graduation portrait in the packet Chuck had given him. Marah Morgan, the oldest daughter. She was tall—five-eight—probably one-twenty-five or less, mid-thirties. Black hair, blue eyes, sunburned cheeks, straight nose. Nice lips. She wasn't supposed to be here.

"Farmhand," he said, straightening. The dog whimpered and nosed his hand again. "Milking, branding, running a combine, tractor—you name it."

"Do you have references?"

He pulled a wad of folded letters from his back pocket, and she took them. Slender fingers, manicured nails, pale polish chipping away.

She scanned the letters, reading quickly. "Can you do any carpentry? roofing?" she asked.

"Sure."

"Will you accept minimum wage?"

He hesitated a moment, scratched his neck, eyed the dog. "Can't you do any better than that?"

"No," she said. "And we won't be needing you long. I'm hoping to put the farm up for sale once I get things in order. Through the wheat harvest and maybe a few weeks longer. Mid-September, at the latest."

"That's it?"

"I expect so."

Her blue eyes studied him, analyzing. He tried to take in the furnishings in the room behind her, rolled-up rug, sagging sofa, lamp, boots on the floor. But he came back to her eyes. Black lashes, he noted. Very long.

"All right," he said with a sigh. "Got a place I can bunk down?"

"Mind company?"

"I'm a loner myself."

"It'll just be at night. A group of archaeologists is staying here temporarily. They're searching for an Indian village. Bureau of Indian Affairs."

"Ah." Exactly what Chuck had told him.

"There are only three," she said. "You'd have a bunk."

"OK." He shrugged. "I'll get my bag. Got anything to eat?"

"Sandwiches."

Without speaking further, Judd turned and walked to the rusted vehicle. The dog followed, tail wagging. He could feel his mind slip into gear. Was it true Gregory was looking for Indian settlements? Or was that a cover for something else he was hunting? If it were Indians, which tribe? Chuck would want the information.

Judd reached into the bed of the pickup and grabbed his duffel bag. He was looking forward to the farmwork. Liked that kind of thing. Never had enjoyed doing desk time. Necessary but dull. Filling out forms, writing reports. He slung the duffel over his shoulder.

"Hi!" The tiny voice came from waist level.

Judd looked down. A child stood looking up at him, huge blue eyes, blond hair in braids, bare feet, about seven years old, he guessed. An unexpected factor. He'd have to give Chuck a hard time about it.

"My name's Pearl Kathleen Harris, but everybody calls me Perky," she said. Her curious gaze rearranged the freckles that bridged her nose. "Who are you?"

"Judd." He started for the rock house. Never had been comfortable around children.

"I live on the farm west of the Morgan place, right over there," she said, skipping beside him. Her long braids flipped up and down. "We grow winter wheat, and we have a dairy, too, just like Poppy."

"Poppy?" He wished she would go home. A child always changed the dynamics. People talked differently, behaved better. Clues stayed hidden.

"Poppy is what I call Mr. Morgan. He's my best friend. Of adults, anyway. Are you his friend?"

"Nope."

"I bet you know his daughter. Are you her boyfriend?"

He shook his head. "I'm working here now."

"Oh, good, because Poppy needs help. He got hurt really bad when he fell off the loft. Did you hear about that?"

"I just got here."

"You picked a good time—the wildflowers are blooming. What's your favorite flower?"

"Umm." He pushed open the screen door and stepped inside. Hadn't thought about flowers in years. "Roses, I guess."

"You're kidding!" She skipped around in front of him, blocking his path. "You're never going to believe this, not in a million years. Poppy's wife had a rose garden and a bunch of other flower beds before she died, and I'm bringing them back to life! You want to help me?"

Judd paused in his forward trek and gave the little girl a closer study. What was she talking about—bringing a garden back to life? Flowers were either alive or dead, weren't they?

"The gardens are hiding," the child whispered up at him, her eyes lit with an inner blue flame. Her breath smelled of bubble gum. "Nobody talks about them. Nobody even remembers them. But I know they used to be there, because I can see their outlines made out of rocks."

He studied a strand of silky gold hair lying on her pink T-shirt as he considered her words. "Well, that's nice."

"There's some other secrets here, too," she said softly. Her hand rested on his arm. "But don't be scared."

Judd nodded, his focus on the voices in the other room, the men talking and then the woman joining in.

"I've hired him because we need help around here," Marah said, her words firm. "It's not just the dairy and the wheat. It's the white house, too."

"That old house ain't worth beans." The voice was deep, gruff, commanding. "I don't know why you're staying over there anyhow. The place is going to fall down on your head."

"The white house is either an asset or a liability. If it's restored, the house will make the farm a more valuable property. I'm planning to repair it."

"Now you're back to selling my farm, are you? Well, I've got news for you, girl, this is all *my* property."

Perky took Judd's hand. "That's Poppy and his daughter," she said, pulling him toward the kitchen. "Sometimes they argue. He wants her to be a farmer. She wants him to be a daddy."

Interesting. Judd followed the little girl whose hand clasped his tightly. She strolled into the kitchen and waved.

"Hey, everybody, guess what!" The adults stared. Perky continued as if she didn't notice. "Judd's going to help me bring the dead gardens back to life! He loves roses."

The adults said nothing, regarding the child and looking curiously at Judd. He shifted from one foot to the other. Then he lowered his duffel to the floor.

"I'm Judd." He addressed the old man, clearly the alpha dog in this pack. "Thanks for the job."

"Thanks for nothing." Ed Morgan tried to lift himself from his chair; then he fell back panting. "Look here, boy, you just put your bag right back in your pickup and head out of here. We don't have the money to pay a hired hand. Besides, I don't need help. I've got her."

The daughter rounded on her father. "I've hired the man, and I'll pay him myself if I have to. I can't do this alone. There's too much work. Too many things that need—"

"You can do this, Marah. I'm counting on you." The words were a strange mixture, half compliment and half command. Ed Morgan glanced around at the men in his kitchen and gave a shrug. "A son wouldn't have any trouble taking on farmwork like this. But that's what you get with daughters."

Perky nudged Judd. "Her name is Dr. Morgan. She's a pediatrician."

"You're a doctor?" Judd said, surprised. She looked like a younger, female version of the old man, as though she'd somehow grown out of the farm's rich soil fully clad in denim jeans and shirt, leather steel-toed work boots, and battered straw hat.

Marah turned from her father, but the hurt and anger remained written in her eyes. "Yes, I am a doctor. I have a practice in St. Louis."

"She loves children," Perky said.

Judd assessed the woman's response to the statement. Her face softened and her eyes misted over. She looked away. Sadness. Loss. Something painful associated with her practice.

"I'll pay you for your work, Judd," she told him, lifting her focus to meet his eyes. "Our agreement stands."

"Who's the boss around here anyhow, girl?" Ed finally managed to hoist himself out of his chair. "I'll be doing the hiring. I'll be giving the orders. Judd, you're working for me, you hear? Now sit yourself down and eat some lunch. These boys'll be around the place while you're working. Greg here and his crew."

"Dr. Milton Gregory," the man said. He stepped forward and shook Judd's hand. Six-two, one-ninety, pale blue eyes, fresh blisters on his right palm. Late thirties, according to records in the packet. Brown curly hair, mirrored sunglasses perched on his head.

"I'm with the BIA," Gregory went on. At Judd's blank look, he continued. "Bureau of Indian Affairs. I'm a medical archaeologist. This is my field crew. Mike Dooley, Bob Harper."

"Pleased to meet you fellows." Judd focused on the lone sandwich remaining on the table. Indifferent to the man. Casual. "I guess I'll be bunking with you."

"I beg your pardon?" Gregory straightened, the friendliness gone. He turned to Ed. "I'm afraid that arrangement won't work at all, Mr. Morgan. My men and I set up our laboratory in the bunkhouse loft. Our work there is absolutely confidential. The government won't allow any kind of civilian interference."

"Well, he's not staying with me," Marah put in.

"I put him in the bunkhouse," Ed snapped, "and that's where he'll be."

"But that's completely unacceptable."

"Tough beans. You got plenty of room. Now get your government backsides out of my kitchen and go dig up your old bones. Me and my crew got real work to do around here. Judd, grab that sandwich, and I'll take you over to the barn. You know anything about milking?"

"Yes, sir."

Ed Morgan unfolded his walker and rolled himself out the back door onto the porch. "Marah," he called back over his shoulder, "clean up that table. And while you're at it, give the floor a once-over with the broom. Make yourself useful, girl."

🐾 🐾 🐾

Back at the farm more than a week now, Marah realized that she had yet to watch a sunset. It was time to rectify that. She drove the old red pickup down the dirt road, pulled up to the gate, got out, and let herself into the pasture. How many years had it been since she had followed this path? Eighteen at least. Probably more. As a child, she had come here to find something that was missing from the big white clapboard house. Peace, maybe. Serenity. Hope.

She approached the ancient gnarled burr oak tree and set her foot in the crook of a low limb. Had it always been so low, or was she taller now? The rough bark felt familiar, comfortable on her hands, as she hoisted herself up into the branches. This had been her secret tree. Her private sanctuary.

Facing east from the highest branch, she would be able to make out the distant house, barn, and outbuildings of the Harris place. Pete was a good man, Marah thought as she continued to climb. From what she had seen, he was a terrific husband and father, a loyal friend. He was so excited about the twins his wife was expecting. Apparently, there had been a miscarriage or two. Perky couldn't stop talking about the babies or praying for sisters.

To the west, Marah knew she would be able to see Indian Hill. The last rays of sunlight always crept over the mound as though the craggy stones hurt to slide past. But after the sun sank below the horizon, the pink sky in its wake softened the rocky pasture, blurred the grass into a sea of gold, and welcomed the rustling comfort of indigo. It was Marah's favorite time of day.

"Hey, Dr. Morgan," a voice said through the oak leaves. "It's me, Perky Harris. What are you doing up here?"

Marah grabbed the nearest branch, adrenaline coursing down her spine as though she'd just been shot. "You scared me to death," she managed.

"I'm sorry." The small, freckled face emerged just above her. "You scared me, too, till I figured out who you were, and then I just thought I'd watch you climb up. I never saw a grown-up climb a tree before. You're pretty good at it. Anyway, how come you're in my tree?"

Marah laid her hand over her heart, thankful it was still beating. Then she joined Perky on the Sitting Branch, her own personal perch.

"*Your* tree?" she asked the child. "This was where I used to come when I was your age."

The blue eyes went wide. "This tree? Out of all the trees on the farm?"

Marah smiled. "Well, there aren't that many trees. We've got one or two near the white house, but this is the best climbing tree for miles around."

"I know." Perky leaned closer. "We have a little group of trees near our house. Mama planted them, one tree for each lost baby. But I don't like to climb them. So I come out here instead."

"Lost babies?"

"We've lost four. Two brothers and a sister. And one slipped away before we knew what it was. One brother died at five months along, and the sister died at six months along. Jeremy was born to us, but he had lots of problems, and he died right away. He never even took a breath. Daddy and I cried. Mama planted another tree."

"These were miscarriages?" Marah asked, peering at the small cluster of saplings in the front yard of the Harris house. She knew Pete and Hilda had suffered some difficulties, but she'd never known the extent of it. From this distance, the trees were indistinguishable from one another, a tiny forest of sorrow.

"I don't know what a miscarriage is," Perky said. "These were our babies that hadn't been born yet, except for Jeremy. And every time another one died, I would ask Jesus why. Why did he take away my brother before I could even hold him? Daddy said it's because Jeremy and the others were precious and perfect, and God wanted them with him."

"I guess that might be it," Marah said.

"Then why did Jesus leave *me* here? Aren't I precious and perfect?"

"Oh, Perky, I'm sure that's not what your father meant. He was just trying to—"

"I'm not perfect. I know I'm not."

"Nobody is, sweetheart."

Perky swung her legs back and forth. "God left me here. He gave me to my mom and dad. You know why?"

"No. Do you?"

"Maybe he wants me to do something for him."

Marah stared at the strange, intense child perched like a little brown wren on the branch of the towering oak. The first few days on the farm, Marah had felt downright irritated with the child. It was all that constant, cheerful chatter, she told herself. Or maybe she felt a touch of jealousy at the warm rela-tionship Perky had developed with Ed Morgan. Marah still couldn't get used to the sight of the girl nestled in his lap. Her father had never welcomed his own daughters with such tenderness. He had never reached out in kindness to them. Never really seemed to want them around. But Perky was different.

As the days passed, however, Marah had grown accustomed to Perky's presence. She had always loved children, and this little girl—with her bouncing blond pigtails and wide-eyed wonder—enchanted her.

"What do you think God might want you to do for him?" Marah asked.

"I don't know yet," Perky said. "But I'll ask him. So, how about some tea?"

She lifted a thermos from the hook of a broken limb and pulled a couple of old plastic cups out of a canvas tote bag. Without waiting for an answer, she poured iced tea into one of the cups and handed it to Marah.

Marah took a sip. It was sweet and refreshing, and she was tired. Bone weary. Long hours at the office, followed by her hospital rounds, had always stretched her endurance. But in a different way. Here on the farm, hauling salt blocks to the pastures, building pens, driving the tractor for hours, or helping with the difficult birth of a calf made her muscles sore yet her body invigorated. It was the time she had to spend with her father that utterly exhausted her.

"What do you think God wants you to do for him, Dr. Morgan?" Perky asked.

"Well, I'm a pediatrician."

"But are you sure that's the right thing? You know, Poppy wants you to be a farmer."

Poppy is not God, Marah wanted to tell the child. *He may think he is. He may act like he is. But Big Ed Morgan is not the sovereign ruler of the universe.*

"I'm supposed to be a doctor," Marah said. "I've wanted to heal people since I was a little girl."

"Only God can heal people. Doctors just help him. That's what my daddy says."

"Your daddy's right. I need to remember that."

"How come you never call Poppy *Daddy?* You never call him anything. It's like he doesn't have a name."

Marah considered the question. "I don't know really. . . . My sisters and I never thought of him as a 'daddy' kind of man. He wasn't around often. We didn't really pay much attention to him, in fact, until he was all we had left."

"But you loved your mom?"

"Oh yes." Marah focused on the pinks, golds, and oranges that spilled across the Kansas horizon. "On evenings like this, Mom would gather all four of us around her rocking chair on the front porch. 'Who can see the first star, my little ducklings?' she would ask us. Then we would search the sky until one of us spotted a tiny twinkle high in the dark blue umbrella. 'I see it, I see it!' we would call out. And our mom would say, 'Thank you, Jesus, for the stars and the moon.'"

Marah ran her finger through the moisture that had gathered on the side of the plastic cup. *Thank you, Jesus.* All those years ago, her mother had found the strength to endure her difficult life. *Through Jesus Christ, our Lord and Savior . . . In Jesus' name . . . Our Father who art in heaven.* The words tumbled around like petals in the wind, soft and fragrant.

"You miss your mother," Perky said.

"I guess I do." Marah studied the cup in her hand. "We used to have such wonderful times together. Every afternoon the twins would climb up onto the kitchen chairs while Deborah and I tried to tie on their bibs. Then Mom would set out plastic cups just like these. Faded pink, blue, yellow."

"Don't forget green," Perky said.

"And green. Then Mom would bring cookies piled high on a yellow plate, all warm and yummy smelling. Chocolate chip cookies, oatmeal cookies, macaroons. Sometimes there might be brownies. She'd make them big and chewy, chock-full of nuts. And then she would say, 'Fold your hands and bow your heads, my little ducklings. Marah, will you say our prayer this afternoon?'"

Dear Jesus, Marah could almost hear her own voice drifting in the silence. *Thank you for the cookies and milk. Thank you for Deborah and Leah and Sarah and Mommy. Amen.*

"You wish your mother was still alive," Perky said.

"I used to wish that. After she died, I tried to keep everything just the way it had been. I washed and hung the clothes on the line, swept and mopped the floors, cleaned the toilet and tub, braided my sisters' hair, shined our shoes, ironed my father's overalls, baked bread, fed the chickens, grew a vegetable garden—everything."

"Because you had loved your mother so much."

"At first that's why I did it," Marah said. "But after a while I did the work because my father expected it."

After the death of her mother, Ed Morgan had become a sort of slow-growing malignancy in his oldest daughter's life, a cancer that fed on her spirit, sapped her strength, threatened even her will to get up and face each day. She had struggled to stand firm against his domination, his snapped commands and unending criticism. In her teen years, she had begun to wither, shrinking into herself like the dying victim of a ravenous disease, until she began to fear there might be nothing left of her. She worried she was gradually turning into a jointed cardboard skeleton with a bony grin and wind whistling through her ribs. And one day she would be folded up and thrown into the incinerator because she had outlived her usefulness to her father.

Finally, at seventeen, fragile and weary and paper thin, Marah had reached out one skeletal finger and touched the elixir of hope a high school counselor held out to her. Medical school. The University of Kansas, a six-year program, and she had the grades to be accepted. Only as she drove to college, her worn leather work boot pushing the old car's pedal all the way to the floor, her blue eyes watching in the rearview mirror as the Kansas dust rose like smoke behind her tires, had Marah sensed her father's power over her ripping away. She was free of him at last. Free and ready to begin living.

"Poppy doesn't act very nice to you." The child's voice abruptly brought Marah back to the present.

"No, I guess not."

"How come?"

"I'm not sure. I guess we don't . . . we don't see eye-to-eye on some things."

"You're mad at him."

"Sometimes." She took another sip of tea. "I wish he'd been different somehow. He certainly wishes I was different."

"How?"

"Oh, he wanted me to be a boy. A son. A part of the farm, just like all the Morgan men going back a hundred years, just like the red winter wheat they'd all worked so hard to grow."

"But you were a weed?"

Marah smiled. "More of a wildflower, I'd say. Whatever I was, it didn't please my father. I didn't fit on the farm. I didn't fit with his idea of a family. After my mother died, I thought he might like me better if I tried to take her place in our family."

"Did you gather your little ducklings around and ask them to find the evening star?"

Marah shook her head. "I found out pretty quickly that I could never really become my mother. After a while, I stopped reading the Bible at breakfast. There was never enough time." She could hear her father's voice echo through the kitchen. *"You girls better get your backsides off to school before you're late."*

"I bet Poppy didn't take you to church either. He says

church is a great big waste of time, and the preacher's full of beans anyhow."

Marah laughed. "That sounds like Ed."

"Dad," Perky said. "Call him Dad. That's what he wants, if he could just tell you."

"*Dad.*" Marah tried out the word. She couldn't imagine applying it to the headstrong old bull who never had a kind word for her.

"Poppy's like my big teddy bear who accidentally got his mouth sewn on all crooked and grumpy-looking." Perky picked up her thermos and swung her thin legs over the Sitting Branch. "Well, I'd better get home for supper," she said. Then she reached out and laid her hand on Marah's arm. "Good night, my little duckling."

As the child clambered down the tree, Marah laid her cheek against a rough branch and gazed across the prairie. A light came on in the rock house. She knew Ed would be opening a can of vegetable soup and getting out the stale saltines.

Dad, she thought. *Dad.*

6

"C'mon with us, Judd. Me and the girl are heading over to the knolls to see what those archaeologist fellows are up to."

Big Ed Morgan leaned out of the passenger window of the pickup's cab, his brown muscled arm a testament to years of hard labor. Judd had been tinkering with the power takeoff on the old tractor. He knew how dangerous the thing could be, especially if a man was less than fully alert. Since he'd come to the farm, Judd had rarely slept through the night, rising every few hours to check the dew point. When it was right, he would drag himself out to the barn, climb onto a mower, and head out to open a field of alfalfa.

Ed's bedroom light never went off. Usually, he yelled through the window for a status report as Judd walked toward the barn. Sometimes, he pushed himself outside on his walker, rolling over the tough grass and hard-baked earth to check on his crops and herd.

"If those archaeologists are digging holes in my pasture," Ed said from the pickup, "we're going to run them off, pronto."

Judd set his screwdriver in the toolbox. Perfect. A chance to watch the team at work. Catch them off guard. He knew Gregory wouldn't let anyone catch a whiff of what he was really doing out in that field, but a look at the site might be revealing.

"Sure, I'll go with you." Judd began to climb into the bed of the pickup with the scruffy dog, but Ed stopped him.

"Ride up here with us, boy. No sense bouncing around in back."

Marah rolled her eyes as Judd wedged into the cab, his knees jammed against the folded walker and his shoulders scrunched between the window and Ed. The woman had come around once or twice while Judd was tending the cattle, but she rarely spoke more than a word to him. That was all right. He sensed she was living in a place that didn't allow visitors. He knew that place.

"Wheat's looking good," Ed said as the pickup bumped down the rutted dirt road.

"Yes, sir."

"Putting up a lot of hay this year."

"Yep."

Ed fiddled with the knob on the glove compartment. "You don't say much, do you, boy?"

"I guess not."

"Well, where you from, anyhow? A good hand like you doesn't usually roam around looking for work."

"I prefer it that way."

"I never did understand that kind of thing, drifting along with no purpose. You ought to get yourself some land, boy. Put down roots. Raise yourself a family. You could be a successful farmer if you stayed put."

"I guess you're right."

The farmer seemed satisfied with Judd's acquiesence and lapsed into silence. Judd reflected on what he hoped to find at Gregory's work site. So far, despite several evenings with the men in the bunkhouse, he had learned little. Gregory had set up a sophisticated lab in the loft, he was computer operational, and he and his men spoke in a kind of vague, coded language that revealed little about their project. Though they resented Judd's presence at first, they soon seemed to forget about him. He was good at blending into the background.

But trying to eavesdrop from his bunk while pretending to read a weight-lifting magazine was all but a waste of time. Gregory mostly kept to himself, reading medical journals or making notations in a journal he kept in his shirt pocket. The other two men talked only about sports, families, girlfriends. A lot of their conversation involved speculation about Marah Morgan. Their discussions had nothing to do with her career as a physician or her work on the farm, and everything to do with her blue eyes, her figure, and the possible status of her love life.

"You never answered my father's question." Marah's voice

interrupted Judd's thoughts of her. "Where are you from?" she asked, her blue eyes focused on the road.

Judd studied the ripening wheat in the field beside the road. She was sharp, direct, edgy. She missed nothing. He'd have to watch her. "Arizona," he said. "Near Tucson."

"Hot."

"Sure is. Ever been there?"

"No."

"She's a homebody," Ed said. "Stayed here in Kansas all her life until she went off to college in Kansas City."

"Medical school," Marah corrected. "It's a six-year program. College and med school rolled into one."

"What's the difference? You leave home, study your big books. She never came back, you know. Not one time after she lit out of here. Left me with Deborah and the twins to take care of. After all a man does for his family, they go off and leave him without a backward look."

"She's here now," Judd said. For some reason he couldn't let the old man continue unchallenged.

Ed stared out the windshield.

Marah glanced at Judd. Their eyes met for an instant, and then she focused on the road again. Though she hadn't spoken, he had read a change in her expression. He also noted that the tinge of white left her knuckles.

"There they are," Ed said. "Pull over, girl."

The pickup came to a stop near a large green canvas tent. Army issue. Unmarked. Vietnam, he guessed. Desert Storm tents were tan. Purchased from a military surplus store, no doubt. Marah would be the first to wonder, but how soon?

As Judd reached for the door handle, Ed gave a snort. "Beans," he said. "What's Perky doing out here?"

🐾 🐾 🐾

Milton Gregory bent over and dug in the dirt until his fingers closed around yet another metal bullet cartridge. He must have found at least a half dozen today, none of them the right era. The physician had been in daily communication with the leaders of Team A, the research branch of his organization, and they continued to assure him he was looking in the right place. All records indicated the past presence of an Indian village in this very spot. Yet the futile search went on, the days of June ticked by, pressure mounted, and September 15 approached. He wondered if there was something more he should do, some other location he should be searching, some clue he hadn't uncovered.

As Gregory straightened to drop the shell casing into the bag over his shoulder, he spotted the movement of Ed Morgan's battered red pickup pulling up next to the tent. What now? He didn't have time to deal with these people, answer their questions, play the part of tourist guide. And then he noticed the little blond-haired girl picking wildflowers nearby.

Dropping the metal detector, Gregory set off across the pasture. As much as he resented the interruption, he had expected it. Curiosity always drew the public. The other two members of his team were out in the field, too far away to hear him call. His head pounded in the heat, and he took his sunglasses from his eyes, brushed his arm across his damp fore-head, and slipped the glasses on again. It was hotter than he'd expected when he had studied the area. Kansas. Though he had enjoyed the change of scenery at first, he would be glad when this portion of the project was complete.

As he neared the tent, Gregory checked the pistol at his waist, a Python loaded with .38 Special lead wadcutters. On impact with the skull, they would expand for an instant kill. He tugged his cotton T-shirt over the weapon, though he didn't mind if they saw the bulge.

"Hi, Poppy!" The girl skipped over toward the pickup. "Hi, Dr. Morgan and Judd."

"What're you doing out here, Perky?" Ed said. "You ought to be home helping your mama."

Perky, that was her name. Odd. Gregory had spotted the child a few times wandering around in the pastures, but she always kept a good distance from the project site. He felt a trickle of sweat run from one sideburn to his chin.

"I'm picking flowers," Perky said. "Mom asked me to get some for the table, so I just started walking, and before I knew it I was out here on the knolls. It's like *Blueberries for Sal* when she wanders over the hill and meets the mother bear. And it's really scary."

"You read too many books, girl. Nothing scary out here." Ed reached out and gave her pigtail a tug.

As the child tiptoed on her sandaled feet to spread her arms around the man's barrel chest, the farmhand began moving toward the tent. Gregory stepped into his path.

"Good morning, Judd," he said. "What are you doing out here on this fine day? I expected you'd be tinkering with one of your tractors at this hour."

"Morning, Dr. G. Ed and his daughter wanted to come out and take a look. See what you found."

"Certainly. You're welcome, of course. Allow me to give you a tour of our work site."

"You hiding naked girls in that tent?" Ed said, wheeling his walker across the rough ground. He laughed at his joke.

Gregory's mouth twisted. He would have to be patient. "An amusing thought, Mr. Morgan. But as you know, this is a government project."

The three adults followed Gregory into the large canvas tent. It was cooler there, darkened and slightly musty smelling. Their tour guide pointed out the shovels and maps. He waved a hand over the microscopes and other equipment. There was not much to see. The real work would take place in his laboratory. If they actually found the village.

"You're not digging any holes in my pasture, are you?" Ed Morgan asked as the group moved out of the tent again. "Bad enough we have all these worthless rocks. Don't need any holes my cattle could fall into."

Gregory slipped his hand behind his sunglasses and ran a finger over the nose bridge to brush away the beads of perspiration. "At the moment, we're using metal detectors."

"Metal detectors?" Marah Morgan, the unknown variable, stepped forward. "How much metal would you find in an Osage village? Didn't they use baskets and leather? Natural materials?"

"The Osage owned rifles during the period in question, Dr. Morgan. Belt buckles and stirrups would have been common in the village. And, of course, we're searching for hinges and hasps from wooden storage boxes."

"So, where you keeping all the stuff you found?" Ed asked. "The skeletons and all that."

"Yes," Marah said. "You told my father you were searching for the village site in order to rebury the skeletal remains. We're all curious about the results of your work."

"Unless you ain't got any results." Ed seemed to find this possibility highly humorous.

"At this point," Gregory admitted, "we don't have any actual findings. No human remains. Once we locate the exact site of the village, of course, we'll have to close it to visitors."

"I'm no visitor," Ed spoke up. "This is my land."

"I realize that, sir. But government regulations—"

"Government, beans." The farmer took a step closer and punched a forefinger in Dr. Gregory's face. "Let me tell you about the government, Greg. When I was growing up on this farm, we had to do set-asides, planting our wheat and then getting rid of 5, 10, even 15, percent of it. How do you think that feels, working your land only to destroy a good part of what you done?"

"Well, I'm certain it was—"

"You think the farm bill in '96 changed a thing? Sure, now I can plant whatever I want, and I don't have to get rid of it. But the prices are at rock bottom. And what does the government do about that? Nothing! Look at those poor hog farmers. You think the government cared a lick about all the small operations that went belly-up? You think they're doing anything to stop those corporate farms from running us family farms out of business? Don't tell me about the government. I've had government up to my ears all my life."

Gregory nodded, summoning his patience, willing his voice to remain calm. "I realize farmers have had trouble—"

"Trouble? You know why I don't have any farmhands but Judd over there?"

Gregory glanced at Judd, who was shuffling around, kicking at pebbles in the dirt. The farmhand was clearly disinterested in the conversation. A dullard, the physician had decided. As far as he'd been able to ascertain, the man hadn't completed his high school education, read nothing more erudite than fitness magazines, and was able to contribute little more than a grunt to any conversation. Dr. Morgan, on the other hand, was alert and curious. If he hadn't been so preoccupied with his work, Gregory would have found the woman more than interesting. After their tour of the tent, she had set off to inspect a fence that rimmed the pasture, and now she was tugging on a strand of loose wire. He had lost sight of the little girl.

"You ought to see the rules and regulations those government folks put on my back," Ed was saying. "I can't hire anybody without checking them over like they might have lice or something. Only reason we could take Judd on is because he's working minimum wage, and he's just going to stay around a couple or three months. I mean, if I want to hire some permanent hands, I got to have papers and records and employee compensation and withholding taxes—stuff I don't even know what it is, you know what I mean?"

"Of course, Mr. Morgan. But my team consists of scientists, and none of us—"

"Why do you always wear those glasses with the mirrors?" The voice came from waist level. Gregory looked down to find the child staring up at him. "Don't you want anybody to see your eyes?"

Gregory stiffened. "I wear sunglasses for protection, young lady."

"From what?" She looked doubtful.

"Sunglasses protect the eyes from dangerous ultraviolet solar radiation."

"My mommy says the eyes are the windows of the soul. It seems like you're hiding your eyes behind those mirrors."

"Lenses. And these sunglasses are very important in bright light." For some odd reason Gregory felt disconcerted by the child. "Now if you'll excuse me, I'd better get back to—"

"I'm glad I don't have to wear sunglasses with mirrors," Perky went on. "They make people think you have a secret."

Gregory wished the girl would wander off again. Her chatter was more than annoying. In the heat, his head felt like it was going to explode.

"No secrets here," he said, realizing that Morgan and the farmhand were listening. "Just looking for that Indian village."

Perky shrugged. "Is that what you do for a job? Dig things up?"

"I'm an archaeologist, my young friend," he said, patting her on the head. "I'm very dedicated to my work."

"But what good does it do?"

"Good?" He smiled down at the girl, aware that the other two men had focused on his words. "I believe that the past can have a profound impact on the future, Perky. The more we know about our past, the greater our opportunity to avoid the mistakes of our ancestors. What my colleagues and I are doing out here in this field may one day make a difference in the future of our world."

"Wow." Perky pushed his hand off her head. "Then I guess you better wear your sunglasses, huh?"

Gregory chuckled. "And now I'm afraid I must ask all of you to leave our work site. Project requirements call for us to have this entire pasture surveyed by nightfall."

The others looked at him in silence, and he sensed their admiration.

"A man's got to do his job," Ed said finally. "That's what I always say. Even if it is a government job. Digging up Indian bones. I wonder how much of my tax money is going to this all-fired project you believe in so much. C'mon, Judd. Perky, you jump in the back with Gypsy. Marah, get over here, girl."

Behind his sunglasses, Gregory's eyes narrowed. The farmer wheeled toward the pickup, followed by the others. As Judd passed, he touched the back of Gregory's shoulder.

"You were good with the kid," Judd said. "You're doing your job. Just like the rest of us."

As he walked away, he was whistling.

7

"What're you doing out here?"

The gruff voice snapped Marah to attention. She turned from the window she had been washing on the white house. Every muscle in her back felt taut and knotted from the long hours she had already spent in the fields that day.

Ed was wheeling his walker across the stretch of yard between the two buildings.

"I'm washing windows," she said.

"No point. First storm that comes along, they'll get all streaked up again."

Marah decided to ignore her father. Like a peppy newscaster announcing bad weather, she put a friendly lilt in her voice. "You're almost out of Windex. I'll buy some next time I'm in town."

"Clean windows won't keep the rain from coming through that leaky roof. You're wasting your time, girl."

Marah grabbed the paper towels and tore a sheet from the roll. She gave the glass a squirt. Then she started on the next set of panes. *Dear God,* she lifted up. *I don't want to be so angry. I want to find some way to get along with my father. Perky says I should call him Dad, but I can't. I can't do that. I need your help just to stay calm, Lord.*

After praying, Marah thought she ought to feel a sense of peace and strength. Instead, she felt panicky. Her father was getting closer, and she would have to talk to him. What if he said something hurtful or thoughtless? She had asked God to help her with her attitude. So why did she still feel so tangled and miserable?

"That Judd's a good hand," Ed commented as he rolled himself toward the porch. "I'm glad I took him on. He's a strong ol' cuss. You should have seen him loading salt block this afternoon. Where were you anyhow, girl? We could have used help."

"I was taking seed to the elevator," Marah said.

"Our bins full already? I bet you didn't check."

She glanced over at her father, who was as strongly disapproving and critical as ever despite the weakness of his huge frame leaning on the walker. Why was he coming over here to the white house anyway? He had moved out several years before, and it was clear from the condition of things that he hadn't been back since. Furniture and debris blocked the halls and stairs. Mice scurried across the floor at night, and the leaky roof made the ceiling sag.

Marah hadn't had time to clean up either of the two farmhouses, and she fought the urge to blame her father for the mess they were in. Did this man ruin everything he touched? No, she couldn't think that way. Despite the condition of the white house, she felt comfortable staying in the old place again. Like her special tree, it had become a haven from her father.

"What did you think about our visit to that archaeologist yesterday out on the knolls?" Ed asked, lowering himself onto one corner of the porch. "Judd likes him OK. Says Greg and his boys keep to themselves most of the time."

"Dr. Gregory is obviously a dedicated scientist. He knows a lot about the Osage, despite the fact that he hasn't found their village yet. I like him pretty well, although I do wish—"

"Nice enough fellow, I guess," Ed cut in. "I don't know what he thinks they're going to dig up out there. I wandered around on those knolls when I was a kid, and I never did find anything but a few arrowheads. My granddaddy used to say there were some Indians around when he was a boy. But the government sent most of them away to live on an Oklahoma reservation, and then they struck it rich. Oil, you know. Ha, that ought to teach the government a lesson or two. All the same, I wouldn't live in Oklahoma for beans. I hear it's practically a desert down there. A man's got to have land he can farm. I always told your mother, I said, I'm staying on this farm till I die, and you can bury me with my overalls on. That's the way I intend to go."

Marah turned back to the window and began to wipe away the Windex. She wished her father would let her work. These windows hadn't been washed in years, and she wanted to concentrate. Or maybe she just wanted the silence.

How many times had she listened to Big Ed Morgan ramble, spouting his opinions about Indians, oil, Oklahoma, farming, and a hundred other topics on which he considered himself an authority? He could talk on and on and never notice that his was the only voice, as monotonous as the droning of bees building a honeycomb inside a wall. Busy with himself and his own thoughts, her father never asked questions. Never sought opinions. Never considered that anyone else might have something to offer.

All her childhood, Marah had listened to this man talk. When she was very young, she had believed everything he said. Like a devotee at the foot of a guru, she had drunk in his words, had absorbed his philosophies about the world, and had even heard herself repeating to her sisters things their father might have said. As though she were just a miniature version of him.

Then one day she had begun to doubt. She remembered the moment with the clarity of sunlight shining through a crystal prism. Her mother had dug a clump of purple coneflowers from the prairie and was transplanting them into one of her garden beds.

"They're wilted," Ed had said. "They won't grow."

"They'll grow," Mom countered him.

"They're weeds and they're ugly and they won't grow." He had walked over to the clump and jerked it out of the small hole Mom had dug for it. Then he tossed the coneflowers across the yard. "Better get to cooking supper, Ruby. Those things are dead."

Marah had watched as her father stomped back into the house to pour himself a glass of lemonade before heading back out into the field. Later, as he drove away in his pickup, she noticed her mother slipping across the yard to the spot where Ed had thrown the coneflowers. Mom lifted the clump gingerly in both hands, as though it were a pie she had just baked. Glancing around to make sure her husband was gone, she set the clump back into the brown hole, pushed a little dirt around it, and tipped a pail of water over it.

The coneflowers perked up right away. They weren't ugly at all. They had tall green stems, beautiful purple petals with firm brown centers. They weren't weeds, and they didn't die. They grew. That autumn after the petals had fallen, Mom snapped off the brown spiky centers and cast the seeds over the ground of her garden bed. The next spring there were twice as many purple coneflowers. And Big Ed Morgan had never noticed a thing.

After that, Marah stopped believing every word her father said. Finally, once in a while, she even tried to dispute him. A backhanded swat to the cheek taught her that was a bad idea. And so she shut up, quietly building the wall that eventually separated them.

"I tried to tell Greg he wasn't going to find anything but arrowheads and maybe a few broken pots out there," Ed was saying now. "Pile of rocks is all that's on the knolls. He's got his boys poking around Indian Hill, but I bet all they stir up is a copperhead or two."

Marah closed her eyes, blocking the window but not the

sound of his voice. Since coming back to the farm, she had found herself trying to top her father again and again. Though she promised herself she wouldn't let him bait her, she got trapped in his words every time. She had prayed to be softer with him, less angry, more accepting. But when he spouted off, she jumped right in with both feet. And she knew she couldn't win. No matter what she said, he did things exactly the way he wanted. Exactly the way he always had.

"If they start digging holes in my pastures," he said, "I'll give them what for. You know I will. Your mother used to do that. One day I drove out there to the knolls where she'd been digging up things to plant, and you should have seen the holes. Well, she'd dig up a plant—roots, dirt, and all. Leave a great big hole in the pasture. I had to put a stop to that nonsense right then and there. I don't know what she ever saw in those flowers anyhow. Not good for a thing."

Marah pursed her lips to keep from responding and squirted another window. She remembered her mother, small boned and always a little frail, lifting heavy stones from the fields and loading them into the bed of the pickup, then using them to outline her flower beds. What had driven her to make the effort?

Ed was getting worked up. "I'll shut those boys down. I'll throw their hides right off my property. I don't need no government bums messing with my land, I'll tell you that."

"When did her gardens die? Was it when you made her stop transplanting wildflowers from the pasture?"

"What?"

"Mom's gardens. When did they die?"

He was silent a moment. "I reckon it was after she passed on. Nobody to tend them, you know. I sure wasn't going to water and hoe a bunch of flowers. Fact is, she filled those beds with what I'd call weeds. I'd as soon plow them under as tend them."

"They weren't weeds. They were wildflowers."

"What's the difference, girl? They weren't good for a thing. In my opinion, if something's not a cash crop or feed for the livestock, it doesn't have a place on this farm."

Marah paused in her washing and stared at her reflection in the window.

"Wildflowers, weeds—whatever," Ed said. "What Ruby saw in those plants I'll never know."

"God, I think."

"Huh?"

"I think Mom saw the hand of God when she worked in her gardens. He was her source of strength. Maybe when she tended her flowers, she felt close to God."

"Who knows? God didn't do her any favors when he—"

"She had a Bible, didn't she? A black one. I wonder where it is."

"Probably in the white house somewhere. There's so much junk down in the basement, you couldn't find anything." He rubbed the back of his neck, his large hand slipping beneath the sweat-stained chambray collar. "Nah, that's not right. We buried that Bible with your mother. We put it right into the casket. It was the preacher's idea, I seem to recollect."

"I wonder why. Surely he didn't believe she would need the Bible in the afterlife."

"I think he said that book kind of summed up Ruby's life," he said thoughtfully. "It was who she was inside, and he said she ought to be buried with it the way people sometimes get buried with their wedding ring on. I think he was right."

"Why didn't you let me go to Mom's funeral?" Marah asked.

"Your Aunt Opal in Winfield had taken all of you in by that time. I drove the other girls over there when your mother got so sick, but I kept you around to help out. After she died, I figured I'd have more on my hands than I could manage. You stayed in Winfield nearly a month, don't you recall?"

"No," Marah said softly. "I don't remember anything that happened during that time. I was only eight, you know. At least I don't think I remember."

"Well, you didn't miss much. We had Ruby a big funeral. Long-winded preaching and loads of people from miles around. More folks than I ever saw at one time. Seemed like she'd helped a lot of them in her time. You know how she always donated pies for the church bake sales and quilts for the raffles. She was one to do things like that, visit sick folks and all. She took you along, don't you remember? I always figured that was how come you decided to be a doctor. All those sick folks you visited with your mother."

Marah felt her heart rate increase. For the first time in her life, she was conversing with her father. An actual dialog rather than an argument. *Thank you, Lord!* And they were discussing her mother, the long-buried past, the silent memories.

"Was that how Mom got sick?" she asked, wondering again about the silence that had surrounded her mother's death. "Did she contract an illness from someone she had visited?"

Ed reached for his walker. He made as if to rise; then he paused. "Well, I reckon that was it. Ruby must've come down with something she picked up along the way."

"What was it?"

"A fever first. I never saw such a fever in my life." He knotted his fingers together, clearly agitated by the memory. "Ruby was burning up. That's about the time I sent the little girls off to Winfield. And then a real bad rash broke out all over Ruby's face and arms. The doc thought she had the chicken pox or shingles or something."

"He examined her?"

"Beans, girl, how should I remember? I reckon we did take her in to see the doc. But maybe not. She never was much for doctors."

"Actually, *you* never were much for doctors. Mom liked Dr. Benson. She had a lot of respect for him."

"Well, if you know so much about it, how come you're asking me all these questions?" He pushed himself up on his walker. "That's how you were from the minute you were born—opinionated and stubborn."

"I was not."

"And ornery. You were ornery, too, wanting to have your

way all the time. Your mother said it was just because you were so smart in school. Too smart for your britches, is what I thought about it. I'd try to set you straight, but you wouldn't listen. You had to put your two cents in on the matter. You always were a lippy little critter."

"Lippy?" She stared at him, the wad of wet paper towels in her hand dripping onto the porch floor. "I'm not lippy. You're the one who talks even if nobody's listening."

"There you go, spouting off again." He began pushing the walker across the yard. "Arguing back, just like your mother."

Marah squeezed the paper towels. She didn't remember her mother arguing. Mom was always submissive, wasn't she?

"I never can talk without you trying to bite my head off," Ed said. "Might as well just keep my thoughts to myself."

Marah felt stricken with panic, as though she were a hungry child whose dinner plate had been swept away before she was finished eating. She needed more. More information about the past. More time with her father. More memories of her mother.

"But was it chicken pox or shingles that Mom had?" she called, walking to the edge of the porch. *Dear God, now what have I done?* She ached to grab her father, hold him back, keep him for just another moment. "Please tell me about Mom. What diagnosis did Dr. Benson give her?"

"I don't know," he hollered over his shoulder. "You're the big city doctor. It was a fever and a rash. You tell *me* what it was."

Marah wrapped her arms around the porch post. *Chicken pox. Shingles. Measles. Strep. Fifths.* Her brain ticked off every virus or bacterium that might cause a fever and a rash. Might cause serious illness. Might lead to death.

But as she watched her father disappear into the rock house, Marah's head swirled suddenly with remembered sounds. Yes, her parents had disagreed with each other. They had quarreled. She remembered now. There had been many nights when she'd listened to those sounds, the sounds of her parents' heated discussions, arguments, fights. She had been so young. Too young to remember clearly. But as she clutched the post, she seemed to feel a shudder of the struggle between her parents. It had been bad between them. Then worse. And then Ruby Morgan had died.

🐾 🐾 🐾

Judd slung his denim jacket onto the pickup's cracked vinyl seat and climbed in after it. Chuck hadn't budged an inch about the vehicle. It was Judd's assigned transportation; it fit the job description, and that was that. Never mind that the whole thing might fall apart a mile down the road.

Judd hadn't been able to contact Chuck personally since coming to the farm, but he had mailed a packet detailing what he'd learned about Gregory's doings on Morgan Farm. Via a delivery of tractor parts from the Ace Hardware store, Chuck had returned a letter of new information he had gathered on the whereabouts of the rest of Gregory's colleagues.

Judd pumped the clutch on the old truck. Once they left the

rehabbed school building in Wyoming, roughly half of the group had moved to a hotel in Chicago. Mostly they just sat around eating pizza, though they spent a good bit of time in the Native American exhibit at the Field Museum, too. Judd knew they stayed in contact with Gregory, though he hadn't been able to overhear any of their conversations in the padlocked loft room of the bunkhouse.

The other half of the group had split up, but they were being traced as they worked their way toward what appeared to be a common destination on the East Coast. Chuck suspected they were headed for Washington, D.C. That city and Chicago both headquartered branches of the American Medical Association, the probable focus of Milton Gregory's ultimate quest. Judd wondered if Gregory intended to take the results of his project straight to the AMA. If so, he would need to be intercepted along the way. Judd would voice his concerns to Chuck, he decided as he turned the key in the ignition.

"Wait a second!"

Judd glanced up as Marah waved at him from the porch of the old white house. Looking more like a young colt than his image of a pediatrician, she jumped off the porch and jogged across the yard. "Are you going into town?"

"Thought I would," he said.

"Will you be gone long?"

"Couple of hours."

She looked away, tucking a strand of dark hair behind her ear. "Would you mind if I tagged along? I need to talk to some people about new flooring and a countertop for the kitchen. And I thought I'd buy some paint and cleaning supplies." When he didn't answer right away, she went on. "The red pickup is out at the Watson farm. And my car's over at Pete Harris's place. He's checking the water pump."

Judd hadn't heard the woman say this much since he met her. He didn't want to take her to town. Didn't want to have to make conversation. Didn't want her around when he made his contact with Chuck.

"Or I could wait a couple of days," she said, her focus shifting. "Um, it's no big deal."

"Hop in," he said. "I'll take you."

"Thanks." She didn't exactly smile, but the blue in her eyes lightened. "I'll get my purse."

As he watched her jog back into the house, he thought about how long it had been since he'd allowed himself time with a woman. The few instances after Marianne, he found they wanted too much of him. Wanted his attention and devotion and time. Wanted his love. He didn't have that to give.

When Marah bounded back outside, long legs in blue jeans, black hair glossy in the sunlight, he wondered at himself. Wondered how he'd managed to shut down so completely. After Marianne, people said he would get over it. He would loosen up, start to date, eventually forget the pain. The opposite had been true. Now, he knew, he was tight and closed and protected. It was the way he wanted it.

"Excuse me," she called through the window, "but I can't get the door open."

Inwardly castigating Chuck, he climbed out of the truck. He might be late, and Chuck would wonder. But he was often late with his contacts. Chuck was used to it by now.

Judd wrenched the rusty handle. The door came open with a bone-jarring screech and sagged down on loose hinges. *Not my pickup*, he wanted to say. But she climbed inside and attempted to hoist the door back into place. They managed it together, but Judd wondered if the thing could take much more.

The muffler had fallen off long ago, so the roar of the engine hindered conversation. Judd steered. Marah leaned back and looked out the front window. After a while, she fiddled in her purse and pulled out a pack of bubble gum.

"Gum?" she asked. "Perky gave it to me."

He hadn't chewed bubble gum in years. He put out his hand. It was Bazooka, with the little comic and the smell that sent a man back to his boyhood sandlot. He chewed, savoring the sweet juice that dripped down the back of his throat.

In a moment, Marah blew a bubble.

Judd glanced over in surprise. She sucked the bubble back into her mouth, a grin sneaking across her lips. He blew the next bubble. It was a good one, bigger than he'd expected. He prided himself in its perfect roundness.

And then she stuck her finger in it.

"Hey!" The bubble deflated, collapsing onto his chin. "Aw, great."

She threw her head back and laughed as he tried to pull the gum off the stubble of his beard. Why hadn't he shaved this morning? This was going to look good—pink bubble gum stuck to his face.

"Sorry," she said, the gleam still in her eyes.

"Sure you are."

"I couldn't resist."

He shook his head and craned up to look at himself in the rearview mirror. Then he remembered he didn't have one. Marah slid toward him across the seat. Without a word, she peeled fragments of gum off his chin, rolled it into a ball, and threw it out the window.

"I'd blame Perky," he said, enjoying the sight of her face so close. Smooth skin. The surprising hint of freckles just beneath the porcelain surface. "But it's your fault."

"You blew the bubble." She slid away again. "Risky business. Perky says if you're going to blow a bubble, you might as well expect it to pop."

"Did she mention anything about mischievous pediatricians with sharp fingernails?"

"These nails aren't sharp." As she held up her hands, Judd studied them. The neat polish had chipped away. Calluses were starting to form. Marah Morgan's manicured life had changed since she returned to the farm. He wondered why she had done it. Not out of love for her father. That much was clear. Duty, maybe. He understood that.

Judd recalled Milton Gregory's passion when he spoke about

his project. The mission drove Gregory with a fire Judd didn't recognize in himself. Sure, Judd felt a commitment to his work. It had significance. Purpose. But nothing burned inside him.

Gregory was way off base, his fire misplaced. His passion dedicated to the wrong things. But at least the doctor believed in something. Judd couldn't say that. He had no faith in anything or anyone but himself. The hollow man.

"What did you think of Dr. Gregory's setup?" Marah said over the roar of the engine. "The other day when we went out there."

Judd nodded. Time to find out what she thought. "He's got a lot on his hands."

"Perky told me she doesn't like him. She thinks he's hiding something."

"Hiding?"

"I don't know what he'd have to hide. Perky has such an active imagination. She reads constantly, you know. Still, I did kind of wonder about the laboratory equipment in the tent."

"Just some microscopes and stuff, wasn't it?"

"Yeah, and I know he's a medical archaeologist. But it looked more high-tech than I would have expected."

"High-tech?"

"You know, the kinds of things a coroner might have or a medical examiner who was going to perform autopsies. After all this time, any remains Dr. Gregory digs up will be skeletal. I mean, what's there to see in bone fragments beyond healed fractures or the possible evidence of syphilis or something?

You'd think Dr. Gregory would just tag the bones, pack them in boxes, and send them off to Oklahoma."

Judd could feel his heart begin to hammer. Stay calm. Stay ignorant. "I guess you'd know about that medical stuff. It just looked like regular microscopes to me."

"Well, the microscopes, sure. But there was a container of physiologic saline on the folding table. That's what we use in IVs at the hospital. In a lab, we would use it to emulsify a specimen so we could culture it. I noticed some syringes, too, and growth medium, and culture plates. I mean, it's like Dr. Gregory's planning to experiment on the remains. Weird."

Experiment on the remains. It made sense. But why? What would Gregory find? What could he use from the skeletal remains of dead Indians? Or maybe there was something else on the Kansas prairie that drew the man. What was he looking for? Judd mentally kicked himself for failing to learn more about medical equipment. Too much time in that New Mexico motel stockpiling explosive fertilizer. He'd have to give Chuck the list of equipment Marah had just itemized.

"Sometimes I wonder if those men really are with the BIA," she said suddenly.

Judd chuckled. "I sure don't know what they're doing, but it seems like *they* do."

"Maybe they're some sort of environmentalist group."

"Oh yeah?"

"Examining endangered grasshoppers or something." She laughed, her face brighter and younger than he had ever seen it.

He steered the pickup onto the single main street of the small town. So, she suspected. But what would she do about it? How far would she go? She was smart. Too smart. Troublesome to have around if the situation got tense. He wondered when she planned to go back to St. Louis. Soon, he hoped, though he had enjoyed the bubble gum.

"You can drop me off by the hardware store," Marah said, nodding toward it.

He pulled into a space. Two-story building, plate-glass windows, hand-painted signs, no fire escape. Pay telephone booth outside the convenience store across the street. Two gas pumps, Coke machine, tires for sale. This would do.

"The door," she said.

He looked over at the pickup's jammed door, thought about reaching across her, his arm at her waist, his face near hers. What did she smell of? Fresh air, denim, and something else. *Flowers*, he thought.

Better not.

Getting out, he studied the sidewalks, mostly empty of foot traffic. Movie theater across the street. One film showing. A Dairy Queen next door. Drugstore beside it. He opened her door, considered helping her out but decided against it. She said she'd meet him back at the pickup in an hour.

As she walked into the hardware store, he strolled down the street. He was early after all. Chuck wouldn't be ready for the call, though he would expect more news. Judd had the make of the tent, the van's license plate number, the information about the medical equipment. But he still didn't know why Gregory's men were there.

The night after Ed's trip to the knolls, Gregory had held a lengthy meeting in the second-story loft area of the bunkhouse—the room he had converted into his laboratory. He kept the door shut and the windows locked, but Judd had tried to listen in. Though he caught some of what they were saying, again they spoke in carefully coded language.

They talked about Team A, the agent, the site. Gregory had become impassioned during his speech, intense, almost angry. He spoke repeatedly of September. "September, men," he said several times. After the meeting, Mike and Bob wore a more determined look. Did he see fear there, too? The following morning, they had gone out to the knolls before sunrise.

Judd passed a narrow bookstore. Bibles and religious paraphernalia were arranged on a purple cloth in the window. He hadn't grown up in a religious home. Didn't understand that kind of thing. Didn't think about it much.

Wanting to pass the time until contact, he stepped into the store and lifted a Bible from the display. He flipped through it, wondering how the words on these thin pages could have inspired wars, dethroned kings, created martyrs. To die for something you believed in—now that was fire. He carried the Bible to the counter and paid for it. Maybe it could help rekindle his interest in life. In his line of work, men who lost interest usually ended up dead.

Outside, he crossed the street and walked toward the convenience store. He bought a small vanilla cone at the Dairy Queen. Had it eaten by the time he arrived at the phone booth. He laid the bag with the Bible in it on the narrow steel shelf inside the booth. Then he dialed. Gave the code. Someone picked up the extension.

"Hello?"

"Chuck?"

"Hunter, is that you?"

"Where's Chuck?"

"Uh." There was a silence.

Judd's skin began to crawl. "Where's Chuck?"

"Just a minute."

He was put on hold. He jammed his free hand into his pocket and leaned one shoulder against the side of the phone booth. Marah emerged from the hardware store. Spotted him and waved. He turned his back on her.

"Judd?" He recognized the voice. Chuck's superior. "Listen, Judd, I've got some bad news. It's about Chuck."

"Where is he?"

"He and some of the other men were checking out the site in Wyoming, the old school building where Gregory and his people used to hang out."

"And?"

"Booby-trapped. The thing blew."

"Chuck?"

"He didn't make it."

Judd felt a curtain, dark and gray, descend over his eyes. He gripped the receiver, seeing Chuck's face—the brown eyes, the crazy grin, the carrot orange hair. Chuck had always kidded about his hair. Kidded about everything. Claimed his wife loved that orange hair. Sheri and their three children.

"I'm coming for the funeral."

"No. There won't be one. They had a memorial service last week."

Judd knew what that meant. There hadn't been enough of the body to bury. He had seen such devastation. Appalling to find only a man's foot, the shoe still on it. Or his finger.

"Anyhow," the agent said, "we're setting you up with another contact. He may want to meet with you."

Judd held on to the rounded edge of the shelf, the blood gone from his fingers. "And until then?"

"You can call here, of course."

"Oh."

"You OK?"

"Sure."

"All right, then. You're on your own."

Marah hoisted two cans of paint into the bed of Judd's
old pickup. She knew he had seen her when she waved.
His snub bothered her, and she wasn't sure why. She set
a sackful of brushes, rollers, and masking tape into the
bed beside the paint.

Draping her elbows over the side of the pickup,
Marah studied Judd from across the street. He seemed
like a decent man, hardworking and conscientious.
She couldn't say much for his face. In fact, she wasn't
sure she'd actually looked at him closely before the
ride to town. He was not handsome in a classic sense,
not the way Milton Gregory was with his curly hair
and snazzy sunglasses.

Judd's nose was crooked, and Marah suspected it
had been broken long ago. Such injuries rarely healed
well. His smile was crooked, too, a sort of lazy,
lopsided grin. Nice teeth, a strong jaw, and a good

mouth were points in his favor, but she didn't even know the color of his eyes. Why wouldn't he look at her? It was as though he didn't want to be seen too closely. Didn't want to be known. Perky would probably say he, too, was hiding.

That was fine with Marah. She shouldered her purse and walked across the street toward the Dairy Queen. There was no point in considering anything more than a casual friendship between them. He was a drifter, a poor farmhand with nothing to his name but a rusty pickup and a duffel bag full of old blue jeans. He seemed to have no family, no friends, no connections. She was a well-educated, respected professional. Who also had no friends or connections—at least not here in Kansas. But other than that, they had nothing in common. Besides, once she'd had time to refurbish the old white house, she was planning to put the farm up for sale. She hoped someone would buy it by the time she left in mid-September. Their paths—hers and Judd's—would never cross again.

When Judd finished with his call, Marah would use the pay phone to check in with her pediatrics clinic in St. Louis. Although she could afford the extra minutes on her cell phone, she didn't want to use it if she didn't have to. And the telephone on the farm was far from private. She didn't like her father knowing the details of her work life. More than once, she'd heard his discourse about the worthlessness of doctors. He believed physicians had no motive for what they did other than money, and that both annoyed and insulted her.

At the same time, she didn't want to let on to her father or anyone else how much she was enjoying the time away from the office. Mowing a field of alfalfa, running the combine, or working cattle left her tired but content. The wheat harvest had always been her favorite time of the year. Despite her expectations, she was enjoying her stay.

As Marah reached the Dairy Queen, she saw Judd suddenly sag against the telephone booth. He gripped the curved shelf with one hand, as if to support himself. Her physician instinct taking over, she started for him. Something had happened. Was he ill?

"Judd?"

She heard the receiver clank down, but he didn't turn. Head low, he wedged a shoulder against the side of the booth.

"Judd, are you all right?"

He didn't speak.

"I'm just . . . I'm going for some ice cream," she said. "Would you like something?"

He shook his head.

She stood for a moment. This wasn't good. Had he gotten some bad news? Did he feel sick?

"I could get you a cone."

He swung around, his eyes narrowed, rimmed in red. "I said no. No thanks. I already had one."

She stepped back, her heart pounding. "Fine. I was just concerned."

Before he could speak again, she turned and went into the

Dairy Queen. She had lost her appetite, but she ordered a small vanilla cone anyway.

"These sure are popular today," the woman at the counter said.

Marah tried to smile. "It's hot outside."

"I guess that must be it." The woman eyed her. "I'll bet you're a Morgan."

"Marah. I'm Ed Morgan's daughter."

"Marah Morgan? Well, I'll be. I remember when you were knee-high to a grasshopper."

"I guess I've changed a little."

"Some, but not much. Those blue eyes and that black hair. You Morgans are easy to spot." She handed over the cone. "We had a fellow I didn't recognize come in here a few minutes ago. He bought him a vanilla cone, too . . . well, speak of the devil."

Marah followed the direction of the woman's focus as Judd stood in the door of the small establishment. His face was composed now, emotionless.

Marah started toward him, uncertain what he might say next. Experience told her to watch out. Be wary.

"Marah," he said, placing a hand on her arm.

She gripped the small cone. "It's OK." Don't pry, she told herself. Don't ask questions. Stay out of his life, out of his line of fire.

"I'm uh . . ." He hung his thumbs in his pockets, his head low again. "Someone died. I just found out. Killed. He was a good friend."

"Oh, Judd." Sympathy poured through her. She wanted to

reach out to him, but how could she? She couldn't predict what his reaction might be, and she felt herself holding back and shutting off, the way Big Ed Morgan had taught her. Why couldn't she break past that? What was blocking her?

"I need some time to think it through," Judd said.

"Would you like to go back to the farm now?"

"That'd be good."

She dropped the remains of her cone into a trash barrel and led the way out of the Dairy Queen. "Do you mind if I make a quick call? I need to touch base with my office."

"Fine." He headed across the street toward the pickup.

Hurrying to the phone booth, Marah wondered how Judd's friend had died. *Killed*, he had said. That was different, worse. Maybe it had been a car wreck or a farm accident. Maybe a murder. *Oh, Lord, what tangles my feet every time I want to take a step toward someone?*

Judd intrigued her. He was silent and strong and pent up. His laughter in the pickup earlier that afternoon had seemed rare, as though he didn't find many things amusing.

Men like Milton Gregory, Sam Girard, and many of the other physicians she knew didn't intrigue Marah in the least. They were educated and suave and caught up in themselves. She found them easy to dominate. Or easy to ignore. Certainly they were easy to date, because they neither gave nor expected much.

As Marah punched in her calling card number, she saw Judd climb into the front seat of his pickup and grasp the steering wheel. This man was different somehow. Things had happened in his life, and he had felt them deeply. The death of his friend had moved him to tears.

Marah sensed warning flags waving madly inside her like the poles on a downhill slalom course. *Watch out. Dodge this one. Stay clear.* And she intended to do just that.

She spoke to her office, fielding queries regarding her patients and asking the staff to let Dr. Jordan know she was still planning to return in September. Yes, she realized they were moving into the new medical building. Yes, she understood how chaotic things were without her. But she had no choice.

As she hung up, she wondered if she had told the truth. Could she leave the farm? Probably. The wheat was healthy; the harvest would be bountiful. The cows had calved. Her father maneuvered fairly well on his walker. Judd was reliable and efficient. The two of them could manage for a time, at least until the crop was in. So what was to keep her from returning to St. Louis?

Turning the question over in her mind as she turned to go, Marah spotted a small white sack lying on the shelf of the phone booth. She picked it up. Judd must have left it. Feeling a bit like a curious child encountering a cookie jar, she opened it and peeked inside.

A thin Bible, its pages gold rimmed, its binding black leather, lay inside. A Bible? She glanced across the street. Judd hammered one fist on the steering wheel and then leaned back in the seat, breathing deeply as if he couldn't get enough air.

Was he a religious man? Or had he bought the Bible as a gift for someone else?

As Marah crossed the street, she remembered her mother poring over the pages of her Bible. Comfort she had found in its words. Strength. Hope. Endurance. In her hurry to get to Kansas, Marah had inadvertently left her own Bible in St. Louis, and she hadn't been able to find one at the white house.

"Here," she said, holding the sack through the open window. "I think you must have left this in the phone booth."

He stared at the package in her hand. Then he shook his head. "Take it," he said. "I don't need it."

She stood aside as he climbed down and walked around the pickup to open the broken door.

🐾 🐾 🐾

A quiet Saturday would be good for putting the white house in order and preparing it to be painted, Marah decided early one morning a few days later. She had spent so much of her time in the fields and the barn. Though she had explored no farther than the living room, kitchen, and downstairs bedroom and bath, she knew the entire house was a wreck.

Humming, she made herself some toast and a pot of coffee for breakfast. Then she began in the dining room by righting chairs and shoving the old round oak table back into place. She fitted the drawers into the sideboard, though they were empty now of her mother's stoneware. The strawberry-patterned dishes hadn't been worth much, purchased one by one in the grocery store as a premium. But Ruby Morgan had tenderly washed, dried, and placed each one back into the sideboard after every meal.

Who had made this mess? Who had allowed the home to fall into such disrepair? Her father, that was who. Ed Morgan never cared about anything or anyone but himself, Marah thought as she climbed onto the table to dust the hanging lamp. He let his wife slump into illness and silence. He let his children, unloved and angry, slip away one by one. And then he let the white house fall to ruin. Even the farm of which he was so protective had been deteriorating for years, the barn walls chinked with holes, the herd of cattle down to a few dozen head, the fences broken and sagging.

The more Marah turned the realities over in her mind, the more tangled her emotions became. Where did this twisting pain come from? And why did it lurk inside her like some sort of undiagnosed tumor sending out malignant tenacles that threatened to choke her spirit? A Christian ought to have rooted such ugly things out of her life, Marah felt. People who had given their hearts to Christ were supposed to be beautiful inside, not filled with lurking pathogens.

As Marah swept and mopped, thumped filthy rugs on the back porch, washed the faded wallpaper, and scoured the sink, she turned the matter over and over in her mind. But she didn't arrive at any answers.

At noon, the rumble of thunder drew her attention as she

was eating a sandwich. A storm was brewing. Through the
dining-room window, she could see gray clouds lining up like
Confederate soldiers on the horizon. Morgan Farm lay right in
the center of tornado alley, and several times during Marah's
childhood the four little girls had raced down into the cellar to
wait out the fury. Though she was the oldest, she had always
been terrified to go there, afraid of spiders and musty corners.
Afraid also, because her father never accompanied his daughters into that dark place. The moment a tornado threatened, Ed
raced out into the pasture to move a pickup or ran to the barn
to shut in his cattle or climbed a silo to close the hatch.

Marah could remember clutching her sisters' hands as they
emerged from the cellar after a tornado had torn across their
farm. Sometimes they found tractors hurled from one field to
another, barns shattered, metal grain bins twisted like aluminum soda cans. They learned that the wind could peel the shingles off a roof, lightning could strip the bark from a tree, rain
could wash gullies through the pastures. They also found out
their father always survived. All the same, Marah had grown to
hate storms.

Determined not to let such memories dampen her progress
toward a fresh, clean house, she realized she lacked several
supplies she would need for the afternoon. The day she had
gone to town with Judd to buy supplies, the upsetting news
he'd received had cut short their shopping expedition. Pete
Harris had fixed her water pump, so she decided to make a
quick run into town by herself. A stop at the grocery store

would take care of the Pine Sol and Comet. If she could get the walls washed down by evening, she might be able to start painting after church the following day.

Keeping an eye on the gathering clouds, Marah climbed into her car and set off down the gravel drive. Freshly painted walls would make the whole house look and smell better. When she returned from town, she would ask Judd to come over one day next week to help her shore up the staircase. Then she could start on the upper rooms.

Marah had been telling herself she wanted to restore the old white house so it would fetch a better price on the real estate market. But she couldn't deny the joy she had felt this morning while she brought the place back to life. It felt like coming home.

As she drove through the farm gate and onto the main road, she again spotted her mother's four-o'clocks beside the mailbox. Mom had always placed canning jars filled with flowers on every flat surface in the white house. The dining-room table, the coffee table in the living room, the kitchen windowsills, even the old wicker tables on the porch usually sported blossoms in pink and yellow.

Speeding toward town, Marah thought of Perky, who had been working so hard to restore Ruby's flower beds. Every evening after dinner and milking time, the child would hunt for Judd, then drag him to the gardens. The two of them would dig, prune, and plant. They rebuilt stone borders. They pulled out weeds. They added fresh topsoil. They hauled in manure. And Ruby Morgan's red roses had begun to bloom again.

A hiss of lightning split the charcoal sky just ahead of Marah's car. She gripped the steering wheel as thunder rolled like a drumbeat across the prairie. Wind was blowing the wheat almost flat, and it buffeted the car, as if trying to wrest control of the vehicle from her hands. Her heart hammered. She could see a line of dark rain in the distance and a faint jade tint to the clouds. No doubt, as her father had predicted, the roof of the old house would leak. Rain would blow through the broken windowpanes. The yard outside would turn into a muddy morass.

She could picture her father in the rock house now, brewing up a pot of coffee as he always did when a storm threatened. He would move from room to room, window to window, checking the sky for hail or funnel clouds. There was no early-warning alarm system so far from town, and each farmer did his part to alert the neighbors. Even with no one to listen, Ed would keep up his running commentary: *"Sky looks green over there to the west. Yessir, I do believe we're going to get us some hail this time, and would you take a look at that lightning. Beans, that's a wicked-looking cloud."*

How often as a child Marah had felt the urge to race across the room and hide in the shelter of her father's arms! He was not loving or kind, but he was strong. She knew he could protect her. Yet he wasn't available. Never. The moment real danger came along, he went rushing out the door to take care of the farm.

No, Marah thought as she steered her BMW down the road

toward the flickering sky. She didn't need her father's protection. She had found a heavenly Father who was far more reliable.

Marah's mother had introduced her four little ducklings to Christ, to her own source of strength, her refuge. Through years of Bible reading, Marah had come to know every story printed between the black leather covers. There were tales of bloody battles, lists of ancestors, laws that detailed the way people should dress and eat, prophecies that spelled doom and destruction. But had she ever found in the Word of God the same kind of comfort her mother had known? Had she ever experienced the hope that had kept Ruby going despite the daily unhappiness in her marriage?

A burst of light split the afternoon air, lifting the soft hair on Marah's arms. A second later, a crash shattered the silence, rumbled through the car, sent adrenaline pouring through her veins. Instinctively, she put her foot on the brake.

She pulled off onto the shoulder as hail began to pelt the windshield. A jagged tongue of lightning licked the treetops along the nearby river. Marah swallowed and glanced in the rearview mirror. As she focused on the road ahead of her again, she saw a black funnel drop down from the clouds.

The tornado spun toward her like a child's top out of control, now dancing above the road, now churning down into wheat fields, now plowing through a shed and sending splinters flying into the air. Staring immobile, Marah clutched the steering wheel as the funnel cloud lifted, nearly vanished into the green sky, then shot to the ground again, whirling in a direct line toward her car.

Without stopping to think, she spun the BMW back onto the road, made a screeching U-turn, and pushed the gas pedal to the floor. Marah didn't need to think. She already knew there were no ditches in which to take cover along this stretch of road. No houses with storm cellars. Not even a side road down which she could flee. This barren expanse of prairie between Morgan Farm and town offered her nothing in the way of protection. It promised nothing but a flat-out race between her silver BMW and a snorting, raging black fury.

Eyes on the rearview mirror, she pushed her car down the highway. Her whole body leaned forward, pressing against the steering wheel as if somehow she could force the vehicle to go faster just by sheer willpower. Behind her, the tornado bounced and swerved, carving a curving path toward the river. And just as swiftly, it snarled right back onto the road again. Did tornadoes look for easy paths to destruction?

She spotted the Morgan mailbox and slowed just enough to thread her car between the two fence posts. Dirt swirled around the car, obscuring her vision, as she tried to follow the gravel drive to the white house. Hail hammered the roof of her car, bounced across the road, began to pile up in mounds in the yard. In the rearview mirror Marah could see nothing but swirling dirt and crackling light. She imagined the tornado licking at her tailpipe, eager to suck her up, gargle her around in its black throat, and then spit her out again.

As the BMW skidded to a stop beside the house, Marah thought she caught a glimpse of her father across the yard, moving through the rain and hail on his walker, heading for the barn. Dashing onto the porch, she pushed her sopping hair out of her eyes and called out to him.

"Hey! What are you doing?"

But she knew what he was doing. What he always did. What he would never stop doing.

"Hey!" she called again. She peered at him through the rain as the locomotive sound of the tornado roared in her ears. A small tree limb suddenly flew out of the fury, slapped into Marah's leg, and tumbled onward. Wincing in pain, she debated only a moment. Even if she ran to her father, she knew he would never go with her into the storm cellar. And he would never leave the farm.

She dashed into the house just as a nearby fence lifted from the ground and began to swing and whip like a barbed-wire lariat. Throwing her shoulder against the front door, she managed to bolt it shut. Then she headed for the cellar.

The green door's rusty hinges resisted, squealing their protest at the unfamiliar movement. Marah yanked and lifted at the same time, forcing it open. She stepped onto the top stair and tugged the door closed behind her. Then she pulled the cord to the single basement lightbulb.

Nothing.

The power must have gone off in the lightning, Marah realized as she raced down the rickety staircase. How often had that happened during her childhood? She sometimes imagined that their house had been electrified with chicken wire or fencing wire, something that shorted out at the least surge of power. The old flashlight they had kept downstairs still might be lying somewhere within reach.

The cellar had been dug deeply into the rich Kansas soil by Marah's grandfather. Its floor and walls were made of dirt, and she remembered how grass and tree roots poked into the darkness like gnarled fingers.

Marah made her way across the bumpy floor toward the wall where she recalled the electrical box was located. What if it was just a bad bulb? She listened to the storm pounding overhead, wondering if a tornado could rip the whole house away and leave her shivering like a tiny bug in her dark hole.

As a child, she and her sisters had planned out what they would take into the cellar when storms came. The twins each brought a favorite blanket and a metal Tonka truck. Deborah carried her Raggedy Ann doll and a book of fairy tales. Marah's treasures had been her white Easter purse and her Bible. The purse had been a gift from her mother before she died, but it also had a practical aspect. Inside that precious patent leather purse with its gold chain strap Marah kept the grand sum of two dollars and fifty cents, with which she and her sisters could start their new life in case their father and their house blew away in the tornado.

Marah almost wished she had that old purse and the Bible now as she felt along the rough wall, aware of spiderwebs and imagining brown recluses lurking in the darkness. The only light came from a small, mud-spattered window at the far end of the cellar. It took Marah an eternity to locate the metal electrical box.

As she pulled open the cover, she thought she heard a movement near the storage shelves. Something shuffling. The rattle of a glass jar. Pausing, she listened, but the only sound was the roar of the storm above her.

Deciding it had been her imagination, she ran her fingers over the open box, feeling for switches she could flip. Instead, she found a row of round knobs, each an inch in diameter. And then she remembered her father descending into the basement with a box of screw-in fuses. These fuses couldn't be flipped like the circuit breakers in her town house in St. Louis. They had to be replaced with new ones—and she didn't know if there were any in the house.

Letting out a breath of frustration, Marah leaned back against the dirt wall. Well, right about now her father was probably lying in the pouring rain somewhere; rain was no doubt gushing through the roof of the old white house; and her silver BMW was likely being beaten to a pulp by hail—assuming the tornado hadn't whisked it off to who-knew-where. She wished she'd brought Judd's little Bible down into the cellar with her. Even though she didn't have enough light to read by, the feel of the leather cover would comfort her.

The smart thing would be to find that flashlight, she decided. With light, she might be able to locate a box of fuses.

If she could get that bulb back on, she could wait out the storm
by rooting around in the old cartons her father said had been
stored in the basement. The contents had probably been
damaged by time and the elements, but it might be interesting
to see what she would find.

Marah headed blindly across the cellar floor toward the row
of storage shelves her father had built. By the dim light of the
window she could see their vague outline and the rows of
canning jars that lined them. She remembered her father carrying lumber down the basement steps and hammering for hours.
In those days, they'd had no electricity. Mom had lit an oil
lamp for him.

The smell in the basement disturbed Marah, as it always had.
Dank and musty, it made her think of graves. Death had always
made her uncomfortable. As a child, she had declared to her
sister Deborah that she would do everything in her power to
keep people from dying. But that was before her mother's death,
before Marah understood that she might battle death, might
even hold it at bay, but ultimately, she was helpless against it.
As Perky had reminded her, only God could heal people.

Thinking of her mother, she continued toward the wall
where the shelves stood. Ruby Morgan had been buried in the
town cemetery, and her granite headstone recorded no more
than the dates of a woman's birth and death. Nothing of the
mother who had cuddled four little girls in her lap.

Marah paused and lifted her head, catching a whiff of something different in the cellar. Something vaguely familiar, like

fabric and perspiration. She tried to identify it. Standing still in the darkness, she wondered if the odor was herself. If she had somehow become rank and earthy in her time back on the farm. If she had taken on the scent of her father.

Her father. That's what she smelled. But he wasn't in the cellar, was he? She'd seen him outside in the storm.

Then who was in the cellar with her? No one, of course. The house had been empty when she left for town. She had come down here alone. Marah shook her head, deciding the tension was playing tricks with her mind.

She located the shelves and ran her fingertips across the dusty jars. How long had these been here? Peering closely, she could just barely make out the wording on the labels: Peach preserves, Blackberry jelly, Green beans, Tomatoes. A familiar handwriting. And the dates? These jars had been filled by her mother.

Marah took down a jar of pickles. She had always loved her mother's bread-and-butter pickles. So sweet and tangy. Was this how people lived on? she wondered. Things they created remained for the world to enjoy. Their bodies decayed, but they lived on through the gardens they had cultivated or the pickles they had canned.

Her mother would laugh at this notion, of course. Pickles were not the measure of her soul, she would say. Ruby Morgan had taught her daughters that each person had a soul that could never die. Certain her body was nothing more than a shell,

Ruby had entrusted her soul to Jesus Christ. And she believed that when she died, her soul would rest in his arms.

Marah believed that, too, she thought as she cradled the pickles. As she reached out to search for the flashlight, she heard the sound of someone breathing.

A deep, heavy sound. A ragged gasping.

Before Marah could react, heavy footsteps sounded suddenly across the cellar's dirt floor. Something scraped and toppled over. Glass tinkled.

"Who's there?" Marah called out.

The room fell silent. Trying to breathe as her heart pounded in her ears, she grabbed on to the old shelves for support. Someone was in the basement with her! Who? Why?

For an instant she had the horrible thought that the intruder lurking in the cellar was there to harm her. It was the kind of thing she'd read about in magazines. Strange men crept in and strangled unsuspecting women. Or drove them away some-where and raped them. Or left them to die in the desert. Terrifying things that only happened to other people.

But Marah had seen horrors in her medical practice. Children who had been burned by cigarettes. Babies with frac-tured skulls. Unimaginable evils, yet those horrors were true.

Fear prickling up her spine, she searched the darkness, trying in vain to make out something definite. Was it a man or a woman? The person was across the room now, near the boxes that Ed Morgan had stored in the cellar. Marah could hear a soft scraping. Something dragging, scooting along the floor.

"Who are you?" she said.

At the sound of her voice, there was a male grunt. Footsteps started up the staircase. Creaking and stumbling. Marah hurled the pickle jar across the darkness toward the sound. It slammed into the staircase and broke with a muffled crash. Above her, the basement door screeched and banged shut. The sound of boots pounded overhead—someone running through the house.

Her heart slamming against her ribs, Marah raced up the steps. In darkness, she fumbled for the round iron knob, found it, turned it. The door didn't budge.

"Hey!" she shouted.

The door was heavy, she remembered, its hinges nearly rusted tight. She jiggled the knob and lifted the sagging door as she pushed against it. Still it wouldn't move.

"Who's out there?" she called. She rammed her shoulder against the wood. Nothing.

She recalled the metal skeleton key that had always sat unturned in the lock. Had the man locked her into the basement? She shoved on the door again. It was definitely locked. She jiggled the knob, wondering if she could loosen it somehow. She was angry now, angry at whoever had dared to invade her home.

"Hey!" she hollered again. "Unlock this door!"

She hammered on it, hoping someone would hear the noise. Who would have done this? Who could have been down in the cellar? Judd, maybe? Had the farmhand slipped into the white house looking for something to steal? Marah knew he lived hand to mouth, but she could hardly imagine him a thief.

Or had the intruder been one of Dr. Gregory's men? What would they have been looking for? The idea seemed implausible. Their focus was the fields and their research.

Maybe someone had been passing by the farm. Maybe they'd seen the storm coming and had entered the cellar to escape the tornado. Maybe that was it.

Listening with her ear against the peeling wood, Marah could hear the patter of gentle rain and nothing else. So, the storm was over. The house was still standing. She felt a sudden urge to find her father and make sure he was all right. But someone had locked her in the cellar and had gone away. Nobody would look for her all day. Maybe not even tomorrow. If it kept raining, no one would be out. She might not be missed for days. If only she had her cell phone. She wished she had grabbed it when she got out of the car. But at the time, all she could think about was reaching the safety of the house.

Marah sank down onto the top step and tried to breathe. OK. She was going to be all right. She would find a way out.

Footsteps.

Marah lifted her head, relief spilling through her. The steps crossed the living-room area as she stood to listen. Then she heard the footfalls approach the kitchen. She listened to the noises overhead. But what if it were he—the man who had run from the cellar? The man who had locked her in?

Grabbing the rail, Marah decided she wasn't taking any

chances. She stumbled back down the stairs and jumped the last few steps, her ankle twisting as she landed on the basement floor. She could hear broken glass crunching beneath her sneakers as she raced through the darkness.

She found a dirt wall. Felt the tree roots and clutched them for support. One root was sticking out, dry and old, and she pulled on it until it snapped. Holding the wood like a baseball bat, she listened. The footsteps continued into the bathroom.

Then she remembered the basement window. The small pane of muddy glass stood high on one wall near the storage shelves. If she could push out the glass, she might be able to climb into the yard. Anything to get out of this place.

Now the footsteps moved from the bathroom into the dining room. Marah moved to the shelves and pushed some jars to one side. The window was high. Maybe too high. She put one foot on the lowest shelf and tested it with her weight. It held. Laying down the tree root, she grabbed on to the upper shelves and began to climb toward the window. The rotting boards sagged under her feet. One began to creak, then crack. She moved to the next. Higher and higher.

Finally she could touch the grayed frame that held the window in place. Termites had gnawed the wood, their dark tunnels obvious along the unpainted surface. The frame should be easy to break. She reached for it and gave a shove.

The shelves beneath her feet swayed, pulled loose from the wall, and crashed to the floor. Marah clung desperately to the windowsill, her feet dangling.

"Marah?" The voice came from overhead.

It was Judd.

"Marah, are you down there?" He knocked on the basement door. "You all right?"

Of course I'm down here, you creep, she thought. *You locked me in, didn't you?*

She couldn't hold on much longer. Her fingers were going numb. If she fell, she would land in the broken glass and splintered lumber spiked with rusty nails.

"The basement door's locked," he said, sounding as innocent as a baby. "How did you get down there?"

Oh, Lord, she mouthed as her arms began to tremble. *Help me, Lord.*

"Marah?" he called again. "I heard a crash. It sounded like glass. Are you all right?"

"I'm at the window!" she shouted. "The basement window. Get me out of here!"

She could hear his boots thudding overhead as he raced out the door. As her arms weakened, she tried to find toeholds. One foot located a knobby root. Letting out her breath, she put some of her weight on it. It held. The blood began to flow back into her arms. Thank God for tree roots in the basement walls.

Judd's face emerged beyond the muddy windowpane, concern written in his eyes. He felt around the edges of the glass. A knife appeared in his hand.

Marah stifled a cry.

As she clung to the sill, one toe balanced on the tree root,

Judd ran the knife through the old putty. She could see the silver tip sliding in and out. He tugged on the frame, loosening it as chunks of debris tumbled into Marah's hair. The window slid out, and a breath of rain-washed air puffed into the basement.

"OK," he said, extending his arm. "Give me your hand."

She reached for him, and the root snapped. As he grabbed for her, Marah tumbled to the floor.

The Twenty-third Day of the Yellow Flower Moon, The Year of 1869

I try to hold the pen, but it is difficult. My thoughts hop inside my head like robins searching for worms, first here and then there. At times I see visions, terrifying dreams, but I know these have not been brought to me by Wah'Kon-Tah, the almighty spirit, Grandfather the Sun.

They are brought by the ge-ta-zhe.

The agent came from the fort again today. He walked through our village and looked at all of those who are dying. He came into our lodge and looked at my mother. He says she will die soon. He says I also will die. He is sorry, he tells my father, but he cannot get any medicine to fight the ge-ta-zhe. When the medicine comes from the city, it is always dead.

I do not believe there is a city. I do not believe there is medicine. I think the Heavy Eyebrows agent is a liar. My heart is filled with bitter anger for him, just as my body is filled with the ge-ta-zhe. Both eat at me, and there is nothing to be done.

My mother thinks clearly again. She is no longer consumed by terrors of the night. But my father says this is only a false peace before the end. The ge-ta-zhe has left her mind, and now it marches like an army across her skin. On her face, the ge-ta-zhe leaves its footprints—small, flat, red spots that destroy the beauty of my mother. Every day more spots appear as the ge-ta-zhe walks across her. Its feet burn and blister her skin, so that each spot rises like a boil. My mother weeps from the pain of the blisters.

I want to cry for the loss of my mother's beauty, for the loss of her strength, for the loss of her gentle touch. I want to cry for her pain. But most of all now, I want to cry for myself.

Once, I hoped to be a warrior like my father. I longed to be a great buffalo hunter. I wanted to marry a strong, quick-walking girl who would build a lodge for our children. These things will never happen. The ge-ta-zhe will march across my face with its burning feet, and then I will be buried beside my mother. And I will be no more.

From The Journal of Little Gray Bird, unpublished
Central Kansas Museum of the Native American archival
collection

9

"Marah?" Kneeling in the deep mud, Judd edged his shoulders through the open window. "Marah, are you all right?"

A groan and the sound of some shifting boards told him she was alive.

"Don't move. I'm coming down there."

"No!" Her voice was weak but insistent. "I can do this. I just need to . . . uhh . . . to get my leg . . . oh, beans . . ."

"Hold on. I'm going for a rope."

"A rope! No, no don't—"

"To get you out. The door's locked." He wished he could see her more clearly. "Are you bleeding?"

"I'm not sure. You're blocking the light."

He moved away from the window opening.

"Yes," she said. "OK, I'm bleeding. I'm definitely bleeding. I seem to have a laceration on the tibialis anterior."

"Glass?"

"I think so. It cut through my jeans."

"Apply pressure to the calf muscle. Use your shirt, if you need to. Don't tie it too tightly, or you'll cut off the blood flow. I'm going for the rope."

Judd searched the immediate area for a length of rope or a piece of garden hose. Finding nothing, he sprinted across the muddy yard to the toolshed near the house. He grabbed a coil of rope and ran back to the window.

He could hear Marah moving around, shoving boards and glass out of the way, clearing a space around herself. He tied the rope around a nearby tree and tossed the end through the window. "I'm coming down," he said as he edged through the opening.

He'd been in tighter places. Didn't know how he'd manage to get her out, but he would. He pulled from his pocket the small multipurpose tool he always carried. Knife, screwdriver, wrench, even a toothpick. He flicked on the tiny but intense flashlight that doubled as a key ring.

"You sure made a mess down here, Marah," he said. He dropped to the floor near her and kicked away the broken boards that separated them. "How'd you get locked in?"

"Somebody was in the cellar when I came down here." She was sitting up, holding her leg. Her blue eyes flashed warning beacons: *Don't come too close. Don't try anything.* And he realized she suspected him. "I called out, and the guy ran up the stairs and turned the key."

"There was no key in the door just now," Judd said, kneeling beside her, looking into her eyes. "Your visitor must've taken it."

"You were a visitor." She flinched as he removed her hand and inspected the wound. "I heard you walking around upstairs."

"I came over after the storm to tell you about a phone call. Someone from your medical group looking for you."

"Who?"

"No idea. You're supposed to call your secretary."

He stripped off his T-shirt and ripped a length of the cotton fabric. Then he pushed up the hem of her jeans. The wound was a clean cut, straight and not too deep. He didn't think stitches were called for, though it was hard to tell in this light. Strange to touch this woman's skin, Judd realized, his palm cupping the muscle of her calf, his thumb on the soft flesh near her injury. She didn't seem to mind, but to him it was unfamiliar, like stepping into a place he hadn't been in years.

Though he was aware of taut sinew, evidence of Marah's physical labor on the farm, he couldn't deny the accompanying female smoothness, the overlying silken skin—like the rose petals Perky instructed him to touch with his fingertips in order to feel their velvety softness. Blood had run onto her white sneaker, soaked the canvas fabric. Judd always carried a few antiseptic pads in his wallet, so he tore one open, cleaned the laceration, and bound it. When he pulled her jeans back down over her leg, she let out a breath, as though she'd been holding it the whole time.

"How did you know to do that?" she asked.

He looked up, surprised at the hostility in her voice. "Do what?"

"The way you cleaned it. The antiseptic pad. The bandage. You did it the way a doctor would. Who taught you that?"

"The United States Army." He replaced his tools. "Spent a few years doing my duty. You learn things."

"But you knew the muscle. When I told you the laceration was on the tibialis anterior, you knew it was a calf muscle. People don't just know that kind of thing."

"Must have heard it somewhere. Still get the tibia and fibula mixed up, though." He shrugged. Getting sloppy. He didn't like that in himself. "What's the deal on the light down here?" he asked, hoping she would drop the topic. "Isn't there any electricity?"

"Power's off."

"You came down here without a light?"

"I was a couple of seconds ahead of the tornado." She placed her folded hands over the cut on her leg. "So where were you when the storm hit?"

He realized she wasn't going to let the subject drop. She still didn't trust him. "I was out in the pasture. When I spotted the funnel, I headed for the rock house."

"You sure you didn't come over here?"

"I told you I wasn't in your cellar, Marah."

"And why am I supposed to believe that?"

"Because I said it." He leaned down and began moving the

shelves, clearing space under the window. Broken jars lay everywhere. Pickles and beans and tomatoes.

"Then who was down here?" she asked.

"Did you get a look at him?"

"How did you know it was a man?"

"You told me. You said, 'The guy ran up the stairs.'"

"It was a man's boots. A man's breathing. A man's running." She paused. "Maybe you were down here looking for something."

"Like what?"

"I don't know. We have things stored in the cellar. Old papers and books. My mother's collections. Maybe some of it's valuable."

"I'm not a thief, Marah."

"OK," she said. "Whatever."

He stood, hands on his hips for a moment, trying to figure the best way to move her. If he lifted her in his arms, he could boost her up through the window. Or if he went back through the window first, he could pull her up after him.

"You ready to head out of here?" he asked.

He figured he would give her the option. Holding out a hand, he felt the warmth of her fingers as she grasped his palm. But when she pulled herself upright and put some weight on her leg, she winced in pain.

"Give me just a minute. I think I twisted my ankle." Sitting on the floor again, she began massaging the spot. "When I jumped off the bottom couple of steps, I felt it turn."

"I could try breaking open the cellar door. You might get out easier that way."

"No, don't break it. My father would have a fit. He built . . ." She paused, still rubbing. "So, did you see him when you were at the rock house?"

"He wasn't there. I figured he'd gone over to the barn."

"He does that in storms." She let out a deep breath and fell silent. Judd studied her. She seemed troubled. But he had a feeling it wasn't the intruder in the basement that had thrown her. It wasn't even the locked door. It was the father.

"You think your dad went out in the rain on purpose?" He stepped over a jar of canned corn. "On his walker?"

"He always does. He wants to make sure things are put away. Tied down." She shrugged. "He used to leave us when we were little, my sisters and me. Tornadoes would come, and we'd run down here into the cellar to hide. I was in charge of the others. When we came out after it was all over, we had to look for our father. We never knew if we'd see him again."

"I'm sure he's fine."

"Yeah." She buried her head in the crook of her arm. "Oh, beans. Being down here makes me feel like I stepped back in time or something."

Judd hunkered down beside her, wishing he knew how to respond. He wasn't trained for this. Trained for everything, they had assured him. Parachuting, triage, combat, desert survival, jungle survival, torture survival. But not tenderness. Not comfort. They didn't teach it.

"Marah." He reached out and touched her arm.

She brushed away his hand. "Don't. Just leave me alone, OK?"

He sat back and tried to think. She shouldn't matter. Didn't matter. He was on assignment. Had to get to the bottom of this. But here she was, all alone, and he felt a strong urge to hold her.

He noticed a jar lying on its side. Maybe he could change the subject. "Who made the jelly?"

"My mother. Before she died." She shook her head. "The jars all shattered when the shelves fell."

Great, he thought. He was really making her feel better now.

"Here," he said, holding out the jar to her. "They're not all broken. Look, it's some kind of preserves. Blackberry, I bet, or maybe strawberry."

She stared at the jar. "When I came down and started look-ing for a flashlight, I saw the pickles. My mom made them years ago. Bread-and-butter pickles."

"Look, here are some pickles." He handed her another glass jar.

"She died when I was only eight."

Judd nodded, remembering Chuck, wishing he could stop thinking about his friend. He was having a hard time adjusting to the loss. The best thing he'd been able to do was push the murder to the back of his mind, the way he pushed away every-thing that caused him pain.

"Here, let me check your ankle," he said. He took her leg

again, ran his fingers over the delicate bones, turned her foot this way and that.

"Ouch! Good grief, what are you trying to do, break it for me?"

"You'll need ice." He could feel some swelling. Gently, he set her foot back on the floor. "So, how did your mother die?"

"My father said it was some disease the doctor couldn't identify." She was massaging her ankle. "A fever and a rash. But I don't know. I think maybe *he* was the real problem."

"Your dad?"

"Mom had failed to meet his expectations. She hadn't given him sons, and we could never be who he wanted us to be. His disapproval sort of withered her. Killed her, in a sense."

"I can see how that could happen," Judd said, aware of the hard places inside his own heart.

"Me, too. Something ugly settles down inside you."

"Ugly? Not in you."

"It's there, like a tumor."

"I can't believe that." He wished he could reach out to her. Touch her somehow. "You're a good person. Perky's crazy about you. She says you tell her stories up in a tree. And I've watched you. You care about everything you do. You're working hard for your father. There's nothing wrong with you."

"Something's been tangling me up. Something to do with my father. My mom would probably tell me to give the whole thing to God. I've been a Christian for a long time, but I'm still not sure how to do that."

Judd shifted on the broken boards. He didn't know much

about God. All he knew was that he ought to be getting Marah out of the basement and checking the upstairs rooms for footprints.

"Why don't you just ask him to help you get over your bitterness?" Judd said.

"Ask who?"

"God, or whoever."

She sat in silence, and Judd wondered what to do next. Had he said something wrong?

"Bitterness," she said softly. "So you think I'm bitter toward my father?"

"Maybe."

"Like I haven't forgiven him. But what am I supposed to forgive him for? He doesn't think he's done anything wrong." She let out a deep breath. "Well, I guess I'm ready to give my evacuation from the cellar another shot."

As he helped Marah to her feet again, Judd thought about the bitterness in his own life. He'd never been able to forgive his wife for betraying him, for leaving him. In fact, he realized now, far from forgiving her, he'd actually been nurturing that hurt, feeding it with all the other wrongs that had been done to him through the years. Chuck's murder was the latest.

Judd blamed Gregory, hated him, nursed that anger. It kept him strong and hard and distant from pain. But in talking to Marah, he began to wonder how it would feel to let the bitterness go. She'd said her mom believed that God could take care of things like that. But how did a person even find God? Judd thought of the Bible he'd bought in town, and he wondered if that might be the place to start.

Marah's slender arms slipped around his chest, and Judd realized she was ready for him to help her up through the window. Trying to stifle the sensation her nearness evoked, he bent and scooped her into his arms. He couldn't think of Marah as a woman. She was too pure, too distant from him. From the moment he met her, he'd known she was different. Something had set her apart.

He was filth. All the killings, the lies, the hatred, the treachery hung heavy inside him, like lead weights that would one day drag him to hell. He had never believed there was any other future for him anyhow. He'd lost hope in heaven. Lost hope even in himself. Who was he anyway? Was he Judd Hunter? Or had he become one of the others, one of the many masks he wore so well?

Steadying the rope, he boosted her up the wall. She grabbed the edges of the window opening and worked her way through to the outside. Devoid of her warmth, Judd followed as fast as he could. But when he knelt in the muddy grass, he saw that she was already limping away from him. Hurrying toward the front of her house.

He turned toward the bunkhouse, wondering why the bright sunshine that followed the stormy morning failed to lift his spirits. Usually he enjoyed a sunny day and, even more, the prospect of an investigation. Footprints. Subtle inquiries. A mystery to solve.

Maybe Chuck's death had cast a pall over everything, he mused as he crossed the yard. Was Chuck in heaven? Judd doubted it. The two of them had done some pretty crazy things together. Things that didn't get a man into heaven.

On the other hand, if a woman like Marah needed to ask for God's help, maybe there was no way anybody could be good enough to get into heaven. Maybe it all depended on letting go and turning things over to God. But could a person turn over his whole life? A life like Judd's? He doubted it.

🐾 🐾 🐾

Feeling shaken and slightly sick, Marah limped into the bathroom. She closed the door and bolted it shut. What was wrong with her? It had to be the man in the cellar, she told herself. Or the talk about her father and her bitterness. But she knew it had something to do with Judd, too. The way he had held her leg, touched her blood, bandaged her wound. The way he had picked her up, almost cradling her against his chest as he lifted her toward the window. The way he had spoken to her, so gently, helping her to see through the tangles.

But what if he'd been the one in the cellar looking for something to steal? Maybe his kindness was simply a cover-up for having been caught red-handed. Maybe he *had* locked her in after all.

Still, how could Judd be a thief? He said he wasn't. He insisted he had come to the house to tell her about a phone call. And he *had* rescued her. Something about him made her feel he was telling the truth. Marah knew she wasn't easily fooled. But she wasn't easily disturbed by the nearness of a man's bare chest either. How had he thrown her off kilter?

She peeled out of her damp, muddy jeans and sank down onto the edge of the tub. "Lord," she murmured, "I need to forget about what happened in the cellar. I need to get Judd out of my thoughts. I need to focus on things that really matter. Can you help me with that?"

Sometimes she felt like a little girl when she talked to God, asking him for assistance and relying on him to take care of her. But she had always liked that. Liked the reality of a loving heavenly Father. After her talk with Judd in the cellar, she realized she hadn't been as close to God as she wanted to be.

She focused her attention on her leg. Her injury wasn't as bad as she had feared. The laceration was long but not deep. A few butterfly strips would hold it together. Though she'd had her tetanus booster the previous year, a trip into town to visit Dr. Benson might be a good idea.

Marah washed the wound again and applied antibiotic ointment, all the while turning over in her mind the kindness Judd had shown in treating her. He had torn up his own T-shirt, hadn't he? But he wasn't a man she could think about too much, she told herself again. He was just a farmhand. A farmhand who knew where the tibialis anterior was, who carried sterile wipes in his wallet, who could climb a rope with ease. He might even be a robber, sneaking into people's homes when they weren't there. Even though he'd seemed kind enough, she knew she shouldn't trust him.

After binding the wound again, Marah pulled on a pair of clean slacks and a fresh shirt. She needed to get over to the rock house and see if her father was all right. And she ought to phone her office to find out who had called. If, indeed, anyone had called.

Maybe one of the archaeologists had been in the cellar. Was one of them a petty thief? That hardly seemed likely. If not, maybe they'd actually gone down there looking for something. But what would they hope to find in a damp basement filled with a bunch of old canning jars? She wondered about the storage boxes. Had any of them been opened? moved?

Marah respected Milton Gregory, and she knew he wasn't the type to steal something from the house. He was too upright, too educated and formal to stoop to burglary. She sensed the man was attracted to her, and the thought had crossed her mind that he might be interesting company for an evening. They'd both been trained in medical fields, after all. She'd vaguely considered asking him to accompany her to a movie in town. But in the end, she couldn't work up all that much interest.

Bob Harper and Mike Dooley, on the other hand, might have found reason to enter her house after they'd seen her leave. She didn't like either of them very much. Bob was a chain-smoker, and both men often flirted with and teased Marah when their paths crossed. Once, Mike had hung his elbows through her pickup window to keep her from driving away. As the pickup rolled along, he kept walking beside it, faster and faster, until finally she had no choice but to stop again. He had laughed and called her "doc," and she'd been obliged to keep listening to him until he finally stepped away from the pickup. She hadn't liked his behavior, and later she told him so. He'd seemed offended. Another time, Bob had invited Marah to the Dairy Queen for a cone. She'd told him she was too busy, and she was. But she knew he'd gotten the message that she wasn't interested in him. Maybe one of them had been in the cellar. It wouldn't surprise her much.

As she set out across the yard, Marah spotted the archaeological team lounging on the back porch of the rock house. They had taken to hanging out there sometimes, eating lunch, making phone calls, using the bathroom and shower, and asking Ed all kinds of questions about the farm. Now they were passing around a bag of tortilla chips and a jar of salsa. Mike offered the bag to Dr. Gregory, but he waved it away. Marah noticed he was wearing his sunglasses.

Nearing the house, she could see Perky Harris standing on the front porch chatting with Judd. He was wearing a navy T-shirt, a clean pair of jeans, and his Stetson. As Judd knelt to talk to the little girl, the farm dog leapt onto his knee and began licking his cheek. Judd laughed and gave Gypsy a hug around the neck; then he took Perky's hand and stood. Together they descended the porch and walked across the muddy yard to the flower beds they'd been tending.

As Marah walked toward the porch, her calf muscle shrieked in pain. She grabbed the rail for support and glanced across at the garden. Judd was watching her, his brown eyes alert.

"Your father's in the house," he called to her. "He rode out the tornado in the barn."

"Anything damaged?" she asked, changing her course and heading for the soggy patch of dirt.

"Hail flattened some alfalfa. Other than that, it looks like the funnel skipped us."

Marah let out a breath of relief. "Hey, Perky," she said, "how are you this afternoon?"

"Dr. Morgan!" Perky leapt to her feet and threw an arm around Marah's waist. "I was hoping you'd visit the garden. Look what's coming up! Judd says it's purple coneflowers and tickseeds and sunflowers. *Tickseed*—isn't that an awful name? They were in here all along, but they were a tangled-up mess, so we weeded them out and made them into tidy clumps. And next year we're going to have flowers. The tickseeds will be first to bloom!"

"Tickseed coreopsis," Judd clarified. "They're gold."

Perky's delight lifted Marah's spirits, and she gave Judd a smile. When he winked in return, something stirred in the pit of her stomach, and she felt her heart rate double. Embarrassed by her response, Marah knelt and ran her fingertips over the emerging wildflowers.

"My mom and I checked out gardening books from the library in town," Perky was saying, "and I looked up everything.

Judd reads the books at night in the bunkhouse. The tickseeds are going to be so pretty."

"It's a native wildflower. This is how the leaf looks." His large, deeply tanned hand reached down near hers and grazed the tiny green leaves. "Now the purple coneflower, that's echinacea. Some people say it cures colds. And we think we've got ashy sunflower right here."

"Poppy says the cows like to eat ashy sunflowers, but we told him he couldn't give these to his cows because they're for the garden. He says he doesn't know why we're working on the gardens because they're just full of weeds. But he comes out here and bosses us around anyway. He says he's the only one who remembers where Mrs. Morgan planted everything."

"He remembers my mother's gardens?" Marah asked, glancing up in surprise.

"Sure. Poppy told us that bed over there always had gayfeathers, loads of them, and your mother wouldn't put anything else in there, because she loved the purple so much."

Marah rose, staring at the small rock-encircled bed with its straggly plants beginning to take hold. She could clearly recall the tall, thick, purple-flowered spikes of gayfeather that she and her sisters had pretended were fairy wands. "I didn't know he ever looked at Mom's flowers," she said.

"Oh yes he did," Perky said, flipping her blond braids over her shoulders. "He told us your mom would drive the old pickup out onto the prairie and gather rocks and dig up wildflowers and tote everything back to the house."

"I remember."

"Poppy hated Indian paintbrush, but she would plant it in her gardens anyway. He says it's a bad weed, and you have to work hard to get rid of it. But she liked the orangy red color."

Suddenly Marah could see her mother's flower beds in all their glory. She hadn't known the names of the blossoms, even though she and her sisters had helped their mother plant them. She hadn't realized they were all native wildflowers brought in from the pastures and prairies. Hadn't considered the hours of labor they had required from her mother. Hadn't thought much about the heavy stones, though she knew her mother had hauled them by herself. And all the time, Marah's father had been watching his wife, studying her work, perhaps even admiring the results.

Had he loved her after all? Even just a little?

"Our gardens are going to be beautiful," Perky said. "We're going to have all the colors of flowers. Red ones and yellow ones and purple ones. That's how our gardens are going to be, aren't they, Judd?"

"I guess we'll see," he said.

"Of course they are. Even though they might look half dead right now, God's going to make them grow and bud out and bloom all over the place."

She pointed around the muddy yard, gesturing at each of the rock-rimmed beds. Marah half expected them to spring to life in brilliant Technicolor as she watched.

Judd gave a low chuckle, covering Perky's shoulder with his

hand. "I don't know, Perk," he said. "I'm pretty sure God didn't have much to do with getting these particular plants up out of the ground. As I recall, it took a shovel and a hoe and a lot of muscle."

"That's our part," Perky said. "But only God can make the flowers."

Judd pondered that for a moment. "I guess you're right." He turned to Marah. "How's the leg?"

"A little sore," she said. "I'm going to the house to make that phone call now. I was just wondering if I could talk to you for a minute."

"I'll walk with you."

"Me, too," Perky said.

"You stay here," Judd ordered, pointing a finger at the determined child. "Stay here and talk to the plants. Maybe they'll grow faster."

He took Marah's arm, supporting her gently as they walked toward the rock house. "That Perky is a piece of work," he said.

"She adores you."

"Me?" He seemed genuinely surprised.

"Sure. You don't think you're adorable?"

He laughed. "Uh, never thought of myself that way."

"Well, you can be helpful anyhow." She drew in a breath. "Judd, I really feel like I need to know who was in the cellar this afternoon during the storm."

"It wasn't me."

"If not, my choices are pretty limited. I know it wasn't my

father or Perky. Do you think it was a stranger? Someone who wandered in to get out of the storm?"

"Maybe," he said. "Or maybe not."

He pushed open the door to reveal the collection of archaeologists who had moved in from the porch and were now gathered around the kitchen table eating an early supper. Marah looked into Judd's brown eyes. He didn't blink, didn't nod, gave no sign, and yet she realized he was speaking to her. He was telling her that one of Dr. Gregory's men had been down in her cellar.

"About time you hauled yourself over here, girl," her father said. "You better call your big city office, and don't put it on my bill. I'm not paying for your chitchat. What have the two of you been doing over there anyhow? Don't you mess with my daughter, Judd. I got my own plans for her."

As the men laughed, Marah walked into the living room and found the telephone. Her father had taken to hiding it under the sofa pillows so he wouldn't have to listen to the ringing. She wondered when he'd had his last hearing exam. Probably never.

"Shirley?" Marah recognized the voice of her favorite receptionist. "It's Dr. Morgan."

"Oh, Dr. Morgan, thank heaven you finally called. We've got such a mess here, we may have to just shut down the clinic."

"What's going on? Where's Dr. Jordan?"

"You haven't heard? Dr. Girard said he was going to call you."

Marah recalled the physician she'd been dating before she left St. Louis. He had phoned once or twice, but Marah never found the time to reciprocate. She considered their relationship over, and she hoped he was moving forward with little regret.

"I haven't heard from Sam lately," she told Shirley. "What's happening there?"

"Oh, Dr. Morgan, it's just terrible. We all thought you knew. Dr. Jordan flew to Atlanta to a meeting at the CDC. They wanted to talk to him about those children in that fire. You know the ones I'm talking about?"

"Yes." Marah remembered, of course. The image of those two small charred bodies fighting for life continued to haunt her.

"Anyway, Dr. Jordan was in Georgia, and he came down with something."

"Oh, no. What's wrong?"

"He died."

Marah gripped the receiver. "Died?"

"Yeah, just like that." Shirley's voice faltered. "We've all been really upset. They told us there was nothing anyone could have done."

"Died?" Marah said again, unable to believe it.

"I'm sorry, Dr. Morgan. I really thought Dr. Girard was going to call you."

"You said he came down with something."

"Nobody knows what it was."

"He was at the Centers for Disease Control and Prevention, for pete's sake. If anybody could figure out what Dr. Jordan had contracted, it would be the CDC."

"But they couldn't. It was a high fever, they told us. Really high. And then his skin turned bright red, like a rash almost. But it wasn't a regular rash. They checked him for chicken pox, rubella, strep—you name it. They're pretty sure it was a virus because he didn't respond to antibiotics at all. They said he was delirious for several days, and then his internal organs failed all at once. Just like that. His family had the funeral, and we all went. It was so sad to realize he was never coming back. I could hardly stand it. I'm sorry, Dr. Morgan. I'm really sorry, but with you and Dr. Jordan both gone, things are awful around here. Patients are getting angry over all the cancellations, and the other two doctors are about to go under with all the overtime they're putting in. We don't know what to do."

Marah brushed a finger across her cheek and nodded. "I'll call you back, Shirley. Give me a little time. We'll work this out."

She hung up the receiver and lifted her head. Judd was watching her from the doorway.

10

Milton Gregory stepped out of the bunkhouse to escape his two assistants, who were spending the evening sipping beer and watching the secondhand television set they had purchased in town. He'd always had trouble understanding how men could enjoy sitting on their backsides and playing cards or staring at a ball game or drinking alcohol. Such activities bored him. Besides, he valued a clear mind.

A movement on the bunkhouse porch caught Gregory's eye. It was the farmhand who shared the bunkhouse. Gregory found the man intriguing, as wrapped up in his own silent world as a single-minded ant gathering food. It would be interesting to probe him, Gregory thought, just as he once had examined the insects in his specimen collection.

"What are you reading there, Judd?" Gregory asked. He sauntered down the porch toward the single bulb that dangled from a wire overhead. He was grateful for the dim light. He'd never enjoyed the scrutiny of others.

"Evening, doc." Judd looked up from his book and gave a slight nod. He held up the slim volume so Gregory could read the title: *Native Wildflowers of the Prairie.* "It's one of Perky's gardening books." He was leaning against the bunkhouse wall, the back legs of his chair on the floor and the other two in the air. It was a cool night; Judd was wearing his black Stetson.

"I never would have taken you for a flower man," Gregory said.

Judd chuckled. "I'm hooked."

"I can see why." He rested a hand on the porch railing. "You've been having a lot of success with your gardening venture. I was admiring your work the other day after the storm. Things are really popping up out there. Personally, I can't tell a flower from a weed."

"It all depends on your point of view. Ed Morgan thinks everything but red winter wheat is a weed."

"He's probably right." Gregory settled in a slat-backed chair beside Judd's. The big-shouldered fellow reminded him of an old-time cowboy, the sort who didn't say much but could not be pushed around.

"That storm was something," Gregory said. "Did you get a good look at the tornado?"

"Yep." Judd stuck a finger in the book to keep his place and closed it. "I'll tell you what—when I spotted that funnel dropping out of the clouds, I took off for the rock house. Were you fellows out in your tent when it hit?"

Gregory pondered how to answer. Though he wanted to be friendly, he felt his work on the farm needed to remain as private as possible. The other afternoon, Marah Morgan had asked him about the equipment she'd seen in the tent. Her questions revealed the depth of her knowledge. And her curiosity.

But Judd was not as quick-witted as the young pediatrician, and Gregory sensed the man might be of some help. The farmhand was capable and conscientious, and from previous conversations, it appeared his thinking might be aligned with the team's ideologies. More important, Judd knew the farm better than any of them. He traveled the entire acreage at least once a week. Maybe he could help them find the site of the village.

"We never left the bunkhouse," he told Judd. "Couldn't see much point in heading out to the field that morning."

"Nope. I bet that old tent leaks like a sieve."

"It sure drips." Gregory studied the bare bulb. "I noticed you talking to Dr. Morgan the day of the storm. Have the two of you got something going on?"

"Not hardly. I figure she'll be heading for St. Louis any day now. Some doctor friend of hers died, and her clinic needs her to come back." He laid the book on the porch and crossed his arms over his chest. "She's a strange lady. Somehow or other, she got herself locked up in her own cellar. She's sure somebody was down there with her. Can you believe that? It happened the day of the tornado. I went over to the white house to tell her about a phone call, and I ended up having to haul her out through a basement window. She accused me of locking her in."

Gregory smiled, interested in the information about Marah Morgan. "Locked in her own basement?" he said.

"Yeah. Weird, huh?"

"So, she's planning to leave. Did she say when?"

"I don't know. Soon, I bet."

"Good."

"What, you don't like her?"

"She's certainly attractive, but I can't tell if she's been much help to her father. Mike and Bob have done most of the work cleaning up the old man's kitchen. Besides, I see the woman as a possible hindrance to our team's project."

"Does she hang around a lot?"

"Sometimes. We're on a tight deadline, you know, and the fewer distractions, the better."

"She pokes her nose into *my* work, that's for sure. I'll be putting together a pen, and the next thing I know, there she is looking over my shoulder to see if I'm doing it right. I don't want anybody looking over my shoulder. Not Marah Morgan. Not the government. Not even God."

Gregory nodded. He wondered if this was the door he'd been looking for with Judd. "I don't know that I'd mind a pretty woman standing a little too close once in a while," he said. "But many people seem to resent government intervention."

"Yeah, why do you think I drift around, working here, working there? I know you have a government job, doc, but I sure don't like paying taxes when the politicians just give handouts to people who won't lift a finger to earn a living. Welfare—now how's that supposed to be equal rights?"

Gregory nodded. This was the sort of talk he liked. Never mind cards and television. He much preferred to discuss issues that mattered, ways to make a difference.

"Equal rights are a joke," Judd said.

"In many ways, I'd agree with you," Gregory assented. "The federal courts do tend to exert their supremacy over the will of the people."

"Folks are powerless these days. You take the ninth amendment, for example."

"Equal protection under the law."

"The government doesn't protect its citizens," Judd said. "It preys on them."

He lowered his chair to all four legs and leaned forward, elbows on his knees. "Gun control. Taxes. And those tree-huggers who keep farmers off their own land so they can save butterflies or owls. Yep, doc, a joke is what it is."

"If only it were funny." Gregory noted the suspicious squint in the farmhand's eye.

"But you folks work for the government," Judd said in a low voice. "Some Indian bureau, or something."

His heart hammering in his chest, Gregory regarded the man in the same way he had studied a candidate for dissection. What would he find inside the brain cavity? Intelligence or an insipid dullness? And what sort of heart beat within this man? Was he passionate and driven or weakly compliant? Most important was his intestinal fortitude. Did he have courage? Would he give his life for a cause?

Gregory knew the questioning must be conducted carefully. Yet he instinctively liked Judd. The man spent his days working hard on the farm and his nights sound asleep in his bunk. He never snooped or pried or asked questions. And he didn't even know the significance of the BIA.

"It's the Bureau of Indian Affairs," Gregory said.

Judd shrugged. "Whatever. Seems strange to me you'd work for the government when you know what they're up to. Ignoring people's rights, taking property without paying folks what they're due, taxing people until they can't breathe. Even depriving people of their livelihood."

"I'm not sure what you mean by that. The government employs a lot of people."

"And puts a lot of others out of work, too."

"How?"

"The Environmental Protection Agency flat ran my family into the ground. I grew up mostly in Arizona. But we lived in Wyoming up until I was about ten, and my daddy was a logger. The EPA discovered some little fungus growing in the forests where my dad worked. They said it was endangered, as if a mushroom ever knew anything about danger."

Gregory laughed. "Good point."

"Anyhow, my dad kept getting laid off while the company wrangled with the government, and finally he took to drinking. My mom stuck it out for a while, but then she jerked us kids out of there and moved us clear to Tucson. My dad took up with another woman, and that was that. I grew up thinking that if the government believed a fungus was more important than my family, I didn't want any part of it."

"I can't blame you." Gregory paused for a moment, remembering. "In many respects, my own story is not all that different. I was a medical doctor at one time. I practiced in an affluent area of Los Angeles. My patients were wealthy women. Wives and daughters of millionaires, film industry executives, even the stars themselves. And then I was shut down."

"How come?"

"I listened to my patients' concerns. And then I took care of their problems."

"You were a psychiatrist or something?"

Gregory smiled. "In a sense. Actually, I was involved with the physical restoration of health and beauty."

"Oh, you were one of those plastic surgeons."

"Cosmetic surgery for the inner woman, you might call it." He decided to leave it at that. "At any rate, things worked out badly for me. I lost my medical license."

"Did the government do that to you?" Judd asked. "Did they destroy you?"

Gregory held back the emotion those words unleashed. "They certainly tried."

"Then how is it you work for the Indian agency?" Judd asked. "If I were you, I'd be looking for justice."

"I've found a way to refocus my medical skills," Gregory said quietly. "I believe justice will be done. In the meantime, I have goals to accomplish."

"Like what you and your boys are doing out there in Big Ed's pasture?"

At this point Gregory knew he must be discreet. Anyone could uncover the details of his past. But the future still lay securely hidden in his hands.

"We are working on a project," he said, "a project that will benefit mankind for generations to come. Those of us who believe in this cause are engaged in a deadly battle against the growing tide of evil in this world. Combatants in battle need weapons. Our task on this farm involves the development of a highly effective tool."

Gregory watched Judd's face as a look of understanding began to dawn. "Are you talking about a weapon?" he asked. "Like the Oklahoma City bombing?"

"Let's just say what we're doing will be more significant than the Oklahoma City bombing. A great deal more significant."

"Whoa."

Gregory had to laugh at the expression of wonder and admiration on his friend's face. "So, Judd," he said, "would you care to help us?"

※ ※ ※

Judd felt nothing as he drove his pickup out to the field where the team was working. No anxiety. No anticipation. No joy. Nothing. Milton Gregory had encouraged him to drive out to the site, spend time with the men, observe them at work. Though he had not revealed their purpose on the farm, Gregory had said he might find Judd's participation helpful.

How many times had Judd done this kind of thing? He pulled on a persona like a ski mask, covering himself completely. His voice, his walk, his mannerisms, and most important, his convictions changed. He became someone else.

He pulled the pickup to a stop near the old army tent. Judd knew he was good at his work. But sometimes he wondered if it was because he had lost the real Judd Hunter. The "hollow man," his wife had called him. Empty.

Was it easy to pull on a mask because he had nothing to hide? because he was nobody?

Judd saw Mike Dooley wave at him from the pasture. Drawing the invisible mask over himself, tucking away the unspoken pain, he thought about that afternoon with Marah in the cellar. She seemed to think God could heal her. Make her new again. And Perky believed God could create living flowers out of dried-up garden seeds.

Judd felt dry. Empty, dry, hollow. He wondered if anyone could bring him to life.

"Hey, Judd!" Mike called. "Glad to see you. Dr. Gregory said you'd be coming out. He told us about his talk with you last night."

"So how's it going out here?"

"Not having a whole lot of luck. Dr. G moved us over closer to the river. But the place is so rocky that it's hard to walk around. Ed Morgan told us he'd never bothered to turn this field into pasture. Too many stones. So it's been sitting here like this for years. Dr. G's holding out a lot of hope for it."

"I don't know what the doc thinks you're going to find out here."

"Something important, that's for sure." Mike shifted from one foot to the other. "But Dr. G wants to make sure we're careful what we say."

"Stands to reason." Judd shrugged. "Well, keep up the good work, and let me know what I can do to help out."

He turned back toward his pickup, but he expected Mike's response. "Wait up, Judd," the young man called. "Dr. G's down there near the river. He said he wanted to see you if you dropped by."

"I guess I could talk to him for a couple of minutes."

Mike walked alongside him for a few steps. "He's an amazing man, isn't he? He's a doctor, you know. A medical doctor. He's brilliant."

Judd knew. "That's what I hear."

As he meandered toward the river, Judd reviewed his information on Milton Gregory. Trained at the most elite universities, practiced in the finest hospitals, lived in a mansion on a hillside in southern California. He was divorced at the time the malpractice suit hit.

After the state stripped him of his license, his properties had been sold to pay his legal bills. His medical practice had evaporated, and he had vanished. No one saw him for years. And then suddenly, at an abandoned schoolhouse in Wyoming, Milton Gregory popped back into view.

This time he had a new agenda. A project he had developed would affect the lives of hundreds of thousands. And he was smart enough to accomplish his plan. September, it appeared, was his deadline.

"Good morning, Judd," Gregory said, straightening from his crouch at the river's edge. He wore his usual garb—green khaki slacks, a T-shirt, and the mirrored sunglasses. He lifted the glasses from his face, folded them carefully, and studied Judd with pale blue eyes.

"Thought I'd pay you a visit." Judd paused a moment, kicked a pebble. "Good talking to you last night."

Milton Gregory's quick eyes studied Judd up and down. "So what do you think? Would you like to help us out?"

"I'll do what I can."

"Here's a description of the area we're looking for. The coordinates and the type of terrain." He handed Judd a scribbled note. "Study it, and I'll tell you more at the bunkhouse tonight."

Judd glanced down at the tidy handwriting, easy to analyze. Chuck would have been grateful. But of course, Chuck had been killed at Milton Gregory's command.

"Keep an eye out as you go on your rounds today," Gregory went on. "Let me know if you find anything."

"Sure. Glad to. What am I looking for?"

"Indian artifacts. Arrowheads, stone mortars for crushing grain, even burial mounds. We're searching for human remains, in particular."

"Bones?"

"That's correct. Bones."

Judd knew he was close to hitting the jackpot. "I'll keep my eyes peeled."

Gregory held up a finger. "A word of caution, Judd. Don't let any of this go outside the team."

"No problem."

"Good man." Gregory clapped Judd on the shoulder.

As Gregory turned back to resume digging, the sound of a pickup drew their attention. It was Marah. Judd glanced across at Gregory. The man's eyes narrowed.

"I guess our resident pediatrician is still with us," Gregory said.

They walked across the pasture together, neither speaking. The physician lifted a hand in greeting as the woman climbed down from the pickup. When Perky and Gypsy barreled out the passenger door, Judd's gut knotted. He didn't want the little girl involved in this.

"Hey, Judd!" Perky skipped toward him, the dog dancing beside her. She was carrying a small green metal spade, her favorite gardening tool. "What are you doing out here?"

"Same to you, Perk. Aren't you supposed to be helping your mother?"

"I already did my chores, goofus. Gypsy and I are going to look for wildflowers while Marah talks to the archaeologists. She thinks one of them was down in her basement the other day, and I think so, too. You know those spiderworts you showed me in the prairie book? Well, I'm going to try to find some, and then you and I can dig them up and put them next to the purple coneflowers."

She looked at him, wide-eyed and trusting. He gave her pigtail a tug.

"OK, Perk," he said. "But stick close. I'm heading out in a minute, and I'll take you with me. This morning I dug up some roots I want to show you. See what you think they might be."

"Deal!" Perky skipped off, her skinny legs vanishing in the tall grass.

"Hey, Marah." Judd tipped his hat.

She gave both men a polite smile. "Judd, Dr. Gregory."

"Good afternoon, Dr. Morgan," Gregory said. "Seems like this old pasture is turning into Grand Central Station. Were you looking for Judd? Or did you need to see me about something?"

Marah glanced away as Perky and Gypsy began clambering over a pile of stones nearby. "Look, Dr. Gregory—"

"You can call me Milton."

"Milton." She let out a breath. "I've been doing some think-ing about your two colleagues."

"Mike and Bob? Shall I call them over?"

"No, it's just that I . . . well, you may have heard that some-one was down in my cellar the other day."

"Judd mentioned that."

Her focus shot to Judd's face. "You did?"

"I mentioned it," he repeated.

"Well, anyway, I'm concerned about it. I wonder if you saw Mike and Bob during the storm."

"Are you suggesting one of them might have been in your home for some reason?"

"I'm not sure."

"The three of us were together that day. Working in the lab." He raised one eyebrow. "Marah, what reason would my men have to be in your cellar?"

"I don't know, but if I'm honest, I'd have to tell you they make me uncomfortable. In fact, I've been feeling pretty uneasy about letting all of you continue to work out here."

"Uneasy?" He frowned. "We've given you no reason for concern, have we? I have no idea what happened in your cellar, but I do know that my men and I have been working day and night on our project. None of us has had time for anything else."

"Day and night." She set her hands on her hips. "Right. I see all of you over at the rock house a lot."

"An occasional break from the heat. Can you blame us? We've been combing this land for weeks."

"And what have you dug up? Nothing. Not a single bone."

"Dr. Morgan," Gregory said, "I'm sure in your own profession you're aware of the time research and experimentation can consume."

"You don't have a clue where that Indian village is, do you?"

"Of course we do. We know it was somewhere in this area. But it takes time to explore this much land."

Judd stood by, one eye on Perky, who was pushing at stones in order to work her small spade into the crevices where wild-flowers grew. He tried to think of some way to cut into the conversation between Gregory and Marah. He needed to steer her off this track, calm her down, assuage her fears.

"I just don't think my father and I can continue to support your project, Milton," she was saying. "He and I discussed the situation this morning, and we believe you've had more than enough time on our land."

"I'm sorry to hear you feel that way, but I'm afraid you have no choice in the matter. Our presence on your farm is legal. Your father signed documents giving us permission to work here."

"I'd like to see those documents, please."

"I'm unable to provide them, Dr. Morgan. I sent everything to bureau headquarters to be kept on file."

"Then I'll ask your headquarters for a copy."

"Why don't you let me take care of it? They'll respond more

quickly if I issue a request." He gave her a smile. "Listen, Marah, I acknowledge your family's discomfort with the team's presence here. That's often the case when BIA teams are given an assignment on private property. But I assure you we're working as efficiently as possible."

"He's right, Marah," Judd said. "They're doing all they can to—"

A shriek from Perky cut off his words. Perched high on a stone outcrop, the child was swaying back and forth, threatening to lose her balance as a small landslide tumbled to the ground.

Judd leapt forward. His foot caught the edge of a boulder. He lunged.

And Perky toppled, plunging into a pit in the stones and landing in the embrace of a pair of dry, withered, long-dead arms.

11

Marah raced toward the rocks as Judd scrambled to the top of the outcrop. She could hear Perky scream-ing, hysterical with fear. Rattlesnakes, she thought. Copperheads. She envisioned a nest of them, writhing and slithering over the little girl, sinking their fangs into her soft skin, flooding her neurovascular system with poison. Who would stock antivenin? Dr. Benson might have a supply in town. But if the child had been bitten more than once, they'd need to airlift her to Wichita. Marah would have to get to a telephone immediately.

"Judd, be careful!" she called.

"It's OK, Perk," he was saying as he leaned down into the hole. "I'm here, honey. I'll get you out."

Marah reached the top and peered over the edge. The empty eye sockets of a skull stared back at her. Stifling a cry, she jerked back, her hand over her mouth.

"Oh, Judd!" Expecting snakes, facing a skeleton instead, she felt adrenaline course through her like a bolt of lightning.

"Give me your hand," Judd said. "Come on, Perk."

Marah could see that the child was almost catatonic with fear. She lay quivering, eyes wide and mouth white-rimmed, atop the deformed figure that embraced her. Abandoning his attempt to reach the little girl, Judd clambered down into the pit with her. "Come here, honey. I've got you now. You're going to be all right."

As he lifted Perky into his arms, she let out a wail and began to cry. He kissed her forehead and looked up at Marah. "Can you take her?"

"Of course." Letting out a deep breath to steady herself, she knelt at the edge of the craggy hole and reached downward. Judd handed up the child, all skinny legs and wet cheeks.

"Hey, sweetie," Marah murmured, lifting Perky into her lap, cradling her like a baby. "You're safe now. I've got you."

"It grabbed me," Perky sobbed.

"No, no, it just seemed that way."

"Is it alive?"

"No, honey." Marah stroked a long gold braid as Perky clutched her T-shirt like a little opossum holding on to her mama for dear life. "You'll be all right."

By now, Dr. Gregory, Mike Dooley, and Bob Harper were climbing the rock pile. Judd boosted himself out of the hole and hunkered down beside Marah and the child. His face was ashen.

"What do you make of it?" Marah asked him.

"It's a skeleton, but—"

"It's not a skeleton," Perky said. "I saw it up close. It's a person. A dead person."

Marah shifted the little girl onto Judd's lap and leaned over the gaping hole. Perky was right. This was no ordinary bleached, white skeleton, the type Marah had studied in the labs of her medical school. Tufts of long, glossy black hair clung to the skull. The empty eye sockets stared upward, as if searching the sky, hoping and waiting for something that had never come. A covering of pebbled, brown, leathery skin stretched across protruding white bones. The nose had decayed, but contorted lips curved over a set of strong white teeth. It might have been a smile once. Now it was a grimace.

Whatever the figure had been wearing was long gone, leaving only traces of multicolored beads and hammered metal adornments scattered over the body. Hardened skin revealed female breasts, delicate fingers, perfectly shaped ears. Bony legs and feet clad in the remains of moccasins had been curved under the figure, but she was sitting upright, as though she had settled there in the pit to await the arrival of someone important.

"It's a lady," Perky whispered, peering into the hole.

"It's a mummy," Marah said. "The mummified remains of an Indian woman."

"Dr. Gregory!" Mike shouted as he lay down on his stomach and gazed down into the cairn. "Bingo, Dr. G! We've got our redskin!"

Milton Gregory joined the others on the rocks. "The remains must have partially mummified," he said in a low voice. He looked across the top of the pit at Mike and Bob, as though he were consulting with other physicians during surgery. "This is unexpected. According to our research, the Osage did nothing to preserve their dead. I thought we would find a skeleton."

"There might have been a long period of dry weather after her death," Marah said. "It wouldn't be unheard of for Kansas. We've had dust storms."

"But that was the 1930s," he murmured, turning to her. She could see her face reflected in his silver sunglasses. "This woman died long before that. Only a succession of arid summers and snowless winters could have permitted the mummification. It's perfect."

"You want me to haul it out of there?" Mike asked.

"Don't touch it," Gregory said. "We need to get our gloves first." He turned to Marah again. "You'll excuse us now, Dr. Morgan. This is what we've been looking for, and we have a great deal of work to do. You can tell your father that we won't need to trespass on your property much longer."

Marah looked away, inexplicably annoyed. Her nagging doubts about the archaeologists' work clearly had no foundation. Here was the skeleton they'd been looking for. Yet somehow she didn't feel any more congenial toward the men.

Milton Gregory was nice enough, though he had been stubborn about staying on the farm. But she was liking his colleagues less and less. First there was the basement incident. Then she had begun to be irritated about other little things. Mike and Bob not only flirted with her, but they ate her father's potato chips and ice cream without asking permission, used his pickup for trips into town, and loitered uninvited in the old rock house on Sunday afternoons. The two struck Marah as unprofessional in their behavior, so much so that she'd even considered writing a letter about them to the BIA. And what had Mike Dooley just called the woman in the pit? *Redskin*. What sort of archaeologist referred to Native Americans as redskins?

Perky began to whimper. "I don't like that lady down there. She's scary."

"I don't much like her myself," Judd said. "Let's head out, what do you say?"

He rose with the child still in his arms and began to climb down from the rocky cairn. Marah followed, almost reluctant to leave the archaeologists to their find. Not only had her medical curiosity been aroused by the discovery, but it bothered her that the men showed such little respect for the remains.

The mound of stones was a grave they had opened. The Indian buried inside had been alive once. She had been a child and then a teenager and then a woman. She had taken pride in her long black hair and beaded moccasins. Perhaps she had married and given birth to children. And after her death, someone had lovingly placed her in that cairn. Marah hoped the Osage tribal leaders would give her a proper reburial after her remains were taken to Oklahoma.

"She had skin and hair," Perky said as Judd lifted her into the pickup cab. "Her fingers were scratchy."

"They were just dry," Marah explained, brushing the tears from the child's cheeks. "The heat and the sun dried her up. But she's not alive, Perky."

"I know!" she wailed. "She's dead, and she grabbed me."

Marah let out a breath of sympathy. "Come on, honey, we'll go over to the rock house and you can tell Poppy all about it while I wash you up. You'll feel better, I promise."

As she shut the door of her pickup, she sensed Judd eyeing her. She walked around him toward the driver's side, but he followed, taking her arm.

"Marah?" He searched her face as she turned toward him. "Maybe you'd better stay clear of this place now. You and Perky."

"Why's that?"

"Well, it . . . ." He hesitated, as if searching for the answer. "It might be best."

"You think I'll bother them, don't you?" she said. "Look, I know you didn't like it that I asked your friends to leave the farm. But, frankly, I'll be glad when they're gone."

"What makes you say they're my friends?"

"Well, you're out here with them. You spend a lot of time with them. It's obvious that you—"

"Nothing's obvious. Nothing." His brown eyes were deeply shadowed by the brim of his hat. He tightened his grip on her arm. "You don't know me, Marah."

"I know what I see."

"Never trust your eyes."

"I was trained to use my eyes, Judd. That's one way I diagnose my patients. My eyes tell me the truth. And the truth I see now is that Milton Gregory is comfortable out here with you but not with me."

"Well, you're trying to run him off your land."

"That's because I don't like him." She paused and studied the physician as he walked away from the tent. He was pulling on a pair of latex gloves. "Milton's all right, I guess. But I'm not crazy about those two goofballs he hangs around with."

"It's because you think one of them was sneaking around in your cellar."

"Unless you want to confess to it."

She tried to read the expression in his eyes. What was Judd trying to tell her? Her instinctive reaction was negative, as though he were her father trying to control where she went and what she did. But something about the way the man was talking to her now—standing with his back to Milton Gregory, lowering his voice until it was almost inaudible—sent a ripple of concern down her spine.

"I wasn't in your cellar," he said, leaning closer, almost menacing in his intensity. "And I don't think you ought to come back out here."

"This is my farm." For some reason she felt suddenly angry with him. He was pushing her. Trying to tell her something without saying it. Trying to bend her to his will. She'd never seen Judd this way, and she didn't like it. "I can come back out here if I want to. Obviously, you're here, aren't you? I can't think of any protocol that makes you more acceptable on a government archaeological site than I am. I'm medically trained. I might be of help. But you. You're just—"

"Who am I?"

"Let go of my arm." She brushed his hand away. "I don't know. Who *are* you?"

"Who are *you?*"

She studied him, wondering at the word game he was playing. What answer did he want? "You know who I am," she said, uncomfortable with the way his eyes penetrated her. "What do you mean?"

"In the cellar the other day, you told me you were a Christian. Aren't Christians supposed to look beyond the surface and see things more deeply?"

"Yeah, so?"

"So, what I see is that you really trust in your own eyes to show you what truth is."

"Maybe." She was even more uncomfortable now, realizing how weak her walk in Christ really was. Judd was right. She relied on her own intelligence and strength too much of the time. Even now, distrust ate at her. Bitterness tried to grasp her heart. She still wanted to keep people at arm's length.

"OK," she said. "Maybe I'm still upset over the deal in the cellar. Something about Dr. Gregory and his men bothers me. I can't figure out what it is, but—"

"Truth," Judd said. "It's truth. Listen to the truth inside you. Trust that."

She tried to read the meaning in Judd's words, silently willing him to go further, to explain what he was talking about. But he just stared at her, saying nothing. Finally, he tipped his hat.

"I've got a tractor acting up on me," he said. "Hope Perky gets to feeling better. Tell her I'll show her those roots when I come in for dinner." He turned and sauntered off toward his own pickup.

Marah stood for a moment, watching him, and then she opened the door and climbed into her truck beside Perky.

🐾 🐾 🐾

At the sound of the farm pickup pulling to a stop in front of the rock house, Ed Morgan looked up from his seat on the back porch. He'd been trying to carve a doll's head for Perky, not that the girl played with toys much. She always had her nose in a book. And lately she'd been spending all her free time digging around in Ruby's flower beds.

Ed set the head on the arm of his chair and hollered through the house. "Who's there?"

"It's me, Poppy!" Perky called. "Me and Dr. Morgan. I fell into a pit with a mummy."

"A what?" He scowled at the aluminum walker, wishing he weren't still hog-tied to the thing. He'd had quite a time getting the barn shut up tight before that tornado hit the other day. Gypsy ran in, barking. "Hush up, Gyp. What'd you say, Perk?"

"A mummy."

Beans, he couldn't make sense out of that one. And it sounded like the kid was about to bawl. Something had upset her but good. He'd better find out. As he rose from the old chair, the doll's head toppled to the porch and rolled under a table. *Double beans.* He ought to be out checking for weeds in the winter wheat, not hunting for a toy in the dust and spiderwebs. Was this what his life had come to? After all these years, was this all there was?

Disgusted, Ed unfolded his walker and wheeled himself into the kitchen, Gypsy dancing along beside him. Perky was sitting on the counter while Marah ran a sinkful of suds.

"Hey, you're using up all my soap there, girl," he barked at his daughter. "You got enough foam there to wash Perky and half the folks in China. You think that stuff's free or something?"

"I'll buy you another bar of soap," Marah said in a low voice.

He had a feeling she still hated him, even though he'd all but offered to leave her the farm after he passed on. "Now, what's this you say happened, Perk? Something about your mother?"

Perky's face brightened beneath her tears, and he thought he saw the hint of a smile. "No, a *mummy.* Like in Egypt, only without the wrappings. I was trying to get loose a clump of spiderworts for me and Judd to plant, so I tugged on a big rock. Then it suddenly rolled away before I could stop it. After that, there was sort of like a landslide, and I fell down into the hole. There was an old dead Indian lady in there, and she was all dried up and scary with strings of long black hair and scratchy fingers."

"A lady?"

"And then she grabbed me with her bony fingers."

The girl's face crumpled up like a wad of old tissue and she began to bawl. Ed never had been able to watch Perky cry without getting all blubbery himself. Even when she was a baby and Pete would bring her over so he and his wife could take in a movie show. The minute that kid would go to bawling, Ed would have to pick her up and rock her, carry her around, feed her ice cream and—

"Hey, you want some ice cream, Perk?" he said, laying a hand on her skinny little arm. "Poppy's got chocolate, your favorite."

She sniffled and gave him a nod. Good, now that was something he could do. He wheeled over to the refrigerator, hoping those archaeology fellows hadn't cleaned out his ice cream supply. He could hear Marah talking to Perky, all soft and sweet. He couldn't remember his daughter ever using that tone with him. She always growled and snarled like a vicious wolf pup.

"Now, then, we'll wash your feet like this," she was cooing, "and dry them with this towel. There you go."

"I think she touched my hair."

"I'll brush it for you."

"But I like my braids. Can you make the braids again?"

"Sure I can. I always used to braid my sisters' hair for church."

"Why didn't your mom do it?"

"Well, after she died, you remember, I was all they had."

"What do you mean, all they had?" Ed said, holding out a bowl heaped with chocolate ice cream. "Those girls had me, don't forget. I was their dad. I kept them fed and clothed."

"I was the one who cooked the food. I was the one who fed my sisters." Her blue eyes had that Morgan fire in them now. She was hot, even though he could sense her trying to stay under control. "I was the one who mended their dresses and let down their hems. It wasn't you who kept them fed and clothed. It was me. I was all they had."

"Well, what was I, pig slop?"

"Poppy, you forgot the syrup," Perky said.

Ed looked down at the bowl. "Beans and double beans, Perk. Why didn't you say so sooner?"

"You and Dr. Morgan were yelling too much."

"We aren't yelling," Marah said as Ed wheeled over to the cabinet where he kept the Hershey's. "We're discussing the past."

"You were yelling," he said to his daughter. "Yelling and fussing at me, just like always. So what else is new? I never heard a nice word out of you since the day you were born."

"And I've never heard a nice word out of you."

He turned, ready to bust her backside to kingdom come, and then he noticed that her eyes were brimming. Now didn't that beat all? Tears. He'd never seen Marah Morgan cry in his life. Not once.

"What'd I say?" he asked.

"You neither one talk nice to each other," Perky said, sliding down from the counter. "It's just awful."

She stood between them for a moment, but Ed couldn't bring himself to speak. Marah was looking out the window, and one of those tears spilled over and rolled down her cheek.

Finally Perky sighed. "I'm going home," she said. "My mommy can braid my hair. Dr. Morgan, thank you for washing me up."

As Perky headed for the door, Ed gave a grunt. "Hey, where you going without your ice cream, little gal? I just put the Hershey's on."

Perky waved from the front porch. "Give it to your daughter," she called. "I bet she'd like it. I gotta go tell my mom and dad about the mummy."

"Well, beans." Ed looked at the bowl. "I guess you wouldn't be wanting some ice cream, would you?"

"Chocolate ice cream with chocolate syrup? That is so—" She choked off whatever she'd been about to say. "Yes, I'd like it."

"Matter of fact, it doesn't sound too bad to me either. Awful hot outside." He took down another bowl, shoveled half the ice cream into it, added a spoon, and handed it to his daughter. "There you go."

Unable to stand any longer, he sank down onto one of the red vinyl-covered dinette chairs. Gypsy dropped to the floor beside him, her long tail stirring up dust. When Marah took the chair across the table, Ed suddenly remembered how it had been all those years ago, the four little girls and him sitting down for a meal. Marah had been right about what she'd told Perky. After Ruby's death, she'd been the one to do all the cooking and serving, all the mending and fixing up. But he had expected it of her, the duties of a daughter. It had never occurred to him that she'd been unhappy.

Uncomfortable, he dug into his ice cream. The thick chocolate slid down his throat, creamy and cold, like a snowfall after a long dry summer.

"You've never given me ice cream," Marah said.

"No?" Ed studied his bowl. "Look, I know I kind of dote on Perky, but she's a good little gal. Always has been. Brings me stuff her mama bakes and draws me pictures at school. I just gave her the ice cream because of the scare she got falling into that hole today. That's all. It doesn't have anything to do with you."

"I just never saw you that way."

"What way?"

"Kind."

"Well, beans, girl, I was working all the time you were growing up, you know. I had to keep food on the table for you kids. I had to keep the cows milked and the wheat growing. And don't think you did everything for those sisters of yours. It was a team effort, you and me."

Marah leaned back in her chair. "A team effort? You and I were never a team."

"Well, we were family. That's how families do. They work to make sure everybody's got enough to live on."

"Is that what makes a family? I thought it had something to do with respect and kindness. I thought it was about love."

"Love?" He gave a laugh. "That's a fairy-tale word, girl. I figured you'd have learned that by now. Families are put on this earth to take care of each other and to see that there's a new generation to follow. That's what your mother and I set about to do, and that's what we did. And I reckon she'd be proud of the way things turned out, except for you being so stubborn about doing your part on the farm."

Marah drew in a deep breath, and Ed could feel her anger building. Well, let her get mad then. If she wanted to spout off her fool ideas about love, let her get a family of her own. Then she'd see.

Ed Morgan had nurtured a crazy notion of love once, dreams of a future with a golden-haired woman who was so beautiful she made his head spin. But his big dreams had vanished like smoke when the love of his life moved out of town. And that was that. He'd joined the army, fought in Korea, and tried to forget. Tried to forgive. During the long period of recovery after his injuries, he kept thinking she might show up. If she would only come back to town, everything would be all right again. But she had never returned, and after a while, Ed knew he had to go on with his life the best he could. So he married Ruby and built his family, just the way a man ought.

"Is that why you and Mom fought so much those last couple of years?" Marah asked, her voice more gentle than he expected. "Was it because you never loved her, and she finally understood that?"

"What makes you say we fought? You were just a pup back in those days. You didn't know anything."

"I heard you argue. I heard you slam doors and stomp around

the bedroom in your boots. More than once, I saw Mom crying after you left the house."

"Well, then you were sticking your nose where it didn't belong."

He couldn't believe his own daughter was sitting there accusing him of things that were none of her business. A curl of dismay slid down deep into his stomach like a worm burrowing into a cabbage. What had Marah heard of the words that passed between him and Ruby during those arguments? Did she know how badly he had hurt his wife? Or the terrible accusations, the blame he shouldered, the insults Ruby had hurled at him? Did Marah know the truth of those last days?

She pushed away the bowl of ice cream, most of it melted into a brown pool. "I was old enough to see and hear the destruction of my family," she said.

"Nothing's one person's fault, girl," he snapped, fumbling for his walker. "I did the best I could."

"Did you?"

"Yes, ma'am, and don't you think I didn't."

"And what happened when it didn't work?" Marah leaned across the table, her cheeks fiery pink. "Mom died, didn't she? You couldn't fix the marriage, and you were tired of Mom and all her baby girls and all her failures, and then she just conveniently—"

"I did wrong. I know it. I never said I didn't." He dropped back into the chair. "I know I blamed her for you girls. But how was I supposed to run this farm? I needed sons, and all she could do was—"

"The male determines a baby's gender. Read any medical textbook. It wasn't Mom's fault that you had female children. It was yours."

"Well, that's a pile of beans if I ever heard one." He gave a snort. *Medical textbooks, ha.* "Anyhow, the point is that I could have done better by your mother. I'm a man, a human being, and I admit I made my share of mistakes. I hurt Ruby. I know I did."

He hung his head, feeling bad about everything. He didn't like to think about the past, he sure didn't want to talk about it, and he didn't want Marah to keep at him this way. But he figured he owed her an explanation.

"I gave your mother more pain than any woman should have to bear," he admitted. "At the time, I told myself she deserved it for hurting me. I blamed her for keeping me from my dreams. But later on I realized it wasn't her fault that the doctors had to take out her parts before she could give me a son. She did the best she could, and she was a good wife all in all."

Ed clasped his hands and rested his forehead on them. Marah was staring down at her melted ice cream, and not a thing he said seemed to make her feel any better.

"Since you heard the arguing," he went on, "I reckon I owe you an apology, too. I told your mother I was sorry, but it didn't make a difference. She never could forgive me."

"And then she just died?"

"I suppose all that trouble between us took its toll. Ruby lost her strength long before that fever came on. Unforgiveness just ate her up inside. She turned hard and angry and cold. She got kind of like you are now, Marah. I sure hate to see you taking after your mother."

"I've been upset. I know that." Her eyes were accusing when he lifted his head. "But you're hard and angry and cold, too."

"Maybe so. Maybe both of us are, just the way we share the Morgan blue eyes and black hair. Sometimes I think bitterness is what killed your mom. It was like a sickness that ate up her life. And mine."

"Mine, too," Marah said. "It's the Morgan family tradition."

She fell silent for a long time. Ed thought about his bed and how he would like to lie down on it. For the first time, he felt old. The memories his daughter had dredged up were like millstones around his neck, weighting his every step, dragging him down. He wished he could get rid of them, but he didn't know how.

"Are you saying you were somehow responsible for Mom's death?" Marah asked finally. "Do you blame yourself?"

"It was the fever that killed her," he repeated, tired of talking now. "She had a fever, and she died."

"I want you to know I'm going to track down her medical records." Marah's voice was low. "I'm going to get the coroner's report. I'm going to talk to doctors, neighbors, friends—anyone who knew her. I'm going to find out everything."

"You do that," he said, rising and pushing his walker toward the bedroom. "Find out what happened, and then come tell me. That's all I've ever wanted anyhow. The truth."

12

"Ugly is what she is," Mike Dooley said as he and Bob Harper stood near the mummified remains of the Indian woman lying on the folding table. "Ugly as sin."

"On the contrary, this corpse is a treasure, Mike," Milton Gregory said. He knew the heat inside the green tent was nearing a hundred degrees, but he hardly felt it in his excitement over the discovery. He sensed that his small group hovered on the verge of something amazing. Something too incredible for the common mind to absorb. Like a child facing a large, still-wrapped birthday present, he shivered with the curl of anticipation that slipped through his belly.

"To our cause," he told the others, "she is as valuable as pure gold. The most I'd hoped to find here in Kansas was skeletal remains. I knew a large collection of bone fragments would be necessary in order to obtain the quantity of material we need. You'll remember that my previous efforts gave us only a single vial of the agent, and it refused to multiply in sufficient quantities within the growth medium. What we did get was weak and ineffective, producing the fragile results with which we're all familiar."

"I remember," Dooley said. His voice was flat.

"Don't be so discouraged, Mike. With actual mummified flesh at our disposal, we have hope. Ed Morgan's rocky prairie pasture is going to let us reap a bountiful harvest."

Gregory bent over the corpse and adjusted the lenses in the protective metal-and-glass headgear he had built. As the distinctive characteristics he was hunting came into view, he felt his heart begin to thud inside his chest. It was a welcome reminder that he was alive, thriving, and with each heartbeat coming nearer to his goal.

"Observe the skin," he instructed his colleagues as he ran his latex-gloved fingertips down the flesh of the corpse. He felt almost as though he were back in medical school, only this time he was the instructing physician in charge of his two intent young interns. "You will note the evidence of an extensive maculo-papular rash. This rash must have evolved rapidly into pustules that covered the victim's face, chest, and arms. I'm guessing these may be hemorrhagic skin lesions, which are characteristic of the more virulent strain of the virus."

"So, if people get this disease, they'll look like her?" Dooley asked.

"Much worse, I'm afraid. Her skin has dried and hardened.

It's almost like leather now. A newly infected victim would be covered with a red, pus-filled rash. Not a pretty picture."

Gregory took a scalpel from the array of tools on the table and sliced a one-square-inch section of dried flesh from the mummy's chest. He squinted as he scrutinized the tiny flap of skin through the microscope lenses that protruded from his helmet.

"Very evident pustules," he said. "In my earliest attempts, I chose to propagate the virus in a liquid suspension. Though a tissue culture is one option, I believe I'll continue with the original growth medium. It's cheaper and easier to obtain. We'll take the samples here to our laboratory and emulsify them. Then we'll grow our culture and do a PCR analysis. This sample may contain enough material to accomplish our goal."

"That chunk of mummy skin?" Dooley said. "But it's so tiny."

"Great power can be contained in small packages, Mike." Gregory shook his head as he placed the sample into a sterile container. "If I had the time and equipment, there is so much more I could accomplish. The effects of this disease can be absolutely devastating. Do you realize that in the right hands, the genetic material contained in our target virus could be synthesized and inserted into the genomes of other viruses? Viruses such as Ebola, herpes, yellow fever, and of course, HIV?"

"But what would that do?"

"For one thing, it would enable a person to create diseases with unstoppable powers. For example, this virus combined with Ebola would produce a virulent hemorrhagic illness in which the victim would bleed from every pore of his skin and every organ within his body. He would disintegrate into a bloody, decaying pulp of living flesh. The pain would be beyond belief. Most important, such a disease would be highly contagious. There is no known vaccine that could prevent its spread and no medication that could contain its destruction."

"So, even we wouldn't be protected from it?" Mike's voice was tremulous.

"Nobody would be protected." Gregory began to remove another square inch of flesh from the corpse's cheek. "It would mean the destruction of the world."

🐾 🐾 🐾

At the thud of Judd's boot on the porch, Marah dropped the pile of papers she'd been reading.

"Beans!" she said, grabbing for the scattered pages and knocking her glass off the arm of her chair. Iced tea splashed across the floorboards. She swept up a few sheets of dripping paper and lifted her head.

"Oh, it's you," she said, letting out her breath. He read a mixture of fear and irritation. "Why didn't you say something before you stomped on the porch?"

"I didn't know I stomped." He glanced down at the scattered papers. "Sorry about that."

When he bent to help her gather them up, she pushed his hands away. "No, leave them alone. Don't touch anything."

He straightened and crossed his arms over his chest, watching her pick up the mess. Her dark hair was pulled into a ponytail that bounced at her neck. Paint-spattered jeans told him she'd been working on the old clapboard house, unwilling to abandon it as her father had recommended. That was something Judd had learned about Marah Morgan. Against all odds, she did what she felt was right. The roof might fall down on her head, but by gum those walls would sparkle with a new coat of white paint.

Marah looked fragile today, Judd decided. In spite of her fierce determination, she seemed thinner and more vulnerable somehow. Maybe it was just the skinny blue T-shirt. Or the white sneakers he remembered from the cellar. He wondered how her leg was healing. And he wondered why he cared.

"There," she said, setting the damp papers on a table nearby. "Sorry I snapped at you. I've been trying to piece together the truth out of this jumble of my mother's medical records. It's so frustrating. Mom was in and out of the doctor's office a lot, and I can hardly read the writing on these documents. The dates are blurred, and the diagnoses are obscure. It's a mess."

"You don't know how your mother died?"

Her blue eyes darkened to indigo. "It was a fever. With a rash of some kind. Not even Dr. Benson seems to know much about it."

"And you're concerned."

"Wouldn't you be?"

Judd nodded. In fact, that was the reason he had come to see

Marah on this hot afternoon. He needed answers. He wanted time away from the farm in order to get some perspective on the situation with Milton Gregory and his team. To visit the site where Chuck had spent his last hours. To talk to his friend's family. His new supervisor had approved the request, hoping Judd could gain insight from looking around the abandoned school that Gregory and his men had booby-trapped before they left for Kansas.

"I guess knowing how she died might help you sleep better at night," he told Marah.

"But what if I find out someone was responsible for her death?"

"Responsible?"

"Maybe someone blew the diagnosis. Or didn't take proper care of her. Or prescribed the wrong medication. What if I find out my mother didn't really have to die?"

"Then you make the person pay."

"Pay?" Her dark eyebrows lifted. "Are you serious?"

"An eye for an eye and a tooth for a tooth. Isn't that in the Bible you've been reading?"

He glanced down at the book he had bought on the day he learned of Chuck's death. Tea-stained now, it was just visible under the stack of medical records.

"It's in there," Marah said. "But there's a lot more. Things about doing good to those who do evil to you. Forgiving other people because God forgave you."

"Uh, yeah." He rubbed the back of his neck. This wasn't

what he needed to discuss. He needed to ask for time off. Needed to get on with his mission.

"This is your Bible, Judd," she said. She picked up the book and held it out to him. "I've been reading it. But I think you might need it."

He took the slender book. "Thanks, but I'm not exactly the religious type."

"Then why'd you buy it?"

He shrugged. "Curiosity, I guess. From what I've heard about Christianity, I don't think I could go along with much of it. Doing good to people who do evil isn't my style."

"So, you've never done anything wrong, huh, Mr. Perfect?" She was smiling now, teasing him. Judd wasn't particularly comfortable with the topic of conversation, but for some reason he didn't want the moment to end. He liked Marah a lot, he realized. Liked her, respected her, enjoyed her. But she wasn't why he'd come to Kansas. He needed to remember that.

"I'm not exactly perfect," he said. "Close, though."

She laughed. "Oh, admit it. You're a sinner just like the rest of us."

"Well, I've done some things that were a little rough."

"Then you'd better read that Bible you bought. It's the path to forgiveness."

"Are you saying I need to be forgiven? Or I need to forgive someone else?"

"Both, probably."

He frowned, realizing she was right. The knowledge made

him uncomfortable. If he forgave the wrongs done to him, he might lose energy for his job. It was anger that kept him strong. But even if he could get to the point of forgiving his enemies, which he doubted, he couldn't imagine God forgiving him. Judd had always imagined God as a man somewhat like his own father, whose favorite slogans ran along the lines of "Use it or lose it, moron," "Shape up or ship out," and "Stupid is as stupid does." Not exactly the merciful type.

"I may look through it," he said as he tucked the Bible under his arm. "Either way I need to ask you if I can take my unforgiven backside off this farm for a few days. There's some business I need to see to. It won't take more than a week."

"You know, I've been thinking a lot about Dr. Jordan," she said, as though she hadn't heard a word he'd said. Her blue eyes were focused on the distant prairie. "He was a physician I admired and respected a lot. A man of great faith, too."

"I see," he said, though he wasn't sure he did.

"I was remembering one time when Dr. Jordan told me to read the Bible. 'Just read it,' he'd said. And I did. I read it to a little girl who was dying. She'd been burned so badly, and it was a horrible death. Who could forgive someone for causing such pain to a child? God's the only one. And that's what I'm having trouble with."

"What do you mean?"

"My bitterness you mentioned in the cellar. See, I know I've been forgiven. Christ took away the punishment I deserve for the wrongs I've done. But I'm not sure how to forgive other people in return."

"Why would you want to?"

"Here's a better question." Her eyes flicked to his face. "How dare I *not* forgive, when I've been forgiven of so much?"

"You've got me stumped there," he said. Judd couldn't imagine ever feeling forgiven. Nor could he remember the last time he'd been challenged to dig so deeply into himself. He was reluctant to look into his heart, because he knew he wouldn't find much that was good in it. At the same time, he envied Marah's certainty about her own status. Forgiven by God himself, absolved by the Creator of the universe—what a concept.

"I didn't mean to run on like that," she said suddenly. "I've been doing a lot of thinking these past few days. My parents. My work. The past and the future. I don't know why I dumped it on you."

"I don't know why I enjoyed it so much." He searched her eyes, wishing he could read her better, wishing he could understand what made her tick. "Talking to you, Marah," he said. "Listening to you. Sometimes I feel like I'm visiting a place I've never been. I like that place."

She glanced away, clearly uneasy, and he knew he'd said too much. Setting her hands on her paint-spattered knees, she let out a deep breath. "Anyway, I know you didn't come here to listen to me ramble. You said you needed to go somewhere?"

"A short trip. I have to take care of a few things."

She stood and began picking up the medical forms, her

shoulder blocking her face. "I can't let you take time off right now, Judd. I'm sorry, but you'll have to stay and work the farm while I'm gone."

"*You're* going away?" He could just about spit.

"I leave Wichita tomorrow morning for Atlanta."

"Atlanta? Look, I've got business—"

"It's about the death of the man who told me to read the Bible. Dr. Jordan was attending a conference at the Centers for Disease Control and Prevention when he suddenly got very ill. He headed our pediatrics group in St. Louis. At the request of the other doctors, I contacted the CDC to ask for details. They were vague. Not even the family has the details. We think we deserve to know what happened. So I've decided to fly there to talk to them in person."

Judd stared as she stacked the papers in a neat pile and started for the front door. She couldn't do that. He needed the week off. His supervisor had arranged everything. Now Marah was heading to Atlanta and leaving him alone with Ed Morgan and the Gregory brigade. And the Bible.

He couldn't think of any less pleasant companions.

🐾 🐾 🐾

Milton Gregory spotted the little girl in the distance. She was crouching over one of the newly rebuilt garden beds that surrounded the two old farm houses. As she spaded tiny weeds from the dirt, her knobby knees stuck out froglike. A single

gold braid ran down her back, following the curve of her spine.
Nearing her, Gregory could see the sprigs of hair that had
worked loose from the braid, like a roughly made hemp rope.

"Hey there, Rapunzel," he said, stopping just at the other
side of the rocky enclosure. He didn't want to frighten her by
appearing unexpectedly. "What are you working on this afternoon?"

She looked up and squinted in the bright sunshine. "Oh,
hey, Mr. Greg. I'm just getting these little weeds out of the
garden. Poppy says they're rosinweeds, and even though they
bloom, they're bad, bad, bad."

"What's so bad about them?" He moved closer now, coming
alongside her to study the small flat leaves.

"They're called increasers. That means they grow in places
where nobody's taken care of the land. When the good plants
die out, increasers move right in and take over."

"But if they bloom—"

"No, no. They might look pretty on the outside. But Poppy
says they're nasty little plants. Things that look nice can be
very bad. Sometimes it's hard to tell the difference, but I'm
learning."

Gregory smiled. "Well, in that case, I hope I haven't brought
you a bouquet of increasers."

He withdrew his hand from behind his back and presented
Perky with the collection of wildflowers he had picked from
the prairie that morning. She gasped in delight as she jumped
to her feet to claim the gift.

"They're beautiful!" she said. "This is rose verbena and wild sweet William and beardtongue! Look how pretty. These are all decreasers, Mr. Greg. You did good."

"I'm relieved." He gave her braid a tug. "I thought I'd give you a little present to cheer you up after that nasty tumble you took the other day."

"Thank you . . . but where are the roots?"

"Roots?"

"These aren't any good at all without their roots. I can't plant them. They'll just die. Didn't you know that?"

He cleared his throat. "Well, of course I knew that. But I didn't bring the flowers here for planting. I thought you might want to put them in a vase of water."

"Why?"

"Because they'll look pretty."

"Oh." She turned the clump of flowers around in her hand. "Wildflowers don't last very long in water. They need roots, Mr. Greg."

"I'm a doctor, Perky," he said. "My name is Dr. Milton Gregory. Your friend Poppy calls me Greg, but that's not really my name. You should call me Dr. Gregory."

"OK." Her disappointment in the flowers was palpable.

"Anyway, I was wondering how you've been getting along these days. Are you feeling all right?"

"I'm fine."

"Well, I knew the mummy gave you quite a scare. I guess you've recovered from that."

"I think about her sometimes. The Indian lady. At night I get kind of scared of her. But in the daytime I wonder about who she was and if she had a family and all. There were lots of beads down in the pit, you know, like she'd had on a pretty dress before she died. Sometimes I think about her sewing all those beads onto her dress. Maybe she was a mommy with lots of children who liked to play with the beads while she worked. What have you done to her, Dr. Gregory?"

"Done to her?" He stepped back, taken off guard by the question. "Well, nothing. I mean, I've examined the remains. That's my job."

Perky nodded solemnly. "You take care of that lady, OK? Because somebody loved her a long time ago."

He stared down at the little girl. She laid the bouquet on a stone near her feet, and he noticed the flowers were already wilting. This wasn't going at all the way he'd hoped.

"Anyway," he said, "I really wanted to make sure you were feeling all right. The nightmares you mentioned. You haven't had any fever, have you?"

He reached out to lay a hand on the child's forehead, but she drew back. "I told you I'm fine."

"As I said, I'm a doctor, Perky. I do care about your welfare."

"I don't have a fever." Her voice held a note of stubbornness now. Defiance.

"Your eyes seem a little bright. Would you mind if I took a closer look?"

She was silent a moment. "OK."

He leaned forward and put one hand on her forehead. With the other, he pulled down her lower lid and studied the eye with its bright blue iris. Though she was hot, even a little sweaty, he decided it was probably from the afternoon sun. The temperature outside was nearing a hundred. But the child's skin was not flushed, and her eyes looked clear.

"Where are your mirror sunglasses?" she said suddenly, and he realized she'd been looking into his eyes even as he examined hers.

"I must have left them at the bunkhouse." He drew back and brushed his palms on his khaki pants. "Well, I think you're doing fine."

"Your eyes look like flat pans of water."

"I'm not sure that's a compliment, Perky."

"It's just what I saw when I looked at you. Your eyes don't have any color hardly at all. You'd think you could look right through them, but you can't. They're flat, like pans of water."

"Pans of water. Well, that's genetics for you." He shrugged. "Speaking of water, you might want to put those flowers in a vase. I'll bet Poppy has something you can use."

"I'll go ask him," she said. She whisked the drooping bouquet from the ground and set off for the rock house, her long legs skipping across the yard. Halfway there, she suddenly swung around and gave him a wave. "Thanks again for the flowers, Dr. Gregory. They're just beautiful!"

He smiled. "Take care of yourself now, Perky."

13

Marah had visited the Centers for Disease Control
and Prevention in Atlanta more than once, and she
knew it was going to be difficult to get information
on Dr. Jordan's death. A layperson had almost no
chance of penetrating beyond the surface dissemina-
tion of information available through the CDC's
brochures and Web site. Physicians could send
samples of problem specimens and receive identifica-
tion of the particular microbe, information on dealing with it, and instructions for preventing its
recurrence. If a doctor needed on-site help, the CDC
would send their disease cowboys, as they were
called, to arrive within a matter of hours. But Marah
had come to realize that the CDC was also a bloated
government bureaucracy employing more than seven
thousand people in nearly two hundred different
occupations. A lone doctor seeking obscure informa-

tion could find her feet tangled in so much red tape that she might never escape.

As she exited the taxi at 1600 Clifton Road, Marah smoothed down the "doctor outfit" she had worn on the day she first returned to Morgan Farm five weeks earlier. Her elegant suit felt awkward on a body now accustomed to a chambray work shirt and jeans. Her unpolished nails were short and stubby. Her so-called energizing panty hose felt like a pair of tourniquets. She pulled her purse strap over her shoulder, hoping she could make her high heels negotiate the walkway to the six-story red brick building.

The CDC complex reminded Marah of the old wardrobe in the C. S. Lewis children's classic. From the front, it was plain, even boring. With its six rows of long windows, the facility appeared hardly adequate for housing anything more interesting than a locally run business. But the CDC building was perched on the top of a hill that dropped off behind in such a way that the main structure was actually below eye level.

Each division within the agency was referred to as a "building," though the structure was really a jumble of added-on basements and subbasements, most of which were several stories above the pavement. In these buildings, a mind-boggling complex of laboratories, animal housing rooms, specimen freezers, and countless offices fought for space as though they had become a physical emblem of the behemoth agency they represented.

"I'm Dr. Marah Morgan," she said to the receptionist. "I have an appointment with Dr. Redkin."

The woman pushed her glasses up her nose and typed the information into her computer. "Dr. Redkin is in a meeting, Dr. Morgan. I'll make a note of your arrival. He'll be with you shortly."

"Shortly" lasted three hours. Marah sat in the waiting room, attempting to be patient, wondering if her St. Louis practice had fallen apart in the weeks she'd been gone, pondering her relationship with her father, and trying to figure out why she couldn't get Judd out of her thoughts. She remembered her mother. She debated calling her sisters. And finally a short woman in a lab coat motioned her to follow.

"Dr. Redkin is sorry to have kept you waiting," the technician said. "I'm sure you know how busy the EIS stays."

"EIS?"

"The Epidemic Intelligence Service. It's a branch of the CDC." She paused before pushing the elevator button. "I thought you were here about the death of Dr. Luis Jordan."

"Yes, but . . ." She paused. "Yes, that's right."

Epidemics? Marah fell silent as they stepped into the elevator, which whisked them to Building 6, once an animal house. Ushered into Dr. Redkin's office, she was abandoned again. As she studied the windowless room, Marah began to feel as though she were a small mouse caught in a maze.

The heavy door featured a tiny square of glass through which handlers once had studied their animals. At the top of the door, rectangular vent spaces permitted no more than a breath of stale air. A three-inch-wide lip of concrete rimmed the room at floor level. Marah wondered if this had been installed to keep water from the seams when the janitors hosed out the rooms.

"Hantavirus," Dr. Redkin said, stepping into the room and slamming the door shut behind him. "We've had another outbreak in New Mexico. Terrible thing, four people sick, one dead, and not one physician identified it in time."

He threw a file onto the metal desk and held out a beefy hand. "Redkin," he said. "You're Dr. Morgan from St. Louis about the Jordan affair. Still don't know much. Unusual symptoms. We took tissue samples, of course, but we're hitting a brick wall. Any information you have for us?"

Marah blinked. "I came here to get information from you."

"Aha." The man was very young, soft-bellied, with an enormous walrus mustache and a mop of untrimmed brown curly hair. "I thought you had worked with Dr. Jordan and were coming to tell us what you knew about his last days."

"His last days were spent here. Our physician group has been given almost no information about his death. Both from a personal and a professional stand, we want to understand what happened. I've been escorted here to epidemiology. That sends up a few red flags for me, Dr. Redkin."

"Standard practice. The microbe samples were . . . unusual. So the information was transferred to me."

"Unusual in what way? Dr. Redkin, if Dr. Jordan died of a

contagious viral or bacterial disease, our office needs to know about it. Patients and physicians were exposed to him."

"We realize that, of course." He looked disgruntled. "The EIS certainly would not let a potentially hazardous situation get out of hand, Dr. Morgan. Had we felt there was a serious concern, we would have contacted you immediately."

She felt like the conversation had become part of the maze in which she was trapped. "But what were Dr. Jordan's symptoms?" she asked. "Why were they so unusual? And why haven't you been able to identify the microbe samples?"

"Let me ask the questions, Dr. Morgan." He shoved a stack of papers from the corner of his desktop and sat down. "You worked closely with Dr. Jordan, didn't you?"

"Yes."

"His patient records don't reveal any unusual cases for a pediatrician. For the most part, he treated the common, everyday problems kids face—colds, sprained ankles, ear infections, flu, and the occasional case of pneumonia or streptococcus. Is that correct?"

"Yes, but—"

"I understand you occasionally asked Dr. Jordan to consult with you on cases in which you were concerned about the proper course of treatment."

"That's right. He'd been a pediatrician his entire career. He was very knowledgeable. He never would have put himself into a situation of risk, Dr. Redkin. He was always careful."

"Can you recall any patient of yours who seemed to exhibit

unusual symptoms? High fever, unexplained rash, pustules covering the face or chest—"

"Pustules?"

"Before he died, Dr. Jordan's flesh was covered with pus-filled blisters."

Marah sank back into her chair. "But he kept his immunizations up to date. He wouldn't have contracted measles or chicken pox. There was nothing unusual that I . . ." She paused, remembering the tiny hand of her burn victim. "Demetria."

"What?"

"Two patients were assigned to me, victims of an arson fire that had gutted their day care. It was a state-run facility in St. Louis, understaffed, records poorly kept, conditions overcrowded. Both children were badly burned. At first, I thought we had them over the hump. But then they went downhill. Raging fevers."

"How high?"

"106."

"Rash?"

"Hard to tell. The epidermis was charred, of course. But we felt something was going on beyond the primary injury. I called Dr. Jordan to consult on the case. By that time the first child had already died. The second, Demetria, was comatose. She died not long after Dr. Jordan examined her."

"And how many days passed until his own death?"

She tried to recall. "Three or four weeks."

"You saw no signs of illness in Dr. Jordan shortly after his examination of the patient?"

"No, nothing. He was fine. I took a sabbatical, and while I was away, he flew here to confer with you people."

Dr. Redkin swung his leg back and forth, kicking the metal desk with his heel. "Were you aware that the subject of our meeting with Dr. Jordan was this very day-care fire of which you spoke? Did you know that there were two such arson fires this spring, and that in each of them, the survivors eventually died not from their burns but from something that caused high fever and unexplained rashes?"

A chill slid down Marah's spine. "Two fires?"

"St. Louis and Kansas City. Conveniently close, don't you think?"

"Are you saying one person might have been responsible for both fires? But the newspapers said the St. Louis blaze was set by the disgruntled boyfriend of an employee."

"Maybe." He stared at the tiny window in the door. "The EIS doesn't like this situation, Dr. Morgan. We're especially unhappy that Dr. Jordan carried his unidentified pathogen onto an airplane, through two airports, straight into the CDC, and then to a public hospital in one of the most populous cities in the United States. We don't know if or when he was contagious. And most of all, we don't know what killed him."

"What about the other treating physicians? Nurses and caregivers who tended the cases in Kansas City?"

"No signs of illness so far. That leads us to believe we may be barking up an empty tree. On the other hand, Dr. Jordan did die."

Marah twisted the strap of her purse around her hand. "Look, this is not the steaming jungle of central Africa. The United States doesn't normally generate unnamed pathogens. Whatever killed Dr. Jordan has to be identifiable. I'm sure you tested for measles, chicken pox, streptococcus, bacilli—"

"Of course." His voice held a note of annoyance as he continued. "Dr. Morgan, inside the laboratories and freezers of the CDC reside all of the world's known viruses and bacteria. All of them. We have data that date back to the founding of the CDC in 1946 and many, many years before that. If this was a known pathogen, I believe we would have identified it."

"Maybe it's something new. Or very old."

"It's not HIV, hantavirus, Ebola, Marburg, or any of the new ones. It's not yellow fever, malaria, diphtheria, or any of the old ones. Smallpox was eradicated by the World Health Organization in 1977. Syphilis manifests differently. We've checked current bioterrorism favorites such as anthrax, bubonic plague, and botulinum toxin. It's none of them. Nor is it a hemorrhagic fever virus like Machupo or Crimean-Congo. It's nothing that we've seen."

Marah drank down a deep breath. "Then you're telling me you don't have any idea what killed Dr. Jordan."

"That's what I'm telling you. We were hoping you could tell us."

She thought of the two burn victims. "I didn't see any pustules on my patients before they died."

"Maybe there's no connection. It's too late to request tissue samples from those patients for comparison unless we want to go to the trouble to petition for exhumation of their remains. That's always a tricky business and often unsuccessful. We won't attempt it unless we feel we have a crisis situation on our hands. At this point, that doesn't seem to be the case, although Dr. Jordan's skin was covered with pustules. Hundreds of foul-smelling blisters. His internal organs were also affected, Dr. Morgan. It was a painful death."

She shut her eyes, envisioning her beloved mentor dying in such agony. Again, she thought of her mother, the high fever and rash that had killed her so mysteriously. And then she recalled the mummy in the cairn on Morgan Farm.

"I don't know what to tell you about Dr. Jordan," she said finally. Dr. Redkin was staring at her, dejected. "I guess you'll just have to wait and see if anyone else comes down with this thing before you know if you have an epidemic on your hands."

"Have you been feeling all right, Dr. Morgan?"

"Fine. I'm perfectly healthy, and I handled the patients in question as closely as Dr. Jordan did." She stood, realizing what she had said wasn't exactly true. "No, that's not right. Dr. Jordan had closer contact with the child than I did. He bent over her bed. He stroked the only healthy skin on her body. He was a compassionate man."

"His compassion may have led to contamination."

"He was a wonderful physician." She stared at the floor for

a moment. "There's something else I wanted to ask you about. Your description of Dr. Jordan's death made me think of it."

"What's that?"

"On my father's farm in Kansas, we found the skeletal remains of a female Native American. The Osage tribe based some of their villages in that area for a number of years. Anyway, the remains had more or less mummified, and I noticed some flat, round markings on the skin. They covered the face and chest area. Does that sound like anything you can think of? I thought measles, maybe."

"Doubtful. Measles pustules are minuscule. I doubt they'd be visible. Who found the remains?"

"A group of anthropologists from the Bureau of Indian Affairs. They're planning to reinter the remains in Oklahoma."

He frowned. "Odd. The BIA usually contacts us for information before a dig. Some pathogens can remain viable in human remains for hundreds of years, you know. We make sure that any archaeologists excavating once-populated areas are adequately vaccinated. I don't recall a BIA request regarding a Kansas dig. One of my colleagues may have information on the group that's working at your father's farm. But you shouldn't handle the remains, Dr. Morgan. Diphtheria, for example, can be lethal."

"There's a child on the farm. She accidentally fell into the hole and landed on the mummy. Should I be concerned for her health?"

"Her mental health more than anything, I'd imagine." He smiled. "I'll bet that scared the living daylights out of her."

"Yes, it did."

"I wouldn't worry about it. Just keep an eye on her."

Marah started for the door. "Dr. Redkin," she said, turning, "do you have a current monograph that details those pathogens you named earlier? Hantavirus, Ebola, bubonic plague—that kind of thing?"

"I can give you some information, but I told you we've already analyzed samples of Dr. Jordan's tissue." He pulled open a file cabinet and took out a collection of brochures and medical documents. "These ought to cover the spectrum. Any ideas you have about what killed Dr. Jordan would be appreciated."

Marah tucked the paperwork in the crook of her arm. "It's not his death that mystifies me the most," she said. "It's the death of my mother."

🐾 🐾 🐾

Judd was mowing a field of alfalfa when he saw her waving from the road. Marah had been back on the farm two days, but they hadn't spoken. While she was away, he had thought about her a lot. Thought about her smile and her glossy black hair and her bright blue eyes. Thought about how she made him feel when she took him into her confidence. Thought about his own past and his future. Even thought about God.

But after analyzing the situation up one side and down the

other, he had decided that the woman irritated him. Caught up in her own goals and plans, she regarded Judd simply as a farm-hand. Someone to order around. Someone to do her bidding. Stay on the farm, she had said. Help my father. Read the Bible. Judd had not enjoyed telling his new supervisor that he wouldn't be able to meet in Wyoming at the time specified.

Worse, Milton Gregory had toned down his enthusiasm where Judd was concerned. They'd found the mummy, Gregory said. So they didn't really need help after all. Judd hadn't been allowed back onto the site. Wasn't welcome at Gregory's secret night meetings. Never had a chance to set foot in their bunk-house laboratory. And he still didn't have much of a lead on what the group was up to.

As Judd drove the mower around the field toward Marah's pickup, he again turned the possibilities over in his mind. Maybe Gregory wanted the skeleton for some bizarre ritual. Judd had contacted headquarters about the possibility. His supervisor said it didn't fit the man's profile. Judd wasn't sure he agreed. Head-quarters wondered if Gregory might be planning to use the remains as a means to extort money from the Osage Indians in Oklahoma. They were a wealthy tribe, it seemed. Oil.

Marah had noticed medical equipment and supplies in the tent. Was Gregory doing something that related to his work as a physician? Clearly he planned to experiment on the corpse. But what would he find in the remains of an Indian woman that would be useful?

Bright as sunshine and wearing a conciliatory smile, Marah

was approaching the mower. Judd cut the noisy engine and climbed down. "Hey there," she said.

Gypsy leapt out of the pickup bed and greeted Judd. He rubbed behind her ears, her favorite spot.

"The field looks good," Marah said.

"Hay's dry."

"Yeah." She crossed her arms. "Well, I had an interesting trip to Atlanta."

"Good."

She shifted from one leg to the other, clearly hoping for more from him. He'd decided against having any further conversations with Marah. Too distracting.

"Anyway," she said, "I could use your help in the white house this morning. The staircase has pulled away from the wall, and I can't climb it to clean the upstairs rooms. Could you help me shore it up?"

He glanced at the field. Gypsy had taken off in pursuit of a bird. "I really need to rake."

"Look, Judd, I know you were upset with me for leaving after you'd asked for time off. I had to go to Atlanta, even though it turned out to be a complete waste of time."

"No good, huh?"

"The CDC doesn't have a clue what killed Dr. Jordan, and you'd think they would know, if anybody." She shrugged. "So you can go on your trip now, if you want. Tomorrow or this afternoon. Whatever. But I do need help with the staircase."

"Is it just me you treat this way?"

"What way?"

"Like a well-trained dog." He headed for Marah's pickup. "Give him the occasional biscuit, and he'll do whatever you want."

"You're my employee."

"Same thing." He slid onto the seat as Gypsy barreled in beside him. She was panting but happy. He slammed the door. "Guess you learned that from your old man."

She climbed into the pickup. "I don't know what you're talking about. I'm not mistreating you. And I am nothing like my father."

She switched on the ignition and stepped on the gas. A cloud of dust rose behind the pickup. Judd studied the purple fields of alfalfa, all demanding to be mowed, raked, baled. So much for infiltration of Milton Gregory's group. Out here on the Kansas prairie, he was a farmer, pure and simple.

"It's just that I need to get the white house finished up, so I can put the farm on the market," Marah was saying. The wind through the open window whipped her black hair around her chin. "I've got to take care of this situation. My father is never going to get off that walker, you know. He can't run the farm, and I'm not planning to stay here the rest of my life. I'm a physician. I have my work to do. My practice. I carry a heavy caseload, and things are a mess in St. Louis. I have to work so I can support myself. I have a car payment and a mortgage, and I need to buy groceries and—"

Marah pulled the pickup to a stop beside the old clapboard

house. "I sound just like him, don't I?" she whispered. She leaned her forehead on the steering wheel. "Beans and double beans."

🐾 🐾 🐾

"So I came right home and checked on Perky," Marah said as she handed Judd a nail. The afternoon sun was slanting through a window, heating the back of her T-shirt. "But she's fine. Not a symptom in sight. I doubt there's anything to be concerned about. What bothered me was that Dr. Redkin couldn't recall hearing anything from the BIA about a dig in Kansas. He said it was standard procedure for them to contact the CDC first."

Judd hammered the nail into a strip of molding that had come loose around the staircase. It was the final step in making it safe to use again. "So you're saying that Indian woman could have died from some kind of disease?"

"Dr. Redkin mentioned diphtheria. He said some viruses stay viable in skeletal remains for hundreds of years. But Perky would have been immunized against diphtheria. The DPT vaccination is required for every child entering school, and I'm sure Pete Harris wouldn't allow his daughter to—"

"What else?" He stopped hammering. "What other diseases could live in those remains?"

"I don't know." She felt a wall of defense rise against the sudden intensity in his brown eyes. Sometimes Judd seemed like a different person, his casual demeanor vanishing in the wake of a surge of passion. It was disconcerting.

"How would I know?" she said. "I'm not an archaeologist."

He leaned toward her. "But you're a doctor."

"It's not something you need to worry about, Judd. You were down in that hole with the mummy for only a few seconds. I'm sure it would take more contact than that to expose you. Besides, any disease those Indians would have been carrying is treatable today."

He nodded and let out a breath. It was hard for Marah to imagine Judd being worried about catching some vague pathogen. He didn't seem like the hypochondriac type. When he spoke again, his voice was easy and conversational.

"I wonder what that Indian woman died of," he mused. "She wasn't old—I didn't see a strand of white in her hair. Must have been some kind of disease. Or maybe an injury killed her."

"Don't forget childbirth," Marah said. "Though I did notice those odd markings on her skin."

"Markings?"

"Spots. They were all over her face and chest."

"Spots." He dropped the hammer into his metal toolbox and climbed the bottom three steps. His voice dropped to a murmur, as though he were speaking to himself. "Measles, no. Everyone is immunized. Mumps, rubella, diphtheria, tetanus, pertussis. No, vaccinations are routine in childhood. Something else. Something rare today."

Concerned that he was back to fretting over contact with the mummy again, Marah followed him up the stairs. "I don't know why you're so worried, Judd. Your chances of exposure were minimal."

He glanced behind him. "What about smallpox?"

"Even if that's what the woman had, I imagine somebody has doses of the vaccine stashed away." She edged past him, stepping onto the second floor landing for the first time since her return to the farm. "I think the military may still vaccinate in some cases."

"They do. I was immunized before I went on active duty in the Gulf War."

"I didn't know you fought in the war." She stared at him, adjusting her perception of the man. He'd told her he had been in the army. But fighting? Combat?

"Yeah," he said, "I was over there."

"So see, you're protected even from smallpox. Although I can't imagine why the army felt the need to immunize soldiers. Smallpox is history. It was eradicated in the seventies." Marah walked into a sunlit room, its matching beds with their pink chenille spreads still piled high with teddy bears. "Oh, would you look at this? It's like time stopped in here."

"What else?" Judd said behind her. "Bubonic plague? Or what about tuberculosis?"

"This is where the twins slept." Disturbed by his obsession over possible contamination, Marah decided to ignore him. She crossed to the window and looked down on the backyard. The barn was not a hundred feet away, sagging and in need of a new coat of paint. Its doors slid apart to drive a tractor through.

"The curtains fell apart in the wash when I was about twelve," she remembered. "I felt so bad, but there was nothing I could do. They were old and fragile by then. We didn't have the money to buy new ones, so my father hung roll-up blinds. I sewed doll dresses from the scraps of curtain fabric. It was pink dotted swiss, faded and threadbare. Sarah loved hers, but Leah said they were ugly."

Wistful at the memory, she passed Judd, who was scribbling in a notebook he had taken from his back pocket. She moved down the hall to the large bedroom where her parents had once slept. In the months before her mother's death, Ed Morgan had taken to sleeping on the couch downstairs. Marah had never understood why, but she had thought it had something to do with all the arguing that went on in this room. Now the bedroom was as empty of life as a discarded shell picked up on the beach.

The old rocker in the corner had belonged to Ruby Morgan's mother. The mirrored dresser had come from a wealthy great-aunt in California. Mom had polished the silvered glass every morning. Now it was so coated with dust that Marah couldn't make out her own reflection.

"My father sold all Mom's dresses and shoes at a tag sale," she told Judd. "He said we'd never have a dime from our mother any other way. But we didn't care about money. We just wanted her to come back."

"There are different kinds of flu," Judd murmured as Marah walked toward the door. He lifted his head from his notebook.

"Did Indians die of flu? I wonder if some strains of it could live in skeletal remains. Is flu bacterial?"

"Viral." Marah paused outside the door to the bedroom she had shared with her younger sister. She touched the peeling white paint on the door frame. There was the dent in the wood from the time Deborah had thrown a clock at Leah in a fit of anger. Mom had nearly had a cow over that.

"Here's my room," she said, stepping inside. She turned on the single bulb that hung from the ceiling. And there stood the big bed where she and Deborah had slept for so many years. Fingering the ragged quilt with its faded patchwork of embroidered names, she thought of the women in her mother's missionary support group at church. They had made personalized quilts for each member of the circle, and they promised to pray for each other every morning of their lives.

"Look at these old boxes," Marah said, noting the unexpected presence of several sagging cartons stacked near the wardrobe. She lifted the flap of one and sifted through the pile of yellowed papers inside. There was an old journal written in carefully inked penmanship. A map lay beneath it, and she recognized the river that ran through their farm. Down the sides of the box, pieces of old glassware had been wedged. Blue plates and a china platter with pink roses. Marah thought she remembered the platter from Thanksgiving dinners. This must be a collection of her mother's things, she realized, the old family records her father had mentioned. Some afternoon she would come up here and go through everything.

Marah moved across the room to her old desk. "Here's where I did my homework," she said softly. She ran her hand across the flat, smooth, pine boards. Then she lifted the desktop to find notebooks, ruined crayons, and pencils sharpened to the nub. She picked up a fat pink eraser and lifted it to her nose.

The scent of pleasant memories flooded through Marah. Like the big burr oak tree in the pasture, this old desk had been her refuge. Here she had lost herself in books about volcanoes, woodland creatures, oceans, faraway lands, and imaginary creatures. When she was older, she had pored through medical textbooks that Dr. Benson let her borrow. Fascinated by the human body, she had allowed herself to dream of a future as a physician. At this desk she had learned to recite her multiplication tables, to recognize a preposition, to identify the major body organs, and to calculate square roots. Here was the source of her intellectual growth.

Her spiritual and emotional nourishment, Marah acknowledged, had come from her mother's faith. She wandered back to the window and leaned her forehead on the pane of the double-hung window. Had she learned anything of value from her father? she wondered.

It seemed like the minute she tried to talk to him, the spring of bitter water inside her bubbled up and overflowed, drowning the meekness of spirit required for reconciliation. She heard her voice grow harsh and angry, watched her father's face harden, felt her body stiffen with hurt.

How much had this unforgiveness hurt her? Probably a lot more than it had ever hurt her father.

Turning from the window, Marah spotted the metal heat register set into the wooden floor of her bedroom, one of two on each side of the room. Drawn by her memories, she passed Judd and crouched down beside the register near the door. Her fingertips traced the intricate scrollwork of twining ivy leaves and vines. Why did she recall every twist and curlicue? As she stared down at the floor, she felt something inside her waken and stir to life.

"Marah?" Judd said. "I asked you a question about the mummy."

She looked at him, but her eyes were focused on something many years in the past. Something about the heat register. Something compelling and wonderful and horrible all at the same time.

"If the Indian woman died of a disease," Judd said, "how would the virus or the bacteria be released from the skeleton? Would it just seep out, or would there need to be active invasion of the remains?"

Marah leaned over the register and peered through the network of metal lace. That's right, the living room was just below the room where she slept. She noticed the old couch in the corner. Her father's stockinged feet always rested on that end of the couch, the part she could see from her bedroom. At night, after Deborah fell asleep, Marah used to creep across the floor and peer down at her father's feet. His work boots would be lying nearby, muddy and worn. The television was always

playing, cowboy shows usually. Ed loved *Bonanza*—Ben Cartwright with all his strapping sons helping out on the Ponder-
osa. And then Mom would come into the room with a piece of
pie. Always pie. Never cake or ice cream or cobbler. Chocolate, cherry, coconut, lemon chiffon, apple, or pecan pie. Pie
on a clean white plate with a small silver fork and a napkin.

Marah glanced over her shoulder at Judd. He was still scribbling away in his notebook. *What a strange man.*

"You know, I used to look through this heat register when I
was little," she said. "I could watch my parents. My mother
brought pie to my father every night."

"Pie?" Judd hunkered down beside her and peered through
the grate. "Not much of a view."

"But I could hear everything."

The television, the fork scraping on the white dish, and the
arguments:

Why, why did you do it, Ed?

Let it go; let it go, Ruby.

What about the children? Didn't you think of them?

It's those girls.

Not the girls, Ed. That's not the problem.

Come here, Ruby.

No, don't touch me! Take your hands off me!

Feeling as though she had fallen into a sort of trance, Marah
rose from the register and walked across the room. "Here's the
other one," she said. "It looks down into the bathroom."

Folding to her knees, she set one hand on each side of the

metal grate and peered through it into the black-and-white tiled room. The bathtub. Easy to see. Two little girls, Sarah and Leah, and Mom bent over them scrubbing two heads of dark silky hair. Big Ed Morgan peeling off his overalls. *Don't look, Deborah! Get away from the register when he's taking a bath!* And Mom by herself, leaning under the faucet to shampoo her long brown hair, froth and suds sliding down her arms into the shiny porcelain tub. And Mom again, setting one toe in the water, then her foot, and then her beautiful slender body. *Will we look like her someday, Marah? Will we be as pretty as Mom when we get older? Oh yes, Deborah. We'll be just like her.* And Mom again, this time red and heated with fever, barely able to lift her leg over the side of the tub, breathing hard and crying softly. *Hot, I'm so hot, Ed. I'm burning up. Don't touch me, Ed! Get away from me!*

Marah laid her palm on the register. If only she could have gotten down there in time. If only she could have . . . could have what? What had happened in the bathroom?

"I remember once when my mom was in the bathtub," she whispered. "I needed to go to her, but I couldn't. I couldn't get to her. I wasn't in time."

"In time for what?" Judd asked, kneeling beside her.

"I don't know." Marah pushed her fingers down through the grate. "I can't remember. I was too little. I was too little to do anything to help her. And I couldn't get there in time."

"Marah," he said.

"This whole house is full of her, but she's gone. She left me here, left all of us. All we had was the old quilt and the jars of pickles and the faded curtains. And he was so angry."

"Your father."

"Mostly he was mad at me. I wasn't a boy. I wasn't Mom. I wasn't good enough, and I couldn't please him no matter how hard I tried."

"Why did you try to please him?"

"I thought if I could just do everything right, I could win his love," she muttered, the knee of her jeans pressed into her cheek. "With my father, it's what you *do* that counts."

"You don't need his love, his approval, Marah. You're a doctor. You have your career, your life in St. Louis, your plans."

"I think I do need my father's love. For some reason, I've spent my whole life trying to earn it."

"What about your faith? Isn't that enough?"

"It's enough. But there's something inside me that still wants my father's love. He wants me to be better and do more—and I can't. It'll never be enough."

"Aren't you expecting the same thing out of him?"

"What do you mean?"

"Cut your dad some slack, Marah. He's never going to be the kind of father you want. He probably has no idea what your picture of a loving dad is like. Why don't you try to love him for who he is instead of wishing he were different?"

"Who he is?" She lifted her head. "He's impatient and stubborn and demanding and—"

"Sinful. But you said God forgives us anyhow. So, forgive your father, Marah."

She looked into Judd's deep brown eyes. Who was this man?

"If you could step outside your hurt," he said, "you might see that Ed Morgan is really a pretty interesting guy."

"Interesting?"

"Have you seen the toys he's whittled for Perky? There's a doll with jointed arms and legs, a bed with tiny flowers carved in the posts, and a little table and chair. Your dad keeps his old machinery going by rigging it in some ingenious ways. He listens to the farm report every morning on the radio, and he's been investing his profits for years."

"Profits?" Marah shook her head. "I didn't know there was ever any extra money to invest."

"I bet he's got a tidy little sum tucked away. And have you watched him with his dog? He's got Gypsy trained to do everything he tells her. One morning he wanted to go out into the pasture, so I loaded him into the truck. It took some doing, but I got him propped up on his walker out in the middle of the cattle herd. And then he showed me how he and Gyp work. It was incredible. That dog can just about make those heifers do the cancan."

Marah smiled. "I've never seen that."

"Well, you ought to start watching. You might find out that your dad is an OK guy. You might figure out how to forgive him. You might actually start to love him even though he doesn't deserve it."

"Grace," she said.

"Who?"

"Grace. It's the undeserved gift of forgiveness and love. God gives us grace. You're saying I need to give my father grace."

"It couldn't hurt."

"No," she said, "it couldn't."

For a moment, seated there on the floor of her childhood bedroom, Marah thought she glimpsed the possibility of freedom. "You know," she said, meeting Judd's warm eyes, "you're an interesting man."

He grinned, lopsided. "I was just thinking you're an interesting woman."

"Am I?" For the first time she could ever remember in the presence of a man, a flush of heat rose to her cheeks and a quiver settled down deep in the pit of her stomach.

"Pretty, too."

"Oh." She said, and suddenly she realized she wanted him to touch her hand or to lean forward and kiss her cheek.

"So, could I ask you something?"

"Sure." She held her breath, feeling off-kilter.

He cleared his throat and swallowed. Then he focused on the window. His eyes narrowed. His grin faded.

"That trip I need to make. Could I take a few days off next week?"

"That's what you wanted to ask me?"

He didn't answer.

"OK. Sure." Disappointment swept through her.

Judd got to his feet. As he walked across the bedroom floor, she could hear the wooden boards creak. He stepped out into the hallway and vanished as completely as though a door had been shut between them.

Marah looked down through the heat register and stared at the empty bathtub.

᠙ ᠙ ᠙

Judd shut the car door behind him and walked toward the shattered school building. Though it was the end of July, he felt a cool Wyoming breeze sweep down from the Bighorn Mountains. He studied the remains of the elementary school in silence, willing himself to feel nothing about this place, to maintain professional detachment. This was the former headquarters of Milton Gregory's group, the focus of Judd's current mission, the site of an explosion. He couldn't think about Chuck, about his last minutes alive, about his bright red hair and his grieving family. This was a job. Just another assignment.

"The explosive demolished the cafeteria and the front offices of the old school." Bill, the new supervisor on the case, walked beside Judd. Five feet eight at the most, one hundred and seventy pounds. Thatch of gray hair. Acne-scarred skin and a paunch that bore testament to years behind a desk. "It was a simple device, pressure triggered. Took out three of our best men and most of the evidence."

Passing through the iron gate, they walked into the barren

school yard. The slide had been curled like a Frito in the explosion. The swings lay tangled near the fence. Glass from the shattered windows covered the sprigs of green grass that had taken root here and there around the yard. The front of the building had opened outward in the blast, exposing its underbelly to the sky. Rain had fallen more than once in the weeks since it happened, and as Judd stepped into the ruins, he noted the peeling wallboard and dampened wood floors.

"We think Gregory ordered his people to clear out most of the equipment before they left," Bill said. "Have you been able to get a close look at his setup there in Kansas?"

"He put up a makeshift laboratory in the bunkhouse," Judd said. "Keeps the door and windows locked at all times, even when they're working in there. The lab's on the second floor, kind of a loft arrangement. One night after everyone was asleep, I shimmied up the outside wall and took a look through the window. Couple of microscopes, lots of flasks, beakers, syringes, petri dishes. There's a big box in the middle of the room. Metal, I think."

"How big?" They were strolling down the darkened hall between classrooms now, looking into empty rooms lined with wooden bunks. The scent of smoke and sulfur clung to the walls. "Is it a container? Did you see a hinge?"

"Definitely a container. Three feet square. Glass windows."

"Windows?" Bill frowned. "Wonder what it's for."

Judd bent down and picked up a scrap of paper. He held it up to a thin shaft of light shining through a seam in the boarded windows. It was lined notebook paper, the kind students use. Nothing written on it. The FBI investigators had been thorough. He doubted he would find anything they had missed.

"Gregory was experimenting with something explosive here in Wyoming," Bill said. "We have an idea he's continuing that work in Kansas. He's isolated out there, and he's got plenty of space to try out things."

Judd leaned one shoulder against a splintered door frame. "He's not stockpiling fertilizer, Bill."

"We're thinking chemicals. Maybe explosive chemicals, maybe toxic ones. Remember the Japanese subway bombings? Members of Aum Shiryinko carried six packages onto Tokyo subway trains, punctured the packages with umbrella tips, and released gas among the passengers. Twelve people died, and five thousand were injured."

"Sarin gas," Judd said. "It's a cholinesterase inhibitor."

"That's right, and Milton Gregory's a scientist. Chemistry is going to be the direction he takes. Look where he sent the rest of his people. Chicago and Washington. Both those cities have sophisticated rapid transit systems."

"What about San Francisco and New York? Why's he avoiding them?" Judd shook his head. "No, I don't think Gregory's interested in random terrorism. He's more focused than that. I'm betting his target is D.C."

"Why did he send some of his people to Chicago then?"

"A decoy. He knows Big Brother is watching him."

"What about the noxious gas angle? Do you think that's what he's doing in Kansas?"

Judd studied the floor. "He's digging up Indians in Kansas, Bill."

"Maybe that's a front. Maybe he's onto you."

"He's paranoid and wary, but I don't think he's got me pegged." He let out a breath. "Would you mind bringing me the evidence report? I'd like to take a look at what our boys found here in the school."

"Back in a minute."

As the agent returned to the car, Judd rolled his head back on his shoulders to ease the throbbing in his temples. An idea had been developing in his mind during the past few days. It was like a puzzle, but the pieces didn't quite fit yet.

For some reason Marah Morgan's face appeared in Judd's thoughts, her beautiful clear skin and wide blue eyes. She had no idea that a whirlwind was swirling around her little farm. She thought the only problem she had was figuring out how to forgive her father. Something unexplained ached inside Judd's chest. It hurt so much, he finally sank to the floor and leaned his back against the crumbling wall.

In the darkness he thought of Marah and the disease of bitterness she felt sure was eating her up. Did she have any idea of the vast, stinking vat of poison that had infected the entire world around her? People like Milton Gregory were walking pathogens, spreading their vile ideas and contaminating everyone they touched. People like Marah believed Jesus Christ could heal every sin. They were wrong.

Some people's evil was too great. Too contagious.

And others were nothing more than living scabs, already too far gone to be saved. That described him, Judd decided. Empty of any life worth rescuing. His wife had called him a hollow man, and she was right. In the little Bible he'd bought in town, Judd had read about Jesus calling people tombs—clean and pretty to look at on the outside, but full of death and rottenness on the inside. Judd wasn't sure he had even that much left. He was more like the Indian mummy under a pile of rocks—just an empty skeleton with a few strips of dried skin and hair.

But Marah had said the Indian woman's remains could still contain disease. Maybe Judd was diseased, too. Diseased with sin. Could God put skin and flesh on the hollow man and breathe life into him as he had done in the valley of dry bones? Could God heal the disease within?

"Here's the file," Bill said, holding out an accordion folder.

The disease within. Judd looked up, and the words spilled out of his mouth even as the pieces of the puzzle fell into place.

"It's disease," he said. "Gregory's not going to spread chemicals or gas. He's going to infect Washington with a pathogen that will wipe out most of the population. And he's harvesting it from that Indian."

Bill swallowed. "Are you sure?"

Judd nodded. "Milton Gregory is a bioterrorist."

The Twenty-sixth Day of the Yellow Flower Moon, The Year of 1869

Yesterday my mother's skin split open. Each small footprint of the ge-ta-zhe tore from side to side, releasing fiery water in a gush that made my mother scream and weep in her agony. She cried aloud, begging for death, wishing it to come more quickly. My father could do nothing to help her. He lies on his own pallet, wet from the sweat of his fever and groaning in madness.

I cannot help my mother or my father. I curl in a ball near my mother's body as the ge-ta-zhe begin to march across my own skin with their burning feet. My fingers can hardly hold the pen with which I write. I await the ending of my life.

As my mother shrieks in pain, we can hear the others of our village moaning with sorrow. They sing the Song of Death:

O-hooooo, it is I who cause them to lie yellowing on the earth.

It is I who attack them thus.

A-e the he, Ah-he the he

It is I who take from them their remaining days,

Ah, HOOOooooooooooooooooooooo.

One by one the villagers carry their dead to the rocky field near the river. There they rest each body, sitting up to await the coming of Wah'Kon-Tah, Grandfather the Sun. They cover the dead with stones, making a large heap that will protect from rain and rot. My teacher at the mission school calls this a cairn. But I know it is a grave.

Today my mother's skin is covered with hard pebbles the size of corn kernels. Her whole body looks like the street of the town where I go to school, a cobblestone street. She can no longer speak words, and her eyes are swollen shut. Her beautiful, long black hair hangs damp and uncombed. I weep when I look at her.

In the month of the Yellow Flower Moon, the goldenrod dances across the prairie. But I cannot see the goldenrod or the compass weed, the broom weed or the partridge pea. I am too weak to crawl outside our lodge and watch the yellow butterflies floating over the bluestem grass. Never again will I watch the goldfinches darting in the trees or the yellow-headed blackbirds beginning to flock.

My mother will not gather the seeds of the columbine or pick the ripe corn. By the time the pumpkins turn orange and the squashes grow full and hard, she will be dead. One day purple coneflowers will nod over her grave.

From The Journal of Little Gray Bird, unpublished
Central Kansas Museum of the Native American archival
collection

14

Marah knocked on the bunkhouse door. "Dr. Gregory? Is anyone here?"

Knowing his team was hard at work in the field near Indian Hill, she didn't really expect the archaeologist to be inside. But if she could avoid a trip to the knolls, she would. After all, it would take just a moment to invite the three men to the picnic she and the Harris family had decided to hold this coming Sunday after church.

Hearing no one and curious to see how this group of men chose to spend their free time, Marah decided to take a quick peek in the quarters. She opened the door and stepped inside. Unmade bunks lined one wall. Magazines lay scattered on the floor along with a collection of empty beer cans and overflowing ashtrays. A television had been set up on a plank between two upturned feed buckets, the long ears of its antenna turned toward town.

Grimacing at the smell of unwashed bedding and filthy jeans, Marah crossed to a single neatly made bed along another wall. Judd's bed, she surmised. She missed him more than she'd expected and wondered where he had gone. She hadn't realized how much of the farm's workload he was carrying. But it was more than that. She had come to enjoy talking with him. Spending time with him.

On the table near the bed lay an opened book, something on the history of the American Revolution, and a few of his personal items. She noted the bottle of Tylenol and a Bic pen. She picked up a pair of mirrored sunglasses.

Stiffening, Marah set the sunglasses back on the table. This wasn't Judd's bed. It belonged to Milton Gregory. She had seen him without his sunglasses only once or twice, and then from a distance. Somehow the thought of handling his possessions gave her a strange feeling. Milton was an unusual man, distant and preoccupied with his work. Marah didn't like his colleagues, but she found the scientist himself intriguing. There was a sense of mystery surrounding him. Why had he chosen the profession of archaeology instead of a more lucrative medical practice? Where had he come from, and who was his family? Most of all, what was he doing out there in the pasture?

If she turned her thoughts to Milton Gregory, Marah wondered, maybe she could put Judd out of her mind. It was possible she'd just gone too long without an evening out. The idea of a trip to town with the dedicated scientist lifted her spirits. She would find Milton and see if he'd like to take in a movie after the picnic. They could talk about their respective careers and their plans for the future. Maybe he would tell her about his work on the Indian remains. At the very least, she would stop thinking about a man who was unavailable in every sense of the word. And that would be a relief.

Marah walked quickly across the floor to yet another bunk, its mattress covered with a sleeping bag. Clearly Judd had taken the duffel bag on his trip. Nothing else of him remained in the bunkhouse. Soon, she realized, he would go away for good. He would roll up his sleeping bag, sling his duffel over his shoulder, and drive off in his rattletrap pickup. And that would be that.

Trying to fight down the sharp ache that rose inside her, Marah decided to give the loft room a quick check. Maybe one of Milton's assistants was in the small laboratory she knew they had set up there. As she reached the landing at the top of the wide, ladderlike stairs, she turned the iron knob. It didn't budge. She glanced down and realized that the door was padlocked.

Curiosity prickling down her spine, she bent over and squinted through the cracks between the rough-hewn boards of the barn wall. Inside the loft room, she could make out a microscope, a stack of petri dishes, and a few unmarked flasks and containers. An odd, unpleasant smell emanated from the room. Something rotten. Or dead.

Marah moved to another crack and peered inside. A metal box sat on a low table. Two round holes had been cut in one side, which also held a small rectangular pane of glass near the top of the box. She'd seen something like it somewhere, though she couldn't quite place it. Beginning to feel a little sick from the odor, she stepped backward and felt a hand clamp around her arm.

"May I ask what you're doing?"

Marah caught her breath and turned, grabbing the ladder rail for support. "Oh, Milton," she said. "I didn't hear you."

A pair of round lenses jutted from the eye sockets of a metal helmet he wore. Sheathed in a latex glove, his hand released her arm. "Marah? What are you doing here?"

"I just came over to invite everyone to a picnic at the Harris farm," she said.

"A picnic?" He tugged the helmet from his head.

At the sight of the man's mop of curly brown hair and his blue eyes, Marah let out her breath. "Before the plowing starts, the neighboring farmers always get together for a picnic. Everybody brings a covered dish. Pete Harris does the barbecue."

She glanced down to find Mike Dooley and Bob Harper swathed from head to toe in rubber hip waders, full-length camouflage jackets, latex gloves, and helmets similar to the one Milton wore. They were carrying sealed metal boxes. For once, Bob was without his ever-present cigarette.

She looked back at the head archaeologist. "What's going on?"

"Our work," Milton said. "This project is highly sensitive, as you can imagine. Dealing with human remains is always a touchy matter, and especially so in this case. The BIA doesn't want to do anything that might offend Osage tribal leaders."

"I see," Marah said. "I guess you have to prepare the remains for reburial."

"Exactly, and as you know from the incident with Perky, the Osage interred their dead in stone cairns. They were not buried. In this instance, we aren't dealing with bone fragments, Marah, but with partially mummified human remains. We can't return these remains in any fashion that would indicate we handled them with less than respect and reverence."

Marah nodded, relieved that her concern about the treatment of the remains was unfounded. "I understand, of course."

"Now, if you'll excuse us," he said, indicating the ladder, "we have a lot of work to do."

Marah made her way down the steps and past the two archaeologists holding their small metal boxes. As she started out of the bunkhouse, she remembered her mission.

"About the picnic," she said, turning. The men were staring at her from behind their helmets. "It's this Sunday after church."

"After church," Milton said. "We'll be there."

"What we've got here is a bunch of rotten eggs." Mike Dooley held his nose as he lifted the lid of the incubator. The sulfurous odor billowed out into the laboratory. Milton Gregory swore as he grabbed the lid from his assistant and knocked the six eggs to the floor.

"Nothing is working," he snarled. "A simple embryo incubation—that's all I wanted. Any high school moron can do it."

"I think it might be the electricity, Dr. G. I know Bob

rewired the building, but I'm wondering if the voltage still may not be coming into the bunkhouse full strength. Or maybe it's this incubator we bought."

"What difference does it make?" Gregory grabbed a bucket and mop from the corner. "Clean that up, Mike."

"Yes, sir." Dooley gave the physician a look of reproach as he started for the door. "But how do you know the agent didn't grow inside the eggs even though they rotted? Maybe we've got viruses all over the floor."

"The agent requires a living host, Mike," Gregory said. "When eggs are dead, they rot. The smell in this room comes from dead, rotten eggs with no living virus."

"Well, what about the meat?"

Gregory closed his eyes, thankful for the mirrored glasses that prevented his colleagues from seeing the utter discouragement he knew must be written in them. "Nothing," he said quietly. "We have rotten brain and heart of bovine to go along with our rotten eggs. Maybe we should forget about our project and just make breakfast."

Dooley gave a laugh as he shouldered the mop. "I wonder if Ed has a can of air freshener over at his house. This place stinks to high heaven."

Gregory spun on his heel and grabbed Dooley's collar. "You will not talk to Ed Morgan. You will not say a word to his daughter. I don't trust either one of them. Marah Morgan was snooping yesterday, there's no question in my mind. Stay away from them. Do you understand me, Mike?"

"Yes, sir."

"We have two weeks to harvest, grow, and concentrate our agent." Gregory dropped his hand from Dooley's collar and let out a breath. "Two weeks, three at the most. And that includes refrigerating and transporting it."

"Do you want me to ask Perky for some more fresh eggs? I don't think it was her fault they rotted on us."

"Don't talk to that kid either. I caught her wandering around on the knolls the other day. Probably curious about the mummy. If she were to see the dissection we've been perform-ing, she'd tell Marah." Gregory switched on the computer and watched it boot up. "Clean up that mess, Mike. We're all about to faint."

The physician pulled out a chair and sat down, relieved to rest after the hours he'd spent in the tent dissecting yet another specimen. His team had found three more sets of remains thus far, two of them with flesh still clinging to the skeleton. He had been so sure the scabby pustules would contain the virus he sought. Yet all of his efforts to culture and grow it were proving futile. Yesterday his men had brought in three boxes of promising skin, bone fragments, and even strips of clothing.

Gregory moved the cursor on his computer to the Internet server's icon and clicked the mouse. As the static and beeps of the phone connection filled the room, he could hear Dooley beginning to mop. Bob had vanished as soon as he could get away. Probably out having a smoke. He didn't blame the man. The smell in the lab was nauseating.

"We've got a message from Team C," Gregory told Dooley. "They're in position in Washington and awaiting word from us. They've learned the name of the heating and cooling company that services most of the federal buildings. It looks like they'll be able to infiltrate the company without much problem."

"I wish I was still with Team C," Dooley said. "Although I've got to tell you that I'd feel a lot better if we could have used a different test group the first time around. That whole thing really got to me."

"Then you're weak." He opened a second message. "Keep your focus on the cause, Mike. If your attentions wander—"

As the words on the screen registered, Gregory stopped speaking, unable to form the syllables.

"What's up?" Dooley leaned over his shoulder to read.

"The farmhand. Judd. He's one of them." Gregory pointed to the screen. "Our scout from Team A spotted him at the Wyoming compound."

"I thought Team A was in Chicago."

"We left a man behind, remember? That's how we knew we'd taken out three of them in the blast."

"Does this mean Judd knows what we're up to? I never would have thought of him as a Fed. He seemed like a good guy, sympathetic to the cause."

"Of course he did. That's his job." Gregory shut down the computer and pushed back from the table. "He'll be back," he said, rising. "And he'll have more information, and he'll try to shut us down."

"We'd better get rid of him."

"It's not that simple. They're onto us, don't you see? If the farmhand is killed, if there's a murder, then there'll be an investigation. The local police, the county coroner, the FBI will be crawling all over this place. We can't afford to draw attention to ourselves. We need the next two weeks."

"So we just continue what we've been doing, without letting on that we know Judd's a mole?"

"There may be another way to handle him. I'll have to think it through." He began to pace. "In the meantime, I'm going to try the viral growth medium again today. If it works, and if we can grow enough . . . I'd give my life for a scanning electron microscope to check for virulence of the organism. But I have the PCR analysis. I'll do that and hope we have enough. Then I'll use the ultracentrifuge to spin down the sample . . . and we can put it into an atomizer. If the refrigerant system doesn't fail us—"

"Dr. G?" Dooley was standing nearby with his stinking mop bucket. "Judd will be back here before you can get the agent ready. What if he tries to stop us?"

Gregory shook his head. He couldn't be stopped. Not now. Not this close to success. "I'll think of a way to deal with it. A way that doesn't focus the blame on us."

Dooley nodded. "Whatever it takes, Dr. G."

"You're a good man, Mike. I hope you know that."

"Yes, sir." He was smiling as he carried the bucket of rotten eggs down the steps.

❦ ❦ ❦

"Dr. Morgan, guess who's here?" Perky skipped across the Harrises' green lawn, her long pigtails bouncing. "Judd! He got back in time for the picnic! I saw his pickup right after lunch, so Daddy and I swung by the bunkhouse and invited him. And guess what he brought me? A rose. Not just a flower but a whole bush with the roots and everything. It's called Pink Pearl, because my real name is Pearl Kathleen, and he bought it just for me!"

Marah laughed and took the child's hand. "A whole rosebush just for you? Wow."

"He's over there talking to Poppy and my dad." Perky pulled up short and spoke in a low voice. "I better warn you that Poppy isn't too happy about Judd being gone. He said that with you running things, the whole farm is going south. He told Judd all about the field of hay that got rained on because you went to town on Wednesday."

Marah pursed her lips. It wasn't the wet hay that had irritated her father; it was the fact that she had gone into town to speak to a real estate agent about selling Morgan Farm. But what choice did they have? Marah had worked hard to get the white house back in shape, painting walls, washing windows, and repairing the staircase. The wheat harvest was in, and the hay was winding down. The cattle were in decent shape, and the calves would be ready to wean soon. After they went to market in October, the rest of the herd would be available for sale.

Marah had been here for three months. She'd spoken to several people but hadn't been able to sell the place yet. She'd even spoken to Pete about buying the farm. He didn't want the land, he said, but he'd be interested in the cattle. Marah had to get back to St. Louis, so she had decided to turn the farm over to the Realtor. Once it sold, she'd just have to come back and move her father into a retirement home. Under the circumstances, it was the best they could expect.

"Don't worry about Poppy," Marah said to Perky. "We'll work things out."

"You want to see my rosebush?"

"Sure." They wandered over to the porch where Perky's mom sat in a large rocking chair with a quilt over her lap. "Hey, Hilda!" Marah said, waving. "You look about ready to pop."

"I am," she called back. "Pearl, did you get out the plates and cups like I told you, honey?"

"Yes, ma'am. They're on the table."

"I've got the sodas in the bed of my pickup," Marah said.

Hilda nodded, a smile of contentment spreading across her face. Marah looked out at the crowd gathering under a small stand of trees. *One tree for each lost baby*, she thought. *Dear God*, she lifted up, *please give Hilda and Pete two healthy children this time.*

"Here it is," Perky said. "It's called Pink Pearl. It's a tea rose."

Marah knelt by the black plastic pot with its long thorny canes. "It has rosebuds."

"Judd and I are going to plant it together. He says if we put in some good manure and water it down right, then we ought to see those buds open up in a couple of days. I'm going to give the first rose to my mommy. And I'll give you the second one." She blinked, her long lashes fanning her freckled cheeks. "I'm going out to our tree tomorrow, because it's almost the end of August, and school starts next week. I don't want summer to end. I'm going to take my favorite book up into the tree and drink iced tea and think about my rosebush. Want to come?"

"That sounds like a great idea. What's your favorite book?"

Perky scrunched up her nose. "Don't you know? The Bible, of course. I have a Bible that's just like a storybook, and I'm reading it straight through from the front to the back. It's blue. What's your favorite book?"

"Well, the Bible, too." As she said the words, Marah realized how often in the past she had chosen to bypass a daily quiet time of reading and prayer. But lately, here on the farm, she had found herself drawn often to the small Bible she'd bought in the same shop in town where Judd had purchased his. Though she used to spend what little free time she had reading best-sellers, Marah realized that these days, given a spare hour or two to climb a tree and read a favorite book, she might very likely choose the Bible.

She took a seat on the edge of the porch as Judd sauntered over with a plate of barbecued beans and a couple of hot dogs piled high with relish and mustard. She hadn't wanted to see him, had hoped he might just stay gone. But now, here he was again, looking good in his blue jeans and denim shirt.

"Looks like I made it back just in time," he said.

"I guess so."

He sat down beside Marah. "I don't know how you could have let that rain fall on the hay, though. A batch of wet hay and the whole farm goes south."

She laughed. "It's good to have you back, Judd."

"Good to be back."

He fell silent as he chased baked beans across his paper plate. Marah studied the gathering of farmers, most of whom she recognized from picnics long ago. Familiar faces, older now, weathered by sun and wind and the pain of life. Among them were many of her family's close friends: the Hollanders, the Johnsons, the McLeods.

"Hey, Perky, where's your Aunt Barbara?" Marah asked, recalling the striking blonde who sometimes passed through Kansas on the way between her homes in New York and Los Angeles. "She always used to come to the picnic."

"She's Daddy's aunt, not mine," Perky said, her voice tight.

"I thought you liked Aunt Barb."

"No." Perky looked away. "She was a troublemaker. She made my daddy cry."

"Aunt Barb? She brought those expensive candy bars to the picnic every year. She was always giving out presents. I thought everybody liked her."

"No," Perky repeated. Her small brow furrowed. "After she left and Daddy cried, Grandma and Grandpa said Aunt Barb would never be invited back to the picnic. And she wasn't. So that's that."

"I guess it is." Marah glanced at Judd. His focus was on Milton Gregory and his two colleagues just arriving for the picnic in their gray van.

Perky followed the direction of their gaze. "There they are," she said. "Those stinkers."

"Perky!" Marah couldn't suppress a giggle. "What a thing to say."

"It's true. Haven't you smelled them? They stink, especially Dr. Gregory. I don't like him."

"You just don't like his sunglasses. They make him look different. You should never judge people by their appearance, Perky."

"Or their odor," Judd added.

Marah could see the grin tugging at his lips. "You're no help," she said.

"You haven't smelled the bunkhouse lately."

"What's going on over there anyhow? I went to find Milton the other day, and he had the loft room all locked up. And now that I think about it, the place did smell funny."

"Not funny," Perky said. "Rotten."

"They must be using a strongly odored chemical in their work," Marah continued. "Milton told me they're doing some specialized things to the remains. They have to preserve the mummies in order to transport them to the Osage tribe in Oklahoma."

"When did you talk to him?" Judd asked.

"Tuesday, I think. I went over to invite his team to the

picnic. You know, I was really pleased to hear how seriously they're taking their work. The Indians they've found have been dead more than a hundred years, but their descendants are alive, and they demand respect. It's almost like preparing a body for a funeral."

"Did he tell you how many bodies they've found?"

"No, but Mike and Bob were carrying three boxes." She paused, thinking. "Of course, those boxes were too small to have contained a whole mummy. I wonder what was in them."

"Did you notice anything in the lab?"

"The same kind of things I spotted in the tent. Microscope, flasks, petri dishes. There was some kind of a metal container." She thought again, searching her mind to identify the image. "That's it! It was a biohazard hood. I saw one in a lab once when I was in medical school, but I never used it. This one looked homemade—a metal box, a glass window, and a couple of armholes. But I'm sure that's what it was. A biohazard hood."

"Biohazard," he repeated.

"I wouldn't worry about it. It's probably standard equipment." She remembered Judd's concerns over the possibility of catching something from the mummy. "Listen, I need to tell Pete to get those sodas out of the pickup. You want to help?"

He was eating the last of his second hot dog. "Just a sec," he said. "Perk, don't forget our plan now. First thing tomorrow morning, we'll head over to Mrs. Morgan's rose garden and plant Pink Pearl."

Perky grinned. "A tea rose. And Dr. Morgan and I are going to have tea tomorrow, aren't we?"

"We sure are. Right after supper—you and me. And don't forget that blue book."

"What blue book?" Judd asked as he accompanied Marah toward the tree where her father stood chatting with Pete Harris.

"The Bible," she said. "It's Perky's favorite. How about you? Been reading that one you bought?"

"Now and then." He tossed his paper plate into a trash can fitted with a black plastic sack. "That Jesus was an amazing guy. If you believe what they wrote about him."

"Do you believe it?"

He shrugged. "I'd like to. But walking on water? Raising the dead? It's a lot to swallow."

Marah didn't know how much more to say. She was reluctant to reawaken the intimacy they had shared. If they spoke about serious issues again, things that were deep in their hearts, she might find herself wanting to spend more time with this man. She couldn't afford the risk. On the other hand, she had been praying for Judd. "Knowing that Dr. Jordan was a Christian has helped me a lot in coming to terms with his death," she said. "How about your friend? Was he a believer?"

"Chuck? I don't know. We never talked about religion. It didn't seem important, you know."

"I know. But it is."

"Yeah." He swallowed and shoved his hands into his pockets.

Marah sensed he was struggling with something, wanting to ask her about the something that concerned him. But he pushed it down, and she could almost see him drawing a mask of lightheartedness over his face.

"Hey, Pete, we've got trouble here," Judd called across the lawn. When the young farmer looked over, Judd pointed a thumb at Marah. "She wants to put us to work unloading sodas from her pickup."

"Oh no, not that!" Pete had one arm draped around Ed Morgan's shoulders. "Not sodas."

"I'm not surprised." Resting his weight on his walker, Ed eyed his daughter. "She was always trouble, that one. Well, go on, boys. You'd better do as she said. You never want to mess with a daughter of mine, that's for sure."

As the two men walked away, Marah strolled over to her father. "It's good to see you out and about," she said. "Looks like we're going to have a crowd."

"We always have a crowd."

"Perky said Pete's Aunt Barbara doesn't come anymore. She told me Aunt Barb once made Pete cry. Do you have any idea what that was all about?"

"No, and don't ever mention that woman's name around me again, you hear?" He gave her a look that would have wilted Perky's roses to the ground. "Well, there's Jimmy Johnson and his wife. I'd better go say hello."

15

"Can I sit on your lap?"

Before Judd could react, Perky plopped down, stretched out her skinny legs, and leaned back against his chest. He was seated under a tree near the blanket where Marah, Pete Harris, and some of the other farmers had gathered. Judd had told himself he didn't want to get involved in their conversation because he needed to keep an eye on Milton Gregory. But it was more than that. The scene around him—families gathered, children playing, grandparents chatting—felt foreign and somehow painful.

"I hate baked beans," Perky announced. "It's like green eggs and ham. I hate them in a barn. I hate them, hate them on a farm. I do not like baked beans and ham. I do not like them, Sam-I-Am."

Judd chuckled. "Have you tried baked beans, Perk?"

"They're brown."

Judd smiled as he looked down at the little girl's small head and the neat part that ran through her golden hair. Perky was real and honest. With her child's eyes she could probably see right through Gregory's silvered sunglasses.

"Do *you* like baked beans?" Perky asked Judd.

"Sure do. But I hate okra."

"Yuck. I don't even know what it is, but I hate it, too. It sounds nasty. If you ever get a wife, you better tell her not to cook okra."

"I'll do that."

Judd thought of Marianne and instantly wished he hadn't. He'd heard she had been married twice since their divorce. Had three or four kids now. She'd never been much of a cook, but that's not why he'd married her. Their marriage had been based on sex more than anything. It brought them together and kept them together. But it didn't last. Once Judd left for the Persian Gulf, Marianne moved on. Sex hadn't built a strong foundation for their marriage. He wasn't sure what would have.

"Your parents have been married a long time, haven't they, Perk?" he said. "What do you think keeps them going?"

"God," she said instantly. "That's what they told me. God is the glue of our family. He holds us together. We've asked him to be with us through all of our lost babies and through all of our fun times, too."

"So, it's going to church together, that kind of thing?"

"No, it's God, just him. Church is just where we go to

worship him with all our friends. But Jesus lives in our family every day."

"I guess God would be a pretty strong foundation for a marriage."

"Are you going to get married, Judd?"

"Me? No. I doubt it."

"Why not? Are you already married? Did you get married before?"

"You're sure being nosy today."

"Well?"

"Yes, I got married once. I've been divorced a long time."

Perky tilted her head. "You must be so sad."

Her words hit Judd in the heart like a sledgehammer. Sad? No, he hadn't let himself feel sorrow. Anger, yes. Rage. Fury. Revenge. He had channeled all of it into his work. But now, with Pearl Kathleen Harris gazing up at him with her big blue eyes, all he could feel was sadness. He had no wife. No children. No home. No future. He was empty and hollow and completely alone.

"Don't cry," she said, reaching up to touch his cheek with her small hand.

He drew back. "I'm not crying."

"Yes, you are. I can see it. Your face is crying." She turned around, wrapped her arms around him, and rested her cheek against his chest. "You're lonely."

"No, I'm not. I'm fine." But he could feel a lump moving up

his throat. "Hey, Perk, you'd better go see if your mom needs a refill on her lemonade."

Perky lifted her head. "I love you," she said.

She climbed off his lap and darted past the folding table loaded with sodas and lemonade. Judd watched her braids fly as she scampered up onto the porch to fetch her mother's empty glass.

The child loved him.

Was she the only one? Once he'd been so sure of Marianne's love. Hadn't they said the words again and again? Maybe the loss of that love was the cause of the emptiness he felt. Maybe he should try to fill the space with someone else.

Judd looked across the lawn at Marah Morgan. She was laughing at something Pete Harris had told her. Head thrown back, she looked so alive, so beautiful. Could Marah be the answer he was looking for? Should he ask her out, date her, maybe even marry her? The thought intrigued him. A home, children, even church and God thrown into the mix. All the things that Perky's parents brought to their marriage. He could do that with Marah. One day he would be just like Chuck— showing off his kids' school pictures, bragging about his wife's talents. . . .

Chuck was dead.

Marah could die. Their children could die, as Pete Harris's babies had been lost one by one. People couldn't be counted on to stick around. They were unreliable. And then what? Even if Judd won Marah's heart, he might lose her someday. Then he'd be empty all over again.

As he watched her rise and set off for the dessert table, he knew how Marah would answer his questions. It would be the same answer Perky had given when Judd asked about her parents' long marriage.

God.

The only one to fill his emptiness was God. The only sure foundation to a happy marriage was God. The only glue to a happy family was God. The only way to survive loss was God. The only hope for life after death was God.

Judd lifted his focus to the tree branches overhead, thinking about the evil that had diseased the world around him and the good that lay waiting within his reach. Marah spoke as if talking to Christ was easy, asking for help, telling him what she needed. Why couldn't he do that?

"Apple pie?" Marah said, passing a plate under his nose. "There's nothing like a Kansas apple pie."

Startled, Judd looked down. "Whoa, I was somewhere else. What've you got there?"

She handed him the plate. "Why don't you come join us? Pete's telling stories on me. It turns out I was a really bratty little kid."

"Am I surprised?" he said, standing and following her toward the checkered tablecloth spread on the ground. "You're a bratty adult."

"Now you sound like my father."

Judd glanced across the lawn to where the farmer had joined his friends pitching washers. Milton Gregory was in the watching crowd, his hands deep in his pockets and a smile on his face. Leaning on his walker, Ed took aim with a metal washer at a can set in the ground. A clang sounded, and the men hollered their approval. Ed laughed.

"Not a bad mentor," Judd said, joining Pete and Marah on the checkered cloth.

"If you want to wind up an ornery old bull alone in the pasture," Marah commented dryly.

"Aw, your dad's not that bad," Pete said. "He's more bark than bite."

"You haven't felt his teeth."

"Well, I'll admit he's a little rough around the edges," Pete went on. "But he wasn't always that way. Back before your mom died, your dad used to come pick me up in his truck and take me swimming at the reservoir. He'd bring a picnic lunch, and we'd sing songs."

Marah's mouth fell open. "He sang?"

"Sure. I used to ask him to bring you along, but he said you were too little. He was scared you might drown."

Judd watched this information filter across Marah's face. He understood her struggle. Her father appeared to scatter his kindnesses to others—Perky Harris, Pete, his farmer friends. But with his own daughter, any tenderness remained locked deep inside.

"I've always thought it was your mom's death that changed

him," Pete said. "Ed got real hard and angry. He didn't come around to take me swimming anymore. Your mom was such a sweet woman, so patient. The guff she took from her husband would've driven most wives away, but she loved him. She'd have done anything for him."

"She couldn't do the one thing he wanted," Marah said. "Give him sons."

Pete looked away. "I guess not."

"They were unhappy together a long time before Mom died."

"Ed and Ruby? I never would have thought that."

"Pete, how did my mother die?" Marah asked. "You're older. What do you remember?"

Judd studied Pete Harris's face. The man knew something. Judd had seen the look on the face of a hundred guilty suspects. Pete knew more than he was letting on. Couldn't meet Marah's eyes. Kept his head tilted down.

"Chicken pox, wasn't it?" Pete said.

"I don't know." Marah was leaning forward, wanting more. Wanting truth. "My dad told me Mom had a rash and a fever. But I thought it might be something else. I remember things. Fighting. Something happened in the bathroom one night, and I—"

"Sometimes it's better not to know the past, Mar," Pete cut in. "If you find out too much, it can hurt. Sometimes silence is better."

Marah fiddled with the crust on her apple pie. "I used to believe that, Pete. But I'm beginning to wonder if it's right.

There are so many things I don't know. What were my parents fighting about? How did my mother die? What made my father so cold and angry?"

"But the truth can hurt, Marah. It can hurt real bad. So bad it's not worth knowing."

She studied her friend. "Pete, what are you trying to tell me?"

He shifted. "I guess I'm saying I don't want to see you suffer, Mar. You've always been a good friend. If I could talk you into letting go of the past, I would. I dug around in my own life, and I didn't like what I found. You might not like the truth either."

"What did you find?"

"Things I wish I didn't know."

She appeared to mull this over for a moment. "But I feel like I *need* to know," she went on. "I've prayed until I'm blue in the face about this, and I can't seem to figure out how to forgive my father. Maybe it's because he hasn't asked for forgiveness. Or maybe it's because I don't know what to forgive him for. Or maybe it's just because everything is so buried, so hidden behind gruffness and animosity—"

"Or maybe you just ought to drop it."

"But how? How can I do that?"

She looked at Judd as though he would know the answer. But he hadn't had any success at forgiving Marianne for walking out on him. And he wasn't about to forgive Milton Gregory for murdering Chuck. "Don't ask me," he said. "I guess I'm in the same school as Ed. Push it down deep, cover it up, and keep everybody at arm's length."

Marah let out a breath. "And then what are you left with? Nothing. Nobody to love, nobody to be with. Emptiness. I'm tired of it. I can't go on this way. I finally realized what has to happen. I've either got to forgive my father or turn the opposite way."

"What're you talking about now, Mar?" Pete asked, his eyes filled with concern. "If you can't drop it and you can't forgive, then what are you going to do? What's the opposite of forgiveness?"

Judd watched Milton Gregory walking toward the dessert table. "Revenge," he said. "The opposite of forgiveness is revenge."

🐾 🐾 🐾

"I'll settle him in," Marah called back through the pickup window. Judd nodded, tipped his hat, and drove off toward the bunkhouse. In the rush of preparing for the picnic, she never had gotten around to asking Milton Gregory to the movies. Now she was glad. Not only had she been preoccupied with her father's needs that afternoon, but she had enjoyed Judd's company so much. Though she was determined to maintain a friendly distance from him, she didn't exactly want him watching her drive off to town with the archaeologist. He might think there was something going on between them, and Marah didn't want to foster that illusion.

"You make me sound like a kid," Ed told his daughter. He

rammed his walker's wheels over hummocks of green grass as he made his way toward the old rock house. "I can settle myself in just fine."

"I know you can." Marah took the walker in one hand as her father leaned on her for support to climb the back porch steps. "But it won't hurt to let me help you just this once. It's late and you're tired."

"I'm not tired. I'm fit as a fiddle, if you'd just leave me be." He retrieved his walker and pushed it toward the door. The low threshold stopped him, and he worked at lifting the wheels over it. Marah stood back, her heart aching for him.

Her father didn't want to admit defeat, yet it was obvious that his health had deteriorated since his fall. Instead of gaining independence from the walker, he had come to rely on it. Rather than building up his strength, his muscles had atrophied from the hours he spent on the back porch whittling. He didn't eat right. He rarely took a bath. And his clothing was in need of washing. But how could Marah reach out to him when he always pushed her away?

"Beans!" he grunted. "You'd think I'd run into a cattle guard here. Help me get over this bump, girl."

Marah put one arm around her father's broad back and set her other hand on his walker. She could feel the ribs through his overalls. As she lifted the walker's wheels over the threshold, she heard him grunt.

"Something like this happens to a man, and he'd be better off kicking the bucket," he said. Wheezing, he shuffled over to a kitchen chair and fell into it. "One minute you're up in the barn, strong enough to lift an eighty-pound bale of hay. And then, with one little snap of twine, you're down and out. Get me some ice cream, girl, before I keel over. And don't forget the Hershey's."

Marah pressed her lips together to keep from responding inappropriately to his barked command. As she walked toward the refrigerator, her father caught her fingers. "Fix yourself a bowl, too. It'll do you good."

"Thanks." Marah looked down at their entwined hands for a moment.

Trying to ignore the unwashed dishes in the sink and the open boxes of cereal on the counter, Marah rummaged in a cabinet for two clean bowls. She rinsed a couple of spoons, dug two helpings of chocolate ice cream from the carton, and poured on the syrup.

Her father pulled out his whittling knife and began to clean his fingernails.

Was she wrong to want to move this man to a retirement center? Marah wondered. He needed to stay as active as possible. But he couldn't look after himself. When she left for St. Louis, what would become of him? He couldn't prepare the fields for the coming year. He wouldn't be able to chop wood for his fireplace this winter. He ate mostly bread and milk. And what if he needed a doctor? Her father kept his phone off the hook most of the time, and he rarely paid his bill. Service had been shut off twice since she'd arrived.

"Dad?" She touched his arm. He smelled musty and old. "I've got your ice cream here."

"Oh." Glancing up, he took the bowl and began to stir the syrup into the ice cream. Sucking on a spoonful, he asked, "How about that apple pie today at Pete's picnic? I've always been a pie man, myself. Your mother could make pies better than anybody I ever met in my life. Sometimes I'd bring in a hatful of fruit—gooseberries, you know, or peaches—and I'd say, 'Ruby, how about you make me up a pie?' Sure enough, I'd come in from work that evening, and there'd be a big old pie cooling on the windowsill smelling like heaven itself."

"I remember Mom would always bring you pie at night after Deborah and the twins went to bed. You'd be stretched out on the couch, and she would come in with a tray."

"Now, how'd you know that, girl? You were supposed to be sleeping same as your sisters."

"The heat register." She felt embarrassed suddenly. "It's in the floor. I could see you and Mom eating pie."

"Well, beans. A little spy. I should have figured you'd be the one."

Marah put a spoonful of ice cream in her mouth, wondering if she had the courage to bring up the subject of her mother's death again. She had learned little from the medical records that Dr. Benson had given her. Pete and the other neighbors would repeat the chicken pox theory. But Ed Morgan knew more than he had told Marah.

"I could see the bathroom through the other heat register," she ventured. "The bathtub, anyway."

His head came up, blue eyes narrowing. "Did you watch me taking a bath?"

"No, no. Of course not."

"Better not. I'd tan your hide for it, girl, and I don't care how old you are." He frowned as he sucked on another spoonful. "What did you want to go spying on the family for anyhow?"

"I was a kid. I guess it seemed like fun."

"Fun." He gave a snort.

"Except for one time. It was the afternoon Mom died."

The blue eyes pinned her. "What did you see in there?"

"I don't remember it very well."

"Good thing. Lay it to rest."

"Mom was crying." Marah lifted her eyes to the corner of the ceiling, focusing on her memories. "I remember how red her skin was. It scared me. She ran the tub full of water and—"

"Leave it be, girl. It's over and done with."

"But I want to know. I need to understand what happened. Mom was alive, and then she was dead. I remember I came running down the stairs, and you were carrying her out of the bathroom. And you told me she was dead. She died in the bathtub?"

"I don't remember it too clear. It was a long time ago."

"But you went into the bathroom with her, didn't you?" She could see the curling lines of the heat register in her mind.

"Mom was screaming. I wanted to run to her, but you were in there. You were with her, weren't you?"

Ed pushed his bowl of ice cream aside. "She called for me. She wanted me."

"Why? The two of you had been fighting and arguing for months. Why did she call for you?"

"I don't know. Beans, girl, she was sick."

"You leaned over the bathtub. I remember I could see your overall straps. Mom was splashing and screaming, wasn't she? And then . . ." Marah searched her memory. For the first time, she actually saw the image from the past. "I must have left the room to run down the stairs. That's when I saw you carrying her."

A sudden, horrifying thought hit her. She focused on her father again. "Did you do something to Mom?"

"Do something to her? Like what?"

"Like . . . did you hurt her? Did she drown?"

"Where in the cat hair would you get an idea like that?" He slapped his palms on the table and pushed himself up. "Of course not."

"It just came to me. She was in the tub, and she was scream- ing and splashing. And you were with her. And then she was dead."

He grabbed his walker and pushed it across the room toward the living room. "She died, plain and simple. Died right there in the bathtub."

"But you told me it was your fault. You said you were responsible for Mom's death." Marah was on her feet now, her heart hammering. "Was it your fault?"

For a moment Ed said nothing. Then he spoke in a low voice. "I reckon maybe it was."

Marah covered her mouth with her hand, afraid she was going to be sick. "Oh, God, please help me."

"It was my fault," he said, turning to face her. "But not the way you think."

"What do you mean by that?"

"I didn't drown your mother. She was sick and hot that afternoon. She could barely get around, and she was starting to break out in hives all over the place. She ran herself a cold bath and climbed in. And right about then, she went to hollering."

"Hollering?"

"Screaming. Crying out that she was dying." He sank down on a kitchen chair by the door and hung his head. "I'd come in from the field to put my feet up for a minute. Been plowing, you know. September."

Marah nodded. Her thoughts whirled even as she tried to concentrate. September was the month Mom had died—that had been in the doctor's records.

"I heard Ruby hollering," he said, "and I ran into the bathroom to check on her. She was writhing around like a shot rattler. I tried to calm her down, took her arms, held her hands. She kept screaming that something was eating her from the inside. I figured I'd better get her out of the tub, so I put my hands under her, and that's when she went limp."

"What do you mean she went limp?"

"Just like that. Stopped screaming, dropped her head back, rolled her eyes up till there was nothing but white. Limp as a dishrag." He was picking at a callus on his palm. "I called her name, but she didn't say a thing."

"Didn't you check her vitals?"

"I listened for her heart. I couldn't hear the beat. So I carried her out of the bathroom, put her on the bed, and called into town for Doc Benson. It was too late, of course, and I knew it. Might have been a heart attack, he said. Or maybe a stroke. We had her funeral three days later."

Marah stared at him. "You told me you did it. Now you're telling me it might have been a heart attack?"

"It was my fault she died." He looked away. "I know the fever did her in, but I was the one that killed her."

"What do you mean?"

"I didn't take her to see Doc Benson but one time after she got sick," he said. "Didn't hold to doctoring. My mama always treated us kids, and we got through just fine. The doc wanted to see your mother again, but I wouldn't drive her to town. Couldn't see the point."

"So you blame yourself?"

He let out a breath. "I *am* to blame. Not just for keeping her home, but for other things, too. The fighting, like you said. The arguing. It tore her down. Broke her spirit the way nothing else could. She might have died of the fever, but it was me that killed her."

Marah tried to comprehend what he was telling her, but she couldn't get past the image of her mother's body lying in this man's arms, a trail of water dripping from her hair as he carried her from the bathroom.

"You were angry with her?" she said.

"The other way around." He made as if to rise. Then he fell back onto the chair. "She was mad at me for what I did to her."

"What did you do?"

"I don't figure you need to know everything, Miss Nosy." His voice grew stronger. "There's some things ought to be kept from children."

"Is that right?" Marah could feel the anger rise like a tidal wave inside her chest. "Well, I'm not a child anymore, and this has affected my entire life. Mom's death changed my world. When she died, I lost my childhood, and if you're responsible, I think I deserve to know how."

"And maybe there's things you're better off not knowing. Ever thought about that?"

"That's what Pete said at the picnic."

"Pete? What did he tell you about all this?"

"Nothing. He told me to leave the past buried. He said sometimes silence is better. Well, I've done that for too many years. I've been so angry at you I can hardly function when you're around. I'm beginning to think silence can be dangerous."

"Because you thought I drowned your mother?"

"Because you resented me for not being a boy. Because you forced me to take care of my sisters when Mom died. Because you never hugged me or held me in your lap or called me anything but 'girl.' My name is Marah. I'm your daughter."

"I know who you are."

"I don't think you know me any better than I know you. What did you do to Mom? How did you hurt her?"

"Barbara," he said. "There, you whipped it out of me. Now you'll have to live with it, same as me and Pete and everybody else."

"Barbara?" She tried to clear her thoughts. "Pete's Aunt Barbara?"

"She's the one."

"You had an affair with her?"

"Not like that. It wasn't ugly and dirty the way you think." He studied the floor. "I loved Barbara Harris."

"But you were married to Mom!"

"Before your mother, I loved Barb. We were sweethearts in school. I took her to the eighth grade graduation dance. Then we courted all through high school. But we had to slip around to do it, because her folks didn't like me. Doc Harris was rich and city educated, you know. I was just a farm boy."

"I don't remember a Dr. Harris."

"He was before Doc Benson. The Harris family moved out of town about the time everything went to pieces."

Marah let out a breath. "What happened?"

"She got pregnant. So, now you know."

"But Barbara never had children with her when she came for the harvest picnics."

"She gave the baby away. Adoption, that's what her parents had her do. I didn't know anything about the baby until later."

"Are you saying I have a half sister somewhere?"

"Brother," he said. "Pete Harris is your half brother."

16

Milton Gregory had hated the picnic. The cozy cama-
raderie, the playing children and chattering grandmas.
They reminded him of things he'd wished for long
ago. Once upon a time, he had imagined himself as a
daddy with children on his knee. Even when things
had grown difficult at home, when his father fled and
his mother was sent away to a place that might have
been a prison or a hospital or something of both,
Gregory had cherished his little dream of happiness.

He could still conjure it up now as he waited
outside the bunkhouse for Judd to return from the
picnic. And he had tried his best to make that
dream come true. His intellectual brilliance had
carried him through high school, college, and medical school. His professional drive had earned him a
palatial home perched high above the surf of
Laguna Beach. His position in society had garnered

him first one wife and then another. But the dream never came true.

His wives weren't kind and thoughtful and loving. They spent his money and had affairs, and finally they laughed as they walked away with their divorce settlements. There had been no children. No romping dogs. No chuckling grandpas or warm-lapped grandmas. So he had given himself completely to his work, to saving the beautiful women from their predicaments. They had become his family . . . until that one. The betrayer.

Gregory had been operating a successful private abortion clinic. Very discreet. Often he was called upon to perform delicate work in order to protect the best interests of his patients. They trusted him, and he bettered their lives. Until one day.

Reliving the memory, Gregory began to pace. It was her third time to come to him. She had allowed her problem to advance beyond the proper time for correction, of course. They often did. This woman was flighty and silly, a starlet who had made a few unnoticed films and commercials. She was ambitious for the top and happy to use her body as a means of barter. And so she kept finding herself in trouble.

Gregory had always believed a woman ought to have the right to choose what she did with her body. And so he removed his patient's "problem," just as he had before.

But that time she happened to see it lying on the delivery table afterward. He hadn't had ample time to dispose of it, and so it was, unfortunately, still alive. He severed the head neatly, yet for reasons he couldn't fathom, his patient went berserk. The clinic was forced to rush her to a city hospital, where she blubbered her experience to everyone who came within shouting distance.

Gregory's practice had been closed immediately, his records seized, and his devoted clientele had abandoned him en masse. Eventually, his license to practice medicine had been stripped away, and he was left friendless and all but penniless. The government had destroyed him.

Feeling the sour taste of bitterness rise in his mouth, Gregory spat on the ground. It wouldn't be long until the enemy was defeated. His latest cultures showed a greater volume of virus particles than he had managed to cultivate in any of his previous attempts. Vials waited now in refrigeration for him to begin the process of concentrating the virus. With the ultracentrifuge, he hoped to be able to spin down the samples so that his entire inventory would fit into four small test tubes. These he would drive to Washington, where they would be put to their awaited task.

"Hey there, Dr. G." Judd's voice startled him as the man strode out of the darkness. "I figured you'd be conked out after all that barbecue you ate."

Gregory forced a smile to his lips. "You noticed."

"I had four hot dogs myself. Forgot how good they taste when you eat them outdoors." Judd stretched. "Well, I guess I'm going to head into town and catch the late show."

"As always," the physician said. "It's gotten to be a regular habit, hasn't it? There must be something special about a Sunday night movie."

"Kind of stretches out the weekend for me."

"I guess so."

"Like to come along?"

"No, thanks. I have some work to do in the lab." Gregory hadn't given Judd's movie habit much thought until lately. Now he surmised the man went to town to make contact with his superior.

"Enjoy yourself," he called as Judd headed for his battered green pickup. Habits, he thought, were never wise.

🐾 🐾 🐾

Marah stared at her father across the kitchen. "Pete Harris is my half brother?"

"That's what I said, isn't it?"

"How did you find out you had a son?"

"Barbara came back to Kansas. It all happened when you were a little kid. She'd been living over in New York or some-place." He snorted. "Doc Harris was rich, like I told you. Big, rich doctor, making his living off folks almost too sick and poor to pay. You know how much he'd charge for a call? Thirty bucks. Thirty dollars just to take a look at a man and tell him to go take some aspirin. And he wouldn't come out to visit, no sir. A person would have to haul his aching backside into that office and sit for a couple hours until—"

"So, Barbara Harris came back to Kansas for a visit and told you about Pete."

Her father nodded. "After he was born, he was adopted by her older brother and his wife who couldn't have kids. By that time, I was off in Korea getting blown to pieces. I didn't have a clue where Barb had gone, just that she'd left me without so much as a fare-thee-well. When I got back to Kansas and was recovered enough to start living again, I heard about the next-farm-over Harrises adopting a boy. I never made the connection that it had anything to do with Barb or me. Good people, those Harrises. They didn't put on airs. No, sir, they raised Pete right. I was proud to find out he was my son."

Marah felt the old jealousy and hurt rise up inside her. "If Pete's the son you've always wanted, why didn't you call *him* when you fell off the loft? Why don't you give your land to *him?*"

"He doesn't want it. Too much for one man to farm. Besides, he didn't take kindly to learning the truth about his 'Aunt Barbara' being his mother. Matter of fact, it upset him real bad. He's loyal to his folks. He didn't find out about the adoption till years down the road, after he was already married and had Perky."

"Barbara told him, too?"

"She came back again for one of the picnics and decided to spill the beans."

"Did she tell Mom about it? Years before? Was that why the two of you fought so much right before her death?"

"No, that wasn't it." He hung his head and turned a screw on his walker. "Ruby knew about me and Barb Harris all along.

Everybody in school knew we were a twosome. And most folks guessed that when Doc Harris up and moved his family, something was going on. I was the only one in the dark, too lovesick over losing Barb to figure out why her daddy had carted her off. Before your mother and I ever married, she told me she thought Barb had gotten pregnant by me. She figured Doc Harris had moved his daughter away so she could have an abortion or give birth in secret. And it didn't surprise her too much when she found out the truth about Pete." He heaved a deep sigh. "No, your mother was angry about something else."

"Tell me."

"Why?" His head snapped up. "It's none of your business."

"It *is* my business. I deserve to know what was going on."

"You don't deserve anything. You were just a puny kid spying on your parents through the heat register." He stood. "All right, smarty. I'll tell you. Then you can live with it eating up your guts the way it ate your mother's and mine, too. Is that what you want?"

"I want the truth."

"Fine. When Barb came back to town and told me Pete was my son, she and I took up again. I'd never stopped loving her, or her me. So we started slipping around together just the way we had back in high school."

"Only this time, you were married."

"Yes, I was, and I knew I was doing your mother wrong. But I loved Barbara."

"And she'd given you a son."

"That didn't have anything to do with it! Pete wasn't hers or mine either. He belonged to his own parents. It was just Barb and me, the bond between us."

"You didn't love Mom?"

"I loved Ruby all right. Took good care of her. Did my part."

"Did your part to have an affair and destroy the little bit of happiness she'd ever known!"

"I did love your mother whether you want to believe it or not!" he shouted. "But I'd have married Barb years before if her daddy hadn't taken her away. She and I were meant to be together. And your mother, well, Ruby was just . . . she was my second choice."

"But she loved you! She gave her whole life to you! She did everything she could to give you sons. And you kept your heart from her because you never could forget Barbara Harris."

"Well, what of it?"

Unable to answer, she started for the back door, wanting nothing more than to get out of this place, get away from him. Stopping abruptly, she whirled around and faced him again, trying to form the words. She had always wanted his love, but he never had it to give. His heart was filled with passion for a woman he could never have. And his family died right in front of him because of his selfishness.

She spat the words at him. "I hate you."

As she started toward the back porch, the telephone rang in the living room. She hesitated a moment, aware that her father wouldn't answer it. She knew him well now. Knew all there was to know.

"You going to get that?" he said.

She looked across at him, saw him crumpled there on the chair. He was old and used up. With the phone jangling inside her head, she felt herself set apart from her father for the first time. Completely separate. She turned and walked back through the kitchen. The phone was in its usual place under a pile of cushions on the couch. She knew exactly where to find it, and she lifted the receiver.

"Ed?" someone said, his voice breathless.

"This is his daughter, Dr. Morgan."

"Oh, Marah, hey. This is Sheriff Dawson. Listen, you got a fellow working for you that drives a green pickup?"

A prickle ran down Marah's spine. "Judd."

"I have to tell you, there's been an accident out here on the main road. Well, the truck just flat blew up, is what happened."

"Blew up?"

"Best we can figure. No one saw it happen, but when some folks came along heading for church, they spotted the pickup on its side over in a field."

"Judd?"

"He didn't make it, Miss Morgan. I'm sorry to tell you that. The truck burned to a cinder. You might better come on down the road toward town, if you wouldn't mind. We're cleaning up. I'd like to talk to you for a couple minutes."

Marah set the receiver down and looked at her father. "It was the sheriff," she said. "Judd is dead."

17

Marah pulled her BMW to a stop beside the old white house and leaned her forehead on the steering wheel. It had been horrible. Judd's truck was almost unrecognizable, a mangled hunk of charred metal lying in a pasture. The tires had melted. The seat on which she'd ridden to town blowing bubble gum was gone. The glass had exploded from the windshield, and shards covered the ground.

Officials hadn't been able to identify any victims. Marah could see it would be nearly impossible. The whole inside of the cab was burned and twisted. Even though she'd been at the site more than an hour, the vehicle remained too hot to touch. The sheriff wondered if the body was even in the pickup. He surmised the driver might have been blown out through the window in the explosion. Though it was dark, the deputies were planning a thorough search of the field surrounding the vehicle.

What had caused such an explosion? everyone wondered. Marah had told the sheriff that the pickup had been in terrible shape, falling apart at the seams. But such a powerful blast? How had it happened? Sheriff Dawson couldn't figure it out, but he promised he'd get to the bottom of it.

Marah lifted her head and stared at the barn in the distance. She couldn't believe Judd was dead. Couldn't accept the truth of it. And yet she couldn't deny it either. He was gone. She would never see him again, never watch that slow, lazy smile, those intense brown eyes, those callused fingers. He wouldn't come sauntering across a pasture toward her and take off his hat as though he were an old-time cowboy and she a pretty young miss. He wouldn't dig gardens with Perky anymore. Or stomp his feet on the porch to knock the mud off his boots. Or take Ed out into the fields to check his wheat. Or rub Gypsy between the ears.

They would have to locate Judd's mother, Marah thought as she slipped out of her car. He had said she wasn't in good health. Where did she live? Arizona? Or was it Wyoming? Walking toward her house, she realized she couldn't even remember his last name. Had he ever told her? He had insisted that she didn't really even know him, and maybe he was right. But she did know him, too—knew so many small things about him. She would miss them all, each tiny detail.

She went into the white house and filled the teakettle.

Unable to keep images of the mangled pickup out of her mind, Marah boiled the water and made herself a cup of hot tea. As she stirred in milk and sugar, she thought back on some of the conversations she'd had with Judd. How had he managed to get to the heart of things so well? He was a man of few words, a man who hoarded his smiles. His emotions were tightly wrapped inside him. And yet he knew what she needed. Knew what to say to her. He had challenged her and encouraged her. More than that, he had *interested* her. Oh, she would miss him.

Wandering out onto the back porch, she sipped the tea, grateful for its soothing warmth. She settled into an old wicker chair and leaned her head back against the faded cushions. An enormous sense of loss filled her, welling up inside like the steam from the kettle of water she had just boiled. It was a pressure she almost couldn't bear. Judd was gone. So was her mother. The vague but persistent mental image of a loving daddy had vanished, too, in the wake of her father's confession. Marah thought of her sisters and how they had rushed off to make their own lives away from the farm. Did they sometimes wish for a loving, supportive father? Or had they given up on that dream?

Deborah had found a husband. And Sarah and Leah were active in the army—their own sort of authoritative yet nurturing father. Marah wondered if she would ever find someone she could love—truly love—with a real, abiding, wholehearted passion. The image of Judd filtered through her mind, and she knew he might have become such a man to her one day. Now she would finish her work on the farm, settle her father someplace where he could be safe, and return to St. Louis. Her patients needed her. And she needed them.

As she set her teacup on the table beside her chair, Marah noticed a shadow moving near the barn. A breath caught in her throat as she reached out for the wooden support post. Judd? Of course not. Maybe it was one of Milton's men. Maybe it was the same person who had been down in her cellar the day of the storm. Someone sneaking around, looking in the barn for something to steal.

Her sorrow transforming into indignation, Marah set out across the yard. Well, she would confront the intruder this time. She would flip on the light, look straight into his eyes, and demand to know what he was doing in her barn.

But as she stepped inside the barn, she heard a gurgle. "Who's there?" Her voice echoed through the cavernous rafters. Her heart pounding, she felt for the switch. When she turned on the light, she had to blink for a moment in the brightness.

And then she saw him. "Oh, Judd!"

Bloody, his clothing tattered and burned, he had curled up in a far corner of the barn. Marah raced to him and fell to her knees. Then she rolled him over onto his back, felt for a pulse, listened for his breathing.

Years of medical training kicked into gear as she assessed his injuries. His breath was labored but steady. His pulse was weak, though, and Marah knew he was bleeding badly. She noted lacerations on his face, but none of them seemed too serious. A long gash ran down the side of his arm, cutting through muscle and sinew. She checked for arterial bleeding and found none. Both his shoes had come off, and the soles of his feet were raw.

"Marah," he muttered, grabbing her hand. "Turn . . . light off."

"What?" She looked into his face again, trying to comprehend. How could she see anything with the light off? She needed help here. She needed a paramedic, an ambulance, a hospital. But would her father hear her cries this far from the house?

"Light," he managed through bloody lips. "Off."

"I'm not turning the light off, Judd. I won't be able to see. Your arm is completely—"

"Light!" he barked, gripping her wrist hard. "Off!"

"OK!" She got to her feet and hurried across to the switch. As she reached for it, a second dark figure caught the corner of her eye. Someone moving across the yard.

"Girl?" Ed Morgan's voice drifted in the night air. "You back from town? I want to know what the sheriff said about that boy. And I'm not done talking to you either—"

"Dad!" Marah shouted, almost screamed the word. "Here in the barn! I need you."

"Well, dog my cats, girl! What're you doing in there?"

"Get in here quickly."

"Hold your horses, would you? This walker isn't worth a plug nickel in the mud. I heard your car drive up, and I thought you were at the white house."

"It's Judd. He's hurt."

"Hurt? I thought you said he was dead, girl. What's going on in there?" Ed muscled his walker across the yard until he reached his daughter. "Beans, girl . . ."

"He's alive, but he's bleeding and burned," Marah said. "I've got to get him into the house."

"He looks just the way I did that day in Korea. Looks like a mortar got him."

"A mortar?" She tried to reconcile the image of this vital man lying here in his own blood with the current reality of her father, bent and gnarled, a shell of a human. "I don't know what happened, but I've got to get him to a hospital."

"No hospital," Judd mouthed, grabbing her wrist again.

"You have a lot of injuries, Judd." Softening her voice, she brushed back the hair from his forehead. "Some of them are significant. I need to get you some professional care. As soon as we can move you out of here, I'll call an ambulance. And then I'll contact the sheriff."

"No." He squeezed her wrist. "No sheriff."

"But he thinks you're dead. His deputies are out there right now combing that pasture—" At the sight of his distress, she shook her head. "For now, let's get you into the house." She turned to her father. "Listen, I need you to—"

"Don't look at me, girl," he cut in. "I can't do doodley."

"Head back to the rock house. Get me a bag of ice and whatever you can find in your medicine chest."

"Are you bossing me—"

"I'm telling you what I need. I need your help."

He looked into her eyes. "All right."

Marah let out her breath as he rolled his walker out of the barn. She couldn't imagine the old geezer being attractive to any woman, let alone the svelte and well-coiffured Barbara Harris.

"How are you feeling?" she asked Judd. "Are you able to breathe OK?"

"I can breathe," he whispered, running his fingers over his neck. "Can't hear much. The explosion."

"You ought to see a doctor, Judd."

"I am." His voice was all but gone, but Marah could read his lips.

"A doctor with some equipment. I don't even have a pair of gloves."

"Take me . . . house," he said with great effort. "Keep . . . voice down."

"My voice? Judd, what's going on?"

He pushed himself up off the ground as Marah supported his shoulders. "The trail," he rasped. "Cover it."

"What trail? Judd, you're not making sense." When she tried to stand, Marah realized her own legs felt like warm spaghetti. What if she hadn't seen him? What if he'd bled to death in the barn? Thank God he hadn't been hurt worse. Thank God, period. It was only God's grace that had allowed Judd to live.

"Put your arm around my shoulder," she told him. "Can you walk?"

He shrugged.

"I think your shoes blew off. What on earth happened?"

"On my way . . . to town." He coughed. "Got to thinking . . . something he'd said."

"Who said?"

"Habit . . . pickup . . . driving funny."

They walked slowly to the barn door and stepped outside. Confusion gnawing at her, Marah helped Judd hobble across the muddy yard toward the old rock house. As they stepped up onto the porch, Ed opened the back door.

"Come on in, both of you," he said. "Put him down on the chair, girl. Not that one! The leg's about to fall off. Now then, let's take a look at you, Judd. Beans, you might as well be one of the boys in my patrol. Those mortars could turn a fellow into hamburger—"

"It wasn't a mortar," Marah said, turning on her father as she rummaged in the cupboard for a clean dish towel. Judd's arm needed to be bandaged as quickly as possible. "There was something wrong with his old pickup. And if you'd get the medicines—"

"Phone," Judd croaked, catching her sleeve.

"You'll have to wait. I need to work on your arm first. It's bleeding badly and—"

"Phone!" he said, clamping her arm. "Now!"

"All right." Frustration mingled with fear as she hurried into the next room and found the telephone where she had left it when she'd taken the call from the sheriff.

With effort, she untangled the long cord from the legs of the old wooden side table and carried the phone into the kitchen. Fumbling, Judd dialed a number.

"This had better be a police station somewhere," Marah said
as she wrapped the towel tightly around his arm to stop the
bleeding. "Or a hospital."

"Tell him . . . ," Judd said and handed her the receiver.

"Tell who?" She listened as a man's voice answered the phone.
"Uh, yes, this is Marah Morgan calling on behalf of Judd."

"Yes?" The man's voice was unidentifiable.

"Well, he was in an accident tonight. His pickup malfunc-
tioned. Somehow it exploded and burned, and we think—"

"Dead or alive?"

She took the receiver from her ear and spoke to Judd. "Who
is this guy?"

"Tell him," he repeated.

"He's alive. I can do some first aid, but he's not in good
shape. There'll be a lot of bruising and swelling. And I suspect
he's going to need stitches in his arm. I certainly—"

The phone went dead.

"He hung up." Marah set down the receiver. "Hung up, just
like that."

"Probably another big city doctor," Ed said. "Figures all Judd
needs is a couple of aspirin."

Marah shot her father a look. "He needs more than aspirin.
What have you found?"

As they went through the pitiful collection of ointments and
pills Ed had managed to dig out of his medicine cabinet, Marah
watched Judd stagger into the living room and stretch out on
the sofa.

"You don't have a thermometer here," she told her father.
"You don't even have any aspirin."

"So, rub some Vicks on him. Mentholatum's what my mama
always used. Worked like a charm."

"I don't believe your mother ever treated you for this kind of
an injury."

As she continued to rummage in the shoe box, Marah felt the
frustration well inside her again. Her father had had an affair with
Aunt Barbara. And Mom found out. And Pete was his son. And
Judd had nearly died. It was all too much, too awful.

"You think he's going to be all right?" Ed asked.

She nodded. "That arm needs stitches, and I don't know why
he won't let me take him to town. Dr. Benson would have
sutures. I could stitch him myself if he didn't want to see
anyone else."

"You could stitch him?"

Marah looked up in surprise at the note of admiration in her
father's voice. Whiskers covered his chin, and he smelled of
bacon grease. But his blue eyes sparkled. "Well, I guess you
could," he said. "I guess you could."

Marah let out a breath as she carried the shoe box into the
living room.

🐾 🐾 🐾

After Marah wrapped Judd's arm in some kind of gauze and put
an ice pack on it, she told him to try to sleep, but he knew he

needed to stay awake. Needed to think. He had let his guard down. Fallen right into Gregory's trap.

He could remember climbing into the pickup. Thoughts of his coming contact with headquarters had been running through his head. He hadn't paid close attention to Gregory's words. Not until he was driving. "Habit," the man had said. Judd knew habits were dangerous. Didn't have any except this one. The Sunday night drive to town to make his contact. And then he'd noticed the pickup pulling to the left a little.

He remembered pulling over, bolting from the truck, thinking he was going to die. He recalled nothing of the explosion.

Coming to, he had found himself in a stubby wheat field, choking on his own blood. Couldn't hear. Couldn't breathe. Couldn't move. But he could think. He knew Gregory had been behind it. Gregory had rigged the explosive. And Gregory would think he was dead—at least for a few hours. Knowing that each moment was precious, Judd had dragged himself back to the farm.

As he crawled across fields and under barbed-wire fences, he had thought about his mission. Thought about Milton Gregory. Thought about Marah and Ed. Thought about little Perky Harris. Thought about his past and his future. There was more to this incident than his brush with death. It was his life.

As he lay on the couch now, Judd thought of the number of times he had nearly died in the line of duty. Each time he had bounced back, full of anger and strength. Determined to tackle his next assignment with even greater gusto. Sworn to take down anyone who stood in his way.

But something had changed on that crawl back to Morgan Farm. Or maybe the change had started when he came to the farm. When he met Marah. When he started reading that little Bible he'd bought. This time, death's touch hadn't prodded him back onto his feet to fight the next battle. Instead, Judd found himself thinking beyond the Gregory case. Beyond the following project he would be handed. Beyond his chosen career, his ideals, even the past that haunted him. Far beyond such things.

"I'm going to check your arm now," Marah said, moving over to him. "I'm lifting away your ice pack."

The woman was as stubborn as her father, Judd had decided. She'd made up her mind to spend the night in Ed Morgan's living-room chair, and nothing anyone could say would change her mind. Judd didn't mind so much. He knew what a scare she'd had, finding him in the barn like that. And he knew that without Marah, he'd be a dead man. The thought sent a stabbing pain that wrenched his gut. Dead, and then what?

But he wasn't dead. He was alive. Alive, and now what?

"You're supposed to be getting some sleep," Marah murmured as she bent over him, gently lifting the gauze that wrapped his arm. "What are you thinking about?"

"I owe you," he rasped. He wondered if his ears would ever stop ringing.

"You hauled me out of the cellar, remember? I figure we're even."

"Hardly."

"Judd, what happened out on the road tonight? Pickups don't just explode like that. I really need to call Sheriff Dawson."

"No." He tried to clear his throat. It felt as though it were lined with sandpaper. "Leave . . . sheriff out."

Judd studied Marah's blue eyes, recognizing the effort it took her to try to make sense of the incident. It was time for the truth. He just hoped he could explain it clearly enough with his sandpaper throat.

"The phone call earlier," he told her. "FBI . . . agent in charge."

Marah sat back in the orange vinyl chair. "The FBI? What are you telling me?"

"I . . . work for . . . FBI. Agent Judd Hunter." He made an attempt to smile. "Surprise."

"You're FBI? Who have you been watching? Us?" She looked appalled.

"Gregory."

"What about him?" she asked. "Isn't he an anthropologist?"

"Doctor. OB-GYN. Abortions."

"So he's not with the BIA?"

Judd shook his head slowly, eyes closed.

"Then what's he doing on our farm?" She stood, her frustration building. "And don't try to hide anything from me. This has been the most horrible night of my life. I went out to your pickup, and I thought you were dead. I thought I'd never see you again. Did Milton do this to you? Judd, I want to know what those men are doing here, and I want them off this place by morning."

"Got to . . . think."

"Think? About what? You nearly died out there. Did you think about that?"

He swallowed. "Yes. Thought about it."

"Oh, I'm sorry," she said softly, sinking back into the chair. "I know you've thought about it."

He shut his eyes, wishing his arm didn't hurt so much. "Not the . . . first time."

"What do you mean?"

"Been shot before. Stabbed."

"Shot and stabbed." She repeated the words as if they were foreign.

"Goes . . . with the job."

"Judd, what happened tonight?"

"Planted something . . . in pickup. Must have . . . found out about me." He sucked down a deep breath. "I just . . . keep thinking."

"About what?"

He rubbed his temples. His head throbbed. "Death," he said. "Life. What's important."

"You're important."

He closed his eyes, wishing he knew what she meant. The only way he'd ever felt significant was through the things he'd achieved. Military prowess. The Gulf War. FBI awards. Cases he'd closed.

"Important," he repeated in his ruined voice. "My . . . great . . . accomplishments."

"Not because of your accomplishments. Because of who you are. The man you are."

"Don't know me," he said, searching her blue eyes.

"I'm not sure I know anyone as well as I thought."

"All . . . got secrets."

"Yes, but I realized earlier . . . when I thought you were gone . . . that I would miss you. And you can't miss someone you don't know."

"No," he said, "you can't."

"Here's what I do know about you. Perky's crazy about you. She's not part of your assignment. You wouldn't be spending so much time with that little girl if she hadn't come to mean something to you. And I know you haven't been faking the hard work you've done on the farm. My father has needed you, and you've been there for him. He and I both care about you. And we've talked, you and I. I've come to believe you're a man of integrity."

"Maybe," he said. "Also . . . man of sin. Done my share of that."

She reached out and took his hand. "Everyone has."

"Pretty far gone."

"No one's too far gone. Sin can build a high barrier. But it can't stop God from loving us."

He couldn't imagine that. What had he done to deserve God's love? Nothing. He'd earned God's wrath, maybe. God's disappointment and disgust. But not his love.

"God loves you because you're his creation." Marah's voice was soft when she spoke, and Judd felt it ripple through him. "It doesn't have anything to do with what you have or haven't done. He sent Jesus here to build a path to him. All any of us have to do is believe that. Once you belong to Christ, he'll never let you go."

It sounded too good. To be sure of God's love, to be forgiven for wrongs in the past, to have meaning and purpose in his life . . .

"I believe," he managed. "I want it. But . . . don't know how."

"That's the easy part. It's a gift. You just accept it."

Easy? If it was so simple, why did he feel as if he needed military training and full battle gear? What hammered inside him, shouting that what Marah had said was a lie? Who was holding him back?

Judd broke out into a sweat as he gripped the edge of the couch. He could feel tears well up in his eyes, a knot form inside his raw throat, his jaw clench and release. It would be easier to go on the way he had, taking care of himself, relying on his own strength. He didn't know enough about the Bible. Didn't completely understand God.

"Jesus," he croaked out, drowning that other voice, the voice of doubt and self and evil. "Jesus, I've done a lot of wrong things. I need peace."

"He forgives you," Marah whispered.

Judd could feel the tears slipping down his cheeks. He hadn't cried since he was a boy, felt stupid about it now but couldn't stop. "Make me new."

"He's doing that, Judd."

He lay in silence a moment, as a calmness he had never imagined possible slid through his chest and curled inside his heart. He squeezed Marah's hand as every corner of the black empty hollowness inside him was swept clean of cobwebs and shadows. Peace and hope and love filtered in, pushing out the old sin and filling him with a bright, radiant light. Judd lay breathless, awed by the power that gripped him.

"Marah," he murmured.

She reached out and brushed away a tear. "You OK?"

"Will this last?"

"Christ's presence inside you is permanent. You're sealed." She bent over and kissed his cheek. "Welcome to your new life."

He could hardly believe it. He felt light enough to float. Where had he put his Bible? he wondered. He wanted to read more about Jesus, about God who filled him up. He wanted to learn what it meant to have a new life.

"Got to . . . do some things," he said, attempting to push up on his elbows. "Need to—"

"You need to rest." She pressed his chest until he was forced back onto the couch. "The real world doesn't stop for Christians, Judd. In fact, sometimes I think Satan attacks us harder than anyone else."

"Feel good . . . right through," Judd said. "Peaceful."

"Judd, I believe that God's power is greater than Satan's. I think that he can help pull us out of this situation. But I also believe that he expects us to do our part. We can't just sit here in this living room and feel good. There's a man out there who wants you dead."

"Not just me," he said. "Lot of people. Gregory . . . harvesting something from those corpses. A virus."

Her fingers tightened on his as understanding dawned on her face. "Oh, Judd, that's what you were talking about that afternoon in the white house. You were asking me all those questions about the Indian woman's death, and I thought you were some kind of hypochondriac. But it was because you knew. Milton and his men . . . they've figured out how to cultivate a virus. And they're going to murder people with it, aren't they?"

"Yes," he said. "Unless . . . I stop them."

Marah felt sick inside. Sick with the realization of this
hovering terror and her own helplessness to prevent it.
"That's why Milton had the growth medium in the
tent. I saw it the day we went out to the knolls,
remember? And the biohazard hood in the bunkhouse.
He's using it to work with the virus. He cultured and
grew the pathogen, didn't he? He's probably done a
PCR analysis—"

"What's that?" Judd pulled himself up to a sitting
position.

"Polymerase chain reaction. It checks the volume of
viral particles in a sample. All you need is microliters.
It replicates the RNA and extrapolates how much virus
was there originally. With PCR analysis, Milton could
calculate the total amount of his supply. He'd know if
he had enough to . . . to cause an epidemic. This is
horrible. Why would he do such a thing?"

Judd thought about how to answer her. Was it even possible to decipher the motivations behind Gregory's actions? The history was clear enough. The medical doctor—stripped of his license—had become ringleader of a small band of outcasts. Judd's new contact with the bureau had sent him a manifesto that had been dug from the ruins of the bombed school building in Wyoming. Milton Gregory, it declared, was dedicated to the total annihilation of the United States government. He was committed to the establishment of a government of, by, and for the people. The document used the normal rhetoric—grievances against the federal government, violation of the sovereignty of the people, the right to bear arms. But there the similarity to run-of-the-mill militia groups ended. Gregory was a physician who had studied disease. It was possible he had a weapon that could destroy millions of people.

"Hate," he told Marah. It was the best explanation he could come up with for Gregory's actions. The man blamed the government for his losses. Hate, anger, and bitterness had eaten him up from the inside out.

"But starting an epidemic? That's pathological."

"Maybe he hasn't gotten far. You saw his lab. Unsophisticated."

"A high school science student could pull this off, Judd. They teach kids how to grow viruses and bacteria. Milton could buy or make most of the equipment he would need."

Judd raked a hand through his hair. "How could he . . . transport the virus?"

"Well, he'd probably need to concentrate his inventory." She tried to recall her days at the hospital lab during her residency. "That would take an ultracentrifuge. It's a piece of equipment that spins down a sample. It concentrates the viral particles so they can be stored in a very small space."

"How much . . . space? What kind of container?"

She stared at him. "Judd, that depends on the virus. If it were something really deadly . . . something we don't have current vaccines against . . . one small test tube would be enough."

Judd slammed his fist into the back of the couch. "What could it be?"

"It's something those Indians were infected with," she said. "Something that stayed alive in their bones, that lives on the mummified skin."

"What's he got, Marah? Have to find out."

She rubbed her hands down her arms, suddenly chilled. "I can only think of one thing. One virus. Something so deadly the World Health Organization spent years stamping it out. Oh, Judd."

"What, Marah? What?"

She took a deep breath. "Smallpox. And the medical community is totally unprepared for it."

🐾 🐾 🐾

Milton Gregory had not slept well. Though he had seen to Judd's demise, he was certain other members of the enemy force would soon make their appearance on the farm. They would poke and prod and ask questions. They would also intensify their attempts to pry into his work.

Drawing his hands out of the thick latex gloves in the biohazard box he had built, Gregory stared through the small glass window at his treasure. Twenty-seven vials of active, living, healthy virus were now sealed and ready. All that remained was to spin down these samples and transfer the concentrated virus into four small test tubes. It would take two days, three at the most. And then he could begin the transportation process.

"What do you think, Dr. G?" Mike Dooley asked over his shoulder. "Have we got some good stuff growing there?"

"I don't know, Mike." Gregory gazed at his vials. "We tested our previous samples. But we don't have the time to test these. Unless you'd like to volunteer?"

"No, sir." Dooley stepped backward, his face draining of blood. "I'm sure you've done it right this time, sir. Your first two batches probably just weren't good enough."

"Not good enough? I sent you out with live pathogen to infect those pathetic examples of governmental ineptitude and then to destroy them. The fault was not in my viral samples but in your inability to set a decent fire."

"You're right, sir." He nodded. "I'm sorry."

"You should be. But this time, we're not going to fail." He smiled, feeling almost fatherly toward his creation. "I have living pathogen here, and plenty of it. In two days, we should be able to refrigerate our weapons and drive them to our target."

"Sir, I'd like to volunteer to join the group in Washington," Dooley said, straightening his shoulders. "I can pose as one of the repairmen as well as any of the rest of them. My dad taught me everything I need to know about heating and cooling systems. I could hook the atomizers into the ventilation ductwork so quickly no one would notice a thing."

Gregory nodded. "We'll see, Mike. I appreciate your loyalty. For now, I want you to nose around the farmhouses. Talk to Ed Morgan, not the daughter. Tell him you noticed Judd didn't come in last night, and you were wondering if he'd seen him. Let me know what you find out about the explosion."

"Yes, sir. I'll head over there right now."

As the man left, Gregory returned his attention to the biohazard hood. He sensed Dooley's loyalty was starting to waver.

For the first time since he conceived his plan, Gregory found himself looking forward to the aftermath of the mission. He and his colleagues had purchased their airline tickets months ago. They would fly to Argentina long before the pathogen had begun to erupt on the bodies of its victims, long before fevers broke out, flesh bubbled and oozed, screams of terror split the night. Thousands would die. Perhaps millions. And as the fragmented and failing United States government worked to contain the epidemic, Milton Gregory would lounge on white ocean shores, observing his handiwork with pleasure.

"Dr. Gregory?" The child's voice shattered his reverie. "It's me, Perky Harris. Are you up there?"

The physician frowned. All summer the little girl had roamed the pastures in search of wildflowers to transplant in her garden beds. She was a bright, curious child, and Gregory had been at his wit's end to keep her out of the tent. Now she was intruding in the bunkhouse.

"What do you want, Perky?" he asked, stepping to the door of the loft laboratory.

"I was wondering if you had seen Judd. I can't find him this morning."

Ha. Good news. Gregory shook his head. "I'm sorry, I haven't seen him. Have you checked the barn, by any chance?"

"He's not there."

"I see."

"I went over to Poppy's house, but he wouldn't let me come in. He told me to go play." Her face reflected her sorrow at this rejection. "And I can't find Dr. Morgan either. Her car's gone."

No doubt Marah was in town. The county coroner perhaps. Or the funeral home.

"Did Judd tell you where he was going to work today?" the child asked. "Was he cutting hay or checking on the cattle? I have to go to town this afternoon to buy school supplies, and he said he would help me plant the rosebush he brought back from his trip. It's my Pink Pearl rose."

"I haven't seen Judd," Gregory said, turning back to his work. "And I would appreciate it if you—" A thought occurred to him. A brilliant thought. "Perky," he said, "did you tell me school is starting soon?"

"Next week. There are only a few days of summer left."

"And have you had your . . . your phlegmoculin inoculation this year?"

"My what?"

"Your shot. It's a special new vaccine that prevents . . . lice. Head lice."

"Yuck. Johnny Miller had those one time. He had to stay home from school for a week, and his daddy shaved his hair clean off until he was bald."

"Lice are a terrible parasite. Schools are going to require vaccines against them this year. Have you had your shot yet, Perky?"

"My mom didn't say anything about shots."

He smiled. "I guess not. She probably didn't want to scare you."

"No." Her face looked pinched and pale.

"Well," he said, "I have a secret that I could share with you. But you have to promise not to tell. It's about the lice shot."

"A secret?"

"As a doctor, I've been sent a couple of samples of a new form of the phlegmoculin vaccine. A noninjectable form." Pausing, he let the information soak in. "If you want me to, I could give you the lice medicine without a shot."

"Really?" She brightened. "But I should ask my mom first. She'd want to know about it."

"You can let her know," Gregory said, "but only when she finally tells you she's taking you to the doctor for the shot."

"How come?"

"Because if people find out about this, everybody will want to see me. In the first place, I'm a very busy man, Perky. You know I'm working on an important project for the government. I can't have hundreds of mothers bringing their children to me for the inhalant. And secondly, I don't have enough of the medicine for everyone. I'm afraid your school friends will just have to take their shots. But for you, because you've been a good friend to me and Bob and Mike, I would be willing to offer you the new kind of medicine."

She looked uncertain. She shifted from one foot to the other. Then she stared out the bunkhouse window.

Come along, child, Gregory thought. *Be my little guinea pig, won't you?* "Well," he said, baiting his hook, "I've got to get back to work. I just thought I'd let you know about it. But if you're not interested—"

"What would I have to do?"

"Breathe. It's as simple as that. Come on, I'll show you. It doesn't hurt a bit."

"I don't know. I should talk to my mom."

"Probably so," he said. "But I'm probably going to be too busy to do this later. You know we're leaving in two or three days."

"You are?"

"Yes, well, I hope you don't get lice," he said, turning toward the lab. "They itch so much after they bite those little holes in your scalp. They're so nasty and small, and you can't even see them scurrying around—"

"Do you have some of the medicine right there?" She was scratching a spot between her two long blond pigtails. "Up in the loft?"

"Sure do. I got a shipment in last Friday's mail. Come take a look, Perky. You'll see how easy it is. Much better than a shot."

He watched as she began to climb the ladderlike stairs to the loft. This would be perfect. The child would begin to evidence symptoms just as his colleagues were inserting the atomizers into the heating system of the federal buildings in Washington. Dooley could remain on the farm to report the effectiveness of the pathogen. Gregory would know, even as he winged his way to Argentina, that his mission would succeed. There would be no anxious waiting, no nervous anticipation. This child would seal the mission with her death.

"I'm storing the medicine in my box," he said, indicating the biohazard hood. "I'll put on my special helmet, so that I don't breathe any of it."

"Why not?" She stepped backward. "Is it dangerous?"

"No, no. Of course not. But I've already had mine, Perky. I wouldn't want a double-strength dose, would I? That wouldn't be healthy."

He slipped the helmet over his head and lowered the protective glass visor. Then he inserted his hands into the gloves and picked up one of the vials. He gingerly uncorked it. Drew it toward the tiny door in the box. Slid back the door. Held the vial out through the opening.

"Now, bend over, Perky," he said. "Lean close to the medicine. That's right. Now breathe in. Breathe deeply."

Perky Harris tilted her tiny freckled nose toward the vial and took a deep breath. Then another. And another.

"That was easy," she said.

Gregory grinned as he pushed the door closed. "Wonderful, Perky," he said. "Now you'll never have lice again."

🦟 🦟 🦟

Marah hit Winfield, Kansas, doing seventy miles per hour. In less than twenty minutes she turned onto Interstate 35, heading north toward Wichita. Judd had given her twenty-four hours—short enough time to keep Milton Gregory from learning he was still alive, but long enough to allow the FBI support system to surround the farm.

The first place Marah stopped was the Central Kansas Museum of the Native American. On the south edge of town, just off the interstate, the small building was not well known as a tourist attraction or educational center. Marah had found it in the Wichita phone book, and she hoped it at least might give her a start.

On the reference desk she set down the cardboard box she had found in her childhood bedroom. Reaching inside, she located the collection of old maps, journals, and mementos her mother had saved through the years. She hadn't had much time to look through it, but she knew the original homestead deed was in there, as well as some artifacts that had been found on the farm. Maybe something in the box would help.

"I need to know about the Osage Indians," she told the librarian, a slender man with pale skin. He wore a crewneck sweater, even though it was August.

"Native Americans, I mean," she corrected herself. "Or maybe it's not the Osage, after all." It hadn't occurred to her that Gregory might have been lying about the name of the tribe. "Do you know which group of Native Americans might have lived in southern Cowley County?"

"The Osage tribe did live in Cowley County in the early 1800s," he said. "But other tribes passed through the area, too, at different times."

"I've brought these old documents. They came from our farm."

He looked down at the cardboard box, his eyes widening. "These are historical records, ma'am."

"I thought they might give us some clues. I'm trying to find out about the Indians who lived in the area. The name of the tribe, how long they were here, what drove them away."

"Unless you want to go through your records right now, we could start by taking a look in our history section."

He led Marah between rows of shelves lined with old musty books and documents. "We have the history of Kansas over here," her guide explained. "Books about the different tribes are in that section over against the wall. I'm afraid not much has been written detailing the history of the Native American in specific regions of Kansas. By that I mean there's not a specific book on the Osage in Cowley County. We do have some archival material, but it's in our rare document section. You'd need clearance to look at it."

"Clearance?" Marah already felt overwhelmed. "I'm in a huge hurry. I have other things to do today, and I need this information desperately."

"Well, I could look through your box while you start searching the books on Kansas history. You could look up Cowley County in the index and see if you can locate the particular tribe you're interested in. Then I'll help you search the shelves on the various tribes. You might find some information on the time period in which that tribe lived there." He smiled. "Or you could look at books on the Osage and trace the history of the tribe to see when they were living in your county and what they were doing there."

Marah stared at the librarian's ivory face and bright brown eyes. He reminded her of a barn owl—wise, alert, canny.

"The Osage tribe," she repeated. "I need to know when they were in Cowley County."

"Follow me." He led her to a small display of books. "We don't have much here, really. You might want to check with their tribal headquarters."

"And where's that?"

"Oklahoma, I think. I have a shelf of very good reference

materials. It wouldn't take long to find an address. You could write them."

Marah sank down onto a stool near the Osage books. "I don't have that much time," she said softly. "I don't have time at all."

As she flipped through the books in the dimly lit corridor, it occurred to her that she was on a hopeless quest. Milton Gregory had had all the time he needed to find the location of that long-ago village. He knew exactly whom he was looking for. And before he ever set foot on Morgan Farm, he had all but pinpointed the spot where the Indians lived.

The most recently written book Marah could put her hands on in the collection turned out to be a lengthy and cryptic history of the tribe. Rather than years, the author referred to the passage of time according to events that had taken place. He gave months names like Little-Flower-Killer moon and Buffalo-Pawing-Earth moon. How was she supposed to find out anything specific with those as reference points? Even the maps were confusing.

"How are you coming along there?" It was the librarian, peering into the shadows at her. "Finding anything?"

Marah let out a breath and stood. "Not much. How about you?"

He shook his head. "There's a lot of mildew damage. Looks like the box has been in the basement."

"No, but—" Marah paused, suddenly remembering the intruder in her cellar. She recalled one day at lunch when her father had mentioned the collection of old maps and documents. Milton Gregory must have sent Mike or Bob down to take a look that day after Marah left for town. She knew how desperate Milton had been to locate the burial site. No one had anticipated the tornado. They hadn't expected her quick return to the house. They must have believed they could rummage around down there for hours looking for Ruby Morgan's old box. Only the box wasn't in the cellar. It had been in the bedroom upstairs all along.

"Listen," Marah said. "I've got to have some information, and I need it today. It's very important. Could I pay you to do the research for me?"

"Pay me?" The man drew back, his eyes narrowing. "I don't think so."

"I need to know which Native American tribes lived in southern Cowley County. I need to know when they lived there. How many years ago was it? And most of all, I need to know what happened to those Indians. Did they move away? Or did they die of some kind of disease? Can you help me? I'll pay you for your time. Twelve dollars an hour. Would that be fair?"

"Twelve dollars! Well . . . absolutely not. I'm paid to work here. This is my job."

"But I—"

"I'll do the research for free." He shrugged. "It's not like I'm exactly busy."

Marah could have hugged him. "OK, thanks so much. Listen, I've got to do some things downtown. I'll be back here by five."

"We close at six. Uh, have you had lunch?" He flushed. "There's a deli down the street. I could take some time off."

"Oh no. Is it noon already?" She glanced at her watch. "I've got to run. I'll see you at six. Thanks!"

As she raced out of the library and down to the parking lot, it occurred to Marah that she'd just been asked out to lunch. But all she could think about was Judd. Judd crawling across the fields with his bloodied hands. Judd weeping on the living-room couch as he gave his life to Christ. Judd lying in the rock house with his burned skin and bloodshot eyes. *Dear God, help me figure this out! Help me stop Milton Gregory.*

Despite the Arkansas River running right through the middle of the city, Wichita had been laid out in a neat street grid that was easy to navigate. Marah drove straight to the Via Christi Regional Medical Center, racking her brain the whole way for the names of physicians she might know there. Via Christi was a large hospital complex with two campuses. Marah pulled into the parking area off St. Francis Street and hurried into the building.

"I need to talk to someone in epidemiology," she told the receptionist.

The woman glanced down at the list on her desk. "Epidemiology? We don't have that. We have units for cancer, critical care, heart—"

"Do you have an infection-control specialist?"

The woman leaned back, as though fearful of catching something herself. "Infections. Yes, there's a woman who administrates a program that keeps the hospital sanitized, and—"

"Could you tell me where to find her?"

"Jenny Bertram. She's on the third floor. Take the A elevator and turn left. Ask the receptionist there."

It took another twenty minutes before Marah was seated in a small gray office decorated with touches of pink silk flowers and crocheted doilies. The petite redhead apologized for eating her sandwich as they spoke.

"My name is Dr. Marah Morgan, pediatrics in St. Louis," she began.

"St. Louis?" Jenny Bertram's face brightened. "I was born there. Do you know a Dr. Luis Jordan? He was my pediatrician."

"I worked closely with him." She looked away. "He died recently. This summer."

"I'm sorry to hear that. I just loved him. He always had a monkey hanging from his stethoscope."

Marah smiled. "He was wonderful."

"How did he die?"

"He developed some kind of rash." Marah caught her breath as she spoke the words. *A rash. Pustules. High fever. Sudden death.* But Dr. Redkin at the CDC said he'd checked for every viral disease. Even smallpox. Or had he?

"Dr. Morgan?" the redhead leaned forward. "Are you all right?"

"Uh, I'm going to need to make a phone call after we speak."

"OK." Ms. Bertram looked uncomfortable. "Is it long distance?"

"Don't worry about it. I'll put it on my card. Here's the situation I need to tell you about." Marah set her elbows on her knees and folded her hands. "I'm from Cowley County—"

"I thought you said you lived in St. Louis."

"I do, but I'm taking care of my father right now. Anyway, not too long ago, three men came onto our farm posing as archaeologists."

"Posing?" she said.

"Yes, but now I've learned that they're really part of a group planning to destroy the government. These men located the mummified remains of an Indian tribe that once lived on our farmland."

"Mummies? I thought that was in Egypt."

"Well, that's true, but these bodies had mummified naturally. There had been a period of dry heat, we think. And the doctor was able to harvest a virus—"

"I thought you said the men were archaeologists."

"Their leader was a doctor, an abortionist who got into trouble and was stripped of his medical license. So he and the other two men harvested a virus from the mummies."

"A virus . . . from the mummies."

"Yes."

"OK." Ms. Bertram gave Marah a wan smile. "Whoops, there's my light," she said, reaching for her phone. "Could you excuse me just a minute? I need to take this call."

Marah rose as the woman punched in a series of numbers and began to speak into the receiver. The meeting wasn't going well, and Marah sensed it stemmed from the convoluted explanation she was giving Ms. Bertram. But how to detail it in a clearer way? And quickly?

There was so much Marah needed to do before hitting the road for home. After she had alerted the medical community in Wichita to the possible threat of epidemic, she ought to call Dr. Redkin at the CDC in Atlanta. Maybe he could rerun the cultures he'd taken on Dr. Jordan. Was it possible Dr. Jordan could have contracted smallpox? If so, from whom? After that, Marah needed to find out if there was any viable vaccine against smallpox still remaining in the United States. Maybe Redkin would be able to tell her. And did any other country in the world store it?

"Dr. Morgan?" Ms. Bertram said. "You were telling me about the mummies."

"Yes." Marah sat down again. "OK, the militia group harvested the virus, and they've grown it. I'm sure they have enough of this pathogen to start an epidemic."

"Wait a minute. Where did the militia group come in? I thought you said the man was an abortionist."

Marah took a deep breath. "Let's skip all that, and I'll get to the point. There's been an FBI agent on our farm. He and I believe that the virus that has been harvested—"

"From the mummies."

"Is smallpox."

"Aha." A knock on the door brought Ms. Bertram out of her chair as a pair of hospital security guards stepped into the room. "Gentlemen, this is Dr. Morgan," she told them.

"Dr. Morgan," one of the men said. "Would you come with us, please?"

"Wait a minute," Marah said, a chill washing down her body. "What's going on here?"

"We'd just like to talk with you, ma'am."

The redhead smiled apologetically. "Smallpox," she said, "has been eradicated from the face of the earth."

"Not in mummified remains," Marah said as the guards approached. "Dr. Gregory has the pathogen in our bunkhouse, and he's going to be transporting it in a few days. Probably to Washington, D.C. But something could happen before that time, don't you see? The FBI is gathering on the farm, and Judd and I are anticipating a possible contamination situation. If you don't listen to me, Ms. Bertram, you may end up with an uncontrollable epidemic on your hands. Now, the FBI is aware of this situation, but—"

"Come on, Dr. Morgan," one of the security guards said. "You can tell all this to Dr. Jackson."

"Who is Dr. Jackson?" Marah asked as they led her out of the office, one guard on each side.

"He's a fine doctor," the man on her right told her. "Here at the hospital, he runs our psychiatric unit."

19

"Got any guns around here?" From his lookout post on the sofa, Judd glanced over his shoulder to Ed Morgan, who was whittling in the kitchen. "A shotgun, or anything."

"Got an old rifle up in one of these cabinets, but I wouldn't be surprised if it's rusted up. It hasn't been fired in years."

"Mind if I look?"

"Beans, boy, neither one of us needs to be up wandering around. You stay put. I'll fetch it."

Judd pushed back the curtain with a fingertip and studied the setting sun as Ed pushed his walker toward the cabinets. From the time Marah left early this morning, the two men had spent the day lying low. Perky Harris was the first to arrive at the house, eager for Judd to help her plant her rosebush. Ed had shooed the girl away—more roughly than necessary, Judd thought. But she hadn't been back.

Later that morning, Mike Dooley had wandered by. Ed could have earned himself a place as an FBI agent with the sad voice he used to tell the young man about the deadly accident on the road to town. After Mike left, Ed spent the day whittling and watching the road. Judd stayed on the couch with the curtains drawn.

"There you go," the farmer said, propping the rifle near the couch, "and a box of ammo I had in a drawer, too. I never was much of a hunter, so those bullets are antiques."

"Thanks." Judd sat up on the couch and inspected the old rifle, hoping Ed would go back to his whittling. He didn't want to talk to anyone right now. His throat felt like it was lined with shattered glass, and his ears were still ringing. But the farmer didn't seem to notice Judd's silence. He seated himself in the orange vinyl armchair and began to pick his teeth with a splinter of pine.

"Wonder where that girl of mine's been gone to all this time," he said. "She ought to be back by now, don't you reckon?"

"Worried?"

"Nah, just wondering what she's up to." He paused. "Well, with all the lunatics running around these days, I'd like to know she's all right."

"She had a lot to do."

"Find out what killed those Indians. I don't know why that's so hard."

"Going to alert the medical community, too," Judd said. "In case there's a problem."

Ed was silent a moment. "You think Greg and his boys might try to give us some kind of disease? I mean . . . if they find out you're not dead?"

"Depends . . . whether or not they've been vaccinated themselves. Probably planning to get it to Washington . . . then leave the country until the epidemic's under control."

"You mean Greg's got himself a disease without a cure?"

Judd took a swallow of water before speaking again. "There's a vaccine for smallpox . . . and ways to control an epidemic. But a cure? Don't think so."

"Beans and double beans. I've got a mind to head over to that bunkhouse right now, walker or not. Who do they think they are, trying to kill a good man like you? And as for this disease they've cooked up . . . it's one thing to disagree with the government, you know, all the rules and regulations they keep hammering down on us. Labor laws and—"

"Poppy?" Perky Harris burst through the front door. "Who are you talking to . . . oh, Judd! There you are!"

"I thought I told you to go home and play," Ed said. "Get on out of here, girl."

"But I've been looking for Judd all day!" She skipped into the house. "I was hoping we could plant the Pink Pearl rosebush you bought me."

She stopped and stared at him, her blue eyes darkening. "Judd, what happened to you? You look like a big ugly monster."

"Judd's sick," Ed barked. "And you better get your backside home like I told you."

Perky's face fell. "Poppy, what's the matter? Are you mad at me?"

"It's OK, Perk," Judd said. "I got hurt last night. I'll be fine."

"What's wrong with your voice? And your eyeballs are red. Your skin is full of cuts. And your arm is all bandaged up. Did somebody hit you?"

"Nobody hit him," Ed said. "Now, get on home to your daddy, girl. And tell your mama to keep you inside tomorrow."

"What's happening, Judd?" Perky whispered, her voice quavering.

Judd took her hand and pulled her onto the couch beside him. Then he set the gun aside and slid his arm around the child's narrow shoulders.

"I'll tell you what, Perk," he rasped. "If you'll stay home for one week, one whole week without coming to visit Poppy or me . . . then I promise I'll plant that rose for you."

She nodded, her head bent. "You don't like me anymore, do you?"

"Of course I like you." He recalled Marah's words about Perky's affection for him. "I love you."

She lifted her head and threw her arms around him. "Oh, Judd, I did a bad thing!" she wailed. "It was like Snow White when the wicked witch gave her the poison apple and she ate it. I smelled the lice medicine even though I hadn't asked my mommy, because I didn't want to get a shot. And now I'm afraid to tell her what I did."

Judd looked across the room at Ed as Perky sobbed in his arms. The farmer shrugged. "She talks like that," he mouthed, tapping his head. "Reads too many books."

"Perky," Judd said, "I'm sure you didn't do anything wrong."

"But I don't like him; I never did. I know he's wicked, and I smelled the lice medicine anyway!"

"Who's wicked?"

"Dr. Gregory."

Judd's heart clenched. "Dr. Gregory gave you something to smell?"

"Lice medicine," she said. "He told me if I smelled it, I wouldn't have to have the shot for school. And I didn't want to have the shot, so I smelled it, but I know my mommy will be upset with me."

"Where was the lice medicine, Perky?" Judd asked.

"In the bunkhouse. Upstairs." She stared at him, her eyes filled with tears. "You're mad at me, too, aren't you? I can hear it in the way you talk."

"No, honey," he said, squeezing her close, "but I'm concerned. Tell me exactly what happened."

"I was looking all over for you, even in the bunkhouse, and then Dr. Gregory said I would have to get a shot for school to keep me from getting lice. But he said he had some special medicine that all you have to do is smell it. So I went upstairs and—" she began to cry again—"and he had it in his box with the gloves attached, and he put on his helmet with the glass, and then he held out the medicine, and I smelled it."

"OK," Judd said, forcing himself to drag breath into his chest. "It's OK, Perky."

"I'm going to tell my mommy right away."

"Good idea, Perk, but not just yet." Judd faced the farmer. "Ed, call her parents. Tell them she's staying over with you tonight."

"I've done that before, but it was just when Pete and Hilda wanted to take a little vacation trip or something." Ed said. "You want her to sleep here?"

"In isolation." Judd hoped his bloodshot eyes could convey the seriousness of the situation. "It would be a good idea."

"Oh." Ed glanced at the little girl. Then he looked back at Judd. "Did that Greg fellow—"

"We're keeping Perky with us. Tell her parents. Don't tell them anything but that, understand?" As the farmer nodded, Judd rose from the couch. "How about a snack, Perk?"

"Chocolate ice cream," she said, brightening. "With Hershey's on top."

🐾 🐾 🐾

"Mummies," Marah repeated. She glanced at her watch. "Look, I've got to get out of here. I realize what I'm telling you sounds odd, but the Indians' remains had partially mummified inside the cairns. There were bits of skin and hair left on the skeletons. I don't know how it happened. Kansas has experienced some exceptionally dry periods in history. Remember the dust storms we all studied in school?"

By now the small room where she'd spent the whole afternoon was crowded with personnel. After convincing the psychiatrist to contact her pediatrics clinic in St. Louis, Marah was finally able to verify that she was not a mental patient on the lam. As she persisted in telling her story, the man became concerned and began to call in support.

"To the best of our knowledge," Marah continued, "Dr. Milton Gregory recognized that living virus existed in the dried pustules on the skin of the mummies. He harvested it, cultured and grew it, and now he possesses a supply of this virus that is capable of causing an epidemic. We think he's planning to transport it out of Kansas, but we can't be sure. And in any case, some of the virus could contaminate local residents."

"Is the Centers for Disease Control and Prevention aware of this situation, Dr. Morgan?" someone asked.

"I'm sure the FBI has contacted them. But no one is absolutely certain which pathogen Dr. Gregory has cultivated."

"It could be influenza or meningitis or measles." Ms. Bertram, the infection-control specialist, was in the room now, apologetic for having sent Marah to the psychiatric unit and very concerned about the hospital in the event an epidemic was really in the offing. "But you think it's smallpox, don't you, Dr. Morgan?"

"I think it might be." Marah looked around the room. "I'm attempting to identify the tribe that lived on our farm and verify the cause of death of those victims. In fact, if I could be allowed to place a call to the museum—"

"Smallpox." As the meeting was taking place, one of the physicians had been working at the computer in the psychiatrist's office. "Excuse me for interrupting, but I've found some information in our hospital files. The last acquired case of smallpox in the world occurred in October 1977. Global eradication was certified two years later by the World Health Organization. Today, the only reservoir of the virus is held in stocks in two restricted laboratories. The mode of transmission is primarily respiratory."

He looked at Marah. "It doesn't say anything about mummies, Dr. Morgan."

"I'm sure it doesn't," she said. "But smallpox is also transmitted by contact with the skin lesions."

"I can see that, but could a primarily respiratory virus survive for long on the flesh of its victim? I must confess, I'm doubtful."

"I don't know the answer to your question, Doctor. All I know is that some viruses do retain potency for hundreds of years."

"The point is," another physician inserted, "that we may have a madman in Cowley County."

"We prefer the term *mentally ill,*" the psychiatrist said. "This situation is bizarre enough without—"

"I don't think we need to worry about political correctness at the moment, Doctor. If we have a lethal virus here—"

"Yes, and if it gets out, we'll have an epidemic, which will mean the media will descend on this hospital. You can't go around using terms like *madman*. It isn't appropriate—"

"Gentlemen," Marah said, standing. "If Dr. Gregory has cultivated the smallpox virus, we need to know if there's any preventive vaccine available in the United States. Where is it located? How quickly can you get it to Kansas? And how efficiently can you vaccinate a large population?" She looked around at the men and women gathered. "Are you prepared to handle an epidemic?"

"That's the domain of the Public Health Department," someone said. "The state should handle this."

"But Dr. Morgan is right," another added. "If this virus gets out, we'll be taking care of the victims here at Via Christi. It's up to us to be prepared—"

"Bingo!" The physician on the computer lifted his hands. "I've got the information we need. The World Health Organization has ten million doses of the vaccine in storage in Geneva, Switzerland. . . . Wait a minute." He paused and leaned forward, examining the computer screen. "In 1990 an advisory committee recommended that most of it be destroyed. They got rid of nine and a half million doses."

The room erupted in cries of dismay.

"There's only one factory in the world that has made any of the vaccine recently," he went on. "And there's probably not any factory capable of making sizable amounts."

"Then what are we supposed to do?" Ms. Bertram spoke up. "No matter how effectively we use our epidemic procedures, we won't be able to control this thing. If it's airborne, everyone who isn't vaccinated will contract it."

"I was vaccinated as a child," one of the older doctors said.

"Probably not going to do you much good," the physician on the computer said. "Research shows that the vaccine may begin to wear off within ten years. How old are you, Doctor?"

"Sixty-two," the man said. "This is an appalling situation! Surely the federal government—"

"Lancaster County, Pennsylvania," the computer physician cut in. "The United States's stockpile of vaccine is in a lab there owned by a pharmaceutical company."

"I'll contact them immediately," Ms. Bertram said.

"Useless. The FDA has put a hold on the vaccine. No one can access it, Ms. Bertram. Not even emergency personnel."

The room exploded into chatter once again as Marah reached for the telephone. Quickly she punched in the number for the museum at the edge of town. It was almost six, and she was whispering a prayer even as the director picked up the phone.

"Museum of the Native American," he said. "May I help you?"

"This is Marah Morgan. I was in this morning—"

"I've got your information. Found it in the archives section." The sound of shuffling papers carried over the line. "The Osage were moved into southern Kansas, including Cowley County, in 1825. In 1865, the Osage in that area were pushed down into Oklahoma."

"Did you find a record of any deaths—"

"I found a little boy's journal in the box you brought in," he cut in. "It's extremely valuable. We don't have anything like it in our collection. I had to do some real detective work to pinpoint the location of his village. The year was 1865, and it was Yellow Dog's village on the Arkansas River in Cowley County."

A shiver ran down Marah's flesh as she pictured the river winding past the rocky knolls just beyond the rise of Indian Hill. "What did the journal say?" she asked.

"The boy wrote about a disease that had infected his whole village. The government agent kept coming to visit, but he never brought any medicine. The deaths were horrible, just really awful."

"What was the disease?"

"The boy called it *ge-ta-zhe*," he said. "I looked that up in an Indian dictionary. It means 'the things on your face.'"

"Things on your face," Marah said. "What's that?"

He paused only a moment. "It's smallpox."

Yellow Dog's Village

I do not know the day or the month or the year. I know only one thing. My mother has died.

This morning, black blood poured from every opening in her body. It soaked the pallet and ran among the buffalo skins. She lay awake, staring at me, speaking no words. I could do nothing to help my mother. After her blood had poured away and none was left, the very entrails within her slipped out onto the pallet. And then her life force left us.

Two young men burning with fever came into our lodge and carried my mother's body to the field beside the river to cover her with stones. Wah'Kon-Tah will take her from the cairn. And my mother's spirit will wander the earth forever.

Now I have done as she asked. I have written the story of my mother's death. No one will forget this horror. Though my people are strong warriors, we cannot defeat the ge-ta-zhe. No one can.

I will lie beside my father now as we wait for the ge-ta-zhe to finish their destruction and leave our spirits in peace.

From The Journal of Little Gray Bird, unpublished
Central Kansas Museum of the Native American archival collection

20

Marah struggled against both sorrow and rage as she sped down the interstate toward home. *Home.* The two old houses. The sagging red barn. The scattered pens and storage bins. How could she have hated the farm so many years? Like the big tree where Marah and Perky held their afternoon chats, this rich land had become her source of strength and refuge. Her roots sank deep into the Kansas soil, and she drew sustenance from its bright sun.

The thought of Milton Gregory spreading his contagious evil across her homeland sickened Marah. She could not allow it. He must be stopped. And with God's help, she would do it.

It was well past midnight when she turned off the main road and passed the mailbox twined with her mother's four-o'clocks and morning glory vine. No lights shone in the distance, and Marah breathed a sigh of gratitude. She prayed that her father and Judd were sleeping now, deeply at rest. They needed it.

Marah's thoughts turned once again to her father. She had despised the man so long. Still couldn't stand him. The way he talked just to listen to his own voice. Barked out commands as though he were king of the universe. Held himself above everyone . . .

No, she thought, picturing Big Ed Morgan asleep in his bed in the rock house. She didn't hate her father. She hated many of the things he had done. His selfishness, and the way he had hurt her mother. But she couldn't bring herself to loathe the man himself.

If she stepped into his cracked and muddy work boots, she saw a man disappointed in life and love. A man without God. As a teenager, he had lost the girl of his dreams, so he had made do the best he could with what he had left. He believed families were for support, not love. And how could Marah argue? Maybe he was right, though something deep inside her believed there must be more. Ed Morgan was bitter, and he had transferred his bitterness to his daughters. But Marah didn't need to hate him for it.

Judd had been right when he had challenged her to try to love her father if she wanted his love in return. It was time to extend her father the same gift of grace—of undeserved forgiveness—that God had given her. For the first time in her life, Marah thought she could.

Judd was another concern altogether. *Dear God,* she lifted up

as she pulled her BMW to a stop beside the old rock house.
*How can I be having such strong feelings for this man? I need to get my
father and Judd off the farm tonight. I need to warn the Harrises. I need to
get out of this mess and get back to my old life in St. Louis. Please, dear God,
help me to think straight. . . . Help me not to feel so tangled. . . .*

Marah climbed out of the car and shut the door softly
behind her. As she crept across the porch of the rock house,
she could hear the floorboards creak beneath her feet. She
didn't want to jolt anyone awake, and she certainly didn't want
her father flipping on the lights. Milton and his men were
suspicious of everything, and they would have to make this
escape in utter silence.

As she pushed open the door, the hinges squeaked.

Suddenly, a hand clamped over her mouth. Powerful arms
dragged her into the living room and shoved her roughly onto
the couch. A rifle barrel pressed into her stomach.

"Who's there?" Judd croaked.

"It's me. Marah."

"Marah!" he said, pulling the rifle away. "What are you doing
sneaking in like that?"

"You could have killed me."

"I thought you were Gregory."

"Does he know you're alive?"

"Not yet."

"Thank God. Listen, Judd, we've got to get out of here."

"Who's here?" Perky's voice, frightened and small, sounded
from the floor.

"It's OK, Perk," Judd whispered. "It's just Dr. Morgan. Go back to sleep, kiddo."

He took Marah's arm and pulled her into the kitchen. Marah's eyes were growing accustomed to the dim light provided by the moon. "Gregory exposed Perky to the virus," he said against her ear. His voice was rough, tattered. "He had her breathe the stuff this morning. Told her it was some kind of medicine against lice."

"Oh, Judd," Marah said, looking into his eyes with a growing realization of horror. Her thoughts instantly flew to Pete, who she now knew was her brother. He and Hilda would be devastated. "She's been infected."

"Maybe. What did you find out? What are we dealing with?"

"Smallpox," she whispered. "I'm almost sure of it. The Via Christi people researched it while I was there, but the outcome is not good. It turns out there are two strains of variola—major and minor. The minor strain is controllable today. Less than one percent fatality. But the major strain is still deadly. We don't know which the Osage had, but—"

"How long have we got with Perky?"

"The incubation is ten to twelve days. But she may be contagious already. We've got to isolate her."

"I'll carry her over to the other house. More rooms. I expect the other agents to get here any time. You and Ed better head out as soon as you can."

"No way. Judd, I'm not leaving that child here to suffer alone."

"You can't expose yourself."

"And you can?"

"I told you I was vaccinated against smallpox before the Gulf War, remember? The guys in the special forces . . . we were protected against smallpox and anthrax and a few other diseases no one likes to think about. The military suspected Saddam might use bioweapons. I can take care of Perky."

"You're not a physician, Judd. And you have to get away from here. If Dr. Gregory finds out you're alive—"

"I'm not afraid of dying, Marah," he said. "I've made peace with that."

She looked into his eyes. He took her arms and pulled her close. For a brief moment, she felt the tension seep out of her. She laid her cheek against his shoulder as his hands moved up her back, gently kneading the taut muscle. When he slipped his fingers into her hair, she lifted her face to his. His kiss was firm, possessive, moving from her mouth to her cheek to her neck.

"I'm staying here, Marah." His breath warm, he spoke against her ear. "It's my job. But I want you to go."

"I can't," she said. "I won't."

"You'll die."

"Who'll die?" Ed stood in the doorway of the kitchen, his hair standing out around his head like a spiky halo. "Nobody's going to die around here if I have anything to say about it."

Marah pulled away from Judd and crossed to her father. "Listen, I want you to throw some things into a bag. A few clothes. Your comb and toothbrush. I'm driving you to a hotel in Winfield."

"Winfield? I'm not going to Winfield. How many times do I have to tell you, girl? I was born on this farm, and I'll die here."

"This is no time for your stubbornness. Now get in there and pack your clothes before I—"

"Who are you to boss me around? Listen to me, girl—"

"What's happening?" Perky tugged on Marah's skirt. "Are you and Poppy mad at each other again?"

Marah stiffened, wary suddenly of touching the child's pale skin or breathing the sweet air of her breath. But Judd knelt and scooped Perky into his arms.

"Come on, my little Pink Pearl," he said. "You and I are going to move over to the other house and settle in. Would you like to sleep in Dr. Morgan's old bedroom? She's got a pretty quilt on her bed."

"Could I?" Perky asked.

"Of course, sweetheart," Marah said. "I'll be over there to join you in a minute."

"Can my mom and dad come, too?" Perky asked. "I miss my mommy. She's going to have our babies soon, and I like to put my hand on her tummy and feel how they move around inside her. I miss my daddy, too. I'm afraid they're going to be mad at me for breathing Dr. Gregory's medicine."

"They won't be mad at you, sweetheart," Marah said. "They'll want Judd and me to take care of you for a while."

"Hey, what am I? Baked beans?" Ed grabbed his walker and

headed for the door. "I can take care of Perky better than either of you. Come on, Gypsy, let's go." It suddenly dawned on Marah why her father was so attached to the little girl. He was her grandfather.

The black-and-white dog pranced around the room as Marah grabbed a few items from her father's refrigerator. She had no idea how long it would take the FBI to round up Milton Gregory and his men. Ideally, she and Judd would be able to transport Perky to an isolation ward in Wichita. But Marah had no illusions about any hospital's willingness to admit a patient with a virulent, untreatable, highly contagious disease.

Oh, God, don't let this child die! Marah breathed as she filled a sack with chocolate ice cream, Hershey's syrup, a box of Cheerios, and some of her dad's hickory smoked bacon.

"I miss my mommy," Perky was saying, her long blond pigtails hanging like frayed ropes down her back. "I want to go home."

"You're just tired, Perk," Judd said, throwing a blanket over her. "We'll put you into Dr. Morgan's big soft bed, and you'll be asleep again lickety-split."

"But I want to go home," she repeated.

"Let's head out," Judd said, settling the child against his shoulder. "Come on, Ed. Marah, can you help your dad over the threshold?"

The small group stepped out onto the front porch and started across the yard. Marah shivered as she helped her father maneuver his walker over the hummocks of grass that had sprouted in the fertile soil. Once they had Perky settled, it would be up to Judd to physically force Ed into Marah's car. If she could get her father as far as Winfield, she would know he was safe. Then she could drive back to the farm and help Judd nurse Perky through the days to come.

"Beans and double beans," Ed muttered. "I'm stuck."

Marah reached across him to lift the front end of the walker over a clump of weeds. As she straightened, a movement in the shadows caught her eye.

"Well, well," Milton Gregory said over the barrel of a large handgun. "Judd, I see you've risen from the grave."

"What do you want, Gregory?" Judd said. He had stopped five feet from the terrorist's weapon. "We've got a child here."

"She's the only one of you we *don't* want. We've already taken care of the little girl."

As Perky began to cry, Marah glanced around at Milton's companions. Mike Dooley's gun was aimed at her. Bob Harper had his weapon trained on her father.

"Take your men and get off this farm, Milton," Marah ordered, stepping in front of Judd. "We've got a sick child and a crippled old man. Judd is worthless to you. So am I. I can promise we don't know what you're planning to do with the pathogen. Just take it and go."

"We have a pathogen, do we, Dr. Morgan?" Milton said. "You know even more about our plans than I suspected. Is it a virus? Or could it be a bacterium? Or maybe we just have a collection of old Indian bones."

"Don't taunt me," she said. "Take it, whatever it is, and leave us alone."

"I'd love to, but I'm afraid I can't. Once Mike came back to the bunkhouse this evening from his second reconnaissance mission with the unsettling news that our dead man was lying on a couch tending a few bad aches and pains, I was forced to make alternate plans." His pale blue eyes were lit by the full moon. "Judd, take the child into the house. Mike, tie the girl to a chair. Bob, go with them. If Judd steps out of line, kill him."

"What are you going to do to her, Milton?" Marah said, clenching her fists as Judd carried Perky toward the white house. "She's an innocent child. She doesn't know anything."

"Relax, Dr. Morgan," Milton said. "We're not planning to harm your little friend. We're merely leaving her here on the farm to await her fate. By the time she's discovered, she'll be swarming with contagion—which should seal the fate of Cowley County, Kansas."

"You demon!" Marah choked out as Perky began to scream and sob.

"Don't hurt me!" Perky shrieked. "Judd, don't let them hurt me!"

Her screams grew fainter as Dooley, rope in hand, shoved Judd through the front door of the house and slammed it behind them.

Ed took his daughter's hand. "I'm not leaving that baby here by herself," he told Milton. "I'll kill you before I let you hurt my granddaughter."

"Kill me with what?" Milton said with a chuckle as Harper

prodded Judd back out into the yard. Dooley emerged from the house without the rope. "You couldn't even catch me, old man. Come on, Bob, Mike. Let's get our hostages into the van."

He led the group around the side of the house to the waiting vehicle. Mike pushed the three captives inside and then tied their wrists behind them and bound their ankles. There were no backseats, so Marah curled down on the bare metal floor next to the wheel well. A portable refrigerator wedged between the two front seats caught her eye. Connected to a large battery, the refrigerator had been sealed with duct tape.

"Judd," she whispered, gesturing at the cooler.

He nodded.

"You can bet I'm going to the sheriff over this, buddy," Ed was saying as Milton climbed into the back of the van with the prisoners. "I don't know what you fellows are up to, but the United States government doesn't allow this kind of thing. I don't care if you do work for the Indian bureau, you've over-stepped—"

"Shut up!" Milton cuffed the old man across the mouth.

Marah let out a cry. "Don't you touch my father!"

Milton jammed his pistol into Ed's temple. "Shut up, all of you. Mike, hand me a vial. The one on the left."

In the moonlight Marah saw the young man peel back the duct tape and open the small refrigerator. Inside, in a shoe box lined with cotton, lay five test tubes no bigger than pencil stubs. Dooley picked up the vial indicated and handed it to Milton.

"Now then," the doctor said as Dooley resealed the refrigerator. "This vial contains enough virus to kill you and a few other people. Maybe most of the people on the farm. Maybe most of the people in the county. Maybe most of the people in the state. If any of you tries to escape, I will have no hesitation in smashing it. Is that clear?"

"What you got in there?" Ed asked.

"Variola."

"Smallpox," Marah clarified.

"Good, Dr. Morgan." Milton smiled at her. "You continue to surprise me."

"You don't surprise me at all."

His face hardened as he seated himself on the refrigerator facing his prisoners. "Mike, start the van."

The vehicle began to move down the dirt driveway toward the road. Marah pictured Perky crying, alone, in the white house. Ed began muttering to himself about government kooks. Judd, seated on the van's bare metal floor across from Marah, stared at Milton.

"You've done impressive work," Judd said. "Better than we expected."

The doctor gave a nod. "My intelligence has always been underestimated."

"But I think I see a chink in your armor."

"Oh, really?"

"Smallpox."

"Smallpox is my weapon."

"Unless you haven't been vaccinated yourself," Judd said.

A nerve twitched beside the man's eye. "Of course I've been vaccinated. We all have."

Marah looked from one man to the other. Though she feared the vial in Milton's hand, she couldn't let his statement rest. "I doubt you've been vaccinated," she said. "The only vaccine in the United States is in a guarded lab in Pennsylvania."

Milton rolled the vial between his thumb and forefinger. "Vaccine can be created, Dr. Morgan."

"Using pox-infected cattle. And you've only just now made your first batch of pathogen." She turned to her father. "You haven't noticed any sick cows on the farm lately, have you, Dad?"

Ed frowned. "What are you talking about, girl? None of my cows is sick, and you know it."

"Cowpox," Milton said. "It takes cowpox to make vaccine. Not smallpox."

"And how many cases of cowpox does the United States see annually?" Marah asked. "According to my research yesterday at Via Christi—"

"They know about this?"

"Your experiment? Of course."

"I don't believe you."

"And I don't believe you've been vaccinated. I think you're as scared of that virus as we are. In fact, I believe that vial you're holding is a decoy. I doubt it contains anything other than tap water, because if it did—"

"Dr. G!" Mike called from the front as the van skidded to a stop. "It's the Feds! Three cars. They're circling us."

As Milton whirled around to see, Judd uncoiled from his crouch on the floor, smashing his head into the doctor's stomach. The vial flew from the man's fingers and bounced against the metal wall. As it fell to the floor, the van started moving again, swerving.

"Doc, what should I do?" Mike cried.

"Get back to the house!" Bob Harper grabbed for the steering wheel. "They're shooting at us!"

As a front tire blew, the van veered to the left. Marah tumbled over onto her father. Judd rolled away from Milton just as the doctor raised his gun. The bullet blew a hole through the van's roof.

Marah screamed and tried to cover her father. "Get down, get down!"

The van sounded like a dryer filled with tennis shoes as bodies were flung from side to side, fists flew, the gun went off a second time. Marah pulled at her wrists until her skin was rubbed raw, but she couldn't loosen the rope. The headlights of the federal agents' cars shone through the back window.

Another tire popped, and still the van kept moving. Milton doubled over on the floor, coughing up blood. Judd balanced on his tied wrists and kicked at the gun. From the sound of the impact, Marah surmised that Judd had made contact with the doctor's jaw. But Milton held on to the gun, and another bullet ripped through a side window. Marah crouched near the back door, praying that she could somehow work the latch. If she could get the door open, she and her father could tumble out onto the road.

"Pull this latch!" she shouted at Ed.

"I can't reach it."

"Turn around. I'll guide your hands."

"My hip . . . it's jammed up on me, girl. You turn, and I'll—"

As Marah attempted to maneuver her shoulders, an arm locked around her throat and a gun barrel pressed into her neck. She froze, hearing the wheeze of Milton's breath against her ear. The van shuddered to a stop.

Milton kicked open the door. In the glare of the FBI cars' headlights, he wrenched Marah out of the van and into the open.

"Don't move," he hissed to her. "You're expendable."

"This is the FBI," a voice called out from somewhere behind the bright headlights.

"And this is Dr. Milton Gregory. I have a hostage here, and I'll blow her brains out if anyone makes a move toward us. Is that clear?"

"Dr. Gregory, you are surrounded. You cannot escape. Release your hostages, and we can begin to negotiate."

Ignoring the federal agents, Milton began dragging Marah backward in the direction of the old white clapboard house. The van's front doors flew open. Mike and Bob hauled their two prisoners toward the house. Milton cocked the handgun he held pressed against Marah's throat. She squeezed her eyes shut. *Oh, God, God, God . . . please help me. . . .*

"We have three civilians," Milton called as he backed Marah up onto the porch and waited for his men to get her father and Judd inside. "Our fourth hostage is one of yours. If you attempt any hostile move toward us, he's the first to go."

"Release the civilians, Dr. Gregory," the FBI agent called. "They're innocent in this."

"Not as innocent as you think," Milton muttered. "You informed Via Christi on me, Dr. Morgan. That alone is worthy of a death sentence."

Marah could feel the sweat rolling down her neck, soaking her collar, as she waited to die. Milton glanced behind him. "Get the refrigerator, and the rest of the equipment," he called into the house. "Mike, Bob—get back out here!"

The pale pink fingers of sunrise were beginning to reach up from the horizon. A lark perched on the electric line. A rooster crowed. Marah tried to swallow against the cold steel still pressing into her neck. She could feel the blood hammering in her jugular, and her head swam. Her father . . . her mother . . . Deborah . . . Sarah and Leah . . . Judd . . . Perky . . . *God, I don't want to die . . . not yet . . . please, Lord . . .*

From the corner of her eye, Marah could see the two men carrying the small refrigerator and a metal suitcase into the house. And then Milton began to jerk her backward to the door. She considered biting his hand. Screaming. Falling down and rolling.

Instead, she allowed him to haul her through the door and slam it behind them. The sound of Perky's sobs threatened to push her over the edge. Milton gave her a vicious shove toward the couch. She tripped and fell, hitting the back of her head against a table. For a moment, she thought she would black out. She lay paralyzed, fighting for breath.

"Get rid of the kid," Milton snapped at Dooley as he flipped on the light. From her place on the floor, Marah could see blood dripping from the corner of Milton's mouth. "Well, what are you waiting for? Kill her!"

"You exposed the girl," Judd said over Perky's sobs. He was tied to a chair near the fireplace. "Don't you want to see if it works? She's your test sample, isn't she?"

Milton hesitated. Marah's chest filled with hope as she realized Judd's appeal to Milton's vanity and pride might actually save Perky's life. She could see Mike standing near the couch at the edge of her range of vision. He looked confused. Milton coughed and wiped a mouthful of blood on the back of his hand.

"Why don't you let the girl go upstairs, Gregory?" Judd said. "Lock the door behind her. You can leave her up there and watch what happens."

Dooley and Harper looked at Milton. The doctor glared at Judd. "You just want me to spare her life. I can see through your little—"

"I'm a pediatrician," Marah cut in. "That child has become a living host for a deadly pathogen. Variola is transmitted primarily through respiration, and contagion may begin the moment infection starts. The first symptoms are high fever and a progressive delirium, but the disease is communicable long before those are evidenced."

"What do you mean?" Dooley asked.

"I mean you'd better not touch the child, Mike. You'd better not even breathe the same air she breathes."

"Oh." Dooley looked worried. "Dr. G, we did fail on our first two test groups. If this little girl doesn't get sick, we'll know we don't have anything to use against the enemy. But if she does, we'll know the weapon is armed."

Milton coughed again.

Dooley squared his shoulders. "Let's put Perky upstairs, Dr. G," he said. "They won't try to smoke us out or gas us with a child in here."

"All right," Milton said, lowering the pistol. "Cut her loose. See that she's locked up."

Marah's chest filled with relief as Dooley opened the suitcase he had brought from the van and pulled on a pair of latex gloves. As he cut Perky free, the girl headed toward Marah.

"Stop, Perky," Marah said softly. "Honey, I want you to listen to me and do exactly what I tell you, OK? Go upstairs to my bedroom and crawl into my big old bed. You can read my books, too, if you want. Mr. Dooley is going to lock the door, but we'll come see you as soon as we can. Will you do that for me?"

"Do it, Perk," Judd said.

"I'm scared," Perky said, turning toward Judd. "What's going to happen?"

"Everybody has to take care of himself right now, Perk. You

stop thinking about me and Dr. Morgan and Poppy, and you watch out for Pearl Kathleen Harris, OK?"

"God is going to watch out for me," she said, walking toward the staircase. Then she looked straight at Milton Gregory. "God's not scared of evil people."

"Quiet, you little—"

"You're a liar." Perky started up the stairs. "God hates lying. He hates tricks. All the things you do, Dr. Gregory, are the things God hates."

"That will be enough—"

"When you play games with God, you're going to lose."

From her place on the floor, Marah watched Perky disappear down the hall. And she couldn't help but smile.

21

"It's nearly ten o'clock in the morning," Judd said as Milton Gregory peered into the living room mirror to inspect the loss of his three front teeth. "You've got to send somebody up there to check on the girl."

Gregory ignored him, prodding the gum as though by some miracle he might see new teeth starting to emerge. Judd couldn't deny the satisfaction he took as the man wrapped his broken ribs and ran his tongue over the empty space in his mouth. The hostage situation had been going on several hours now, with neither side budging.

The yard surrounding the two farmhouses had grown crowded. Media vans with their portable satellite dishes had begun to gather. From the relative safety of their three vehicles, Judd's fellow agents continued to broadcast entreaties to surrender. The county fire truck had been called into service, and two ambulances were parked nearby. The local police force and sheriff's department had added both men and vehicles to the cluttered scene outside. Occasionally a movement or a shout drew the attention of the group inside. But Milton Gregory merely studied his missing teeth and let the minutes tick by.

"Someone needs to check on Perky," Marah said from her place on the couch. She and her father had been ordered to lie there together on the foldout sofa bed. "Let me go, Milton. I'll give you a report on her condition."

"You'd risk your life for that child?" Gregory stared at her. "Or is this another of your brilliant escape attempts?"

Judd studied Marah's face, reading the intensity in her eyes. She had tried, once during the standoff, to climb out the living-room window. Gregory had laughed as he slammed the window on her fingers. Though her knuckles had been crushed and her nails were turning black, the man insisted that she be kept tied at all times, hands behind her back.

"I'm not afraid of you," Marah told him. "I don't worry about my future."

Gregory gave a derisive laugh. "And I suppose Jesus is going to drop down out of the sky and save you?"

"He's already saved me, Dr. Gregory. My future is settled, and it doesn't matter what happens to my body here on earth. So let me check on Perky."

"I find this amusing, don't you, Mike?" Gregory said over his shoulder. "All this concern over the life of one small organism in the vast macrocosm of the universe. Apparently, Dr. Morgan hasn't learned that humans can be sacrificed for the greater good of a worthy cause."

"You're a kook," Ed Morgan said from the couch bed. His walker stood by the front door, too far away to do him any good. "I knew you were a kook right from the day you showed up on my porch."

"Am I a kook, Mike?" Gregory asked.

The young man was seated on a chair across from the couch. In the past few hours, Judd had watched Mike Dooley's resolve go right out the window. He was terrified, and Gregory had used his fear to manipulate and control the man's mind. Bob Harper, on the other hand, was as sociopathic as his mentor. More important, both men kept their guns loaded and ready. Judd had no doubt they would use them.

"You're not a kook," Dooley said.

"Do you think I'm a kook, Mr. Hunter?" Gregory asked Judd.

"Certifiable," Judd said.

Gregory laughed, showing the gap in his mouth. "I'm far more lucid than you." He sat down near the window and lifted the curtain back a fraction to study the scene outside. "You and your friends out there are the crazy ones. You've chosen to give your life to a government that has taken from you everything you loved most."

"What are you talking about?" Judd asked.

"Marianne Hunter." Gregory turned and looked at him as he spoke the name. "Your wife, wasn't she?"

"A long time ago." Judd glanced across the room at Marah.

She had paled. Though nothing much had passed between them, he knew he had come to care deeply for the woman. More than he should, probably. It bothered him to have his past paraded in front of her. How had Gregory found out about Marianne?

"My research team is thorough," the man said, as if in answer to Judd's thoughts. "You lost your wife while you were away doing battle for your country, did you not, Mr. Hunter? In the holy name of the United States of America, you left your home, your family, and your wife, and you journeyed halfway across the globe to the burning sands of Saudi Arabia. There you were employed by the military's special forces division to risk your life for the honor of the land you love. Am I right?"

Judd shrugged. To him, patriotism came as naturally as breathing. He would go to battle again if duty called. Truly he'd never stopped fighting. Only now the mission was to defend the United States against internal terrorism. There were worse things to do for a living.

"And what has the United States government given you in return for your sacrifice?" Gregory asked. "Did it protect your wife for you while you were gone? Or did she slip away into the arms of another man? How did it feel to return home, knowing you might have lost your life for your country, only to discover Marianne heavy with another man's child?"

Judd shifted in his chair. "The government did not betray me."

"Didn't it? I don't believe Uncle Sam was looking after

Marianne for you at all. And how many times have you been shot? Four, is it, or five? You've been stabbed, too, I believe."

"And blown up," Judd said.

"Where was your beloved government all those times you put your life on the line for it? No doubt, it was busy creating forms for Mr. Morgan and the other farmers to fill out, passing anti-gun legislation, accepting extravagant gifts from the tobacco lobby, dallying with the congressional pages and White House interns sent there to serve, dining in luxury with the Russians, selling our weapons to Iran, trading secrets to the Chinese—shall I go on?"

Judd stared at the man.

"Oh, the United States government," Gregory said with a sigh. "That vast army of paper-shuffling, fornicating, lying, spying, gold diggers. And these are the men and women you've chosen to serve. To defend. To give your life for."

"I believe in the ideal. I fight for this country's future—for the hope that the United States will follow the vision our founding fathers had for it."

"And so do I." Gregory's eyes darkened. "So do I, Judd. But you'll never change this country. It's too far gone. We need to start over. Start from scratch. And this time, we need to do it right."

"So we should wipe out everyone with a smallpox virus?"

Gregory glanced at the small refrigerator humming away. "Can you think of a better way?"

"You're not trying to create a better country, Gregory," Judd said. "You're out for revenge."

"How wrong you are, my friend. I believe in the ideal of a free, God-fearing country as much as you do. And I intend to fight—just as you fight—for that dream. But lives must be sacrificed in every battle, Judd. You know that. This war is no different."

Judd closed his eyes and leaned back against the chair. Gregory's words held power. They were mesmerizing. He could see how they could tempt an impressionable mind. *If I joined this man,* he thought, *I could carry the vials of smallpox right out the front door and transport them to their target.* Washington would be wiped out. Then Boston and Philadelphia. The plague would devastate every branch of the federal government. And once the epidemic came under control, the United States would be free to start over. Fresh. New. Get it right this time. All it would take was one step over the line.

Judd lifted his head and looked across the room at Ed Morgan tapping his fingertips on the old rocking chair. Then he glanced at Marah. He studied the small refrigerator for a moment, and then he listened to the sobs coming from the bedroom upstairs.

"Forget it, Gregory," Judd said. "You can join the ranks of Adolf Hitler and Pol Pot and Idi Amin and all the other men who've used genocide to try to win power."

Gregory's face tightened. "Mike, take this fool upstairs," he said. "Put him in the room with the little girl. And lock the door."

🐾 🐾 🐾

Aching hands tied behind her, Marah lay awake on the foldout sofa bed listening to the sounds outside the window. She could hear cars pulling up and others leaving. Urgent conversation. The static calls of agents speaking through megaphones. Though the sun was high in the sky and the situation was growing more intense, nothing had happened to break the stalemate.

Marah knew the small group inside could make a few meals from the food she had in the pantry. But how much longer could this go on? Now and then, Judd called down the urgency of Perky's need for medical attention. Milton Gregory occasionally spoke by phone with the FBI, always refusing to surrender his hostages and constantly making new demands. Marah knew his elaborate plan was unraveling, but he still had some hope of transporting his pathogen. She understood now that he was ready to give his life in exchange for a chance at spreading the disease in his little vials.

Ed lay stretched out beside his daughter, staring at the ceiling. His tears glistened.

"Hey, there," Marah whispered.

Ed rolled over. He was not tied, but he needed the walker to move off the bed. Gregory considered him harmless. "What do you need, girl?" the old man said.

"Quiet, you two." Bob Harper was on guard duty. He dropped his cigarette into an empty ice cream bowl.

Marah scooted toward her father and edged up until she could mouth the words into his ear. "We have to get Perky some medical help."

"Got any ideas?" he whispered back.

She could feel his rough whiskers on her cheek. "I want you to untie me."

Her father laid his hand on her arm. "The last time I did that, girl, he broke your fingers. How are you going to get back to doctoring if you don't have your hands?"

Marah lay in silence. "I thought you didn't want me to be a doctor," she said finally.

"Beans, baby girl, I been figuring you wrong since day one," he said, pulling her close to his chest. "If we ever get out of this mess, you have my blessing to be whatever you want to be."

Marah lay still for a moment, overwhelmed by the sweaty scent of his shirt and the unwashed hair that brushed against her face. And then she knew this was the smell of her father. This was the touch she had longed for. These were the words she had ached to hear.

"Dad," she whispered.

"Sweetheart," he said, tucking her head under his chin. "I don't know how you put up with me all these years."

Marah blinked back tears. "I don't either."

She could hear a chuckle down deep in his chest. "You weren't a piece of cake yourself, as I recollect."

"I guess not."

He held her close, rubbing her back. "I wonder how Pete's doing. I bet Hilda's beside herself. If she loses those twins . . ."

Marah could picture two more saplings in the Harrises' front yard. Or three. And for the first time, she realized that her father, too, grieved those losses. Grandchildren he would never know.

Marah could hear Perky speaking now, begging Judd to take her home. Marah had read enough about smallpox to know it wouldn't be long before the first stage of the disease set in. The little girl was fully contagious. After a while, the characteristic pustules of the disease would begin to emerge on her face and chest.

"I'm hot," Perky cried out suddenly, her voice drifting down from the upstairs bedroom. "I'm hot. Get me some water, Judd."

Big Ed shook his head. "Reminds me of your mother," he whispered. "She had that terrible fever and—"

"Dad." Marah drew back from him as realization shivered through her. "Could Mom have had smallpox? Did she ever go out to the knolls? Out to that pasture near Indian Hill?"

"Well, sure—"

"Collecting rocks for her gardens. She went out there and picked up stones from those cairns, didn't she?"

"But she never said a thing about coming across a mummy. Course I was always onto her anyhow, didn't want her driving the truck out there, didn't want those weeds brought into the yard. Beans, girl."

"Oh, Dad."

He pulled her close again. "I never had any notion of it."

"I suspected, but I didn't put it all together." Marah nestled against her father. "The bathtub."

"She was hot, you know. The fever. And she had that rash. She ran cold water, and then she took to screaming. By the time I got there, she was splashing around and hollering to beat the band. And then she collapsed. Up and died, just like that."

"Her internal organs must have failed all at once. The virus could have taken her before the pustules had time to fully emerge."

Her father was silent for a long time. Finally he whispered again. "It was my fault anyhow," he said. "Ruby was weak and worn out from all our troubles. She hadn't slept for days. Weeks maybe. And when she came down with the fever, I took her to Doc Benson only just that once."

"But Dr. Benson wasn't infected by her, and neither were you. Neither were any of us girls."

"She wouldn't let you get near, remember? Me and Doc Benson both had smallpox shots. They gave them to us when we were kids, you know. Had to have them for school. I think I might have had another one before I went off to Korea."

"You two, shut up," Harper said, standing and taking a drag on his latest cigarette. "I'm sick of all this whispering, and I'm sick of this stupid house, and I'm sick of you."

Marah watched him scratch himself and then wander over to look out the window.

"Dad, Perky's going to die," she said in his ear. "She wasn't immunized, and she breathed the virus. She's going to die."

Ed stroked his daughter's hair. "You reckon you could save her if you got her out of the house?"

"I don't know. I doubt it. But if we don't get her some help, she doesn't stand a chance."

Her father rolled over onto his back and fished around in one of the many pockets on his Big Mac overalls. "I figured I'd use this myself if I got the chance, but that kook never comes near me," he whispered. "I don't want to lose you, Marah. It's why I haven't done this before now. I don't want to lose you, and I don't want to lose Perky. You're my family, and no matter what I said before, I know family's not just about duty and survival. It's about love. I love you, Marah. And if you can save Perky, do it."

As he spoke, he turned his daughter over away from him. Then he pressed something small and hard into the palm of her hand. She lay still for a moment, running her swollen fingers over the object. And then she knew what it was. Big Ed Morgan had given her his whittling knife.

🐾 🐾 🐾

"I need to get a drink," Marah said. "It's very hot in the house."

Milton Gregory studied her up and down. How many times had she been to the kitchen during the morning? He checked his list. Just twice. Once just after six o'clock for five and a half minutes and once at seven-thirty for three minutes. He was bored, and he'd taken to keeping charts on everyone's activities. He didn't trust any of them, not even his two compatriots. Marah Morgan was the worst of them—too quiet—and she kept looking at him with those big blue eyes. He could feel her disgust.

"I don't know why you're so eager to go into the kitchen," he said. "The sounds of your little friend's crying just get louder in there."

Marah clenched her jaw.

"It bothers you, doesn't it, Dr. Morgan, to think of children dying?"

"Yes, it bothers me. Of course it does."

"Because you're a pediatrician."

"Because I'm a human being."

"I suppose you wouldn't have approved of my medical practice, then, would you? You're probably one of those Christians who think life begins at conception. And you certainly wouldn't have liked our previous test projects."

"What test projects?" she said.

He smiled, thinking of her outrage. The hours of waiting had begun to tell on him, Dr. Gregory realized. He felt certain his colleagues must have heard about the siege by now. The news coverage was intense. It was only a matter of time, he was sure, until his coworkers arrived to begin the rescue process.

But if they were unable to breach the enemy barricade, Gregory had already formulated a secondary plan of action. He would simply instruct Judd Hunter to carry the girl out among the opposition. They would swarm to tend her and their comrade, of course, and that would begin the epidemic. Though it wouldn't start in Washington, unfortunately, the plague would certainly affect the members of a target federal agency.

Within a matter of weeks, the media, civilians, and FBI who were exposed to the virus here in Kansas would spread the contagion to others around the country. And Gregory's goal would be accomplished.

The only problem would be getting himself out of harm's way. Marah Morgan had guessed correctly. He had not been immunized against smallpox.

"Mike," Gregory said. "Why don't you tell Dr. Morgan about our previous test groups? She'll be interested."

Dooley looked like he could use a good night's sleep. Gregory decided it might be interesting to toy with him. Anything to pass the time.

"But that kid keeps on crying upstairs."

"She's afraid. Perhaps she's already in pain."

"I wish she'd be quiet."

"Were the children quiet in Kansas City? The ones you burned?"

Dooley's eyes widened, and he glanced at Marah. "Please, Dr. G, let's drop it."

"You *burned* children?" she said.

"Barbie One." Gregory wanted to smile, but he hated the thought that they could see his missing teeth. "'Put another shrimp on the barbie, mate.' Ever heard that one, Dr. Morgan?

Well, Mike Dooley here learned everything there is to know about the barbie. Tell her, Mike. Tell her about your barbecue."

"It was part of the test program," he said, his voice subdued. "It wasn't a barbecue, Dr. Morgan. We took vials of the agent—"

"My previous attempts at cultivating smallpox," Gregory clarified.

"We took the vials into day-care centers and hooked them to atomizers in their heating and cooling systems. They were government-run programs, you know. Welfare mothers keep having babies and having babies. It's one of the things we hate about the enemy's tactics. So we decided we could sacrifice a couple of them for our project."

"A couple of what? Children?"

"Day-care centers." Dooley shrugged, but Gregory could see that his acts were bothering him. "We waited to see if the agent would work, but it didn't look good in either place. Just in case, we set the buildings on fire. Destroy the evidence, you know. It was Dr. G's idea."

Marah's nostrils flared as she absorbed the news. Gregory felt a warm glow spread down deep inside him. She understood, now, how clever he was. How he had done everything with scientific precision. How he would not be stopped.

"Where were the fires?" she demanded. "Mike, where did you set those fires?"

"Kansas City, like I told you," he said. "And St. Louis."

"St. Louis!" She shot up off the sofa, struggling to free her hands. "You murdered children, Mike, and some of them didn't die. Two of those kids were my patients. Demetria. She clung to life, fighting for every breath. She wasn't a lab rat; she was a child. A precious little girl. And the fever that burned—"

Her eyes went wide and the blood drained from her face. "Your test succeeded," she whispered, her voice fairly dripping venom. "And your victims infected one of the most talented pediatricians in the United States. You murdered Dr. Luis Jordan."

🐾 🐾 🐾

Marah sat at the end of the sofa bed and stared down at the worn carpet. She had tried praying. Tried grasping the threads of hope she could remember from every Bible passage she could dig out of her memory. But she knew now that Gregory had won this battle.

Not the war, of course. God had already assured Christ's victory against evil at the end of the age. But in this skirmish, sin would be the victor. Demetria and Dr. Jordan and all the little day-care victims had died. Perky would die. Marah and her father would die. Judd would probably die, too. The virus would infect unprotected and unsuspecting people, and they would die.

If the things Marah had learned at Via Christi were accurate, even one case of smallpox would be considered a national emergency. The United States had almost no resources to combat such a threat. The lab in Pennsylvania could produce about seven million doses of vaccine. It would take a hundred million to stop a smallpox epidemic.

"It's your turn for the bathroom," Dr. Gregory said, cutting into her thoughts. "Dr. Morgan?"

Marah lifted her focus from the floor. In the past few hours, Gregory had grown increasingly agitated. He charted the time it took for Bob to smoke a cigarette. He measured the distance around each room and drew elaborate maps of the house. He began to schedule bathroom breaks for each resident. Marah tried to stay focused on hope and love and faith. But her broken fingers ached, and her heart was filled with dread.

"I said it's your turn for the bathroom," Dr. Gregory repeated. "If you don't go now, you forfeit your chance."

Marah stood from the couch as Mike Dooley lifted his gun and prodded her toward the bathroom. With her feet tied, she had to shuffle along like a trussed duck. She glanced at her father. He was dozing on the couch. Upstairs, Perky had stopped crying.

"Thanks, Mike," Marah said as he unlocked the door for her.

"Hey, Dr. Morgan," he whispered, leaning close and glancing anxiously over his shoulder, "can the virus that Perky has come down through the floorboards?"

"Maybe," she said. "The room isn't airtight."

He shifted from one foot to the other, clearly anxious. "You think those federal agents are back behind the house? I mean, if we tried to get out that way, you think they'd be ready?"

"Probably. I've heard them on the roof, too." She studied the gun in his hand. "Mike, the minute anyone opens the door to Perky's room, we're all going to be exposed to smallpox. You'll die, you know."

He let out a shaky breath. "I didn't think it would turn out this way."

"You believed you could kill everyone and get away yourself? Dr. Gregory's been feeding you lies."

"I thought he was right, you know. His dream for our nation."

"You have two minutes!" Gregory called from the living room. He had taken to loudly counting down the time allotted for each activity.

Marah pushed her way into the bathroom, and Dooley pulled the door shut behind her. As she tottered over to the toilet, she passed the bathtub. Staring into the empty porcelain tub, she thought of her father's words. Ruby Morgan had sought this place as a refuge from the disease raging through her body. And upstairs, Perky Harris was dying from the same plague.

Marah lifted her head and stared at the ceiling. And at the heat register. And the curling metal vines. And the tiny screws that held it in place.

Adrenaline surged through her. Judd could lower Perky through the hole between the two rooms. Marah could ease her out the window. Someone could rescue the child, help her, maybe even save her life.

Reaching into the back pocket of her jeans, she prodded with her swollen fingers until she located the small penknife her father had given her. It seemed to take forever to pull out the tiny blade. Frightened she might drop the knife, she prayed as she began to saw on the rope that bound her wrists.

"One minute!" Gregory called.

Marah pushed her wrists apart and the rope snapped. Free! She bent down and sliced the binding on her ankles.

"Mike," she called, "tell Dr. Gregory I need more time in here. I'm not finished."

"OK," he said.

She could hear his footsteps as she climbed up onto the side of the tub and fitted the knife blade into the screws.

"Judd!" she called in a whisper. "Judd, can you hear me? The heat register."

A shadow appeared over the grate. "Marah?"

"How is she?"

"Asleep. She's exhausted." He paused a moment. "What are you doing?"

"I'm opening the grate. I want you to lower Perky through. I'm going to get her out this window."

"Marah, she's contagious."

"I know, but . . ." She hesitated a moment. "I don't care."

"You leave the bathroom. I'll get her down by myself."

"You can't do it alone. These are ten-foot ceilings. There, the grate's open."

She looked up into Judd's face for the first time in many hours. A heavy growth of dark beard covered his jaw. His look was one of longing.

"Marah," he said, his brown eyes flecked with gold, "I don't want you to die."

She glanced away. She didn't want to die either. A few minutes ago, it had seemed inevitable. Now, she felt a surge of hope.

"Wait a second." She stepped down from the tub and drew open the doors of the under-sink cabinet. A packet of latex gloves lay near the scrub brushes, cleaners, and metal pail she had used while cleaning and renovating the house.

Trying to focus, Marah tugged on three pairs of gloves. Then she emptied the bucket of brushes and put it over her head. Wrapping towels around her neck, she stuffed them up into the bucket until her head was completely enclosed. She would be able to breathe, just barely, but she could see nothing.

"Hand her down," she called up.

"Move to your left," Judd whispered.

"Dr. Morgan." Mike knocked on the door. "You done in there? Dr. G wants you to come out."

"I can't," she called. "Not yet."

As she held up her hands, she felt the frail little body slip into her arms. *Oh, God,* she prayed, squeezing tears from the corners of her eyes. *Save this child!*

"I'm coming down," Judd called.

Could he fit through the narrow opening? Marah held Perky close as she listened to the sounds of his efforts. In a moment, Judd was moving beside her.

"Window's painted shut," he whispered.

"There's a knife. Somewhere on the floor. Dad's whittling knife."

"Got it." He worked for a moment. Marah could hear Perky's labored breathing. "Can't budge the window. I'm going to have to break the glass."

"Judd, no! They'll hear."

"No choice, Marah."

The sound of glass shattering jolted Perky awake, and she began to cry. Judd grabbed the child from Marah's hands. She was backing blindly toward the door as it burst open.

"What's—"

Marah turned and crashed into Mike's body. They fell together, and she rolled across the bathroom floor.

"Agent Hunter coming out!" Judd was shouting through the window as Marah scrambled to her knees and began crawling toward what she hoped was the doorway. "The child is contagious. Stand clear."

As Marah stumbled into the living room, she tore the towels from her neck and pushed off the pail. The room had erupted. Gregory was on his feet, pistol aimed at the window as black-clad agents swung down from the roof and burst through the door into the room. Bob Harper began firing randomly. Mike Dooley staggered back into the living room, blood streaming from a gunshot to the shoulder.

"Dad!" Marah screamed. "Get down!"

She could see him sitting up on the sofa bed, bewilderment written on his face. All she could think of was saving him.

He tried to stand, knocking over Bob's makeshift ashtray. She ran toward him, her feet heavy. A bullet slammed into the wall beside him. Bob's lit cigarette ignited the old, worn curtain, and it burst into flame.

Her father tumbled forward.

"Dad!" Marah reached him as the fire began to lick his overalls. "Oh, Daddy, I'm here."

Glass sprayed across the room, and Marah felt a shard slice through her cheek as she lunged forward. She threw herself over her father, praying she could shield him. A bullet tore into her thigh, and she gasped at the pain.

Arms spread and body splayed across her father's curled form, Marah watched as Milton Gregory ripped the duct tape from the small refrigerator. Dooley covered his mentor, firing at the agents who had taken shelter behind furniture. Harper lay wounded, writhing on the floor nearby.

"Mike!" Marah cried out. "Don't let him do this. You know he's wrong. You know it!"

Gregory tugged open the door and grabbed the shoe box with its four tiny vials. Flames roared up the curtains and licked at the ceiling, sending thick black smoke through the room.

Gregory lifted a vial in one hand and reached with the other to pull out the stopper. "Here's to a free America," he said, coming to his feet.

Marah clenched her teeth. As the stopper edged upward, Mike suddenly cried out, "No!" He swung around and shot Milton Gregory through the heart. Instantly, a hail of bullets cut the young man to the floor. Fire caught the edge of the sofa. Smoke cloaked the room.

Marah held her breath and hugged her father close as the tiny vial, still stoppered, rolled across the floor and was engulfed in flame.

Epilogue

Marah limped across October's golden grass toward the open grave. The people gathering in the cemetery were old friends, those who farmed the nearby acreage, those who attended the local church, those who came to the annual summer picnic. She felt their love and their loss.

As she stood staring down into the dirt that would soon hold the wooden coffin, Marah felt a small hand take hers. Looking to her side, she focused on a pair of bright blue eyes centered like jewels in a small face marred by deep pockmarks.

Perky smiled. "Poppy is in heaven now," she said.

Marah stroked the tiny fingers, grateful to have the bandages finally removed from her own hands. She was going to miss her father terribly. Their last few weeks together had been a precious gift, as though God had granted her the daddy she'd longed for for so many years.

"Yes, he is, Perky," she said.

"He believes Jesus is God's Son," Perky said. "He

told me so in the hospital the other day, because I asked him."

Marah smiled. There were no secrets, nothing hidden, nothing left in silence with this child.

"Poppy told me he wanted Jesus to live in his heart," Perky said. "I asked my daddy about it, and he said the thief on the cross went to heaven even though he'd only been a Christian for a few minutes. So I'm sure Poppy's in heaven, too."

Marah glanced across the crowd at Pete Harris. Marah was grateful for his presence, especially since none of her sisters had been able to come for the funeral. Pete cradled one of the twin daughters his wife had given birth to the past week. Hilda held the other baby, and despite the sad setting, the light in her eyes was one of utter joy. There would be no more saplings in the garden.

Perky gave Marah's hand a squeeze before she started back toward her parents.

The doctors had all but given up hope on the little girl as they had worked to save her life in the isolation unit at Via Christi. The disease had run its predicted course. Her fever had grown intense, and she had become delirious. Finally her skin had broken out in a heavy red rash. The attending physician diagnosed the disease as variola minor, the less deadly strain, though it was difficult to be sure.

When Perky had slowly recovered consciousness and the pustules had begun to heal, everyone breathed a collective sigh of gratitude. The plastic surgeon had assured Perky's parents that although their daughter would bear some scarring for the rest of her life, in time he would be able to erase most of the ravages of the disease.

Marah felt a sense of peace descend over her as the pastor of Pete and Hilda's church led the graveside service. She looked out over the land that her father had farmed, thankful for the few short weeks of deep love they had shared. Ed Morgan's hip had disintegrated further after the siege ended and the old white house burned to the ground. Eventually, he had developed the staph infection that had taken his life. But in the meantime, Marah and her father had shared laughter, tears, and more warm hugs than she had dreamed him capable of giving. She knew her life would never be the same without him.

As the pastor began to pray, Marah lifted up her heart in thanksgiving for God's protection. The three remaining vials of smallpox virus had been removed from the house before it burned, and now they rested in guarded storage at the Centers for Disease Control and Prevention in Atlanta. Though Marah had not heard from Judd again after that moment in the bathroom, she had read in the newspaper about the unnamed FBI agent who had rescued a sick child and brought the hostage crisis to an end. She imagined him now somewhere, disguised as a drug runner perhaps or even a pizza deliveryman. Saving the world. She missed him terribly.

"Marah, are you going to be all right by yourself?" Pete asked as the prayer ended and the funeral party began moving toward the cars parked at the edge of the cemetery. "You call me if you need something."

"I'm fine, Pete," she said.

He grinned. "Count on me, sis."

As he walked away with Hilda and their family, Marah stood under the shade of an old oak tree and watched her father's casket being lowered into the grave. She had made up her mind to run the farm in his place. Dr. Benson, eager to retire, had offered her his medical practice next year after the wheat harvest, and she had accepted. In the meantime, she would drill the seed and wait for winter.

"Excuse me." The man's voice behind her startled Marah, and she turned, hand at her throat.

He stood a few feet away in a pair of jeans and a sweatshirt. He took off his hat, just like an old-time cowboy in the presence of a pretty young miss.

"I'm looking for work," he said. "Name's Judd."

Marah's heart flooded with joy. She took a step forward. "What kind of work are you looking for, sir?"

"Farmhand," he said. He walked toward her. "I spent the past two months behind a desk before they decided to send me on another assignment. Another mask. But I've been listening to a quieter voice lately. It's time for Judd Hunter to step out of hiding."

"And you think an old, broken-down farm in Kansas is the place to begin?"

"I know it is."

Marah turned away and watched as the soil her father had farmed slowly filled his grave. The disease of bitterness between them had healed, and it was time for her to begin a new life, too.

"There's a bunkhouse down the road," she said. "You could stay there."

Judd slipped his arm around Marah's shoulders and drew her close. "It's a start."

Acknowledgments

From the moment this book was conceived, I have been surrounded by a host of earthly angels. I cannot thank them enough.

Ron Beers has championed me, believed in the ministry value of my words, and upheld me through the highs and lows of this process. I thank you for Laguna Beach and for everything that came before and after it. This book would not exist without you.

Ken Petersen helped me take a vision and shape it into a reality. For the long meeting in Nashville and for the hours of your time and labor that followed, I thank you. This book bears your stamp on every page, and I am so grateful.

Kathy Olson's gentle words and astute observations have guided me through the editing process many times. Those who know me are aware that I'm directionally, spatially, and chronologically challenged! Kathy puts everything in the right order and much, much more. Bless you.

My Tyndale support system includes too many to name, and I love each one of you. I am especially grateful for the prayers and undergirding of the HeartQuest Team: Rebekah Nesbitt, Danielle Crilly, Anne Goldsmith, Kathy Olson, Jan Pigott, and Diane Eble. And Travis Thrasher—thank you for being my rock of emotional support.

For expert advice, I am indebted to many. While any errors are my own, I thank these people for sharing their time and knowledge with me: DeLoss Jahnke taught me about farming in Kansas. Greg Jentsch, M.T. (A.S.C.P.) provided invaluable medical information before I wrote, and he read through the finished manuscript in order to help correct any errors. Patricia Osman also shared from her wealth of medical information. Mary Anne Stoskopf, a woman I have never met, generously researched several questions for me and told me about her life in southern Kansas. Audrey Hanson McIntosh—a font of plotting ideas—gave me valuable advice on legal matters.

I could not write without the regular flow of tea and sympathy from my friendship support system. Among many, I especially thank Sharon Buchanan-McClure, Sylvia Johnson, Rhonda Maples, Kristie McGonegal, Audrey McIntosh, and Patricia Osman.

Tim Palmer has been my husband, my soul mate, and my best friend for more than two decades. His loving eyes read every word I write, and his hand has helped shape this and each of my books. I love you. And for daily hugs and kisses and unwavering love, I thank Geoffrey and Andrei. I love you, my precious sons.

About the Author

Catherine Palmer lives in Missouri with her husband, Tim, and sons, Geoffrey and Andrei. She is a graduate of Southwest Baptist University and has a master's degree in English from Baylor University. Her first book was published in 1988. Since then she has published more than twenty books. Catherine has also won numerous awards for her writing, including Most Exotic Historical Romance Novel from *Romantic Times* magazine. Total sales of her novels number more than one million copies.

Books by Catherine Palmer

A Town Called Hope series

Prairie Rose

Prairie Fire

Prairie Storm

Prairie Christmas (anthology)

Treasures of the Heart series

A Kiss of Adventure

  (original title: *The Treasure of Timbuktu*)

A Whisper of Danger

  (original title: *The Treasure of Zanzibar*)

A Touch of Betrayal

Finders Keepers series

Finders Keepers

Hide and Seek

Anthologies

Prairie Christmas

A Victorian Christmas Cottage

A Victorian Christmas Quilt

A Victorian Christmas Tea

With This Ring